THE TRAITOR'S GOLD

David Leadbeater has published more than fifty novels and is a million-copy ebook bestseller. His books include the chart-topping Matt Drake series and the Relic Hunters series, which won the inaugural Amazon Kindle Storyteller award in 2017.

www.davidleadbeater.com

T0182207

Also by David Leadbeater:

The Joe Mason Series

The Vatican Secret
The Demon Code
The Midnight Conspiracy
The Babylon Plot

The Matt Drake Series

The Bones of Odin
The Blood King Conspiracy
The Gates of Hell
The Tomb of the Gods
Brothers in Arms
The Swords of Babylon
Blood Vengeance
Last Man Standing
The Plagues of Pandora
The Lost Kingdom
The Ghost Ships of Arizona
The Last Bazaar
The Edge of Armageddon
The Treasures of Saint Germain
Inca Kings
The Four Corners of the Earth
The Seven Seals of Egypt
Weapons of the Gods
The Blood King Legacy
Devil's Island
The Fabergé Heist
Four Sacred Treasures
The Sea Rats
The Blood King Takedown
Devil's Junction
Voodoo Soldiers

The Carnival of Curiosities
Theatre of War
Shattered Spear
Ghost Squadron
A Cold Day in Hell
The Winged Dagger
Two Minutes to Midnight
The Devil's Reaper

The Disavowed Series

The Razor's Edge
In Harm's Way
Threat Level: Red

The Alicia Myles Series

Aztec Gold
Crusader's Gold
Caribbean Gold
Chasing Gold
Galleon's Gold
Hawaiian Gold

The Relic Hunters Series

The Relic Hunters
The Atlantis Cipher
The Amber Secret
The Hostage Diamond
The Rocks of Albion
The Illuminati Sanctum
The Illuminati Endgame
The Atlantis Heist
The City of a Thousand Ghosts

Stand Your Ground

To find out more visit www.davidleadbeater.com

DAVID LEADBEATER

THE
TRAITOR'S
GOLD

avon.

Published by AVON
A division of HarperCollins*Publishers*
1 London Bridge Street,
London SE1 9GF

www.harpercollins.co.uk

HarperCollins*Publishers*
Macken House,
39/40 Mayor Street Upper,
Dublin 1
D01 C9W8

First published by HarperCollins*Publishers* 2024
1
Copyright © David Leadbeater 2024

David Leadbeater asserts the moral right to
be identified as the author of this work

A catalogue record for this book is available from the British Library

ISBN: 978-0-00-865988-2

Set in Sabon LT Std by HarperCollins*Publishers* India

Printed and bound in the UK using 100% Renewable Electricity at CPI
Group (UK) Ltd

For my beautiful children, Keira and Meg. Even if we're apart, I'll always be with you.

Prologue

Gobi Desert, China

1444

It reared up out of the sands, a wide, squat, ugly building that sat a long walk from the city. It comprised pillars of stone and stone cladding, its walls long and wide, its main front door a double leaf of carven oak that sat open day and night except in the face of inclement weather. The sands that surrounded it were already trying to devour it, piled up high against the sides and drifting across the paths and settling on the roof.

The desert was always swelling, expanding, enlarging like a living, breathing, greedy beast, Jin thought. One day, it might reach Beijing, where it would overwhelm the newly built imperial residence, known as the Forbidden City.

But Jin shrugged those dark thoughts away. He straightened his tunic, smoothing it down to his knees, and took a step forward. Then he froze.

Was this the right thing to do?

If he entered that building, he was committing a sin, breaking the law.

No, no, he wasn't. The authorities had been forced to legalise gambling because of overwhelming demand. That was the only reason Jin stood outside its alluring doors right now. The bag he held nestled close to his right hip and, when he walked, Jin could hear the faint jangle of coins.

He walked now, putting his fears firmly behind him, determined to enter the unadorned, unassuming, low-profile, shady and sultry, ensnaring, darkly powerful den of iniquitous entrapment.

Jin stepped right up to the door before experiencing another rush of anxiety. Maybe this wasn't for him. Maybe, if he waited long enough, he might forget his money woes and wake up in another land, another realm, rich and unworried, fresh and clean.

Someone pushed past to his right. Jin got a whiff of rich spices and body odour. The man's long hair looked lank; his shoes were full of holes. The gambling den ate him up like it would an unsuspecting tasty snack. Jin wondered if he was going to risk being next.

No one was depending on him. Jin didn't have a family, a wife or a son or daughter. He lived alone, eked out a living on the land, selling the fruits of his labours in a local town. He wasn't starving. He had enough money to clothe himself and furnish his home, but he wasn't happy with his existence. Jin wanted more.

Hence the three-day trip to the Gobi Desert.

As he stood near the high doorway, almost standing in sin's gloomy embrace, something new enfolded Jin. It swept over him like a strange, alien blanket. It was the din of conversation, of voices raised – some in anger, some in joy –

of men, for it was only men in here, venting their emotions, speaking excitedly, asking questions. Jin found that the noise drew him in deeper still.

Deeper and deeper until he stood in the enormous room, wide-eyed, looking from left to right and up and down, overwhelmed, stunned, unable to process the enthusiastic peculiarity of what he was seeing.

First, it was busy. Jin could barely see between bodies. There were many men in here, short, tall, fat, thin, those who stooped and those who had no control over their manners. Their outerwear was contradictory, from tunics short and long to jackets, some padded. Some wore hats. Some had great curling moustaches, others were clean-shaven. Jin saw immediately that there was a wide range of values in here; some men were clearly wealthy, others without the means to buy shoes. Most of the men were standing around the few who were seated, but it was the seated ones that took Jin's interest.

They were playing the games, and these games were the eyes of the storm, so to speak. The calm within the chaos. Everything came down to winning the games. Jin put one foot in front of the other until he came to a low table on which was being played the first game.

Mahjong.

Jin didn't know if he was proud or ashamed of China's long association with gambling. The earliest record of gambling tracked back to the first dynasty, some 4,000 years ago, and it was said that many modern games such as mahjong and lottery and Pai Gow originated in ancient China. He blinked now and watched as two men played the game, gambling against each other. Noises from other tables filled his ears and the smell of food and sweat mingled in the air, making Jin wrinkle his nose. This place was certainly a

3

shock to the senses. He'd never seen anything like it. Jin was firmly out of his comfort zone.

So far, in fact, that he knew he had to stay here, absorb it, take some time to grow accustomed to this new, fearful, exciting, fascinating place.

He wandered the aisles between the tables. Manners were non-existent inside the den of iniquity, he decided. People jostled you whether you were walking the aisles or stood watching the games. The smell of food made him feel hungry, to want to spend some coins he'd brought for the purpose of turning them into more coins. He could practically taste the excitement in the air. It carried like the scent of nectar.

Jin grew accustomed to the clamour, to the smells. He started concentrating on the games, noted that they were all chance because you never knew who you were going to come up against. Skills, of course, were the best order of the day, but there was always chance. That was the beauty of gambling.

Jin moved among the crowd, seeing tile-based games, card-based games, all manner of games from the intellectual to the crude. He realised after some time had passed that he was procrastinating.

I have travelled far to try this, he thought. *Made a great effort. Why am I delaying matters?*

There was no straightforward answer. Jin was still trying to make sense of it all. He was nervous about sitting at the right table, about taking his place in line, about making a mistake. He was worried that he might lose all his money on the first attempt to play.

Jin steeled himself. He had a backbone. He worked throughout the daylight hours and he worked hard. He made deals for his produce. He stood up to the town's authorities rather than let them ride all over him.

This he could do.

Jin chose one game where the lines weren't so long. He reached inside his bag to make sure his coins were safe. There were pickpockets in here, he was sure of it. He stood behind a broad-shouldered, long-haired man whose eyes never left the game and the men playing it. Some time later, the man sat down to play, and it would be Jin's turn next.

A nervous flutter of excitement flickered through him.

Strangely and simultaneously, that was when the first tremor hit. It was nothing major, and Jin had felt tremors before. It was an odd sensation. The ground moving beneath your feet, the walls shaking, the tables clattering. But it didn't last long. When it hit, there was a sudden lull in the noise that Jin had now become accustomed to, the new silence stinging his ears almost as loudly.

Jin waited with bated breath as the building shook. And then it was done, over, finished. Jin sensed the hesitancy inside the place, the fear that overrode everything. Dust floated from the ceiling, spinning calmly in the air. The sun that speared through open windows caught it and refracted.

Jin looked around the place, met the eyes of hundreds of men. They were wide and seeking, wary. Jin noticed the coins clutched in their hands, the coins scattered all over the gaming tables, the coins that had fallen from piles and struck the floor. They were all silver and gold, shiny and patinaed. Jin had never seen so many coins in his life.

For some reason, it unnerved him. Or was it the rumble through the ground? Jin wasn't sure, and didn't care too much as he saw the broad-shouldered man playing the game before him lose. The man hung his head and pushed away from the table.

It was Jin's turn.

As he clasped the back of the chair, ready to sit down, Jin felt the impact of a second rumble. Like the first, it came from nowhere, from deep within the earth and with no warning. All of a sudden, there was a noise filling Jin's ears – a profound, terrifying, cavernous rumble that abruptly held sway over all; there was an incessant shaking, an unfamiliar effect, that made men stare at the ceiling, the walls, the floor.

This time, the rumbling lasted longer.

The entire place shook before Jin's eyes. He stopped breathing. It was terrifying. He looked to the door, but saw it quivering too, curtains of dust drifting down the gap through which he could see the shifting desert sands. There were people out there, standing and watching, looking towards the distant buildings of the large town.

Jin touched the table to help keep his balance, but was frowned upon by the other players. Perhaps he was too close to the stacks of coins. The trembling continued to run through the building, the deep roaring noise growing in strength. Jin got worried. Perhaps he should leave...

And then it stopped again. As quickly as it had started, the rumbling ended, the walls and ceiling returning to normal. Jin realised he was staring at the block work as if checking for cracks, for irregularities. He saw nothing and tore his gaze away.

Now, some men were leaving the gambling house. They filed through the door, walked down the path outside, headed for the desert. Most of the men, though – they weren't going anywhere.

Like them, Jin felt the pull. He didn't *want* to leave. The thrill was upon him, the thrill of pitting his wits against another and playing that man for money. He didn't want to walk away now, to leave that behind. And in any case, there had been two tremors. There probably wouldn't be any more.

Jin arranged his tiles. He was ready to play. His eyes met those of the man sitting opposite – a man who sat with an emotionless face, a low hat, and a moustache that hung out from both sides of his face. He had arranged his tight-fitting tunic so that it was totally smooth and the rings on his fingers spoke of at least a little wealth, nothing ostentatious.

Jin reached out to move the first tile.

And then it hit. Jin immediately understood that the first two tremors had been mere warnings. He realised that the men who'd prematurely filed out of the building had been the sensible ones.

First, the deep roaring sound came. Then, the walls started shaking, and this time they shuddered back and forth like twigs in a gale ready to snap. The block work wavered. Jin saw the ceiling rippling like a great wave. A terrible sound filled his ears. Men were screaming and shouting, rushing for the exit, getting stuck, falling, trampling each other. The immense sound intensified until it was Jin's entire world, a black gaping wall of noise. He saw the far end of the building crumple; the walls just giving way. He shot to his feet. A chunk of debris fell from the ceiling, landing across the shoulders of a reedy man and crushing him to the floor.

Jin started making his way towards the exit, surrounded by a sea of people. All his horizons shook and trembled. Men yelled in both his ears. The ceiling cracked from end to end, a wide, irregular fissure opening up. At the same time, Jin saw something shifting below him.

The floor was opening.

The great fracture ripped haphazardly through the entire floor. At both ends, the walls sagged. Debris shattered down from the ceiling above, crushing some men, smaller rocks bouncing off others. Jin saw the doorway changing shape, the frame sliding to a forty-five-degree angle even as men slipped through it, squirming, getting stuck, fighting to be the first ones out. By now, Jin could sense that a mob consciousness had taken over.

The first big collapse happened far to Jin's left, the entire ceiling over there slumping down to the ground. Rubble fell in a heap, landing at an angle, clouds of dust drifting through the air. Suddenly, daylight flooded the place. Jin struggled to progress against the great clump of humanity that stood before him. People were still squeezing out of the madly angled doorway, but it was getting harder and harder.

And there were more ominous sounds now, too, even above the roar of the quake. Jin, not having heard them before, knew exactly what they were. They were the sounds of unaccountable stress being put on walls, on stone pillars, the noise supports made when they were close to breaking point.

Then, the state of the walls receded far from his mind.

Because the crevice in the floor opened up even further. It spread past his feet, causing him to fall into it, but, luckily, it wasn't deep. Just a few feet. Yet still his ankle scraped the bare rock and started bleeding, his bones bruised. He yelled and spread out his arms to protect the space around him.

It didn't work. Men barged him aside, stepping in all around him, closing all the gaps. Jin was crushed between them, unable to move. The fissure wouldn't let go of his ankle; he fought to stay upright, to sway more than an inch. His breathing came in brief gasps, his heart hammering inside his chest. He realised that he'd hung on to his bag and all the coins left inside. Somehow, it was still slung around his body.

All the wealth in the world didn't matter right now.

There was a monstrous roar, filling the senses and blotting out all hope. It was the sound of a demon approaching, a destroyer of worlds. Every wall suddenly collapsed; the ceiling came crashing down. The fissure beneath Jin opened a little wider, sucking him down. Debris smashed all around him, crushing the struggling men, breaking bones and shattering skulls. Jin shivered as bones and blood and the contents of broken skulls struck him. There was nowhere to move, no way out. His ankle was stuck, the crevice almost pulsing beneath him as it widened and deepened and then shifted.

He screamed. The ceiling above undulated and then came down in a vast heap. It fell like the terrifying, infuriated gods would fall on the people below, an incensed down-surge of certain death.

Jin threw his arms up. He saw struggling bodies and falling masonry and mushroom clouds of dust and rubble. He heard the ever-present roar, the screaming, the groaning of dying men. He *felt* the whole building sinking, saw it coming down, but not just that. The entire space was descending into the sands, sucked down by some incredible, unnameable force. This was something men could not stand against, something infernal and elemental, a force unlike anything man-made. Yes, the empire believed it had come a long way in the last four thousand years.

But it had never equalled this.

Jin saw nothing as the ceiling descended on him, as the walls shuddered down and the ground slipped away beneath his feet. He was struck by large rocks, broken, beaten, devoured by the fundamental fury of the earth. Nothing known, nothing invented, could have saved him.

The rage of the world he lived in had swallowed his dreams.

Chapter 1

Present Day

Joe Mason laid punch after punch on the frayed leather that hung before him. He'd returned to his old gym for the morning, as much for the sweaty, noisy, aggressive atmosphere as anything else. These days, Mason usually worked out at Sally's house – the place where his entire team was currently living until they worked out something better for themselves. But today, Mason felt like going back to basics.

He'd needed to clear his head, and for him this was the best way to do it. Wearing gloves, striking leather, sweating profusely on the threadbare blue mats – that was the way he worked his issues out. At least for the next few hours.

Mason ducked and weaved and punched. There were a lot of issues to work out. Yes, the team dynamic helped. The way they hunted down or transported treasures all around the world, the way they offered protection to paying organisations and corporations who wanted their relics, their

11

prizes, protected as they conveyed them from place to place. Mason enjoyed the new life; the business that went under the name Quest Investigations was hectic and just getting busier. Sally was having to turn jobs away.

Mason pulled away from the bag and looked to his right. His teammate Roxy Banks stood there, hitting a bag with as much gusto as he. Mason had brought her along as a kind of treat, promising her some good, old-fashioned sweat and toil if she felt up to it. Roxy was a raven-haired, six-foot-two American, and what people termed a loose cannon. This was because of extensive inner issues of her own she was barely keeping from ruining her life. Mason remembered that, the first time he'd met her, he'd had to pull her out from between rum-soaked sheets. It helped her sleep, she'd said.

Mason got a look at himself in a mirror. He was rakish, kind of wiry, not too thin but not too bulky. Mason was often underestimated, with his sandy blond hair, blue eyes and a face that didn't show the hell he'd been through during his life. He was clean-looking and amiable and liked to fit in.

Sometimes, Mason wished the issues that had once almost ruined his life stood out more on his body, on his mien, but that wasn't to be. There was barely a scratch on him. All the trials and tribulations existed in his head.

Every damn day.

Roxy saw him looking at himself and stopped work, grinning. 'Looking at it won't change it, Joe,' she said. 'Like you said to me – you gotta put in the work.'

'Funny,' he said. 'No matter how hard I try, it never changes. No definition. No obvious muscle. I guess I'm just me.'

Mason was strong, but it was an underlying strength. Nothing showed on the surface. He watched Roxy now, a woman who struggled silently with her own demons and always spoke her mind.

'You ready to call it a morning?'

'Are you kidding? I've been hankering for a caramel macchiato and blueberry muffin for the last hour,' she said.

'Unless you wanna go one on one for a few minutes?' He grinned.

Roxy could never pass over the chance to get a few good-natured hits in on Mason. Their relationship was professional in the field and in the office, but there was still that sense of fun and rivalry and good, old-fashioned mischief between them they never overlooked. Roxy stepped up to him now.

'Get in the ring, Babyface.'

Mason slipped through the ropes and did a few practice jabs as he waited for Roxy. Soon, the American was in his face.

'You're going on your back,' she said.

'Not my kind of position,' he replied.

'Yeah, you just wish it was.'

She jabbed him in the ribs for good measure and then backed away. Mason tapped his gloves together. They circled each other warily, and then Roxy came in fast, double-jabbed at his head and followed it up with a cross to his ribs. Mason covered up safely, searching for an opening. When Roxy came in again, he threw a hook to the side of her head, the momentum pushing her sideways. As she staggered, he stepped in quickly, jabbing and crossing, until she backed her way into a corner. Once there, she covered up, but then realised her error and started attacking, trying to fight her way out.

Mason let her throw punches, ducking and weaving. He wanted her to wear herself out, but Roxy Banks was far too

13

wily for that. She knew the game, had been trained to fight and fight hard all her life. She slipped around him with some fancy footwork and threw a jab at the side of his head.

Mason feigned hurt. She smiled and stepped in. He threw a cross to her midriff that doubled her over. She cursed him. As one, they backed away from each other, stepping lightly from foot to foot, eyes narrowed and still searching for a gap, an opening. They were fully concentrated, didn't see or hear the men and women working out, the old timers with their tired but watchful eyes offering suggestions. It all came down to the fight and the focus and the very next move.

Which was made by Mason.

He stepped in, threw a feint, stepped around and clouted Roxy over the head. She grimaced and punished his ribcage. They came together, resting on each other, panting and sweating, face to face.

'You had enough?' she asked.

'Never give in,' he puffed a little. 'Never surrender.'

'I'll buy you a blueberry muffin.'

'That'll do.' He pushed her away, turned his back, and stepped out of the ring. Roxy followed, jumping down to the mats. Mason showed her where the showers were, grabbed his towel from his battered locker and spent two minutes showering before towelling off and then dressing in jeans and a T-shirt. It was a lovely, warm July day outside and he was looking forward to spending a little time walking in the sunshine.

He met Roxy back at the lockers.

'You ready?' he asked, noting her damp, dark locks and fresh, reddish face.

'You're buying,' she said.

'Why the hell am I buying?'

'Because it's your treat. You told me. You said, "Hey Rox, come out with me today. I have a treat for you." Remember?'

Mason grumbled. The truth was, he'd wanted a little company and thought Roxy would enjoy the workout more than the others. Sally was currently too interested in searching through her father's old house and sorting reams of old files and papers and ornaments and paintings and…well, everything an older man might accumulate. It was a tough job, and there was a lot to go through, and every moment she was there reminded her of his death not so long ago. Quaid was engrossed in one of his favourite activities, taking his time buying sentimental old stuff that might include cookbooks and car manuals. He was also trying to ignore several recent calls from Anya, one of his old flames who'd already proven very useful to Mason and his crew. Anya was a lovely woman who gave off a kind of older Lara Croft vibe, and Mason did not know why Quaid would want to ghost her. But then Quaid was an odd bird, always living in the past. And then there was Luke Hassell, the New Yorker who was always brooding, always going over certain events in his tragic life that had shaped him – he thought – for the worse. Hassell's issues were ones that were not easily overcome, not with years' worth of well-meaning therapy.

'I'll buy,' he said to keep the peace and preceded her onto the street.

It was only when Mason and Roxy were fully ensconced in their booth, syrupy coffee for Roxy, proper black and piping hot for Mason, plates with huge blueberry muffins in front of them, that Mason thought to check his phone. Unlike many these days, his phone was not an attachment to his arm, and he didn't enjoy carrying it around with him.

He reached down to the gym bag between his legs and spent a while fishing for it.

'Hey,' he said. 'I have three missed calls from the house.'

Roxy looked up, black eyes flashing. 'You're kidding? Can't we spend just a little time alone together?'

If it had been anyone else, Mason might have wondered if there was a deeper meaning there. But not with Roxy Banks. If Roxy wanted you to know something, she'd give it to you directly, right between the eyes. So there was nothing deeper here, just Roxy speaking her mind and wanting to spend a little time away from the house.

'You think I should call them back? I mean, we'll be home in an hour. What can be so urgent?'

'Could be a new job.' Roxy shrugged. 'Could be Sally, all excited about a new relic and some research she's doing. Or maybe Anya's come across from Italy and married Quaid.'

Mason choked back his laughter. 'Can you imagine that? The way they argue.'

'Did you used to argue with your wife?'

It was a blunt, typically unsentimental question, and it caught Mason off-guard. His ex-wife, Hannah, had always been good to him. They never argued, not even when Mason was beset by his demons and couldn't confide in her. In the end, she'd realised she couldn't help him no matter how hard she tried and the two had drifted, respectfully, apart.

Mason bit into his muffin and chewed slowly as he formed an answer. 'Never did and still don't,' he said and added, 'We haven't spoken in a while.'

'Is there a reason for that?'

'No, just life. Work. The things we do.'

Roxy finally appeared to notice it wasn't Mason's most comfortable subject and pointed at his phone. 'Might be best calling them back.'

Mason had been feeling the same way. He reached out for the phone but, at that moment, it startled him by ringing. He checked the caller display.

'Sally,' he said and answered it. 'Mason here.'

'Joe. *Joe!* Thank God I finally got hold of you. Don't you check your phone?'

'What's so urgent?'

'Oh, so you *do* check your phone? We're going to have to come up with some protocol for answering. For the team.'

Mason was tempted to say, *You're the boss.* He was tempted to say a few things, but managed to hold his tongue.

'Is there a problem?' Roxy asked loudly, her voice ringing out in the coffee shop.

'I'd say. Quaid's gone.'

Mason frowned and gripped the phone tighter. 'Gone? What do you mean, gone?'

'He got a call. From Ireland. Something terrible. Then Quaid got all desperate and…well, he just went?'

'To *Ireland*?' Roxy's voice rose a few octaves, making a few people in the shop glance over at their table.

'What happened?' Mason asked.

'Like I said, he got a call. We're also headed to Ireland. Well, to the airport and then Ireland.'

Mason frowned even harder. He shook his head to clear the wool. 'What, wait, you mean you're *all* headed to Ireland now? What the hell for?'

And now that he knew she was on the move, Mason could detect a rushed quality about Sally, as if she was hurrying around.

'You know Quaid has a lot of contacts across the globe? Good contacts. Well, someone he's really close to has been kidnapped. Quaid's fraught with worry.'

Mason shot to his feet, draining the coffee. 'You're with Hassell?'

'I am.'

'Do we know much about this person?' Mason asked, phone to his ear as he strode out of the coffee shop.

'Only that it's a woman, an ex-flame of Quaid's, and that she's a treasure hunter. She hunts for important relics all over the globe.'

'So, no note? No ransom demand? No phone call? How do we know she's been kidnapped?'

'Quaid is sure of it. Let me explain...'

Mason stood in the street, getting his bearings, and then started walking briskly towards their car. He was acutely aware of Roxy close by, clinging to his side like a limpet.

'And he's gone all the way to Ireland, based on what?' he interrupted.

'He got a call from her, all breathless, saying men were in her house and searching for something. After that, nothing. She's not answering her phone or emails. Quaid has more information.'

Mason didn't want to voice the obvious – that she might be dead. He wasn't the type to tempt fate. Instead, he opened the car door and leapt inside, key in hand, and started the engine. Soon, he was cutting through the traffic as best he could.

'We're on our way,' he said. Quaid, part of their little family, was in trouble. They would not let him down.

'We're already at the airport. We'll meet you here.'

Mason nodded and ended the call. Roxy, in the passenger seat, gave him a look.

'Put your damn foot down,' she said.

Chapter 2

Mason and Roxy met Sally and Hassell at the airport and boarded the plane. During the flight, Mason read up on Dublin from the in-flight brochure: 'Located on the east coast of Ireland, Dublin is the rich gateway to the stunning landscapes and allures of the Emerald Isle. In Dublin, music and pubs infuse its lively and diverse culture, with folk, rock and pop artists playing inside and on street corners. With a long history, a deep culture and a modern outlook, the tourist or locals can stroll from museums and galleries to up-to-date boutiques and malls in just a few hundred yards, or take longer trips to nearby mountains and seaside towns. With its friendly people, its colourful streets and districts and its unique entertainment, Dublin adds up to one exceptional, memorable experience.'

But Mason wasn't here to sightsee; he was here to help his friend. When they landed, Mason checked his phone.

'Nothing,' he said.

'We're at least an hour behind him. What the hell is going on?' Roxy said.

Mason's phone rang. They were just outside the airport, waiting in line for a taxi.

'Quaid here.' He spoke in clipped tones and then reeled off the address of a coffeehouse in central Dublin. 'Get here as fast as you can.'

Mason eyed the long queue, thought *fuck that*, and stepped out of line, ordering an Uber instead. The wait time was seven minutes. He stood for a moment, but then a light rain started to fall, rapidly coating the pavements and the road so that they looked slick and black, and he and Roxy stepped back, sheltering under an overhang and watching the now miserable taxi line shuffle its way forward. It was one o'clock in the afternoon and Mason was aware that he carried no luggage, not even an overnight bag. They had hopped straight on the plane from the gym, and still held on to their gym bags, useless though they now were.

The Uber took them to the correct address and soon Mason, Sally, Hassell and Roxy were climbing out into a light shower, staring through the darkly tinted windows of a ritzy-looking coffee shop. Mason made his way to the door and pushed his way inside. Roxy and the others followed. A hand was raised in greeting. Together, they made their way to the back of the shop, where, at a round table, their friend sat.

'We couldn't have made the trip together?' Roxy grumped, taking a seat.

'That was my fault,' Quaid said. 'When we couldn't get hold of you at the gym, I panicked. Grabbed the first flight I could get. I've managed a quick recce, seen nothing, and then thought it would be best to wait for you.'

Quaid was fifty-one, an ex-British army officer, a superb cook, a man who took his time to get things right but, due to his extensive connections, a man who could make anything happen, anywhere. He was rooted in the past, found it hard to trust modern technology, and had a daughter somewhere whom he never spoke of. Quaid had sparkling eyes and grey sideburns on lustrous black hair, a fact that had often spurred Roxy into asking if he dyed it. The best answer she ever received was a huff, the worst a raised middle finger.

'Your friend?' Mason didn't say much more as the server came over and took their order.

'Yes. Luciane.'

Roxy coughed. 'Can I ask, how many lady friends do you have ensconced around the world?'

Quaid's eyes sparkled. 'Oh, more than a few.'

'Are they all as mad as Anya?' Hassell asked. Hassell had stayed with Quaid and Anya for a week in Italy.

Quaid shrugged. 'I do tend to attract a certain type.'

'So give us the full story.' Mason sat back in his chair, conscious that Quaid and the others looked fretful, impatient and uncomfortable.

'Luciane Harlow lives here in Dublin.' Quaid had decided to give them the full picture, which Mason was pleased about. 'She's, like I said, an old friend. I first met her during my army days when I came across her a fair bit. We met, we talked, we helped each other out with information. Back then, she was a copper.'

'And now?' Sally asked.

Mason watched the brunette carefully, noting the perpetual blue tips to the edges of her hair were still lighter these days. Sally was what might be called a wealthy rebel. Born into privilege, she had shunned it, leaving her father to go her own way and, occasionally, live on the street. When her father was murdered during their search of the Vatican, during which they'd vied with a madman called Marduk to get hold of the Vatican Book of Secrets, Sally had only recently returned home to give him a second chance. Now she had inherited the family fortune and was trying to put it to good use by forming Quest Investigations and searching for relics all around the world, something her father used to do. Sally didn't yet know whether she was honouring his memory or doing her own thing, but she was sure she was exactly where she wanted to be.

Quaid leaned forward, getting Mason's attention. 'Now?' he repeated. 'She's an expert in certain countries' histories.'

Mason waited as Quaid took a deep breath.

'Luciane is a brilliant historian. A methodical researcher. A finder of secrets. She turned to this job after getting injured in the Garda and deciding to leave. The years have found her knee-deep in research, leading to some quite amazing finds.'

'Have you spoken recently?' Sally asked; a shrewd question. The answer might reveal what Luciane was currently working on. 'I mean, apart from the rushed call.'

'Yes,' Quaid replied. 'That's what worries me even more. About a week ago, she told me she had a big secret, a new idea. I didn't push, but she was irrepressible, unable to keep it to herself. She told me she was working on a dusty old legend, the legend of some ancient Chinese casino that vanished into the Gobi Desert. The first of its kind.'

Sally's eyes flashed. 'I like the sound of that.'

'So did she. They cut you two from the same cloth. Luciane is fascinated by ancient relics and treasure.'

Sally nodded. 'That's me, too. So the casino is associated with some great treasure?'

'Luciane told me it vanished after an earthquake but, during those times, it would have been packed to the rafters.

22

We're talking thousands and thousands of coins and jewels and other priceless items. Imagine finding it now.'

Sally leaned back. 'It would be quite a coup.'

'That's what Luciane thought.'

'But what got her so excited?' Mason asked. 'Enough to tell you all about it? Did she explain?'

'She definitely found something,' Quaid said. 'She was eager to the point of being agitated.'

'But she didn't tell you what it was.' Mason pursed his lips. 'Could Luciane have been the victim of a robbery, a home invasion? Maybe the cops are already working on it.'

'I don't think so. She didn't sound like she was just getting robbed. Not the way she spoke.'

Mason wondered how to broach the big issue here – the issue that Luciane might actually be dead. He looked Quaid in the eye.

'Paul…' he began.

'Don't.' Quaid shook his head. 'I know what you're thinking. I refuse to believe it. In fact, I think there's only one thing we can do. Something that will answer all our questions.'

'And what's that?' Hassell asked.

'Follow me.' Quaid rose, left the table and started for the exit.

Chapter 3

Quaid led them straight to Luciane Harlow's apartment.

It wasn't a long drive. Quaid had chosen the coffee shop because it was situated relatively near Luciane's apartment. He hadn't gone in earlier because he'd decided to wait for the full team to investigate once he heard they were just a few hours away. He had watched the apartment from afar, just in case, but had seen no movement. As they were driven in the back seats of a large Uber, Quaid told them a little more of his history with Luciane.

'Met her whilst I was in the army,' he told them. 'She was one of those Garda who were actually helpful, not pissed off that I was hanging around, sticking my nose in. She led us in quite a few good directions, following her nose, and helped prevent several attacks. She put herself out there, which was more than you could say for most. We hit it off almost immediately.'

'And when you say "hit it off"?' Roxy was interested.

'Yeah, yeah, we were really close. And we've stayed close-ish ever since.'

'Do you love her?' Roxy pushed.

Quaid swallowed heavily. 'You know, in my small way, I probably do.'

Mason didn't say, *Then I hope she's still alive*. It was a thought close to all their hearts, but not something they should voice. The vehicle drove them through mid-afternoon traffic, finally pulling over to the side of the road down a narrow street with shops and pubs on both sides.

'She lives around here?' Sally peered out the window.

'Yes,' Quaid nodded. 'Luciane really likes to immerse herself in the excitement, the culture and the diversity of Dublin. She loves the city. In the heart of all the fun is where she wants to be.'

They stepped out onto the pavement, immediately surrounded by a sea of people and their loud conversations. Mason, at first, didn't dare move for fear of stepping on someone. From his left there was the jangle of a shop bell as someone entered the establishment. From further down the road, the faint strains of a guitar and singing. A car with a loud exhaust rumbled by. Mason could smell a bakery and tasty treats and, perhaps, on the edge of the wind, fried food, maybe bacon.

Hassell was standing beside Quaid, but still had to raise his voice. 'Where does she live?'

Quaid smiled. 'Typically,' he shouted, 'above that pub over there.'

Mason studied it. He saw two curtained windows above a colourful façade. Bay windows jutted out into the pavement. The sign above the door read *Kearney's*. The pub itself was painted red and had overflowing hanging baskets and other paraphernalia outside, and a low shelf running along its front. Signs for tobacco and Guinness covered the walls. Quaid was already focused on the single open door.

Inside, the bar was dingy, the headroom rather low. The floors were wooden and a little sticky. There was a stage to the right and a bar to the left, on which many people were leaning. A male/female duo stood next to the mic, strumming their guitars and singing a powerful song that the entire bar tapped their feet and clapped their hands to. The space was loud and chaotic and Quaid lost no time cutting right across the middle of it and heading for a far double door.

'You know your way?' Roxy yelled above the din.

Quaid nodded. 'Obviously,' he said.

Mason followed Quaid through the door and into a narrow corridor lined with paintings of Dublin from one era or another. To their right was a carpeted flight of stairs.

'Up,' Quaid said. 'Second floor.'

They climbed the flight and then another, coming out onto a wide landing where there were three doors. Up here, the music was a little muted, allowing them to think more clearly. Quaid pointed out Luciane's door and Mason turned to Hassell.

'You're the expert,' he said. 'Lead the way.'

Luke Hassell was an infiltration specialist. When they came across him, he was working for the enemy, but soon switched to their side, sick and upset with what the criminal boss was making him do. The criminal boss, a man named Gido, befriended Hassell after he quit the police department, after his girl Chloe was murdered by lowlifes, and gave Hassell purpose, a will to live. It was only years later that Hassell found out it was Gido who sent the lowlifes. He had then killed Gido in a savage act of vengeance. This was what Hassell brooded over, day and night, trying to decide what kind of person a man who'd operated on every side of the tracks actually was.

Now, the man who'd once helped plan a break-in of the Vatican secret archives pulled a set of carbon fibre lock picks from his pocket. Without a sound, he inserted them into Luciane's lock and started twiddling. Less than half a minute later, he turned the round silver handle and let the door ease itself open.

Quaid pushed to the front, ready to go into the room first. Mason laid a steadying hand on the man's shoulder.

'Maybe I should—'

'It's okay. I'm okay. *She's* okay.'

Quaid went through the door and switched on a light. The others were quick to follow. Mason found himself in a typical living room with a two-seater blue sofa, a large television and a low black coffee table. There was a silver lamp on the table made of two curling leaves, which must have cost a pretty penny. Mason saw rugs on the floor and prints on the walls and a chandelier-type light fitting in the centre of the ceiling of the front room, all arranged precisely and neatly. The apartment had the effect of an orderly, lived-in place – and it was empty.

Quaid strode to the centre as Hassell and Roxy went over to the curtains, tweaking them apart to take a look at the street below. Mason knew it was inbuilt for them, instinct, a result of their training, that they had to inspect their perimeters.

'Luciane is a journal kind of woman,' Quaid told them. 'She'd use the computer to streamline her research, but she'd record it all in a journal, a folder maybe. That's where we'll start.'

They spread out. Quaid went immediately and unapologetically straight into her bedroom. Mason took the front room and Sally found a little niche on one side where a computer desk stood. Mason went across to the coffee table and started leafing through a few magazines that lay there, then reached in between the pages. He rummaged through a sheaf of papers on the lower shelf but found nothing and then started shaking the magazines to see what might fall out.

Roxy drifted into the kitchen. Hassell stayed by the window, watching.

They rifled through the place. The muted roar of banging music filtered up through the floorboards and in the double-glazed window. It was around 3.15 p.m. by now and the afternoon festivities down below were in full swing. Mason had counted at least two other pubs nearby, all advertising live music, either folk or rock.

They searched for some time, safe knowing that no one knew they were here. At least, they hoped so. The first thing Mason noticed was that there were no signs of a struggle in the apartment, and, obviously, no dead bodies.

It was a step forward.

Sally sat in front of the small, open laptop and booted it up. Luckily, it opened straight onto the desktop screen with no need to enter a password. Unfortunately, though, it offered nothing. No personal files, no notes, no documents.

'Clearly, she uses this just for entertainment,' she said.

'I have something,' Quaid said at that moment. 'There's a proper computer thing in here and a few notepads.'

'I would call that a desktop PC,' Mason said, walking in behind the older man. 'Something, like the paddle-shift gear change, that doesn't interest you. But then, it's not fifty years old, I guess.'

'Nothing wrong with older models.' Quaid puffed his

chest out. 'They're more sturdy and reliable. Experienced too.'

Right then, Roxy pushed past Mason, followed by Sally. There was quite a crowd in Luciane's bedroom, all situated around the king-size bed with its yellow duvet and lone furry toy nestled next to the pillow. It was a big bedroom and in its far corner there sat another computer desk with a large PC. Quaid had switched it on only to be confronted by a password screen and had then turned his attention to the pile of notepads heaped to its left. He sat before them now, flicking through the pages.

'They're dated,' he said. 'I've gone back to just before she told me about the casino. Looks like she's been researching it for a while, though.'

'Any clues?' Sally asked.

'Well, yes, there are a lot. It's gonna take some scouring.' He opened one book at an early page. 'Look here, for instance. She writes of China and the Chinese culture, and their love of gambling and casinos. But then she switches her attention as though she happened upon something else. And this is bad. She mentions the dreaded SED here.'

Mason racked his brain to no avail. 'The SED?'

'You never came across them in your army days? Lucky you. The SED, made up of mercenaries, is the Special Exercise Division. They're kind of like our SAS, but a secret division of a shadowy militant group called the Shadow Kings. They're covert, low-key, probably do business through the Dark Web. I remember our SAS used to have a covert offshoot called the Ninth Division, sent out only on super-secret missions that couldn't be disclosed to anyone. The SED are like that, but with one glaring difference.'

Mason narrowed his eyes. 'Which is?'

'It ties in with Luciane and what she does.'

Sally walked over to the desktop. Roxy cleared her throat. 'Give us a clue,' she said.

Quaid scrunched his face up, thinking hard. 'Well, do you recall the stories about Hitler and Himmler, back in the Nazi days, where they encouraged the field of pseudo-archaeology? Basically, they directed everyone from normal citizens to specially formed units to search through Germany's archaeological past to find quantifiable verification of an advanced Aryan ancestry. But it wasn't just that they were researching. They were looking for artefacts, all relics from the world's ancient history, hoping to find some supernatural slant or maybe just enrich themselves.'

'You're telling me these Shadow Kings have some secret relic-hunting army?' Mason said with surprise in his voice.

'Damn right, I am. But you make it sound crazier than it really is. The SED are chiefly tasked with finding, looting, buying and generally procuring any ancient relics and treasures and either selling them for a vast profit on the black market or taking them back to the Shadow Kings where they will be placed in private vaults.'

'Who are these Shadow Kings?' Mason asked.

'Anonymous figureheads,' Quaid said. 'Fronted by the SED.'

'And what does Luciane tell of them?' Sally asked.

'There are several pages but, basically, she's saying that they're involved in the search for the casino.'

Mason looked uneasily around the room, thinking of the living room and the manic bar downstairs. Had deadly, secret soldiers cut through there, climbed the stairs and forced their way into Luciane Harlow's apartment to abduct her?

And why?

Was she that close to some mysterious truth?

Mason put a hand on Quaid's shoulder. 'Can you find any reason they may have taken her?'

'All of her research for the past few months revolves around that casino. She's put all her time into it and has made a tonne of enquiries. The SED could have taken her to find out what she knows or to shut her up because they want to keep all knowledge of the casino to themselves. They're cutting investigations off at the source. Maybe.' He shrugged.

'The SED operating in Ireland?' Sally asked dubiously. 'Really?'

'It happens more often than you might think,' Quaid said. 'What's stopping them from sending out operatives? The Russians do it. Why not the Shadow Kings?'

'Okay,' Mason said. 'But this Chinese casino has been buried out there in the sand for centuries. My question is – why now? What has prompted this recent interest?'

'That's where it gets really interesting,' Quaid said, leafing through a few pages, still reading and taking in the information. 'According to Luciane, several coins have turned up that date back to the period. And not just a few. Bags full. And one story told by the men who are trying to sell these coins is that they're from the old casino.'

'It's been found?'

'Not officially, it says here. But maybe. Maybe by a single person or a group. They could be drip-feeding the coins onto the market so as not to make waves. They could be creating interest, getting people excited. Unfortunately, now they've caught the attention of the Shadow Kings and thus the SED.'

'I have to ask,' Roxy said. 'What's so special about this casino? Special enough to get these Shadow Kings all hot and bothered?'

31

'Anything to do with ancient, priceless relics is easily enough,' Sally said. 'It's their bread and butter, how they thrive, how they exist. They have their noses in everything. And don't forget, if they do choose to sell a relic, it will be lost for ever to some secret, private collector. . And because we're artefact hunters, preservers of history, protectors of antiquity, we don't agree with that kind of attitude. We think it should be there for all to enjoy. And add to that, this might be the oldest proper casino ever found.'

Just then, the apartment's front door was flung open. The hulking shadow of a man stood there. In a heavily accented voice, he said, 'What are you doing here?'

And in his right hand, the blade of a knife glistened.

Chapter 4

Mason came alert in an instant. He moved towards the man, seeing the heavyset shoulders, his mind instantly making the connection between the SED, this apartment and the missing woman.

'We're friends of Luciane,' he said evenly. 'Who the hell are you?'

'What are *you* doing here?' Quaid returned the question.

Without replying, the big man walked into the room. He wore cargo trousers, a black padded jacket and an incongruous baseball cap that read 'I heart Dublin'. Overall, his behaviour was passive, but the face and the eyes told quite the opposite tale.

Mason watched the blade. 'Where's Luciane?'

Behind the man, in the doorway, more figures appeared. Roxy moved to Mason's shoulder. The first guy ran his thumb up and down the handle of the knife.

'You are the girl's friends?' he asked in accented English.

Mason didn't answer. He saw no reason to continue the conversation. He knew what was about to happen and was already preparing his mind and body for it. He knew also that the other members of his team were shifting into position too, even Sally, whom they'd all been training lately but who still had a long way to go.

The first man exploded into action. The blade came up sharply as he lunged at Mason, who let it pass between his ribcage and his arm and then trapped it, twisted, drawing the man inward. With his free arm, he then delivered a solid uppercut to the man's chin, a blow practised thousands of times in the boxing gym, striking perfectly. The enemy's eyes rolled up into his head. He flew backwards, and then he collapsed to the floor, flat out. The knife clattered across the bare wood.

Now Mason turned his attention to the oncoming figures. There were eight of them, all crowding through the door, all similarly attired. They all carried exposed knives, and Mason instantly knew why. It wouldn't work for an elite squad of special soldiers to walk down a busy Dublin street and then through a crowded, overexcited bar carrying their proper weapons, their guns. They couldn't risk the exposure. So, instead, they improvised.

And carrying knives didn't make them any less deadly. Mason would rather be in a gun battle than a knife fight.

The room was becoming crowded, but Mason didn't have a lot of time to think about it. The SED mercenaries moved fast, brandishing their weapons, asking questions in passable English. Mason ignored them all, waited for the attack he knew was coming.

He didn't have to wait long. A man dived in, knife swinging down towards Mason's chest. At the same time, others attacked. Roxy met one; Hassell met another, blocking knife strikes left and right. Mason caught the wrist of his attacker, tried to break it, but the man twisted away and then came again, this time with an underhand thrust. Mason darted sideways, out of the way.

There were more attackers than defenders, but the dimensions of the room didn't allow the enemy to attack with their full force. Three at a time, that was it. Mason crouched, eyes on his opponent, waiting for the next move. The guy looked wary, rightfully so; he'd already seen what Mason had done to his companion.

He lunged forward with the knife. Mason kicked out, swiping it from his hand, then led with two jabs and a devastating cross. His blows snapped the man's head back and then to the right. Blood flew from a broken nose. Mason kept up the onslaught, delivering combination after combination, driving the man back into his friends who waited behind. Six fast blows later, the man slithered to the ground.

Only to be replaced by another.

Mason's knuckles were throbbing. The next man's knife flashed in low. Mason caught the guy's wrist in two hands and forced them downwards, pushing them as low as he could get. The two men came face to face.

'What do you want?' Mason asked. 'Where's Luciane?'

'We are here for the evidence,' the man grunted. 'The location. What do you know?'

'You've already been once,' Mason said.

'We kept an eye on the place. Saw you arrive up here.'

Mason head-butted him just as the last word came out of his mouth. Not expecting it, the guy staggered and slipped further down as his knees gave way. Mason felt a blinding pain where he'd hit the man but held on. He didn't want to let go of the knife hand and prepared to deliver another head-butt.

To his left, Roxy had a tight hold on her opponent, her arms around his neck. She was close in, so that he had no room to use his knife, which was currently hanging ineffectually in his right hand, sticking out from their bodies. Roxy was choking her opponent into unconsciousness. She could feel the energy slipping away from him, feel the resistance lessening. Her left arm, around his neck, was exposed to those behind him, but they didn't dare stab at her for fear of striking their own man. She looked up then as she saw the knife fall from his limp grip.

And then he glided down to the floor, unconscious.

Roxy stepped back. Behind her, Sally was ready, her body language positive, her eyes steady. Now Roxy knew Sally had been training hard lately, but she didn't want their historian getting into a knife fight with a bunch of well-trained enemy combatants. Roxy waved her back.

To the far right, Hassell was struggling with an opponent. The man had him guessing as he struck again and again with the knife. Already, Hassell had a red tramline across his right bicep and another shallow one across his left wrist. He was bleeding, his shirt shredded. He was wincing with pain.

Quaid backed him up, though. When Hassell wilted, Quaid struck from the sides, slamming the SED guy around the neck and face. It helped distract him, kept him from attacking too fiercely. He knew that, if he came forward, he was walking into a barrage of punches, so instead he flailed with the knife from a few feet away.

Mason head-butted his current opponent to the ground. The man's eyes were rolling as he fought against unconsciousness, but he was in no state to fight. The next man stepped in, tripped over his fallen colleague, and landed head-first into Mason's devastating uppercut.

Instant lights out.

They were driving the enemy back now, towards the door. It was now five versus five, but some of those rendered unconscious were already stirring. Mason was glad and oddly disturbed to see Sally, at their rear, bending over those fallen, wriggling men, to deliver more debilitating blows, sending them back to dreamland.

The mercenaries squeezed through the room's door and out into the hallway. Mason, Roxy and Hassell formed a fighting line, impenetrable, driving them backwards. The gang thrust with their knives, but the blows were blocked, turned aside, the weapons falling from their grips. Mason didn't let up. They did not know where Luciane was being held, but now they knew all their suspicions had been correct. Before the SED attacked, they'd been living with nothing but conjecture.

Now...it was real.

All because someone had pillaged an ancient Chinese treasure, allowing foreigners to get involved.

They forced their attackers to the top of the stairs and then started down. One man tripped and fell the full length, groaning on the floor below, now effectively out of the battle. Mason, with height advantage, kicked out, sending the last knife spinning through the air and making their enemy double-time it fast down the stairs, almost running.

They hit the bottom, saw the bar through double doors to the right.

For the first time, Mason balked, actively stopped fighting, and thought about what was about to happen.

This Irish bar was about to get a hell of a lot rowdier.

Chapter 5

The four remaining SED mercenaries smashed in through the swinging double doors that led to the main bar.

Mason kicked them through it, not allowing them time to collect their wits, to fight back, to breathe. He'd learned in the army that it was the only way. Stay on top of your enemy, don't give them a chance to regroup.

The bar was rocking, packed to the rafters, live music pounding from the stage. The dance floor to the left was a living, breathing animal, overflowing with men and women waving their arms and bouncing up and down. To the right, the bar was three rows deep as people lined up to order drinks, shouting at the tops of their voices for beer and wine and malt whiskey.

Many people turned their way, most of them at least half-drunk. The mercenaries stumbled through the bar. Mason and his team punched and kicked them through it. There were cheers and grins and more than a few wide eyes. Some people shrank away, others muscled in on the battle. Mason saw an unknown figure stiff-arm an SED man across the back of the neck. He saw another try to trip one of the retreating men, a wide grin stretched across his face. Mason yelled out into the din that they should all leave well enough alone, but the tumult swallowed his voice. People swiped at him. A man holding a beer struck one of the SED fighters on the side of the face, laughing all the while. The soldier elbowed him back, knocking the beer from his hands and sending him clattering back into a pack of other men and women, some of whom hadn't seen what was happening, and starting a shouting match and then a ruckus. Out of nowhere, a blast of violence swept the room. Punches were thrown. People stumbled, fell backwards. The mercs lashed out, perhaps sensing a distraction they could use. Men and women turned, some fighting back without pause, without thought.

Suddenly, there were people staggering and stumbling about, throwing their beer, breaking glasses, punching left and right. The bar area became a melee. Screams ripped the air. Mason and his team, and their enemies, were all caught in the middle of it, trying to force their way through. It became harder and harder, every step a struggle. Mason saw a glass fly, spilling beer as it came. He ducked. The glass flew over his head and struck a man on the side of the face. Then came another, and still more. A woman barged into him from the side; he gently pushed her away. Her boyfriend saw him urging her aside and came in with a drunken barrage of blows. Mason gently put him on his arse. Ahead, their adversaries continued to force their way through the bar, but now a horde of people had come between them and Mason's team, making everything harder.

Screams filled Mason's ears. The chaos had spread to the dance floor, people swinging and swiping out over there. The band had stopped playing and was backing away, holding on to their instruments. The bar manager was yelling for calm. Someone else shouted that they'd call the cops. It was wild, crazy, a morass of humanity embracing its savage side for no real reason other than herd mentality.

Mason jabbed at an SED soldier's throat, making him stagger, but also aware he was adding to the violence that was sweeping the room. Every blow incited more blows. Did he stop? Let the SED escape? Or did he pursue them and try to take them down? It was every man and woman for themselves in here. The background music was still playing, though, an old rock song that somehow seemed to accompany the bar fight quite well.

Mason was about halfway across the bar, in the heart of the madness. Roxy was to his right, fending off drunken revellers who thought it prudent to throw their fists. Hassell was to his left, pushing away body after body, trying to keep them from being swept away in the brawl. Sally was in the little pocket of space to their rear, backing them up and trying not to get trampled. It was an anarchic push. Beer flew through the air in waves, followed by pint glasses and bowls of food, even a bottle of spirit. Somewhere a glass display cabinet shattered. Cutlery flew too, arcing high into the air, glittering as it came down under the sparkling lights.

Mason pushed on, pushed through. He fended off half-hearted, drunken punches. He threw men to right and left, tripped them and leapt over them. A woman struck him on the side of the head with her purse. Another crashed into him, making his legs buckle. The mercenaries backed off at speed, but they were experiencing their own problems, getting held up in the frenzied flow.

Mason picked his way, now over three-quarters of the way through the bar. Between them, they were staying upright, fending off the struggling masses, ducking missiles and punches and even, once, a young man. People were on the bar now, standing and yelling, cheering and throwing wild punches. The musicians had disappeared. Someone else had turned the background music up and now Queen was singing 'We Will Rock You' in time to the senseless affray. Mason saw myriad faces flashing by, some scared, some terrified, others happily grinning and enjoying themselves. Ahead, he saw a stream of people trying to get out of the far doors and into the street.

He walked across broken glass, almost slipped in spilled liquid. One moment, the mercs were out of reach, the next they were suddenly back in his face.

One struck out, catching him across the chin. Mason saw stars but ignored them, reaching for the man's throat, gripping it and squeezing. It was the wrong move. His opponent ignored the grip, striking fast, landing three or four blows that made Mason's head swim. He swore and let go, annoyed at himself for choosing the wrong attack. Roxy was advancing steadily at his side, striking out, taking her time and landing the right blows, as was Hassell to his left. Quaid and Sally did their best to disengage civilians from the confrontation.

They were nearing the far door. They slowed, caught up in the flow that wanted to escape the bar. Mason saw an empty narrow passage to the right that probably led to the kitchens and quickly pointed it out to Roxy.

'Ya think?' she yelled.

'No other option,' he yelled back.

Briefly, he wondered about the SED they'd left back up in the apartment. He glanced quickly to his rear, saw a writhing mass of people and knew they'd be no problem. Now, he looked in front of him again and wondered how they might pull off their next move.

But Roxy was already on it, driving her opponent more to the right, stepping in so that she created the angle. Mason did the same, punching and barging, trying to force his opponent into the narrow passage. The mercs hadn't seen it, and if they wondered about Mason and Co.'s sudden change of tactics, they didn't show it, just continued retreating, blocking, trying to retaliate.

Mason knew his team had the upper hand. Just then a glass hit his opponent on the side of the head, made him stagger as it shattered and spilled liquid down the man's front. Mason took advantage of the nasty distraction. He stepped in, grabbed his opponent under the arms and threw him to the right, making him stumble down the passageway whether or not he wanted to.

This was it. Mason's chance.

He stepped out of the chaos, entered the empty passage, and kicked out. A blow to the man's knee, another to his thigh, and he was falling. Mason grabbed the man's jacket and hauled him backwards across the floor, reached the kitchen door and slammed the back of the man's head against it to force it open.

Once inside, Mason took a quick look around.

There were no staff, all of them having prudently cleared out by now. He saw a gleaming rectangular central workstation, sinks and countertops and shelves all around the walls that were cluttered with plates, pots and pans, and countless bits of equipment.

The man at his feet was breathing heavily, gasping, holding his right knee.

Mason reached down and hauled him upright. He slapped

him on his right cheek, trying to get him to focus on anything but his own pain.

'Are you SED?'

Mason's captive struck out, still strong, still wily, bringing a knee up that barely missed Mason's groin and then sending jabs to the eyes and throat. Mason evaded them all, then smashed a fist into the man's solar plexus before knocking him sideways with a blow to the temple. The mercenary groaned and staggered.

Mason grabbed him and hauled him upright. 'I don't want to hurt you if I don't have to. Are you SED?'

There was a small nod, nothing more. The man's eyes were practically swimming in circles.

'We know you abducted Luciane Harlow. Why?'

The SED man's eyes abruptly focused. He opened his mouth to speak. Mason saw blood on his gums and teeth.

'Fuck. You,' he said.

'Oh, that's nice.' Mason dealt another blow, this one to the man's body. He thought he heard the crack of a rib.

'Same question.'

'We...follow orders. The...orders were to grab the woman. Don't know why.'

Mason could believe that. These specialised teams were often purposely kept in the dark by their leaders and even team leaders and given only the briefest parameters of their mission. Mason remembered the practice well from his own army days.

'I have one more question. Lie and it'll go badly for you. Where is Luciane now? Where is the woman you abducted?'

The man's eyes narrowed, then flitted from side to side as if seeking escape. Mason knew it was unlikely that a special forces operative would give up such information even on pain of death, but maybe he was considering a different alternative. Maybe, as Mason imagined, there were more SED members guarding Luciane, and by then the whole team would have had time to regroup and this guy could escape. That was this man's most likely train of thought.

'You will never defeat us,' the man said.

'I only want one answer from you.'

Mason raised another fist, came within a hair's-breadth of delivering it.

'Wait,' the man said, holding up a hand. 'I'll tell you. But it won't do you any good.'

'Let me be the judge of that.'

'Is she a friend of yours?'

'Very much.' Yes, the guy was fishing, but all Mason wanted was the address.

'She's not far,' the SED guy said. 'O'Connell Street. Past the Spire of Dublin, another monument further and you come to Clarice's Sweet Shop. It's empty, closed down. We're inside.'

'How many?' Mason asked.

'We left her with four guards.'

So that made thirteen total. Mason had what he needed. A quick glance back through the kitchen door's vision panel told him that the bar fight was still under way. It would make an excellent cover for their getaway.

And now, he heard sirens on the street.

Mason swung out with a haymaker, connected solidly with his opponent's skull, and sent the man into oblivion. Then, rubbing his knuckles, he exited the kitchen and went in search of his friends.

Chapter 6

Outside, in the early evening, it was wet and cold.

The rain had continued to fall, slicking the city streets and sparkling through the gaudy, flashing lights that lit up every pub and restaurant in the area. Mason could hear it running into the gutters. The street outside haemorrhaged men and women, all dressed up for a party night, many of them standing in the road as if herded there, looking back at the pub from which they had come. It was chaos out here too, but calmer overall. At least, Mason thought, he could see no fighting.

People still streamed out of the pub. Right then, the street was lit by flashing blue lights and police cars started approaching. Mason moved among the crowd with his friends and kept an eye on the pub's exit. There was no sign of the SED. Maybe they'd already escaped by a back entrance.

Or perhaps they were trying to regroup inside, most of them unaware that Mason had extracted information from one man.

Speaking of that, Mason turned to the others, reeled off what he knew and then looked around, trying to get his bearings. The rain fell lightly, coating the top of his head and shoulders in a fine wet mist. The cool breeze out here actually felt nice, soothing away the aches and pains he'd accumulated and lowering his body temperature. Mason's knuckles throbbed, his chest hurt, his face ached, but he was still very much in the game.

'Everyone okay?' he asked.

Police cars forced their way through the crowd and pulled up to the kerb. Mason, though he knew nothing would happen, didn't want to be around when they got here in force. He turned to Quaid and Sally.

'O'Connell Street,' he said. 'Where is it?'

Sally immediately consulted her phone. 'Two streets that way.' She pointed. 'We can reach it directly by following that street over there.'

Mason led them in the direction of O'Connell, dashing quickly across the road and then up the other street. He kept a wary eye out for the SED, but saw no one. Roxy and Hassell also voiced their worries that the SED numbered thirteen in total and would no doubt outmatch them, especially if they had advanced weaponry stashed at the sweet shop.

'That's why we have to be quick,' Mason said. 'In and out faster than they can react, just like a military op. If we hit the sweet shop now, we have only four enemies to contend with.'

He didn't like it, and neither did Quaid. It was just too risky to be viable. But Mason also knew it was their best way forward.

'Hurry,' he said. 'We can beat them back to the sweet shop.'

They sprinted now, flying through the rain, racing for O'Connell and then turning left when they reached the wide thoroughfare. They passed the Spire of Dublin, the rain slanting into their eyes. It occurred to Mason that they didn't know who was in charge of the SED operation. Who these fabled Shadow Kings were. Were they faceless politicians? Or military leaders, bent on profiting from historical secrets? Rich, powerful, bored men and women? Maybe it was a private individual with connections to an army? Mason didn't know, and that unsettled him a little. In battle, it was always best to know the opponent you faced.

The rain lashed down, coming harder now. It bounced off their shoulders and heads, sparkling under the streetlights. It swirled down the sides of the street. The skies above were prematurely dark, casting long shadows over the early evening.

Minutes later, they reached the sweet shop. The name *Clarice's* hung outside on a quaint, swaying square sign; the windows were dark. White and red banners that read *Closing Down Sale* were stuck across the inside of the windows at an angle. Mason could still see the dark shapes of tables, racks and shelving inside.

The front door, whilst set back in a little alcove, sat in full view of the street.

'Let's try the back door,' Hassell said.

Mason agreed. O'Connell was still quite busy at this time of night, though the area around the sweet shop was a little less travelled. Hassell led the way around the side of the sweet shop, down a side street that ran the length of the building. As they approached the rear, Mason saw an eight-foot brick wall to their left, enclosing the shop's rear, and a small wooden gate set into the wall. The gate had padlock access.

Roxy turned to Hassell. 'What's it to be, bud? Over the top or through the padlock?'

Mason hoped for the padlock option, but Hassell threw them a grim smile. 'We left so quickly I didn't have time to pack my other stuff.'

Roxy sighed loudly. 'You mean you can't connect with anything electronically, don't you? Make some numbers flash and then a *click*?'

Hassell opened his hands in defeat. 'No, I can't do that.'

'No time to waste.' Mason cupped his hands and motioned for Roxy to put a boot in them. Quaid and Hassell turned to check the scene was clear. When they nodded, Mason hoisted Roxy to the top of the wall and then motioned to Sally.

'You're next.'

Up they went, and over the top. Mason lifted Quaid up and then turned to Hassell. 'Your turn.'

'You go.' Hassell laced his own hands together. 'I'm good at jumping.'

Mason blinked at that but, knowing they had no time to waste, took a surreptitious glance left and right before lifting a boot into Hassell's hands and feeling himself propelled up the wall. At the top, feeling the slick, rough brickwork beneath him, he took hold of the edges and pulled his body over, then looked over the other side for any obstructions. Seeing nothing but a concrete yard, he nodded in satisfaction, then turned back to Hassell.

'Ready?'

'Yeah.'

He lay across the top of the wall, hung his arms down and braced himself. Hassell leapt upward, grabbed Mason's hands and used them to climb the wall until he could grab hold of the top. Seconds later, the two men had jumped down to the yard below, which was cast in darkness because of the high walls on all sides. Ahead, Mason saw the back entry to the sweet shop.

Roxy approached it stealthily. They were all aware that their enemy, though only numbering four, were likely armed.

Mason had a sinking feeling when they approached the back door, thinking the lock would be the same as the gate, but was surprised to find a normal keyhole. Clearly, the security mechanisms had been fitted at different times. Hassell stepped up, lock picks in hand, and bent to his task. Seconds later, he soundlessly pushed the back door open.

Mason knew they had no time. He went past Hassell in silence, into the dark interior, finding himself in a storage room. Old cardboard boxes littered the place, some still with a few cartons of sweets inside, others ripped apart or stacked in the corners. He moved to the inner door and waited for everyone to enter the storage room before putting his hand on the door handle.

He twisted it and gently opened the door. Gradually, an inch at a time, the room beyond came into view. He stayed absolutely quiet. The first thing he saw was the empty rows of shelving that ran down the shop, although, oddly, he saw some boxes of sweets here too, as if the sweet shop owners had been in a hurry clearing out and forgotten a few.

The second thing he saw was the huddle of men off to the right, all sitting around a strange irregular shape. Mason blinked and then looked again. Yes, there were four figures and a fifth bumpy-looking outline. As he stared, Mason figured that the four men had all thrown their jackets over the captive, perhaps as a sign to keep quiet. He saw no weapons clasped in the figures' hands.

49

Was the irregular shape Luciane?

He crept forward, conscious that a squeaky floorboard would put an end to their skulking. He felt confident, but naked, without a weapon. With a weapon, they could just stride forward and take charge. Here, though, now, they were at high risk.

They all crept through the door, leaving it ajar behind them. Now, they caught the faint sound of the men conversing, laughing, swopping a story or two. They didn't seem worried about guarding their perimeter. Maybe they'd been here a while and were confident in their environment, or perhaps they were just sure of themselves, of their abilities. Mason ducked behind a shelf and breathed, making ready for the next fight. The others crowded around.

Nobody spoke. Mason could see their bright eyes in the dark. He could hear their breathing. He peered out from around the corner of the shelf.

The men still sat in place, talking animatedly. Mason signalled with his fingers.

Three…two…one…

And moved. He swept around the corner, ran softly towards the four guards, sensing Roxy, Hassell and Quaid just steps behind him. First contact would be imperative. But the closer he got, the harder it was going to be.

These were trained operatives.

And, finally, they showed it. They heard the onrush of approaching bodies, or at least one of them did. He whirled, spotted Mason and let out a yell. Right then, Mason launched himself through the air, striking the man's chest and driving him backwards. As he landed, he spotted a pile of weapons to the left, within reach, all semi-autos, gleaming in the relative dark. Mason used his advantage to swipe out at the man he'd hit, punching with body shots to double him over and then kneeing him in the face. But the guy was tough. He leaned against the wall, panting, his face slicked with blood, and growled.

He came at Mason, hands reaching. Mason batted them away and powered forward with a head-butt. This made the man groan and stagger and throw his hands up. Mason went for the groin, using his knee twice in quick succession, and then finished up with two devastating blows to the temple.

The man slipped down the wall, unconscious.

Behind him, Roxy, Hassell and Quaid had engaged the other three, with Sally remaining spare. Mason guarded the cache of weapons, his ears also listening out for any more company that might arrive. The figure beneath the coats was squirming. Roxy lashed out with a foot, snapping her opponent's right knee backwards and making him yell. When he staggered she pounced on him, raining down a flurry of blows that he couldn't escape, and that gradually rendered him inert. Quaid and Hassell were less competent in combat scenarios, but they were game, striking forward with blows to the throats and eyes and temples that drove their opponents back. The opponents separated either side of the squirming pile of coats and then came up against the wall. Hassell and Quaid waded in.

Mason and Roxy were spare now, and it was a good job. The mercenaries were happy to take the punishment so long as they lured Hassell and Quaid in. Once close, they pushed back with brute force and turned the tables, spinning so that it was Hassell and Quaid who were cornered.

And they drew knives.

Mason thought it best to end it quickly. He spun, picked up a gun and made sure the safety was off.

51

'Drop the knives,' he growled.

The SED guys froze, turned, and saw the man with the gun. Roxy went immediately to pick up another and threw a third to Sally. They spread out around the men, but made sure their own team members weren't in the crossfire.

Mason repeated his request. 'Drop 'em.'

Two knives clattered to the floor. The SED slowly put their hands in the air. When they did, Quaid wasted no time in rushing up to the pile of coats.

'Luciane,' he said. 'Is it you?'

He ripped the clothing away, uncovered the shape beneath. Mason saw a tall, leggy woman with blond curls and a fierce-looking face. She hadn't been cowed by her captivity. Quite the opposite. She was fighting back. Quaid caught a fist that was thrown at his face and now Mason thought he saw the reason for the coats. It had probably been a way of subduing her for a while. After all, they'd had Luciane captive for hours and were probably fed up with the strong-willed woman.

'It's me,' Quaid said quickly. *'Paul Quaid!* It's me. Calm down, Luciane, we have to get out of here fast.'

Mason was already in motion, waving the two SED soldiers aside. They wouldn't be pulling any punches here. Both he and Roxy stepped forward, reversed their guns and smashed their captives across their faces. It took two hits, but the men finally collapsed to the floor.

Quaid pulled Luciane to her feet. 'Are you hurt?'

'Only a little,' she said in a breathy voice. 'They hit me a few times, but I'm fine. Nothing broken.'

'They hit you?' Quaid sounded angry.

'We have to go.' Mason expected to hear the arrival of the remaining SED at any second.

Instantly, they all turned and ran for the back door, sped through the storage room and out into the rear yard, where still a light drizzle fell. Outside, it was silent and dark, fooling Mason into thinking it was later than it really was. He raced across the yard to the wooden gate and looked back, uncertainty in his eyes.

'It's quicker.' Roxy read his mind.

Mason nodded. A little noise at this stage would have to do. He braced himself, then leapt forward and kicked out, smashed the gate right off its hinges, and dashed through the gap into the street outside, eyes on stalks. Luckily, there was no one around. He gestured quickly to the others.

'Move,' he said.

They weren't safe yet, Mason knew. The SED could be anywhere, taking any route back to the sweet shop. Maybe they would recognise Luciane. They had to get her well away from here and to safety. Mason went first, heading back to O'Connell since it was the busier alternative and the road less likely travelled by the SED.

'We should head to a car and get the hell away from here,' Hassell said.

Mason tended to agree. They'd arrived and gone to the apartment above the bar in such a rush that they hadn't checked into a hotel anyway. Where they went next didn't matter. And it was best that they put some distance between themselves and Dublin before listening to Luciane.

So long as it was far from the SED.

Mason led them through the falling rain.

Chapter 7

They traversed the wet, glassy streets of Dublin in a hurry, stuck to walking with other groups and found a quiet area surrounded by monuments before calling an Uber. It wasn't the best getaway under the circumstances, but it was all they had. Mason, as he waited, resolved that next time they would hire their own car.

Escape by Uber happened soon enough, though. They had instructed the driver to take them to the outskirts of Dublin, to a rambling hotel there, and were soon dropped off outside. It was getting on for seven-thirty by now, and darkness had fully drawn in, bringing with it a newer, colder, fresher rain. They wasted no time hanging around outside and hurried up the front steps to the double entrance doors and into the gleaming foyer.

Inside, the hotel was a tired but clean concoction of old wood, worn carpets and lustrous light fittings. The staff leaned over their stations as if they'd been working for two full days without a break, glassy-eyed, as if they'd had their fill of humanity for now. Sally secured them all rooms with the company credit card and then met them in the middle of the hotel's lobby.

'Do you feel up to talking about it all?' Quaid asked Luciane.

'Damn right, I do,' the tall curly-haired blonde replied immediately. 'But first I want a change of clothes, a shower and a bloody good meal.'

'You've not been harmed then?' Quaid asked again, concern in his voice.

Luciane shrugged. 'They hurt me. They questioned, grabbed, punched. They relented when I told them everything I knew, and then I think they weren't sure what to do with me.'

'The SED special forces?' Mason winced a little. 'After fighting them, I think they knew exactly what they were going to do with you. It was just a matter of time.'

Luciane stared at him. 'Well, thanks for that nugget of information. That really settles my nerves.'

'You don't look nervous,' Quaid said.

'You know me. I just get on with it and worry later. Listen, seriously, can you give me half an hour before we do this?'

Mason nodded. Sally pointed out that they had very little luggage with them but, between them, they could probably rustle up Luciane some new clothes. Roxy didn't look pleased.

'Not me,' she said. 'I'm wearing the only pair of jeans I own and nobody's taking my "Ride Me and Die" T-shirt away.'

'What's your bag full of?' Mason teased, indicating her rucksack. 'Cosmetics? Perfume?' He grinned.

'Rum,' she growled.

They split up, found their rooms, showered and changed. Mason sat on the edge of his bed for a while, running through the events of the night. He knew they'd got lucky at the sweet shop, but he figured they'd carved out their own right to some luck with their performances in the bar fight. Sometimes, you got exactly what was coming to you.

They were down in the restaurant less than thirty minutes later, ordering food. Mason didn't say much as the drinks arrived and then the steak. He polished his portion off and tried not to watch Luciane; he didn't want her to feel pressured. He got the impression her captivity had been tougher than she was letting on, but respected her need to downplay it.

After the meal, Luciane sat back and smiled, a look of pleasure on her face for the first time. She nodded as Sally ordered brandies all around, and crossed her legs under the table.

'I'm a capable woman,' she said, for the benefit of everyone. 'Nobody pushes me around. Not sure if Quaid mentioned it, but I used to be in the Garda before, helping the British soldiers on missions. I then changed that life for the better, got into relics and history and archaeological finds. I travelled all over the world, gained respect...' She shrugged. 'It's a good life until you step on someone's toes.'

'Tell us about it,' Quaid muttered. 'We've been accosted all over the world and we've been at it for less than a year. The relic-and-archaeological business seems to attract its fair share of lowlifes.'

'It's the money,' Luciane said. 'It's a relatively easy way of earning tonnes of cash. It brings out the degenerates. And the Shadow Kings – they're the worst degenerates of the bunch. They're a global organisation, known to steal treasured artefacts and either sell them on the black market or store them in a secret vault for their viewing pleasure alone. Once the Shadow Kings acquire a precious artefact you can assume it's lost for ever. It's also how they're funded. They're a legendary group on the Dark Web and will stop at nothing to get what they want.'

Mason took a sip of his brandy. 'What do you mean by that last sentence?'

'Okay, they abducted me. I don't know what division or agency or how, or any of that crap. But I do know that the man who questioned me was evil, ruthless, terrifying. He has a single-minded love for his employers and will let nothing and nobody stand in his way.' Luciane shuddered at the memory.

'What was his name?' Quaid asked.

'Miura. At least that's what the others called him when they weren't calling him "boss". The few times they spoke in English. I heard the name Miura all the time.'

'At least we know who their leader is,' Sally said. 'But what did they question you about?'

'That's the big question, all right. So, when I get the bit between my teeth, when I'm searching for something, some relic, some artefact, anything, I go all in. I make every enquiry, talk to all the major people, investigate thoroughly.'

'And, this time, you caught the attention of the Shadow Kings,' Quaid said.

'Exactly. I found out that, across China and Japan, there are fresh stories emerging of bags of old casino coins being found. Nobody knows where the stories come from; they just keep coming. It feels like someone has found or stolen these bags and is distributing the coins a few at a time, but I can't be too sure of that. I got hold of my contacts in both countries and started asking questions.'

'Like what?' Mason asked.

'Where do the coins originate? Where did they find the bags? What period do they date back to? Who found the coins? That kind of thing. General stuff. I purposely cast a wide net.'

'And that was probably your downfall,' Sally said. 'These Shadow Kings got wind of it.'

'Of course they did. They'd have to be deaf and blind not to. I'm sure they will already have been investigating. But when an international treasure hunter gets involved, that tends to make them sit up.'

'Is that what you are? A treasure hunter?' Hassell asked.

'I'm a hybrid, honey. I don't go both ways. I go *every* way when it comes to treasure hunting, travel every highway, every sea, uncloak every mystery. I'm open to anything. And the Shadow Kings, they want to profit hugely from this casino. I want to find the treasure so that I can share it with the world.'

'So we hear,' Mason said.

'They will kill to get their way, by which I mean they will keep it for themselves and keep any outside interference to a minimum,' Luciane said. 'This guy Miura told me that. He speaks very good English, by the way. He said they had no qualms about sending the SED out into the world to "silence the rumours", as he put it.'

'They don't want anyone relic hunting on their territory,' Sally said.

'With a vengeance,' Luciane said. 'I wouldn't want to cross them again.'

'Hopefully, you won't have to, but they've certainly got their teeth into you,' Mason said. 'They won't stop, especially now that you've escaped. And now they'll be on to us, too. How far did your enquiries actually go?'

'Oh, as I said. Deep. Extremely deep. All my Eastern contacts were involved. They all know how to reach me, my real name, my details. I sure don't skulk in the shadows.'

'I like the sound of this casino, though,' Sally put in. 'From an archaeological point of view. I believe it could be the world's oldest.'

'Yeah, back to the mid-fifteenth century,' Luciane said. 'It certainly grabbed my attention. Something of that ilk could be huge.'

'But the Shadow Kings won't share it,' Quaid said. 'They won't share the discovery. They won't share access to the casino, even with world-leading historians or archaeologists. They're not interested in analysing the artefacts for historical value. Not only that, they've sent killers out to stop others finding it. We know they have other plans for the artefacts. It's all about profit and resale.'

'We'll stop them,' Luciane said. 'And not just the Shadow Kings, but anyone who tries to derail an archaeological hunt of this importance. We will protect this casino at all costs.'

'After everything that's happened, you want to press ahead with your quest?' Quaid said in a slightly disbelieving voice. 'Let's not forget, the Shadow Kings are not to be messed with and do have their eyes on this casino.'

'Of course I do,' Luciane said. 'In fact, I want to do it even more now. The Shadow Kings desperately want the casino, but their motivations are simply terrible. Maybe to sell off the parts bit by bit until there is nothing left…But if we do go after this, I want to do it with protection.' She looked around at them and repeated, 'With protection.'

'I hate to say this, but nobody can protect you against the might of the Shadow Kings,' Hassell said. 'By all accounts, they're scarily powerful.'

'I know that,' Luciane said. 'But we're talking about an offshoot here. Special forces, I believe. Bad, I know, but you already bested them. And the payoff for the world of archaeology…it's enormous.'

Sally smiled as she threw back her brandy. 'I do like the sound of finding that casino.'

'How far did you get?' Mason asked Luciane.

'Put out the feelers all across the East. I made waves. And I was progressing, too. Maybe that's why they felt the need to capture and interrogate me.'

'Wait, wait,' Quaid said. 'Now that we have her back, shouldn't we go to the authorities?'

'And tell them what?' Mason asked. 'That Shadow King mercenaries started a bar fight? That they hid out in a sweet shop that, by the way, will now not contain a single trace that they were ever there? What evidence do we have?'

'They turned her place over,' Quaid said quietly.

'But you know there's no proof. Nothing. As usual, mate, we're on our own here.'

'I won't stop searching for the casino,' Luciane said. 'I have too much riding on it.'

'What does that mean, exactly?' Mason asked.

'All my efforts for the past weeks and months have gone into the search. All my money, greasing palms. I have everything tied up into the hunt for that casino now. And, as I said, imagine the payoff if we do find it first.'

'If they catch you on the hunt, they'll kill you,' Quaid said. 'That's why they're here.'

'They'll kill her anyway, just because she's seen them,' Mason said. 'The Shadow Kings don't mess around.'

'All right, I'm confused,' Hassell said. 'I agree you need to find the casino. I see you won't back down. But let's say you *do* find it. What then? It's in China, so it's already under *their* ownership.'

'A good point,' Luciane said. 'But that's not what it's all about. If I take a good camera I could film a very good documentary around the search. Around the discovery, the place itself. A programme like that would be well received and worth the effort. Imagine it being played on Western screens. It would fare better coming out of a forbidden country as China is thought of than if it were, say, Brazil or America. Everyone's drawn to the forbidden.'

Around them, the restaurant was emptying. It surprised Mason to see that it was after ten p.m. Waiting, he tried to figure out what was the best way to go. In fact, judging by the looks on the faces of his teammates, they were all thinking the same thing.

On the one hand, Luciane wasn't their responsibility. They'd saved her once. They couldn't be held responsible if she ran headlong into danger a second time. On the other hand, there was the casino itself, and all the possibilities it represented. Handling treasure was what they did. Whether protecting an ancient artefact, or transporting it, or hunting it down, that was their job, and they enjoyed doing it. Obviously, they hadn't taken this quest on as a job, but the pull of the ancient casino was in his blood.

'Where are you?' he asked Luciane. 'In your investigation.'

'Making headway,' she said immediately. 'And, unfortunately, I had to tell the soldiers the same thing. I have a lead. There's a man named Kei Aoki, who frequently visits a casino in Japan. He's been dropping quite a few of these coins.'

'And when you say "dropping"?' Hassell asked.

'Dropping. Selling them at local shops. Offering them for sale. Showing them to locals and asking their worth, trying

61

to exchange a few. Word soon gets around, especially if the wrong person finds out.'

'Your contacts told you this?'

'Yeah. Kei Aoki has at least one bag of the casino coins.'

'Why am I feeling a trip coming on?' Quaid asked with a groan.

'Is there a better way than being in the thick of it?' Luciane asked.

'You're saying you want us to accompany you to this Japanese casino?' Sally said with a smile. 'To hunt for clues that may lead us to the ancient casino? One of the oldest known to man and, at least in fame and renown, worth an absolute fortune? That'd certainly look good on our résumé.'

'I still think hunting for this casino is a vast grey area,' Quaid said.

'The thing is,' Mason said quietly, 'this SED are trying to kill people. They're here covertly and they don't care who they hurt to achieve their goal – finding that casino. We know why they want to keep it so secret. They certainly don't have its historical value at heart, that's for sure. We have to help Luciane to stop them.'

'It's risky,' Quaid pointed out. 'The SED already has this information.'

'But they're still in Dublin, looking for me,' Luciane said. 'What do you say, people? Shall we go look for a piece of incredible history?'

'It certainly seems as if this Kei Aoki knows something,' Roxy said.

'He may know everything,' Luciane said. 'We just have to get to him first.'

Chapter 8

Inside the closed-down sweet shop, standing alone in the dark as befitted his station at this time, Captain Miura, a Frenchman of the Special Exercise Division smoked an unfiltered cigarette and stared out the darkened windows. It was dark outside, raining too. The dirty rabble passed occasionally, some running because of the rain, their no doubt nit-ridden heads sheltered by umbrellas, hats and even newspapers. The shop was silent, its innards gutted except for empty shelving and tiered racks. His men all sat in a corner, twelve of them, and they were a sorry bunch, sitting with their heads hanging, their shoulders slumped, in silence.

Miura was a tall man, blocky and powerful. He liked to use his hands for everything, from cooking to killing, if he got the chance. It wasn't about saving a bullet; it was about getting up close and personal, seeing the lights go out. He was hairless, intensely clean, and the perfect Shadow King soldier.

Miura went to his pocket as usual in times of stress. He plucked out a photo of his wife and stared at it, rubbing the image with his thumb. Next, he unfolded an informational note from his Shadow King president and gave it a long perusal. His wife was currently visiting her ill mother in Paris, taking time off her government job. The president? Well, the president was counting on Miura to get this job done.

Indirectly, of course.

Miura didn't know who, above his rank, had been read into the operation. He didn't need to know. All he needed was to succeed. And here, tonight, the chances of that had taken a nosedive.

Miura thought about his father. He, too, had been an officer of rank in the French Army, known as the Land Army. Father had been working at the French embassy in London when he had been set upon by three youths, beaten, robbed and murdered. The animals hadn't needed to take the man's life; he gave them everything they wanted. But that was the way of lands of violence and greed and excess.

Miura, above all, was a soldier. An utterly loyal soldier. He commanded his unit with ruthless devotion and, until today, they had performed faultlessly. *What had happened today?*

They had been surprised, shocked, bested by unknown combatants. They had been out-thought, outwitted, most definitely out-played.

Miura stayed at the window, watching, seeing nothing, his thoughts and attention turned inward. Briefly, he touched his wife's photo again. Amelie was pregnant, three months now. Miura wanted his child to grow up in a world where his employers were powerful and dominant and he would make any sacrifice, perform any duty, to achieve that.

Most of all, they *couldn't* let themselves be overpowered by outside forces.

Miura would help keep the Shadow Kings working at the top of their game. They were secret, active, a true world power that worked from the shadows. He would kill to preserve that power, that anonymity. The president demanded it, and he was a loyal soldier through and through.

The casino.

It was a developing problem. Miura had made sure he'd conducted the woman's interrogation himself, got his hands filthy by touching her, by striking her, by being spattered by her blood. It was disgusting, but necessary. The woman – Luciane – had told him everything she knew, and Miura had been ready and very willing to go much further. He had knives in mind, bricks, fire. He had been almost disappointed when she gave everything up so quickly and easily.

But then they had received disturbing information. A new team had entered the fray by visiting the woman's stinking apartment. They had been nosing around, looking for information...or maybe they already had information.

It was a situation Miura couldn't let develop further. He had sent nine of his men, including himself, in to take care of the civilians. At first he believed the civilians had escaped by luck – the bar fight couldn't have been of their own concocting – but then, when they came immediately to this place, he knew that something deeper was going on. They had taken four men out here too, left them alive but incapacitated.

They were military.

Miura was sure of it. And the military, dressed as civilians, probably meant special forces. Which was another problem. They had rescued the woman, which added to Miura's issues. But at least he'd wrung all the information out of her that he could.

Miura had been looking forward to killing the bitch.

His men, sat in a circle, were smoking and eating their rations, sipping their drinks. They knew enough to stay quiet. They knew that, somehow, an inferior force had bested them. Most of all, they knew it could never happen again.

Miura himself went over to them without speaking, poured himself some tea and took it over to the window. Under the circumstances, it wasn't bad. It soothed the blighted part of his soul that screamed failure. Miura took another sip.

He watched passers-by trudge past the window. He hated their arrogance, wanted to scour it right out of them with something sharp or serrated. But discipline held him back. That, and a love of his job that bordered on fanaticism.

'Captain.' The voice came from behind him. 'The men are restless. They want to know what is next.'

Miura turned slowly, set the tea on the floor. He wanted both his hands free for this. He glared at the man who had the effrontery to approach him at this time, in these moments of failure, the man with the gall to question him. That man was named Liam and, if Miura didn't expressly need him at this time, he would have hurt him, maybe killed him. Miura drew his military knife.

'Was it you?' he asked quietly. 'Was it you who betrayed our position?'

The words were a furious whisper, a death knell. Liam would have to answer very carefully.

'Not me, captain. They did not capture me tonight.'

Miura observed him, trained to spot lies. 'Then who was?'

'I do not know, captain. The men are quiet, subdued. They have not tasted defeat before and, it is worse, at the hands of the non-military.' Liam hung his head.

Miura put a hand on the man's shoulder. 'Do not worry, we do not know that for sure. We will win.' And by that he meant *the Shadow Kings,* not his unit, though he firmly believed they would also win the day.

Liam nodded. 'Of course, sir. I mean, look at these people. Look at them passing by. They think they are the rulers of their world. They are nothing. Their opinions are shit, their observations as worthy as long-dead, rotting creatures. They are nothing compared to the Shadow Kings and those proud to work for them. We are above them all.'

Miura liked it that his men thought the same way he did. Yes, civilians were insignificant. That they thought themselves valuable and meaningful was something that stuck in Miura's throat like a chicken bone. They all needed to be taken down several pegs, taught lessons. The Shadow Kings could do it with ease, anytime, anywhere. They could single out any individual and break them. *Any* individual. And when he had the chance to interrogate one of them again, Miura knew it wouldn't go well for that person.

Miura had been on many special operations. Usually, it involved sneaking around some war-torn country, making sure a particular relic was extracted professionally in any manner that was possible. If that manner contained torture, murder, kidnapping, then so be it. If it required stealth, the SED were up for it.

Miura remembered Liam stood at his shoulder. 'Go back to the men,' he said. 'Tell them we will move soon.'

'To...Japan?' Liam clearly remembered the woman's whispered words, the information she'd spilled to them.

'To Japan,' Miura said, and that was enough information for now. 'Go,' he repeated.

'Yes, sir.'

Miura didn't move, but continued to stare out into the night. Raindrops made tracks down the windowpane before his eyes, obscuring the glass. He took all the hatred and discipline he felt, remembered the woman's words, the way they'd been bested tonight, the men and women who'd bested them, and hoped for a future confrontation. He would take great pleasure in teaching those people the errors of their ways, teaching them the right way to live and learn and exist.

Next, Japan.

Already, he was looking forward to the challenge.

Chapter 9

It turned out they were wrong about the location of the man named Kei Aoki.

Luckily for Mason and the others, it didn't affect their plans too much. What had at first been an international flight to Japan turned to Hong Kong before they even left Dublin.

It was down to Luciane's and Quaid's contacts. The curly-haired blonde and the older man had made several calls to Japan regarding the individual they sought, and had been told that he'd recently relocated to Hong Kong, there to be found frequenting various casinos.

It was a KLM eighteen-hour, one-stop trip that had Mason sitting next to a snoring woman for the entire flight, Roxy almost beheading a man who reclined his seat in front of her, Sally breaking out her laptop to research Chinese casinos, and Quaid and Luciane putting their heads together for a chat about the old, perhaps better, times. Or maybe Quaid was still being recalcitrant. For his part, Hassell leaned back, ignored everything and brooded for the entire flight. It was what he did best.

The plane landed with a squeak of tyres and a rush of air at Hong Kong International around 6.30 a.m. By the time Mason and the others had cleared passport control and walked through baggage claim to the arrivals area, it was getting on for eight. As they waited for a taxi, Luciane turned to speak to them.

'Clearly, we're too early for the casinos, though many are twenty-four hours. We should wait for tonight to find and approach Aoki.'

It made sense. They went to a midtown Western fast-food restaurant and hung out there for a while before listening to Sally tell them about Hong Kong's various casinos.

'Most of the casinos, the lawful ones at least, are to be found in gambling cruise ships, many in the city of Kai Tak, which depart from Hong Kong at certain times and cruise to international waters. They say that Aoki frequents the Celebrity Millennium Cruise, the Silversea Shadow and the Poker House, but we really have to pin the right one down as, once that ship has sailed, there's no way on or off until it docks. That's the first problem.'

'We should get to Kai Tak city,' Quaid said.

'Agreed, but hold your horses. As I said, we don't know which casino Aoki's going to visit tonight.'

'You're saying we have to surveil all of them?' Mason asked.

'All three,' Sally said with a nod.

'Not a problem if we're going through with this,' Quaid said brightly. 'There are six of us.'

'I don't like the team being split up,' Mason said. 'You know that.'

'Don't worry, Babyface.' Roxy put a hand on his arm. 'We'll survive.'

And immediately she knew she'd said the wrong thing. Mason's face dropped, his lips tightening. His major demons came from a moment in Mosul, during the war. Mason felt a bond and a responsibility for his friends, for the people he considered family, and thus for his army buddies. When two had died during a routine building check – a building that Mason had already cleared – he had taken it in the worst possible way, losing his army career and everything else that was good in his life.

Mason knew that sometimes good people, friends, didn't survive.

Roxy believed that Mason had overcome most of those demons by now, by being a part of this team and throwing himself into their missions. But he still carried, and always would, the burdens of his darkest memory.

As did she. Roxy cast her mind back over her own problems. They were profound, like Mason's. But at least she knew exactly what she was trying to do with her life now. Before, it had all been drifting under a haze of rum-soaked indifference. Now, it was a quantifiable goal. Recruited at eighteen by a three-letter agency that officially didn't exist, Roxy had lost twelve years of her life – her *young* life – to duty and orders and death around the world and was now trying to find at least a small piece of the woman she might have become. It was deep, she knew, but she was getting there.

Mason recovered quickly. He smiled at her and she nodded back at him, an apology in her eyes. It was sometimes hard finding the right word to say, so she said nothing.

'We should grab a hotel and get some rest,' Quaid said. 'It's gonna be a long night.'

'The flight wasn't exactly relaxing,' Roxy grumbled.

'Exactly.'

They found a hotel in Kai Tak city, paid for early rooms and split up. Roxy didn't need to unpack; her rucksack contained just underwear and a few other bits and pieces. She showered, closed the blinds and got her head down, determined to catch a few winks before their agreed meeting time around mid-afternoon. When she couldn't sleep right away, she drank water, snacked on a bag of crisps and a small rum from the minibar and then tried again. Soon, her mind was wandering and her eyes closing. Sleep came fitfully. Visions fuelled by terrible memories ran around her head, vying for prominence. She saw old kills, poor decisions, crazy moments. She saw how the agency had corrupted her, taken her youth, her dreams away, tooled her into a machine.

She woke bathed in sweat, glad to be rid of the visions. She never looked forward to sleep. It was always the same.

It could have been any hotel room, anywhere in the world. The walls were beige, the prints old and generic, nothing more than drone shots of Hong Kong. The bed was too hard; the shower smelled, and the bathroom contained those little shampoo and conditioner bottles and several freshly laundered towels. Roxy sat for a while on the edge of the bed. She brewed a coffee, tried not to think too deeply. When the memories resurfaced, they dragged her deep, like a demon rising out of swirling hellfire, grabbing her ankle and pulling her down to nefarious depths. And the memories always resurfaced. They were as much a part of her as her new life, as Joe Mason and the ragtag crew. As her considerable efforts to move forward.

Roxy showered again and then joined the others downstairs for an early dinner. They knew the night would be spent aboard the cruise ships and wanted to be ready for anything. They sat around the table, ordered and ate, and said very little until the coffees were served near the end.

'We all have phones,' Sally said. 'The idea is to stay in contact. When someone sees Aoki, call the others, try to get everyone on the same boat.'

'Do we know what kind of man he is?' Hassell asked. 'How he'll react to us?'

'Not really,' Quaid said. 'My contacts call him ruthless at the table, a career gambler. Of course, he loses more than he wins, which is why he splashed the ancient coins around in the first place. But that doesn't stop him returning night after night.'

'We'll need to have our wits about us for this guy,' Roxy said.

'And don't forget the SED,' Luciane said with a shudder. 'They know exactly what we know, thanks to me.'

Quaid leaned towards her. 'I'm just glad you're safe. I agree with you that sending the SED killers to find the casino was a terrible move. It shows the Shadow Kings consider loss of life insignificant.'

'This is a chat, essentially, not an extraction,' Mason said. 'We can't force him to tell us anything. We're not working for any government and we're not even here officially. Unfortunately, we're relying on goodwill.'

They'd worked it so they had time to spare. Their current clothes weren't going to cut it. They went out, found a department store and bought suits and dresses. For his part, Mason chose the cheapest he could find and determined to leave the tags on for one night only so that he could return the items tomorrow. Roxy called him a cheap Englishman and bought something black that clung to her curves. Sally spared no expense. Luciane, awkward at spending someone else's money, eventually bought a relatively inexpensive flowing dress with a high neckline. Quaid and Hassell went very conservative, the former sharing Mason's view, the latter just wanting to get the entire process over with. In the end, they were back inside their rooms in just over an hour, getting ready.

Add a bit of glamour. Roxy snapped a shiny bracelet over her left wrist and hung a sparkling necklace around her neck. Neither were truly expensive, but to her mind, this stuff was stock. They might use it all again in the future. Her only concession was flat shoes. She wasn't about to go into action wearing high heels.

She was ready. She rose and checked herself in the mirror. She would pass muster, she thought. After all, the casino they were headed for wasn't exactly a real floating palace. She met the others in the lobby below.

'This is different,' Sally said awkwardly.

'We've done it before,' Quaid said. 'Remember Monaco?'

'Yeah, but we fell into that casino by accident,' Sally said, smoothing down the front of her dress.

'By necessity,' Mason said, clearly remembering how they had run for their lives through the streets of Monte Carlo.

Roxy preferred not to dwell on it. She needed to move forward, to keep raising those barriers and build a new life. She looked at the door.

'Shall we?'

'It's time,' Sally said.

They exited the hotel, split up into three groups and walked the few blocks to their various casinos. Roxy, tasked with the Silversea, eventually saw a small cruise ship, maybe five decks high, with an atrium and several lounges and restaurants. There was a wide gangplank leading to the ship and a queue of people spread out along the dock. At her side was Quaid. Together, they perused the queue, studying all the faces and trying to find the one they were looking for. They'd been given a description of the man through Luciane's network of contacts. Luckily, Aoki dressed rather extravagantly and had distinguishing characteristics so shouldn't be too hard to spot. He usually wore a white suit with a red tie and thick gold bracelets that dangled off his wrists. He wore shiny black shoes and had his long hair tied up in a bun. And there was a scar too, a scar that ran from the corner of his mouth to his nose and travelled quite deep.

Roxy and Quaid concentrated mostly on the scar, not the suit, not even the fact that they knew Aoki always visited these casinos alone. They couldn't afford to miss him tonight. They did not know how close the SED was.

Roxy walked to the front of the queue with Quaid, linking arms, pretending to study the ship more closely, and then walked slowly back down the length of the queue. She examined everyone. She clutched a small purse, large enough to carry a small gun but unfortunately empty tonight. They had no weapons with them. Hopefully, they wouldn't regret their absence.

They walked along the queue again, seeing men in dark suits waiting impatiently, thumbing their mobile phones, women staring into space and at their closest counterparts, maybe picking up a few tips for next time. There was muted conversation and some bursts of laughter and more than a few stares from men and women alike.

Roxy held on to Quaid tighter. There was no sign of Aoki.

They reached the end of the queue and took their place in line. The dock area was quiet apart from the cruise ship areas. Roxy knew that Mason and Luciane were just a few berths down, checking out another floating casino, whereas Hassell and Sally had gone a few blocks into town to investigate a static establishment. The one hope was that someone would spot Aoki and allow them all to get back together. After all, Aoki would have to show up soon if he wanted to play in one of these floating gambling houses. Cast-off time was approaching.

Roxy saw the rope drop ahead. People started filing along the gangplank into the casino. She feigned an issue with her shoe and motioned dozens past her, as she bent over to sort it out. Quaid studied all of them.

Finally, he tapped her on the shoulder.

'Got him.'

It was an electrifying moment. Roxy didn't look up. Instead, she quickly snatched her phone out of her purse and rang the other two groups.

'We're on,' she said. 'Get here quickly. We've almost finished boarding.'

Cast-off was in twenty minutes. The teams would have to double-time it if they were to make it.

Roxy looked up as Aoki passed and then slipped into the queue behind him. Sure enough, he wore his trademark white suit and there were three golden bangles dangling from his wrist. He was staring at the Silversea eagerly, craning his neck, as if desperate to get aboard and start gambling. Roxy stayed close. She wasn't about to let him out of her sight.

Chapter 10

Kei Aoki went straight to the gaming tables on the fifth deck.

Roxy and Quaid went with him, trailing along behind another couple. Aoki walked purposefully, as if reaching the tables was all that mattered, and he was first through the door. He nodded to the doormen, to the guy behind the room's bar, to some of the blackjack dealers clustered in a corner. They weren't ready yet. The ship had yet to set sail and reach international waters before it was allowed to operate.

And he didn't have a great deal of time to play. The voyage was four hours, so it wasn't as if Aoki could linger until daybreak as you could in some casinos. He would have to live his obsession at a rapid pace. Roxy spent a few minutes texting the other couples to tell them exactly where they were.

Soon, they were together again.

Mason, breathless, nodded at Roxy. 'Where is he?'

'Getting a drink at the bar. He's itching to start. Can't wait to get behind a table. You know one of us is going to have to join him to make all this look believable.'

Mason starred blankly. 'I'm no gambler.'

'You think I am?'

The others all voiced similar concerns.

Sally bit her lip. 'Roxy is right, though. We need to get close to Aoki and he's gonna be stuck behind one table or another. This needs to be done right.'

They all felt the boat start to rock a little right then. They shared a look. The ship had cast off. It wouldn't be long until they reached international waters now. The staff situated around the room started drifting towards their various stations, getting ready. Roxy stood aside to let several other people into the room. All the women wore flowing dresses with pearls and diamonds at their throats. The men wore tuxes and expensive watches and carried their wives' coats over to the cloakroom. Roxy waited as the room filled up.

A bell sounded. The tables were open for business. Roxy also counted twenty gaming machines about the large room, all of which were suddenly in use. Men and women slid into seats with practised familiarity, leaving Roxy and her friends standing alone.

'Well, that didn't go so well,' Hassell said.

'Hey, I'm a gambling virgin,' Roxy said. 'But I can do this.' She waited for Aoki to choose his poison and then drifted towards the table.

'Roulette,' she heard Mason say.

Truth be told, Roxy had gambled frequently in several of her past personas. The three-letter agency that ran her life for twelve years had sent her into dozens of hotspots where her targets loved to throw down at poker or roulette or one of a dozen different games played in various high-class gambling houses across Europe and the Far East. She was no stranger to gambling, but that wasn't something she

78

wanted to share right now. Doing so would just bring back nasty old memories.

As if it wasn't doing so already.

Roxy watched Aoki play a few rounds, saw him gather the multicoloured chips before him and spread some of them out across the roulette table. From the crowd gathered around, she saw him start cleverly wagering on outside bets, groups of numbers instead of single digits, since they were cheaper and had a higher likelihood of winning. Aoki was content to do this for a few rounds. Time passed. People came and went from the table. Aoki stayed, his golden bracelets jangling, his face totally absorbed, a fancy, colourful cocktail loaded with ice and umbrella sticks sitting before him. Roxy looked up several times and saw Mason and the others place themselves around the room, some looking out for the SED, others watching for any unexpected interference.

By stepping forward, Roxy had become the one most likely to make contact with Kei Aoki.

She continued to watch him, squeezing forward through the crowd that surrounded the gaming table. Aoki appeared to be avoiding a grandiose strategy; he was keeping it simple. A good approach, something Roxy would have done. Roulette was mostly a game of luck. It was always best to know when to walk away.

But that part was where Aoki failed. He didn't walk away. He won some, lost a bit more, and stayed at the table. He finished his fancy cocktail and ordered another. Time slipped by. Roxy knew they'd been on the water for the best part of two hours. It was probably time to make her move before Aoki got too drunk to care.

She watched him some more. Was this really the guy who had flashed the ancient coins to all and sundry, the guy who'd raised so many international concerns? Was this the man who had started a manhunt, a quest for the mysterious Shadow Kings, a crazy pursuit? Aoki looked normal enough. He didn't stand out apart from his gaudy suit, didn't act differently. In fact, he appeared to be a typical gambler, used to losing money. Maybe it was the alcohol that undid him.

Roxy ordered a double rum and Pepsi Max from the bar. She watched the black wheel spin, the thirty-seven numbers flashing by, the small white ball speeding around and around. She saw the ball land on red zero. Aoki smiled widely and added some chips to his dwindling pile. Next, he placed an inside bet, something she knew as split betting, because he bet on two numbers rather than one. She sipped her drink as he sat back and watched the wheel spin. When he lost, he switched again to the outside bet.

Next, Aoki bet on all red.

Roxy waited for someone to vacate the table. Her chance came five minutes later when a rail-thin woman with a plunging neckline got up and stalked away with her nose in the air. Clearly, she'd lost everything, and was headed for the bar. Roxy slipped into the hastily discarded seat and arranged a couple of sets of chips before her. She watched the next game unfold without betting. She watched the dealer, aware of the so-called 'house edge', which revolved around the extra number '0' and gave the house an additional 2.7% chance of winning. She knew that if she'd been playing in France, she could have taken advantage of the En Prison or La Partage rules and only lose half her bet, but this wasn't France. This was as near as dammit to Hong Kong.

She played. She won, and she lost. Mason appeared at her shoulder, watching, and then Quaid on the other side.

She was opposite Aoki and met his eyes once or twice, smiling. She was in entirely the wrong position to start up a conversation. Not that Aoki looked in the mood for a chat. His entire focus was on the game.

More time passed. Roxy took an opportunity to move from her seat and slid into the one beside Aoki. The man barely noticed. He switched from inside to outside betting and then back again. His chip pile diminished, then enlarged, and then faded away again. He didn't know when to stop. That was his problem. Roxy made the easy, safe bets. She caught Mason's eye from across the table.

He nodded, urging her on.

She needed to hurry. The ship was already making its way back to the international waters line and the dock.

As Aoki waited for the outcome of a wheel spin, Roxy leaned over towards him.

'Hi,' she said. 'I'm Roxy Banks.'

She wanted him to look at her, wanted his attention, and she got it.

'Hello,' he said in a peculiar singsong voice that was rather off-putting. 'The numbers are going better for you than for me.' He took another sip of his umbrella-heavy drink.

How did she broach this? Roxy took a deep breath and did what she always did. She came right out with it.

'Listen,' she said, drilling to the point. 'I know your name is Kei Aoki. I'm here because I need your help.'

Aoki raised his eyebrows at her, and then, surreptitiously, swept the entire room with his eyes. He placed another bet before looking back at her.

'With what?' he asked shortly.

'With the Chinese coin collection you've been flashing

around lately. It's aroused a lot of interest, my friend. We need to know where you found those coins.'

Aoki stared at her, his eyes wide, his mind working overtime. He looked cagey, unwilling. He pulled away from her as far as conditions allowed.

'What coins?'

Their words were lost under the general din of conversation that surrounded the table and filled the room. They continued to place their bets, so that anyone watching would think they were just passing the time of day.

A voice rang out across the room. 'Final bets, ladies and gentlemen. The casino will close in ten minutes.'

Which meant they were approaching the international waters line.

And then the dock. Roxy figured she had about thirty minutes to break Aoki down. She leaned forward.

'You know what coins. Look, we're here to help. Your actions have aroused the suspicions of a dangerous entity, and they're not happy. You're in danger.'

'We?'

'My friends and I,' Roxy gestured vaguely at the room. 'We're not here to hurt you, but I can't say the same for the killers known as the SED.'

'They're here?' Aoki looked scared.

'I damn well hope not.' Roxy could tell the guy just wanted to run away, but here, on the boat, he had nowhere to run to. 'Now, where did you get those coins?'

Aoki shrank even further away, almost falling off his chair. His turn came around again, and he put most of his remaining chips down on black eleven as though it was a time-honoured ritual. This would be the last spin of the wheel. Roxy let up for a few seconds and let him have the moment. His eyes were hungry as the little white ball flashed around the wheel and then, as it jangled from plastic hole to hole, bounced in and out of numbers under its own momentum.

The ball bounced out of black eleven and jumped into fourteen. Aoki closed his eyes and sighed. He pushed his chair back from the table.

'I'm done,' he said.

And he stood up and went straight over to the bar. Roxy followed him closely. 'Please help us,' she said as he ordered another drink.

He spun quickly. 'The Chinese coins? I don't know what you're talking about. You have the wrong man. Now, leave me alone before I call security.'

Roxy stared at him. She truly hadn't expected the stonewall. Maybe Aoki didn't understand the genuine danger he was really in. Nevertheless, she backed off to defuse the situation and beckoned to her teammates.

'He's not buying it,' she told them as they gathered around her beside the room's only door. 'Refusing to confirm he knows anything about the coins.'

Sally made a frustrated sound. Luciane stepped forward. 'Maybe I can reason with him,' she said. 'I persuaded my fair share of people when I was in the Garda. I have the skills. And we *need* the provenance of those coins.'

Quaid held up a hand. 'I realise this is your baby. This is everything you've been working towards, but we can't force anything out of Aoki. Force won't work here.'

They were watching Aoki across the bar, and he was watching them as the ship sailed through the international waters line and then made its way back towards the dock. It occurred to Roxy that they might not be the only ones watching Aoki tonight; his position might have been relayed to the SED by any of the assembled patrons. He wasn't exactly hard to find. For that reason, she stayed alert, wary, watching everyone.

'So what next?' Hassell asked.

'I refuse to fail,' Sally said. 'We'll grab him as he comes off the boat.'

'Grab him?' Mason asked.

'I don't mean kidnap him,' Sally said. 'Or maybe I do. But I mean talk to him. He can't run to security then. He'll have to listen to us.'

Mason nodded. 'Sounds like a plan.'

'It's risky,' Quaid said and Luciane nodded. 'It will be our last chance.'

It might be risky, but they saw no other way. If Roxy approached Aoki again, he would call security on them. Roxy could see it in the man's eyes. She leaned against a wall and waited as the cruise ship slowed and then made a turn as it came into dock. The engines were running loud now, and conversation was muted as the guests' evening ended. Many were already gathering at the exit door, standing in line. Roxy saw them leaving the casino room. She watched Aoki. Surely, he would expect them to accost him.

The ship docked. The doors opened.

She turned towards the exit to the casino room. 'Let's go,' she said. 'We can approach him outside. Otherwise, he'll just stay here for as long as he can and then maybe still call security.'

They turned.

And came face to face with the SED.

Chapter 11

Mason gawped for a long second, but the SED didn't even acknowledge him. Their eyes were firmly set on the man at the bar, on Kei Aoki.

Mason counted eight of them, which left five still at large. The eight in question shoved their way through a line of people, into the casino room, and headed straight for Aoki.

The gambler's eyes opened wide, his face blanching as finally he realised the reality of his peril. The men striding towards him would show no mercy, Mason was sure of that. At a glance, he saw they carried no guns, not inside this floating casino.

And, of course, they were still in the full view of the public, linked covertly to a secret organisation. There was no chance of them using weapons in this place and throwing light on themselves.

Outside, in the deeper darkness however...

Mason acted quickly. He grabbed the nearest guy by the back of his jacket, hauled him backwards, and smashed an elbow into his face. That set everything in motion. Roxy leapt over a chair to grab the next man in line, smashed a fist into the back of his neck and sent him stumbling forward. Quaid and Hassell waded in too, grabbing more men, and there was no stopping Luciane. She had her Garda training and wanted to be part of the team. She leapt on another man's back, hooking an arm around his throat.

Sally stood back for now, looking for a chance to help.

The SED turned quickly to address this new threat. The security guards scattered around the room rushed forwards. Mason bent down and hefted his opponent up onto a nearby poker table and let him crash down, scattering cards and chips. The legs wobbled and the table groaned as the man's spine hit its surface hard. Mason saw his face twist in pain and used the moment to pummel him in the ribs and the solar plexus, further weakening him.

To the left, Roxy flung her man into another table. This was the roulette table she'd been playing at for most of the night. The man hit the table, sprawled across it and scattered the box of little white balls on the side, sending them bouncing across the floor. A security guard accosted her, but Roxy gently levered him off.

And for Roxy, gently levering a man off involved him flying across the room and coming down hard on his spine.

Quaid and Hassell tried to choke their opponents into a coma, but it didn't quite work. The SED were too well trained to go down that easily. They squirmed and shuffled and writhed until they managed to get free and then turned. Instantly, Hassell punched his opponent in the face. Quaid caught his across the throat.

Mason slammed his man down once again, this time breaking the poker table. It collapsed underneath the guy, legs shattering. The entire mass came down hard, wood splintering everywhere amid a pile of chips and a few coins someone had left behind. The man kicked out, catching Mason on the right knee. His leg buckled, and he fell, and his opponent was suddenly sitting up so that they were face to face.

Mason dodged the head-butt. He led with an uppercut, sending the guy back down to the ground and then leapt to his feet. His knuckles, already aching from the previous fight, screamed when they contacted the guy's chin.

Mason had a moment to take stock.

His eyes fell on Luciane, since the others all seemed to be on top of their opponents. The researcher had ended up in a fist fight and was currently circling her opponent, but Mason saw blood on her jaw and her chin. She'd been struck, but maybe she'd given as good back. She had every reason to. As he watched, Mason saw the SED guy motion to one of his comrades.

The SED had three spare fighters. For now, they honed in on Kei Aoki. The man in the white suit was still at the bar, half a loaded cocktail at his side. He was looking frantically from his drink to the approaching men, as if wondering if he could throw it at them or maybe defend himself with one of the umbrella sticks. There was a look of sheer terror on his face, the obvious sign of guilt.

The security guards around the room interfered with the SED approach. They could see the men advancing, see the severe looks on their faces. They walked up to the SED, hands held out, and told them to slow down. The mercenaries just wiped them out, kicking and punching and spinning in place. Within seconds there were three security guards on the floor, moaning, bleeding, crying out.

Mason ran for Aoki. 'Back off!' he yelled.

Aoki stared at him, then at Roxy, who was fighting her way to his side. It wasn't enough. The SED guys leapt for him, grabbed his arms and held him upright between them.

But they weren't going anywhere. Not yet.

Mason approached them at speed. At first they still grasped Aoki's arms, pinning them to his sides, but as Mason kicked the first man in the chest, they soon let go and attacked him. Aoki scrambled away, flapping his arms wildly.

Mason backed off, confronted by two men. He stayed wary, didn't commit. They came in with fists swinging, which he blocked and deflected, sending out sharp jabs to vulnerable areas. He led them through the debris of the poker table, hoping they'd stumble, then got behind a blackjack table, struck by an idea.

As they approached, he grabbed it, lifted and threw it end over end at their heads.

The table struck like a battering ram, sending them both crashing to the floor. It hit with a heavy thump that resounded around the room, then it collapsed on top of them. The men groaned, clearly dazed, struggling weakly.

Roxy clearly approved of Mason's tactics. She'd come up against another SED fighter and now made a grab for the nearest table, lifted it and slashed her opponent across the face with it. The man flew sideways, slamming into a colleague, and took them both out of the battle. Roxy continued running to Aoki's side.

'Are you hurt?'

The gambler patted himself, looked at his hands and checked his face. 'No, no, I seem to be okay.'

'Good. Then come with us.'

Aoki hesitated.

Roxy grabbed his arm. 'I told you this would happen. We're the good guys. These other guys – they want to boil you alive.'

Her words had the desired effect. Aoki stopped resisting and started moving with her. Mason was just inches away, struggling with one man and listening to their conversation.

'All the way to the exit,' he said.

'What about the SED?' Roxy asked.

'We can't kill them. Just incapacitate. Now *move*.'

Mason blinked, struck by a fist to the nose. Blood flowed. He ignored it and rounded on his opponent. In that moment, though, his attention had been diverted and his enemy, no slouch, had taken advantage. Already, he was striking Mason's sternum, ribs and stomach. Mason staggered, head down.

A blow sent him to the floor.

He rolled, looked up. There was a boot flying down towards his throat. If it landed, he was toast. His throat would be crushed. So much for holding back.

Mason brought his arm up, but way too slow. The boot was about to strike him. Just then, the boot and the man attached to it were smashed aside by Hassell, who, seeing Mason's predicament, had rushed to help. Both men disappeared from sight.

Mason sat up, rubbing his throat even though no blow had landed. It was the thought of it, a ghost pain. He looked around. Roxy was dragging Aoki towards the ship's exit. Even now, Aoki looked reluctant to go with her. Hassell struggled on the ground with a guy. Quaid was backing off another, face bleeding. Sally was ready to step in to help and did so even as Mason watched. Luciane was bending over an opponent, delivering a solid blow to his head. Mason saw four SED mercenaries lying on the ground, groaning, limbs moving, but largely incapacitated. And he saw one more.

One making a beeline for Roxy from her blind side.

Mason creaked as he forced himself to his feet. His entire body hurt. He could feel blood on his face, dripping down his chin. With a tremendous effort, he lunged, throwing himself in the attacker's way. He bore him to the ground, landing heavily. Both men lay there, stunned for a second, and then turned to look at each other.

The SED fighter reacted first, throwing a lateral punch. Mason took it, head rocking back, a flash of pain making him cry out. His eyes then fell on something he could use.

A table top.

Mason grabbed the discarded item and swung it in a sideways movement, whacking his opponent across the face with it. Right then, he saw a forest of legs approaching and looked up, grateful to see his team suddenly standing by his side.

'This is our chance to get the hell out of here,' Quaid said.

All around, the SED team members were lying prone or struggling to their feet or on their knees. None of them were active.

Mason held a hand up and let himself be dragged upright.

Speaking through a bloody mouth, he turned to yell at Roxy.

'*Move!*' he cried.

Chapter 12

The Silversea nudged gently against the long concrete dock. The gangplank stretched from the side of the ship to the dock, swaying slightly. Roxy hit it first, dragging Aoki by one arm. Mason and Quaid ran across it next, racing for the dock. The others came a second later. Nobody looked back.

There was commotion all around. The docks were in uproar. Casino-goers stood around in their party dresses and smart suits, staring from the ship to the end of the docks where their transport waited, then at the newcomers who were running between them. Nobody seemed sure what to do or where to walk. Mason spied a few staff members around, but they seemed as nonplussed as everyone else.

The air was cool, the sky black and cloudless. Stars sparkled from horizon to horizon. Mason knew they should just run, vanish into the night. They couldn't hope to get a better chance. He was about to turn to his team, shout out a battle order, when his eyes strayed to the right and caught five more sets of steady eyes, glittering with malice, staring right at them.

Crap, he thought. *The remaining members of the SED team.*

They were positioned along the dock for just this kind of eventuality. Mason cursed. He swung back quickly to the ship, saw no signs of pursuit just yet, and then conveyed the only order he could think of.

'*Run!*' he yelled.

They all took off like scalded cats, still pumped up on adrenalin. Roxy had also spied the SED squad, and so had Quaid, but Mason didn't think anyone else had. Still, they all ran, and that was what counted.

The five SED men hesitated at first, clearly unsure whether to stick or twist. Maybe they were waiting for their colleagues. Mason and the others got a good head start, and then he heard a barked order. He spun to see where it came from. Saw a tall, blocky man standing in the middle of the five, stern-faced, with a bald head and hard eyes. The man was pointing in his direction.

And the five SED guys started sprinting after them.

Mason turned, put his head down and ran hard. They pounded up the docks, hearing the constant lapping of water on their right, the sound of other boats and revellers spreading from other docks, the yelling of their own concerned partygoers as they saw the chase begin.

Mason raced for the far end of the docks where all the transport waited.

It was a tough run. They were all injured in one way or another. Aoki was distracted, his terrified eyes spinning from Roxy to Mason and then to their dangerous pursuers. His spasmodic movements almost sent Roxy stumbling to her knees. But they ran through the night, focused, straining to stay that few dozen steps ahead of the enemy, looking back constantly in case one of them pulled out a gun.

It was only a matter of time and opportunity.

And now, as Mason looked back, everything got harder. He could see the other members of the SED team stumbling and staggering off the boat onto the dock. They were searching for the rest of the team, spotted them running and now made their way forward.

His heart hammered. He urged everyone on, keeping it together. They had seconds in which to make a decision that might cost them their lives. Roxy met his eyes. She swept her gaze back to the front as they reached the end of the docks.

Slowed down. Looked left and right.

There were several cars and a few vans parked haphazardly, waiting to pick up their customers. There was no choice. They had to commandeer one of the vehicles.

Roxy knew it, too. She took firm hold of Aoki, ran up to a Maserati, and flung open the door. She reached in, grabbed the driver and hauled him out, turning quickly towards the others as the man protested.

'Come *on.*'

Mason eyed the powerful black car and winced. 'That's only got two bloody seats!'

Roxy stuck her head in the car proper. 'Oh.'

He was already dashing towards another vehicle, shaking his head. Quaid was just a step away from him.

'And if we could get one with a proper gear shift, I'd appreciate it,' he said.

Mason despaired. 'You'll get what you're bloody given,' he yelled back, grabbing hold of a door handle and yanking hard.

The door flew open. A suited man sat inside with wide eyes, a chauffeur. He looked up at Mason, blinking rapidly.

'Can I—'

Mason grabbed hold of his jacket and dragged him out. He didn't speak, just gestured everyone into the car. Doors were flung open. Everyone piled in, squeezing in where they could, two in the front passenger seat. The car was running, though Mason didn't have the key. Never mind, it wouldn't cut out whilst they were driving. He let Quaid take the wheel simply because it was what they were used to doing.

'Typical.' Quaid pulled a handle behind the wheel. 'Bloody flappy paddles.'

'It's a SEAT,' Mason grumbled. 'You don't need to use them.'

'Then what the hell are they there for?' Quaid asked as the car jerked forward.

The SED squad was getting closer and closer.

'To fool old timers into thinking they have a sporty car!' Mason shouted.

'Stop arguing, you two!' Roxy leaned forward, gripping the seats and settling Aoki hard on her knee. 'And get us the fuck out of here.'

Quaid pressed the pedal. The car shot forward faster, turned in front of the oncoming enemy, and then swung around. Two of the SED mercs reached out to grab the back of the car. Quaid gunned it, sending everyone slamming into their seats. In the back seats, they were crammed in, overcrowded, and arms and limbs went awry.

Mason used the side mirrors to watch their pursuers. The SED team fell back and then started searching frantically for their own car. The SEAT's engine roared, the tyres struggling for grip as Quaid showed them no mercy, hands gripping the wheel hard. The car slewed as it raced down the darkened road, lights illuminating the way ahead.

'Where?' Quaid asked suddenly.

'Just drive.' Sally was already pinching and sliding at the map on her phone, trying to find out where they were and where they could go.

'Just lose them,' Roxy snapped.

The scene behind was fading into blackness. Mason saw their enemy commandeer a car of their own and then they turned a corner, blocking his view. He kept his eye on the road behind, seeing only darkness in the mirror.

And then two pinpricks of light.

'They're on our tail,' he said.

'Bollocks,' Quaid said.

'Shake 'em,' Roxy said.

'That's easier said than done,' Quaid replied.

Mason watched the oncoming headlights, saw them grow. 'Shit, they're catching up,' he said. 'Put your damn foot down.'

'It *is* down. Down to the floor.' Even as he spoke, Quaid flung the steering wheel to the left to negotiate a bend in the road, sending everyone on the back seat sprawling across each other. Aoki squawked the loudest as his head came into contact with a plastic bulkhead.

The other car was coming fast, and then, from the shape of its headlights, Mason realised it was the powerful Maserati, which meant only two of the SED team were closing in. He knew they'd just be the first wave.

Quaid snapped the car around another bend, blasting through a warehouse district, long low buildings to both sides. He'd purposely avoided the road that led around the dockside, expecting it to be busier.

Mason gripped the door handle. The other car was coming faster, its headlights filling his mirror. Staring hard, he thought he could see a figure leaning out of the window. A sudden, terrifying thought flashed through his mind.

'Down!' he cried out just as the sound of a gunshot rang out.

The gloves were now well and truly off. Now clear of civilians, the SED had broken out their weapons and were looking to engage with superior force.

Mason heard another gunshot. Again, the bullet flew wide. The cars were both travelling at high speed, every bump in the road knocking them slightly left and right, making it hard to keep a target in sight. Mason nudged Quaid to take it up a notch.

A right-hand bend came up, and then a left. Quaid slewed the car around both, back tyres drifting, but the Maserati stayed with them effortlessly, now just a few metres behind their back bumper. A third gunshot rang out, this one also missing, and Mason began to wonder if the guy back there was wearing sunglasses. Still, Quaid somehow managed to pull out a little lead using the flappy paddles, something Mason would have ribbed him about if their situation hadn't been so desperate.

The next shot struck true. The back window exploded. Mason bent low, his ears ringing, shattered glass flying across his shoulders. Those in the back seat were as low as they could go, hugging the seats, covered in shards.

Quaid came to another bend and took it like a racing driver, clipping the apex. The Maserati fell back a bit. Mason was watching not only the black car but beyond it also, in case any other cars came flying up, but so far there were none. They seemed to have out-driven the rest of the SED team.

'This is a losing battle,' Roxy warned. 'They have guns.'

Mason knew it. There was only one way they were going to escape this chase alive, and that was to risk dying.

'Let them pass,' he said. 'Then hit them from behind.'

Quaid nodded. It was an old manoeuvre, something taught to advanced police and army drivers all across the world. If they were quick and precise, it might work.

Quaid hit a straight. He let up on the gas. Another gunshot rang out. This time, the bullet flew through the open back window and smashed the front, punching a small hole in the glass. Spiderwebs spread netlike from the point of impact all across the screen.

Quaid didn't slow down too much. That would be telling. The Maserati's own momentum brought it up alongside in just a few seconds. Then Quaid hit the brakes and swerved, ramming the front of his car into the rear of the other. The Maserati swerved and spun, swinging its way across the road, out of control, until it smashed head-on into a tall streetlamp, its front end crumpling.

Quaid sped past.

The road behind them was empty.

Mason leant over the back of his seat. 'Are you all okay?'

There were several groans and a few affirmations. Mason nodded. That was good enough. He turned quickly to Quaid.

'Take us somewhere quiet,' he said.

Chapter 13

Quaid drove them to a darkened parking area where they left the car behind. They walked across the street to a dark corner, called an Uber and took it back to their hotel, reasoning that the SED couldn't possibly know who they were or where they were staying. They walked through the double revolving glass doors together, giving the appearance of a group just in from a sparkling night out on the town, and found plush seats to the left of the foyer, where there was a small bar. Despite the late hour, the bar was still open, its soft mellow golden glow highly inviting after all the deadly activity. The seating area itself was dimly lit with gilt-edged lights. Mason settled into an armchair and accepted the double vodka that a waiter brought over on a silver platter.

They shifted the tables and chairs around so that they could sit in a circle. Aoki was antsy, eyes on a swivel, watching everything. Every time the hotel's front doors opened, he shuddered. Mason asked Hassell to monitor their perimeters and then turned to Aoki.

'You, my friend, have caused us quite the problem.'

'Not my fault,' the white-suited man said with a tremor of fear in his voice. '*You* came looking for *me*.'

'I asked you back at the boat for help,' Roxy said. 'If you'd given it, then…maybe all this could have been avoided.'

Mason knew that wasn't necessarily true. The SED would still have forced their way onto the vessel when it docked.

'How about you help us out now?' he asked. 'Tell us about the coins.'

Kei Aoki swallowed hard, then accepted a stiff drink from the barman. At first, he stammered when he started talking, but then his voice strengthened.

'I…I'm grateful,' he said. 'I know…know they'd have come for me anyway, whether you were there or not. Who are they?'

'As far as we can tell,' Mason thought about how best to term it. 'The Shadow Kings' mercenaries – the SED – are covert special forces. We rescued Luciane here from them, and their leader is a stocky bloke called Miura. That's all we know. Why are special forces chasing you, Aoki?'

'I messed up.' Aoki downed half his glass in one swallow, then stared at the thick black carpet under his feet. 'I guess I shouted too loudly.'

Now Luciane leaned forward. 'Listen,' she said. 'I heard about the coins from various sources. I tracked you down, got your name from several of them, in fact. Before I could start looking for you, the SED came looking for me. They grabbed me, interrogated me and made me give up your name and location. I'm sorry. Soon after that, my friends here turned up, and we came to both warn you and get the information from you.'

Aoki took it all in silently, his eyes flicking from face to face as he listened. Sitting there, Mason thought the white suit looked ridiculous and all the gold dangling from his wrists ostentatious. There was no doubt Aoki liked to be seen. Maybe being seen was what had got him into this quandary in the first place.

'How did you believe you would ever hide it?' Roxy asked, no doubt thinking along the same lines as Mason. 'You stand out like a sore...umm, thumb.'

'I'm a gambler.' Aoki shrugged. 'I gamble. Sometimes I win, sometimes I lose. I guess I took a risk shelling those old coins out, but I never thought for one minute that they might spell my death. I wouldn't have done it. Yeah, I'm noticeable. People remember me, my name, my appearance, but that's kind of the point. It's what I'm aiming for. Of course...' He made a face. 'Now it's all backfired on me. I'm a famous face everywhere I don't want to be.'

'Are the SED out to kill all of us?' Sally asked.

'Not if we stop looking for the casino,' Quaid muttered.

But Mason believed they would. They had already proved they didn't care who died, by firing at the car. Of course, during the three confrontations they'd had so far, the SED had reined themselves in, using fists and knives mostly, but those confrontations had been in civilian areas. Chiefly, the bar fight and the casino battle.

'I think they'll do whatever they have to, to get the coins back,' Mason said.

'Wait, they want them *back*?' Aoki said. 'How am I supposed to do that?'

'Can you tell us where you got them from?' Roxy asked.

Aoki turned to her and smiled weakly. 'You saved my life,' he said. 'You all did. Of course I'll tell you.

Look…' and he opened his jacket, reaching inside the inner pocket.

He slipped first one, and then another coin out. After a few seconds, he held five in his hand and then nine. He placed them gently on the table before them, wincing slightly as they jingled against the glass.

Sally practically leapt forward. 'These are the ancient coins?'

Aoki nodded. 'All that I have left.'

'How many did you sell?' Hassell asked.

'Too many. Most of them. They paid for my nights and days for weeks. But that's only going to make matters worse, I fear.'

Mason agreed. 'They won't stop coming after you.'

'That's my problem.'

'I hope you're good at hiding, bud,' Roxy said.

Aoki nodded grimly. 'The exact opposite of what I'm used to. I'm not shocked that you and they tracked me down, actually. I'm a well-known character.' He looked pleased with himself for a moment, and then his face fell.

'Help us out, mate?' Mason prompted gently.

'Yes, yes, of course. The coins. Well, I'm afraid I didn't find them in the desert, which I guess is what you're wanting to hear. I've never even been to a desert. I acquired them from a friend of mine. A man named Kenji Kimura.'

'You bought them from him?' Sally asked, still fingering the coins.

'No. He owed me a large favour. So we kind of traded favours. I ended up with the coins.'

Mason saw a blank wall. 'So you just picked them up from another guy? No treasure hunting involved?'

'I'm afraid not.'

101

'And did this Kenji say where he got them from?' Quaid asked.

Aoki shook his head. 'Again, no. I didn't ask. I think he too sold some coins, though not nearly as many as me. He seemed sure of their worth.'

Luciane sipped her drink. 'I can corroborate that several sources lead back to the different stashes of coins,' she said. 'It wasn't just Aoki.'

'No,' the man said miserably. 'I was just the most obvious.'

Mason ignored his gloominess. 'So Kenji got the coins from some other source. Maybe he's the treasure hunter.'

'Where does this Kenji live?' Luciane asked. 'Is he local?'

Aoki laughed with little humour. 'Are you kidding?' he asked. 'Kenji is a market trader, and he lives in Japan.'

Mason closed his eyes briefly in dismay. He opened them a second later, just in time to see Sally lean forward inquisitively.

'*Where* in Japan?' she asked.

'Where do you think?' Aoki said. 'Tokyo.'

Chapter 14

The Tokyo markets have a certain charm that a local or a tourist doesn't find in the malls. Nakamise Market, on the shopping street of the same name, is famous, infamous and historical, stretching back to the seventeenth century.

They'd jumped on an overnight flight from Hong Kong, landed in the early hours and found a hotel close to the market. It was ten a.m. now, Tokyo time, and they were all suffering from aches and pains, bruises and jet lag.

The sight of Nakamise Market was daunting. The place was choked with locals and tourists, the stalls so deep in humans that getting close seemed to be an insurmountable challenge. Sally had told them there were ninety stalls here, and that most of them sold traditional souvenirs from samurai swords to kimonos and wooden toys. Mason saw a colourful mix of stalls stretching away into the distance, the aisles thronged with people. At a glance, he saw shoes, statues, books and many other souvenirs. It was a cool day, a stiff breeze blowing in from Tokyo Bay to scour the streets and make the canvas flap all around so that it sounded like a million birds were circling overhead.

He stopped at the entrance to the market, taking a deep breath. People pushed past him to all sides. His team was close by, along with Luciane and now Kei Aoki. They hadn't felt right about just leaving the man back in Hong Kong to face the music and maybe the SED. And they hadn't taken him simply to slow the SED down, either. As Aoki constantly reminded them, he'd dealt with several other people concerning the coins. Mason and his team couldn't protect everyone, and the SED would have vast resources at their disposal.

'Do I really have to be here?' Aoki whined.

Mason barely heard him above the general hubbub. It was Roxy who rounded on him. 'No, of course not. But we're kind and saved your ass, because we didn't want the SED to kill you. We want to save people from the actions of the SED. Is that okay?'

'Yeah, yeah, but why *here*?'

'So you can help us find your friend Kenji Kimura,' Sally said, reiterating their plan. 'And you can make the introductions. Okay?'

Aoki didn't look pleased. If it were him, Mason mused, and someone had just saved his life, he might seem a little more grateful.

Crowds pushed past them, some using their elbows. Mason realised they were causing an obstruction at the entrance to the market, took hold of Aoki's arm and pushed the group forward. They merged with the crowds, alert for pickpockets, and walked down the wide aisle between stalls, looking from left to right. Uncounted people enveloped Mason; it was a crush on both sides, and he walked with his head high, his back straight, trying not to get jostled or pushed aside. They threaded their way through the crowds, taking it easy. There was no way they were going to rush this job. It was a step at a time, a twist, a turn and then another step. To Mason, it felt odd. Lately, he had been used to rushing through things at breakneck speed, thinking on the fly, jumping from one mini-mission to the next. But here in the Nakamise market, they were forced to take it slow whether they wanted to or not.

Mason turned to Roxy, who was fighting her way past an elderly couple to her right. Walking sticks were swinging.

'Keep a lookout, Rox. You just don't know if the SED are gonna turn up.'

'Sure, if I can fight my way past all the old people desperate to cut me off at the knees.'

Hassell already had an eye on the market's perimeter. Luciane and Sally were close to Aoki, as close as Mason, and Quaid was trying to clear a path ahead, most unsuccessfully. It wasn't long before he shrugged and gave up.

Aoki stared at the proprietor of every stall, making no sign of recognition. Mason tapped his arm.

'Don't owners have their own spaces?' he asked. 'Surely you know where Kenji will be?'

'Not all of them,' Aoki yelled back. 'The permanent ones, yes, but Kenji isn't permanent. He'll get allocated a stall on a daily basis. Could be anywhere.'

Mason sighed. There was no sign of the market calming down; in fact, it appeared to be getting busier as more and more tourists woke up and finished their breakfasts. But they were making headway. Little steps, yes, but they pushed and shoved their way through the throngs and past the stalls. Eventually they reached the end of the market and stood in a wider space that formed an entrance or exit to the vast row of stalls.

'He's not here,' Aoki muttered.

'What?' Mason was crushed.

'Look, maybe we need to ask a few questions. I see Ren there selling cutlery, and Hiroshi two stalls to his right. Both men are normally here with Kenji. Maybe they'll know something.'

Mason nodded. It was worth a try, and those stalls appeared less busy than most of the others. Steadily, they made their way to the front of the queues.

Aoki leaned over a table full of crockery to shout in Ren's ear. 'We're looking for Kenji,' he yelled in Japanese. 'Got something special for him.'

The man named Ren nodded. 'Yeah, Kenji's not here today.'

'I can see that. Where is he?'

'You know Kenji. He's transitory. Turns up wherever he wants, when he wants. Could be at Kyoto, at the Kitano Tenmangu shrine, or Nishiki, at Osaka.' Ren shrugged.

Aoki translated the conversation. Mason felt a sinking feeling. Why did nothing ever go smoothly?

They stood in the shadow of a building with a sharply angled red roof, leaning against a brick wall. The wind blew all around them, scooping up paper and plastic from the streets, throwing it around. It made the canvas stalls flap and sent unweighted items tumbling.

'What the hell do we do next?' Mason asked.

'It's hardly a dead end,' Sally said. 'There are options.'

Luciane stepped forward. 'Don't give up,' she said. 'You know how important, how desperate, this all is. The SED are killing indiscriminately in their hunt for the casino. We can help people, save their lives. And the casino itself is too important to let them take it for themselves. And if they sell those artefacts on the black market...'

'We're not giving up,' Hassell said with a sharp look at Mason. 'Finding the treasure will safeguard you and all of us. I mean, the actual act of revealing the treasure will protect us from the Shadow Kings because it will all be out in the open, and they surely can't attempt to take it for themselves once the whole world is watching. Finding the treasure will get the SED off our backs once and for all. They probably know who we are by now, anyway, and that we won't just go away. And let's face it, we want that treasure for humanity. To share. To study.'

Sally nodded. 'I do,' she said. 'We do. We want to be part of it and I, for one, don't enjoy being strong-armed by these damn Shadow Kings. What do you say we beat them to the prize?'

Mason didn't like being shot at, but the others were right. They were in this now, right up to their necks, and couldn't back out. They had Luciane and Aoki with them, both of whom had been threatened by the SED, and they couldn't just leave them to their own devices. He turned to Sally.

'If we're gonna do this, it has to be quick,' he said. 'The SED will be busy tracking down others who've handled the coins, maybe even the same people as us.'

Sally nodded. 'Then first we have to fly to Kyoto,' she said. 'And then maybe Osaka, and Nishiki market. It has to be done today, whilst we know Kenji isn't here.'

'Then we'd better get a move on,' Hassell said. 'Double time.'

They ran for it, grabbed an Uber and asked to be taken back to Tokyo International Airport. As they drove, Sally found a flight that left in an hour and booked them all aboard. Flight time to Kyoto was about an hour. The streets flew by, a patchwork of colour and writing and swinging signs. There were flashes of Tokyo Bay to their left, a rolling sheet under grey clouds. The traffic was non-stop – flashing red lights, the occasional honking of horns. The team had little to do on the way, but shot out of the big car when it arrived, and headed for the departure doors.

A short time later, they were airborne. Snacks and drinks were served. Not long after, the plane descended gracefully on its final approach to Kyoto. They had the names of the market that Kenji frequented from Aoki's friends Ren and Hiroshi. They hit the ground running, cleared customs and were soon on their way again. Kyoto gave Mason the impression of *old* Japan, a modern city that hummed and moved to a fast beat, surrounded by thousands of old temples, monks and stunning Zen gardens. He directed their driver to the Kuromon market, a food market containing over a hundred stalls selling a variety of local cuisine and fresh food to enjoy there and then. Kuromon was well established and boasted a 600-metre pedestrian alley. Mason wasn't looking forward to their upcoming search.

They arrived in a short time, stayed together and took stock of the market. It wasn't very different from Tokyo's. They joined the crowds, picking their way through, made sure Aoki saw every stall trader, and kept an eye out for the SED.

Mason kept his fingers crossed but, by the time they'd traversed the entire long alley, they still hadn't found Kenji.

'I'm getting a bad feeling about this,' Mason said at the far end. 'What if Kenji just took the day off?'

'Don't say that,' Quaid breathed.

'It's unlikely,' Aoki said. 'I've seen Kenji at the market seven days a week, in all weathers, even ill. It's why I chose him for the coins. He's dependable, consistent, enduring. I'd bank on Kenji if I had to.'

'That's good, but we're not gambling here,' Mason said. 'We're very much in hard reality. Are you sure Kenji's not here?'

Aoki nodded.

Sally led them back through the throng, calling an Uber as she did so and dialling up the internet on her phone. Soon, she had them booked on a flight to Osaka that left in two hours. Mason checked the time. It was one p.m. now, which meant they would land in Osaka about four, roughly an hour before that market closed. It would be the last market of the day.

Which puts us shit out of luck for Nishiki, he thought. But it would have to do. They arrived promptly at the airport, grabbed sandwiches and ate them as they waited for their flight. Roxy managed a couple of rums and Mason downed a beer to help with the frustration. All this flying around searching for an elusive man who might or might not even be working today was wearisome, to say the least. But this was proper investigation, he thought. It was the hard slog. Hopefully, their labours would pay off.

Soon they were on their flight and headed for Osaka. The plane bounced along unhappily amid patches of turbulence. Mason gripped his armrests and rode it out, running old rock songs through his mind to help take his attention off the shaking.

They landed in Osaka a little after four and were soon on their feet, waiting to disembark, conscious that they didn't have long before the market closed for the day. The door seemed to take an age to open; the people shuffled to the exit and then there was a delay at border control.

Nevertheless, they reached the market area with a good thirty-five minutes to spare. Now the hard work began. The market area was lively, full of men and women walking every which way. It felt cooler here than it had been back in Kyoto and Tokyo – several degrees cooler, in fact. The wind ripped at their faces as if it had claws. Mason zipped his jacket, put his head down and pressed himself into the horde that filled the main aisle between stalls. Aoki was complaining about all the walking, about the long day, and Mason was getting frustrated enough to slap him. It was that kind of day. The others stayed together and remained vigilant, watching their perimeters as usual.

It was a long, crammed walk down the centre aisle. Mason reached the far end first and then turned back to Aoki, speaking loudly to make himself heard above the din of conversation.

'Are you kidding me?'

'He's not here.'

'Bollocks,' Quaid said loudly, making more than one person turn in his direction.

'That just leaves Nishiki, and we can't make it there today,' Sally said. 'Which leaves us in a bit of a quandary.'

'I don't know what to say,' Aoki muttered. 'I haven't missed Kenji. He's just not here, which surprises me. The law of averages and all that.'

'I wonder if we're barking up the wrong tree,' Quaid said.

Aoki looked blank. 'What?'

'The market stall idea seemed the easiest option at the beginning,' Quaid improvised. 'Now I'm wondering if we shouldn't track his address somehow.'

'Yeah,' Mason muttered bitterly. 'We'll get to his home and he'll have left to go to market for the day.'

'Wait,' Aoki said suddenly.

'How far is this Nishiki place?' Roxy asked.

'Too far,' Sally replied.

'I said wait,' Aoki said.

Mason ignored him. He'd had enough of relying on Aoki's suggestions for now. 'I guess we either find a hotel for the night or head back to Tokyo. Maybe we'll get lucky tomorrow.'

'It feels…desperate,' Quaid said.

'Will you all *wait*?' Aoki whispered furiously. 'Will you just *look*?'

Mason blinked at him, saw him pointing and turned to look. 'I don't get it,' he said.

'It's just an empty stall,' Roxy said.

Aoki smiled. 'That's what's important. It's *Kenji*'s empty stall. I recognise the canvas stripes, the chair, some of the stock.'

Mason let the ramifications of that statement sink in. Suddenly, he didn't feel cold anymore, didn't feel frustrated. He was just a man standing in the middle of a market, staring at an empty stall.

'Crap,' he said.

'Maybe he's off to the loo,' Quaid said. 'Give it a minute.'

They waited. Five and then ten minutes passed by and then the traders all around were starting to tie up their canvas sheets, removing the produce from their tables. The market was closing up.

Quickly, they made their way through to the empty stall.

Mason reached it first, looking left and right, expecting the man in question to make an appearance. They were

111

reliant on Aoki here, but the gambler was as alert as they were, and far more scared.

'I don't like this,' he said. 'Kenji would never leave his stall unoccupied.'

There was little else they could do. It was Aoki, still looking worried, who walked across to the next stall and approached the man working there.

'Please,' he said in Japanese, later translating for the team. 'We have come to visit my friend, Kenji. This is his stall. Have you seen him?'

The market trader gave them a wary, searching look. He shouted loudly for the guy on the other side of Kenji's stall to join him and then spoke.

'He saw more than me,' the first man said.

Both men were rail-thin, wearing baggy clothes and hats. Their hands were callused and dirty and their shoes were threadbare. When they proffered their hands, Sally was happy to fill them with yen.

The men spoke. Mason waited patiently for his translation.

Aoki turned quickly towards the team. 'They say Kenji was here yesterday. They say it was a normal day until lunchtime when many men appeared. They shoved their way to Kenji's stall, surrounded him, speaking angrily to him. These men then grabbed Kenji and hauled him away.'

Mason looked around. 'Through the market?'

Aoki nodded. 'In front of everyone. They just grabbed him and removed him.'

'They abducted him,' Sally said.

'Yes, in front of everyone. But everyone was too scared to say anything. They say these men had guns.'

'Has to be the SED,' Quaid said. 'Bastards got here before us.'

'They beat us.' Sally looked despondent. 'They'll kill him.'

Mason felt the same sinking feeling. It was Roxy who grabbed Aoki's arm and turned him bodily back to the two market traders.

'Where did they take him?' she said. 'Ask them.'

Aoki asked the question.

Mason didn't expect much in return, but was pleasantly surprised at the answer.

'They were looking for something too,' Aoki said. 'These men with the guns. They questioned Kenji.'

'And we all know what that was,' Hassell said.

'The men here…they overheard Kenji say that he had what they needed at his home. That's where they took him.'

'And they know where that is, right?' Roxy asked.

'Yes, they share stalls three days a week with Kenji. They are friends. They know where he lives.'

They acquired a few more bits of information. The men told Aoki there were seven men with guns, all dressed in dark clothing like military garb. It became clear these men were the SED and must have come across Kenji's name by interrogating some other poor, unfortunate soul. Like Aoki said, there were more men than just him peddling these coins. Someone, somewhere, had a very large haul.

'We need Kenji's address,' Sally said.

'I have it,' Aoki said. 'Are you guys headed there? Won't those soldiers be there?'

Mason nodded. 'Don't worry,' he said. 'We're not stupid. We have guile on our side.'

Roxy made a show of looking around. 'Is that your invisible friend?'

Mason waved her away and started for the far end of the market. 'Hurry,' he said. 'We have no time to lose.'

Chapter 15

Captain Miura of the Special Exercise Division stood next to a cheap plastic statue, smoking an unfiltered cigarette. Yesterday, he'd watched his men torture some Japanese national. He'd seen the man sweat, cry and bleed, heard his moans of agony, seen the repentance dancing in his eyes.

Miura had enjoyed the show.

There was something therapeutic about watching your enemy squirm and plead, something that went far beyond satisfaction. Miura had watched every cut, heard every broken bone acutely, followed every strike of the ball peen hammer.

The torture was, of course, justified on behalf of the Shadow Kings. It was what certain individuals were demanding. The location of the ancient casino and the retrieval of all its many treasures were imperative to his employers. Miura was the bull leading the charge.

He stood now in a square, thinking. There were people all around. Ignorant peasants, mostly, not even worthy of his gun. He felt they were more akin to lumbering cows, already herded, wandering half-blind from place to place.

He and his men stood far above them, grand servants of the Shadow Kings.

Yesterday had been a good day.

Miura took a long drag on his cigarette, savouring it. The unfiltered sticks were a treat that he allowed himself usually only twice a day. On a mission like this, he deserved them. Miura considered the torture again. It made him shiver inside. And, of course, all done in the man's own home, where he felt most safe. Miura was a soldier, a man of the system. But he had always had these tendencies. From being a small boy to a troublesome teenager, he had hidden some extreme tendencies.

Being a part of the SED gave him the perfect outlet for some of his more bloodthirsty cravings. Of course, you couldn't reveal it too clearly to the men. You remained aloof, tried to appear like ice whilst being on fire inside.

Please take them and go, the victim had moaned. *Please don't hurt me.*

That's my job, idiot, Miura had thought. 'What you have told us has been most helpful,' he had told the idiot to give him some hope before crushing it into the ground. 'We thank you for your help. I am confident that you have given us everything, so well done. Now, men, see that you reward our captive. Reward him well by breaking his bones, shedding his blood and piercing his flesh. What you have done, my friend, is worse than sacrilegious. It is a betrayal of the highest order. You are worse than an animal, worse than the vile things that slither and creep and crawl around our feet. But then...' Miura had gestured beyond the man's piece-of-shit home. 'All your kind are. I hate you all. The subservient. The meek. The worker ants. You stink, you sweat, you move about in herds. The best thing you can all do is die by the metal-toed boot of my shoe.'

He watched. They gagged the captive before the real work began. It was fun, watching him squirm, and, for the first time since he'd taken on this job, Miura had felt contentment wash through him. He'd switched off, drank in the moment...the hours, actually.

Where next? Somewhere else in this godforsaken country. His men were making the preparations right now.

Again, Miura's mind drifted back to the day before and the conversation he'd had with the man as his flesh was being flayed, as they painted his own blood on his face and dripped it into his eyes.

'You see, the Shadow Kings have a choke-hold on your nation. In fact, on many nations. Some say we are nothing more than a powerless shadow society.' He shrugged. 'But we are strong. We will never stand down, never be cowed. We pull the strings across the world and most civilians don't even know it.' Miura had bent down close to the writhing body, so close he could smell the fear washing off the man in sheets, see the sweat popping from all the stinking pores, feel the cowherd mentality emanating from him. He had used a finger to scoop the sweat up and then wipe it on the man's reeking clothes.

'Die slowly, cow,' he had whispered.

Miura took a moment to think of his wife, on her own, in their home. Her government job was important and would sustain her. She was the best cover for his rampant eccentricities. Nobody would imagine the married captain with a wife of that standing would have such proclivities. Miura was proud of himself for thinking that way. And now that she was pregnant...well, it was just the perfect shelter for him.

Miura hated civilians, hated their arrogance. Whenever a mission came up involving potential civilian collateral, Miura saw that it was executed with the severest prejudice possible, at the same time as staying under the radar. His superiors viewed it as loyalty. Miura just took vengeance every chance he got. And now, all this furore centred around the old casino…

…that involved civilians too.

At least, it did now. Who had stolen the coins in the first place? Miura wondered about that. Who exactly came across the site first? Would a Chinese national betray their country so easily, so stupidly? He thought not. He thought that maybe, just maybe, it was all a civilian plot. Some chancer working alone or with a few friends. His team had travelled to Dublin, questioned the woman Luciane Harlow and, before they could interrogate her properly, had somehow lost her. They had initially thought that an anomaly, a loss and a failure that occasionally happened to teams in the field. They had put it down to a one-off, an aberration.

But then the floating casino fiasco happened.

Miura still cringed about it now, despite the recent warming memories that curdled his brain. He remembered boarding that ship, getting struck in the face by some fiery-eyed, raven-haired woman, and had then known nothing else for about ten minutes. By the time he recovered, their enemies were outside in some car being chased by two of his men. It was a washout. A disaster. But then…the two men chasing *lost their prey*.

Miura had swallowed it hard. They were essentially back to square one; the prey called Aoki snatched away from them. And, even worse, it was the same enemy that had thwarted them back in Dublin.

Of course, circumstances hadn't enabled the SED to bring their full force. They couldn't operate with impunity in public. It was a hobble that Miura didn't need. He brought the matter to his superiors every day, asked them respectfully for more leeway. It was a request that, so far, hadn't been granted.

Civilians.

Miura would exact revenge from them. He would make them pay for humiliating him and his men. Miura would never exceed his authority, though; kidnapping and torturing the Japanese national had been part of his purview. Miura knew that, to his employers, he was just another asset, another head to put into motion. But he kind of respected and liked that. The leaders, far and immediate bosses, shouldn't feel the need to explain themselves. And Miura had no qualms about going into action.

He just wished his hands weren't partly tied.

Miura returned to the present, waiting for his men to make a plan, to make something happen. His thoughts turned towards the ancient Chinese casino.

A prize. A national asset, not a dirty place for enemies to pick over. Miura had been told by people who knew that the casino had vanished beneath the sands, destroyed by a gigantic earthquake back in the fifteenth century, that it had been full to the brim at the time. Not just with people, but with all sorts of wealth.

Coins. Jewels. Tapestries. Paintings. Bracelets. Necklaces. A veritable capital of the nation's wealth. It had been the most famous casino of its time, the biggest. Why did Miura need to know all that?

To understand just what it meant to the men in charge. To have no illusions about the importance of his mission.

Miura was happy in any scenario that pitted him against a capable enemy. It gave him scope, choice, fewer fetters. He had little respect for his adversaries. The only scenario he didn't like was where the enemy was winning.

But no more. Not after yesterday.

In his mind's eye, Miura could still smell the fresh blood, still see the torn flesh. It had a kind of beautiful symmetry to it, more fulfilling than any sunrise, any blazing sunset. Miura wondered who else they might capture and interrogate soon. He was sure somebody would come along.

Filled with the peace that the thought of torture and murder brought him, Miura started walking. He made sure not to touch the filth that passed by, made sure not to follow in their tracks. He was a man alone among inferiors. He knew it, had always known it. Above all, he was entirely loyal; he loved the Shadow Kings. At any cost, he would avenge them even if the slight hadn't happened yet. If his bosses pointed him at it, he would kill it.

My superiors demand that I win.

And Miura would win.

Chapter 16

It was after six by the time Mason and his team had called a taxi, given the driver Kenji Kimura's address and then sat in silence as the vehicle wound its way through the suburbs. Here, Mason saw a very different Japan from the Tokyo he'd visited yesterday. He saw dilapidated shacks, dirt roads and children playing out in the street in their dirty rags. He saw malnourished dogs roaming the streets, men and women standing on corners with little to do. Yes, it was a reality often found behind the main façade of, say, a bustling street market, but it was a reality that existed everywhere, it seemed.

Eventually, they arrived. A dirt path led to a row of squat homes just off the street. They all climbed out of the taxi and asked it to wait, but the man inside either didn't understand them or couldn't be bothered, because he drove off at speed. Which left Roxy waving at the vanishing car, looking like she wanted to get hold of the driver by the neck.

'Bastard,' she said.

They walked up the dirt path. Immediately, Hassell and

Roxy had gone into surveillance mode, observing in all directions. The houses – Mason counted nine in a row – were all attached and all the same: two front windows, a wooden door and an inverted V-shaped roof. He walked down the path, stopped at the door and gave it three raps.

He waited. Nobody answered. Aoki came forward and tried to do better, giving the door five good whacks. Still nothing.

Mason, ready for anything, saw the front door ease inwards with a low creak at that point. It wasn't locked, wasn't even fully closed. He reached out and pushed it open.

'Heads up, guys,' he said. 'Be ready for anything.'

He led the way inside, moving swiftly and carefully. Quaid backed him up, followed by Aoki and then Sally and Luciane. Hassell and Roxy stayed outside a while longer and then entered when they were sure the coast was clear.

Mason walked down a narrow corridor, immediately presented with a room to the right and a far door, through which he could see an oven and a sink. He checked the door on the right first, conscious that the light slanting in the front windows was dimming already. The room was empty of life, inhabited by a two-seater sofa that had burst, leaking stuffing, a high, scarred table and an old radio that sat on an incongruous nightstand.

He checked out the floor too, saw the mud on the floorboards. Either Kenji was incredibly messy or a lot of men had tramped their way through here recently. The mud wasn't totally dry. Mason knew they'd already announced their presence to anyone in hiding, but he crept down the narrow passage quietly, and entered the kitchen with stealth.

It was small, dark; just a few surfaces, a cooker and a small fridge that buzzed loudly. There were dirty dishes in the sink. Mason could have believed that Kenji hadn't been home for a few days, maybe a week. Perhaps he wasn't here at all, hadn't been for days, weeks. It would be better for him if that were the case.

Mason turned in a circle. There really wasn't anything else to look at and they couldn't all fit in the kitchen. Quaid and Roxy had gone through the other door in the hallway and found a small bedroom. They called out that it, too, was empty, and that there was a lot of mud on the floor, and dozens of footprints.

Mason checked the kitchen floor. It was the same. He walked over to the back door. Saw that that too was partly open.

It didn't feel right. Surely Kenji Kimura didn't go out and leave all his doors open, leave this kind of mess on the floor. Mason saw myriad boot prints in the mud.

He turned to the back door.

Opened it. Went back out into the bracing wind and the dying of the light. It wasn't night yet, was barely sunset, but the clouds had rolled in and were suffocating a lot of the ambient light. Mason stood on a flagstone and stared hard at the centre of the garden.

He gasped.

The others followed him outside. For a long minute, Mason didn't move. His stomach turned over, the breath caught in his throat. He narrowed his eyes, desperate to unsee the sight that appeared before his eyes.

In one corner of the garden, under the wooden fence that separated Kenji's garden from the next one, a figure lay. They had staked him out, wooden spears bashed through his hands and feet, pinning him to the earth. Congealed blood was everywhere, and bits of clothing, rags. The man was naked, his mouth wide open.

And he was still moving.

Mason ran to the weakly struggling individual. Aoki was with him, the man's eyes wide with fear and expectation. Mason reached the figure and fell to his knees.

He reached out but didn't touch the man. Aoki leaned forward.

'Kenji,' he said. 'Who did this to you?'

Kenji's glassy eyes fixed first on Mason with fear and then on Aoki with recognition. He struggled again, winced with the pain. Mason saw many encrusted stab wounds covering his body like a latticework. The only thing his enemies hadn't touched was his mouth and eyes.

'Kenji,' Aoki said again, voice soft.

Mason sensed the others coming up, gathering around. He looked up. 'Form a perimeter,' he said. 'I don't think whoever did this will be back, but it's better to be safe than sorry.'

'On it.' Roxy and Hassell drifted away.

Mason looked directly at Aoki. 'Can you get him to tell us what happened?'

'He needs a hospital,' Aoki said.

'And he'll get one. But the men responsible for this, and for your own dilemma, are out there. We need to catch up and get ahead of them. Is this how you want to end up? I know I don't.'

Aoki bent to Kenji, close to the man's wide, blinking eyes, and spoke. Through translation, Aoki related the conversation.

'My friend,' he said. 'I am sorry. Who did this?'

'Soldiers,' a whisper came rattling from the parched, bloody throat. 'Soldiers did this.'

'Why?' Aoki asked.

123

'Coins,' Kenji whispered. 'They wanted the coins. You remember?'

Aoki nodded, bending closer still to his friend. 'I remember those damn coins. I'm still paying the price for them. Though not as hard as you,' he added.

'What did you give them?' Mason asked suddenly, not following the conversation but conscious they needed an answer to the question.

Aoki whispered in his friend's ear. 'What did you tell them?'

Kenji struggled weakly. Mason had left the stakes in for now; the blood had encrusted all around them and was no longer flowing. Kenji was badly hurt, but not dead. If he'd been lying staked out in this garden all night, though, things might be different.

'Tanaka,' Kenji said simply. 'Do you remember Tanaka?'

Aoki blinked rapidly. He certainly remembered Tanaka, and now it all made sense. 'Tanaka gave the coins to you?'

Kenji nodded.

Aoki turned to Mason. 'He says Tanaka gave him the coins in the first place. He told this to the soldiers.'

'Who's Tanaka?'

'We'll get to that. Tanaka is a relatively famous guy. I can tell you all I know, but first we have to help Kenji.'

'We are helping Kenji. The SED did this. We're here for him, and we're calling an ambulance. But please, tell me all about this Tanaka as quickly as you can.'

Mason pulled Aoki away from the prone man. He was fully aware that they had to act fast, but he had also thought this whole scenario through to its bitter end. There were no options here. He felt sorry for Kenji, but they couldn't be here when the ambulance and the cops arrived. There would be too many questions. It could put them back days. And if they couldn't be here, they couldn't yet call an ambulance. It was tough, but it was clear enough to Mason. He looked hard at Aoki.

'You give me everything you have on Tanaka and then you're gonna have to stay behind. With Kenji. You can say you came to visit your friend and found him that way.'

'It will look better if I stay behind on my own,' Aoki admitted.

'That's sorted then. Can you pull it off?'

'I'm a gambler. I have the poker face.'

Mason didn't get into the man's losses and debts. This wasn't the time. He had to hope that Aoki was as good as he thought he was.

'Now,' he said. 'Tell me all about this guy Tanaka.'

Chapter 17

Mason and the others were on the road again, this time trundling through the prefecture of Saitama on their hunt for the man named Tanaka.

Leaving Kyoto, they'd flown back to Tokyo, arrived late and then spent a few hours kipping in a hotel. They'd hired a car, a large black Nissan, and then set out on their journey through central Japan.

'His name is Tanaka,' Aoki had told them before they left him behind with the dying Kenji. *'He is a travelling salesman, well known, famous, in fact. He trawls a known corridor from the outskirts of Tokyo to Saitama to Kumagaya, Takasaki and Ueda when he's not flying to Kyoto market for supplies, which he does once a month. He has been doing the same urban journey for more than a decade. His journey follows the corridor of Highway 18. As a joke, people call him Tanaka 18. That's how systematic he is. He visits the same people, same homes, same faces, on his loop that takes him two weeks. Through Kenji, I know two people on that loop. Take your pick.'*

They had a description of Tanaka. They knew what make of car he drove – a dark grey Toyota Hilux, a vehicle Tanaka was synonymous with. They knew his route. Sally had worked out the supposed days he would visit any single place. All they had to do now was surveil the people Kenji knew of, and wait.

All we have to do… Mason thought.

It was loose, he knew. But Tanaka was a creature of habit, had been for a decade, and Mason thought they could rely on him to stay true to form. They drove through Saitama City, passing the great stadium and a few high-rise buildings on their way. Saitama was big. Luckily, both of their addresses lay beyond the city.

They drove for hours, Mason and then Hassell at the wheel for a change. Quaid sat in the back alongside Luciane, the two conversing quietly.

'Thank you for saving me back there,' Luciane said.

'Back there? Oh, you mean in Dublin?' And Mason realised they hadn't had time to stop or take more than a few minutes to themselves since leaving Ireland. They'd been in full-on chase or research mode.

Quaid smiled sideways at Luciane. 'You're welcome,' he said. 'As soon as I knew you were in trouble, I jumped on a plane.'

Luciane slipped her hand into his. 'Thank you.'

'It's no bother,' Quaid said a little gruffly. 'And hey, it's been a few minutes.'

'Since we last saw each other? I guess it has. You look well.'

'I am well.'

'Still active. Still take charge. Paul…' She sat forward. 'What happened to you, honey?'

127

Quaid closed his eyes briefly. 'You mean since we last saw each other? Wow, that's a long story.'

'Tell her about Anya,' Roxy said.

Quaid winced.

'Who's Anya?' Luciane asked.

Quaid turned to Roxy with a *thanks a lot* look and then switched back to Luciane. 'Since we last met,' he said pointedly. 'I grew out of love with the army. Got sick of playing a politician's game, fighting enemies one week who ended up as allies the next, seeing good men die along the way. I became enlightened.'

'You found God?'

'No, no, nothing like that. My eyes opened to the corrupt ways of government. I wanted nothing to do with it. So I left the army. Branched out on my own. Spent years growing already good contacts and helping those in need, buying and selling, accepting a small profit whilst helping the less fortunate in luckless, war-torn countries. I guess I dropped off the radar.'

'You certainly did.' Luciane clasped his hand. 'I tried to reach you more than once.'

'Sorry' was all Quaid could think of to say.

'So who's Anya?'

Quaid swallowed. 'Just a lady I met along the way. Met on my travels. You know how it is.'

Luciane smiled as they went over a pothole. 'I definitely do with you.'

'What's that supposed to mean?'

'A woman in every port, sometimes two. That's the Paul Quaid I remember.'

'They're *contacts*. Extremely good ones.'

'Yeah, contacts,' Roxy laughed. 'Stick with that.'

'Stay out of it. I didn't ask for your—'

But now Luciane was looking around the car, from one team member to the next. 'So how did you come to be working with this team?'

Quaid bit his lip. It was a good question. 'Well, Sally,' he said. 'Her father died recently in a raid on the Vatican. Joe and Roxy were also involved. They tried to save him. Sally hates wealth and privilege, fought against it for years, but she inherited a fortune when her dad died, and has tried to put it to good use. One of these uses was to form this team, Quest Investigations, and now we travel all around the world safeguarding or transporting or hunting for ancient artefacts.'

Luciane nodded at Sally. 'Sounds like a good cause.'

'Hassell?' Quaid sighed. 'Is hard to explain. When we met, he was a baddie. Now he's a goodie.' Quaid smiled as he tried to lighten the conversation. 'He's an expert infiltrator, and he's on a journey of enlightenment. Seeking something. The bad guys did some terrible things to him.'

Luciane looked at Hassell's stoic face and tried a smile. 'I'm sorry.'

'Then we have Roxy,' Quaid went on with the proper introductions.

'Be careful,' Roxy said.

'What the hell can I say about her? She's raw, an ex-assassin or something. Hard ass with a heart of gold. This team just wouldn't work without her. It's really difficult *not* to get on her wrong side, but she doesn't hold a grudge.'

Roxy made a face. 'That's what you think, asshole.'

Quaid shook his head, turning finally to Mason. 'And then there's Joe. He's ex-army too. Mason is the glue that holds us all together.'

'A fighter, like me,' Luciane said.

'We're all fighting something,' Quaid said with a shrug. 'That's who we are.'

Mason kept concentrating on the road as the conversation turned in the back seat. He learned a bit more about Luciane, understood what drove her to do what she did – a love of history, a desire to do something different and a willingness to go out of her way for something long lost, long forgotten in some instances. She loved a lost cause and the art of trying to make it live again.

Mason followed National Highway 18 for some time, sticking behind other cars and not pushing the speed limit. He knew they were ill-equipped, ill-prepared, for this journey, but what else could they do? They were behind the SED now, he was sure, but they were still trying to save Tanaka's life here, still pushing. And going to the police wouldn't help at this point. They would still face questioning long after Tanaka was dead.

Fields and forests flashed by. They drove through some smaller towns, negotiated tight bends and drove for a while alongside a wide gravelled path. For some time, a long eighteen-wheeler slowed them down to frustrating speeds, but finally it turned off and allowed them to accelerate. The morning passed and then they had to decide which of Tanaka's haunts to stop at.

'We have the exact address for only one,' Sally said. 'The one in Ueda, across from the Toyoko Inn. That's our best bet.'

Mason already knew it. When Ueda's name came up on a signpost, he made a beeline for the town and then drove through the centre. Among the impressive temples were shops and restaurants and hotels, all catering for tourists. Ueda boasted hot springs and an ancient castle, rice terraces that hugged the hillsides and a 'silent museum', a moving tribute displaying the works of art students who died in World War II. Mason took his time picking through the town until he found the Toyoko Inn.

And parked, for now, outside it.

As one, the occupants of the car cast their eyes across the road.

There sat a row of white-walled houses with black drainpipes, all overlooked by the tall hotel with its grey marble-effect frontage. Further down the road sat many restaurants, their blue, red and yellow signs swaying in the wind.

Mason kept his eye on the second house in, the one belonging to a man frequently visited by the travelling salesman known as Tanaka.

'We made it,' Roxy said.

'Any sign of the SED?' Luciane asked.

'They're not gonna be sitting out front waving a flag,' Roxy said. 'They're gonna be undercover, like we should be.'

Mason gave it a few more moments. It was just after lunch now, and the weather had turned from warm sunshine to drizzle. It smeared the windscreen and side windows that Mason was trying to see through. He peered hard, saw a simple two-storey house with curtains across the windows – probably because of the proximity of the hotel – and a black front door to match the drainpipes. Most of the homes followed the same design. He looked around the car.

'Bit anticlimactic,' he said.

'It's what surveillance and investigation are all about,' Roxy answered. 'We're on the right track.'

Mason nodded, started the car, and drove into the hotel's parking garage. Soon, they had rooms facing the row of houses and were settling into them, stripping off and getting showers, agreeing to meet in Sally's room in thirty minutes, but also agreeing to keep up a constant twenty-four-hour watch on the house in question. There was no telling what time Tanaka might turn up.

Later, Mason settled in a chair close to the white-curtained window with its pine surrounds. They had agreed to watch the house in shifts, so while half the team went off to grab food, the others watched. They were all contactable via their mobile phones.

Just like that, Mason sat and waited for something to happen.

Chapter 18

Captain Miura of the Special Exercise Division hated the position he was in. To torture a man, to rob him of his dignity, was one thing, but to then follow that man's instructions to the letter and find out there was nothing you could do to move things forward was quite another.

And since they had left him staked out, dying, bleeding to death, there was now no other recourse than to remain in place.

Miura had been looking forward to torturing Tanaka. Or at least watching his men do it. Now, they had to wait for the man to turn up.

'Boss,' said one of his men, relieved for the moment, smoking around a square kitchen table and playing cards. 'How long will we have to wait here?'

A stupid question, but an understandable one. Miura understood. This entire mission had involved an awful lot of waiting around, of waiting for something to happen, from the very moment they kidnapped Luciane Harlow back in Dublin. He saw the frustration, well concealed, that lingered in the eyes of his men. They were used to action, to war-torn battlefields, to the bloody field. They were used to being inserted into hot zones all over the world, to do their job so quietly that it appeared they were never there. The job was hard, stressful, but it had its perks.

This job, however…

It was anything but rewarding.

Miura kept his face blank and pulled on a brand-new unfiltered cigarette, holding the smoke in his mouth for as long as he could before breathing it out in a cloud through which he spoke. 'Hopefully, not long. Tanaka could come to Takasaki at any time. We must be patient.'

And there was the rub. Soldiers were rarely patient. Of course, these were special forces men and had some modicum of fortitude for off-the-book operations, but even they had their limits.

Why choose Takasaki instead of Ueda? Miura was a decision maker. He didn't flinch in front of his men. He made the decision like the snapping of fingers, in an instant, simply to show that he was in charge and confident with it. He didn't want any underhand, sly messages getting back to the employers and authorities who ran his career. Miura had to look like he was in full control, always, and any misgivings he might have he would never air.

He wondered if his filthy adversaries were still on the right track. He doubted it; the man named Kenji had been their last resource and was left for dead. But still…some teams were tenacious and might have other means. Miura hoped they were still on the trail. It would make the next few days more interesting. He thought back now, recalling that they had three men and three women, including Luciane, on their team. One woman, a brunette with blue tips to her hair, had held back, clearly not fully trained though she had showed some signs of being able to fight. The woman with the dark raven hair had been formidable, as had the man who at first sight seemed ineffectual. He had been hiding incredible talents. The older guy and the one with the scar on his right cheek had barely held their own, relying on each other's help. Miura fancied his odds the next time they met, especially if his entire team fought and they had access to their weapons.

And, once captured, he could indulge himself in their agony.

Miura took another long drag of his cigarette. The owner of the house they were inside wouldn't mind. He was currently duct-taped and locked in a cupboard, breathing through his nose. Miura hadn't yet decided whether he would live to see tomorrow.

He liked that kind of power.

He rose now, went to the cupboard and unlocked it. The figure inside lay bunched up in a most uncomfortable position, his hands tied behind his back, his legs taped together. Miura could see the big whites of his eyes reflected in the meagre light – terrified eyes. Miura crouched, leaned forward, and blew smoke into the man's eyes, all the while giving him a smug, severe grimace. He shook his head, enjoying the man's terror.

To compound matters, he took out his gun and held it up so that the barrel glimmered in the half-light. He aimed it at the man, put a pound of pressure on the trigger. The man went absolutely still, wheezing through his gag, panting. Miura placed the end of the gun against the man's forehead.

And shouted *Bang*! The guy wet himself. Miura chuckled and withdrew, leaving him to his own stink. He went back to the window where four of his men sat.

'Anything?'

'Nothing at all, sir.'

Miura sighed. They had been here almost a full day. How long would it be before this Tanaka showed up? Supposedly, he was a creature of habit, a salesman ploughing an identical furrow, week after week, month after month. He knew his customers well and what they liked. He made a living doing the same thing every day. The man would not change his habits. It was just a matter of time before he turned up.

But how much time?

Miura wasn't an idiot.

He had men in both places…both here and in Ueda. Seven here, six there. There was no point in leaving anything to chance.

The thought took him back to his childhood, to the very moment when he'd started forging the man he would become.

A young Miura had been walking with his father through the forest. They had a steady if sparse life. They didn't have a lot, and both Miura's father and mother worked all the daylight hours they could, seven days a week. It was a hard subsistence, but not a hard upbringing for Miura and his sister, Camille. This day, this fateful day, Miura's father had been on the lookout for a special fungus, something that could be ground into one of his mother's potions to successfully treat backache. They had toiled and trekked and sweated their way through the trees for hours, their own backs aching through bending and squatting so much, their heads burning from the sun. When Father had stopped for lunch, Miura had hoped to enjoy it, just himself and his parent alone in the woods, but he had felt detached recently, as if he didn't really belong in this place, in this time. He felt

136

out of sorts, cut off from all emotion. Miura didn't know how to deal with it, so he said nothing.

Then they were continuing through the woods, heading back to the house on a different route, and Father started slowing. So far, throughout the day, Father had shown anger and frustration at not being able to find the much-needed fungus; he'd barely spoken to Miura. Now, Father skirted a hole in the ground, a well. There was a brick circle all the way around it, about three feet high. Father stopped and peered down, wiping the sweat from his head.

Miura never knew why he did it. There was no reason, no rhyme, no decision or intent. He just walked up behind his father and gave him a hard push. The man flew out and into the well and disappeared down it, striking the walls on the way with a heavy smack, crying out in horror. When Miura heard a final thwack, he peered over the edge.

'Father,' he said.

There was no answer. He didn't know how deep the well was. With a practised shrug, he withdrew a torch from his backpack and shone it into the hole. There, at the edge of the beam, a broken figure lay writhing. It was his father, legs at unnatural angles, arms clearly broken, squirming in pain and shock and horror. The man made a high keening sound, something Miura could barely hear. He kept the torch beam on the figure until it stopped moving.

By then, darkness was falling.

Still feeling nothing, Miura made his way back home and told his mother that Father had fallen into a well. Miura, he said, had been behind the man and had barely managed to stop in time. He told his tale in a monotonous litany, his eyes on the floor, his head down. His mother's cries didn't move him. When she asked where the well was, Miura said he couldn't tell in the dark, and when she mobilised the townspeople he pretended to help, led them close to the right place. There they found his father and lifted him free of the well. The man was dead, broken, having bled profusely.

Time passed. Miura knew he was different, full of glee at the anguish of others. While others, including his mother and sister, wept at Father's funeral, Miura could barely keep the smirk from his face. Months passed. They grew further into poverty. His mother couldn't cope with the loss of his father, let alone pick up the slack. After a while, Mother went out into the woods one day and never returned. They did not find her body.

Which all left Miura being brought up by his older sister, Camille. At first it was almost impossible, but, as Miura became a teenager, they fell into a good routine. They supported each other, worked as one. Still, Miura couldn't find it in him to grieve for his parents. He actually felt the opposite most of the time, glad they were dead. In particular, he was pleased with what he'd done to Father. The feelings raised that day excited him.

Miura found animals and murdered them slowly. He taunted the kids of the town, tried to hurt them without repercussion. More often than not, it worked.

But when Miura turned eighteen, it all changed.

His sister died in a car crash. She had been walking along the road to the nearby larger town, the pots and pans they sold hung over one shoulder, when a rogue vehicle came out of nowhere, hit her, and then wrapped itself around a tree. The driver, too, had been killed, which Miura was sorry about because he would have wished to take vengeance on the man. The death of his sister left him all alone but losing her only made him wonder how she felt when the car hit, when her bones broke, when...

It got worse from there.

But he was eighteen.

In France, eighteen was the age where you could enlist in the army. It wasn't compulsory, but Miura saw a chance. If he could excel, they might send him off to kill people, they might actually *ask* him to do it. How incredible would that be? To be told, by your own government, to indulge in the one thing that you loved.

And so it went. Miura shone like a star, head and shoulders above the rest, and soon came to lead his own squad, soon progressed to special forces and then ever further. He was ruthless, skilled, patriotic. He would follow every order to the letter, without question. Civilians were not a problem for Miura; he killed them often on missions where war had broken out, came across them at every step. It was good to kill them, even better to take his time with them.

As captain now, he wasn't required to carry out the torture of an enemy, but Miura still liked to cultivate a hands-on role. He wouldn't expect his men to do anything he wouldn't do.

So, occasionally, Miura still killed.

It would have been his job to fully interrogate the woman named Luciane. He had been looking forward to it, building up to it, practically salivating over it. Yes, he had to keep his inclinations to himself but, over the years, he'd found ways to do that. It had been close a couple of times, but Miura had always come out smelling of roses...

...with thick, red blood on his hands.

Maybe he would get a turn at Tanaka. He didn't want to seem too eager. Perhaps he should wait and see if they

139

captured any members of the enemy team. That could prove fun. Men and women at the same time, in front of each other. Miura liked that idea. It made him twitch uncontrollably, a trait that he was trying to eject.

'Any movement?' he asked one of his men.

'Nothing at all, sir.'

Miura clasped one hand in another, tried to stop the twitching. He couldn't lose control, couldn't show emotion here. His face was blank, his eyes unfathomable caverns. The men, oblivious, were smoking and playing their game of cards. Others had their noses pointed at the house's windows. Miura was safe.

He lit another cigarette. Puffed on it for a while. The nicotine helped calm him, took his excitement and anxieties down several notches. He helped himself by flicking his thoughts towards the ancient casino that this whole exploit revolved around. How long had it lain underneath the sands of the Gobi Desert? Six hundred years or more. Miura couldn't see what all the fuss was about. Why preserve a dirty old relic?

Simply because the Shadow Kings wanted it done. And what they wanted, Miura wanted. He too, would see it done.

Chapter 19

Mason had decided hours ago that remote surveillance, a stakeout, wasn't for him.

They took it in turns sitting behind the thin netting that covered the hotel windows, staring down across the street at the houses opposite. They had three rooms on the right side of the hotel and had to keep swopping as day became evening and then night. They took four-hour shifts. Nobody expected anything to happen during the darker hours, but everyone knew that, if they weren't watching, Tanaka would come and go and they'd miss the chance to talk to him.

Mason found himself with a graveyard shift. He sat in a chair, a black coffee on the table at his side, knowing that Quaid and Sally were taking similar shifts in the bedrooms alongside.

He was anxious. Time was slipping away. He didn't know where the SED was, and he didn't know how long they could practically stake out the house down there, waiting for a travelling salesman. Previously, Mason had been chasing the prize, running headlong towards the treasure and into danger. Now…well, it wasn't exactly stimulating.

Mason sat back, sipped his hot coffee and sighed. The weather outside was a little hostile, drizzle flying in from the east at a slant, spattering the windows and making it harder to see. Not that there was much to see. The entire row of houses was in semi-darkness, some of them illuminated by just night lamps in the windows.

It was just then that he saw something. He sat forward, placing his cup on the table with a little rattle. One door, two up from the surveillance house, had opened. That house sat entirely in blackness and the opening of the door emitted no light, but in the dim pools cast by the streetlamps Mason could see exactly who it was who was exiting.

Three members of the SED. He was sure of it.

And one more standing in the doorway, watching them go. So at least four. The men wore tactical gear and carried guns and crept along carefully and steadily, passing the houses until they came to their target. Mason was sitting forward in his chair. His phone rang. He scrambled it out of his pocket.

'Yeah?' he whispered.

'Do you see them?' It was Quaid.

'I think they're SED.'

'Me too. Wait, Sally's calling too. Let me conference her in.'

Soon they had a three-way call going.

'They sure look exactly like the guys we've already tangled with,' Quaid said. 'And who else could it be, really? This shit with the SED is really starting to piss me off.'

'Agreed.' Mason had been taught well in observation, both by the army and by MI5. He recognised what the men were wearing, their body language, their formation. He watched as three of them reached the surveillance house and paused by the front door, two of them monitoring the street, the other one trying the handle.

'Any ideas?' Quaid said.

Mason quickly racked his brains. 'They have to be here for Tanaka too,' he said. 'Look at them. Did you see that?' Mason leaned forward, eyes scouring the figures below.

'I did,' Sally said. 'They're using a comms system.'

Mason nodded to himself. One of the figures below had touched his ear and spoken. He didn't need to do that. It was pure habit, maybe a bit of complacency sneaking in.

'Those three are communicating with another team,' Quaid said.

'Which means there are another three at least going round the back.' Mason shook his head. 'This isn't an attack; this is a recce.'

'Risky,' Quaid said.

Mason wasn't sure if he meant the SED's recce or his own observations of it. He said, 'I'm sure we can let this go. The SED are just getting the lie of the land. Maybe planting a few bugs. If they have the same lead as us – which we have to assume they do – they wouldn't do anything to jeopardise it.'

Now, Mason watched first one SED guy and then the other two enter the house. They slipped in and were gone in a matter of seconds; the street was empty again. Mason wished he could wipe the drizzle from his window to get a better look.

'Stay still,' he said. 'They might look through the front windows.'

He counted the minutes. Exactly four minutes after they'd gained entry, the SED team was back, exiting the house stealthily and making their way back to their own. He saw nothing of the other team, but had to assume they'd done the same.

'Shit,' Quaid said.

Mason agreed. He checked the time. It was 3.35 a.m. What next?

'The good thing is they haven't spotted *us*,' Sally said. 'Gives us an advantage.'

She was right, Mason realised. They still had the advantage here. A small one. 'Let's gather the team later,' he said. 'This is something we should all discuss.'

It was six hours later, after they'd all taken their turns getting breakfast, that they gathered in Sally's room to debate the fresh course of events. It was Roxy's turn to look out the window, and she sat in place, a steaming mug of black coffee in hand. The rest of them either sat on Sally's bed or stood around the room, their faces glum.

'The moment Tanaka appears, the SED will grab him.' Luciane stated the obvious.

'That's why they're here,' Hassell agreed, the strain hardening his already morose features. 'Question is, what are we gonna do about it?'

Mason was glad the New Yorker had cut straight to the heart of it. 'There are at least six of them,' he said. 'That's two small teams which they used last night. That's my guess. We have to find a way of neutralising the six.'

'They have guns,' Sally pointed out.

'We lure them out during the day,' Roxy said. 'Take them out in the street.'

'Sneak in through the top floor,' Hassell said. 'I could get us in, no worries. Take 'em out one at a time.'

'Pretend to be Tanaka,' Luciane suggested. 'Bait them.'

144

Mason considered all the options. None were without risk. The idea was not to take on six armed men at the same time.

'Ambush,' he whispered.

'What?' Sally asked.

'Divide and conquer,' he said and then turned to them. 'Listen,' he said. 'I have an idea.'

* * *

Later that day, Mason carried out his plan. The sun was up; it was the most dangerous time of the day for them. His nerves were already shot – was he leading his team to their deaths? Was the casino in the desert worth it? Should they leave this Tanaka to his own devices? Mason couldn't stop the questions peppering his brain like bullets from a Gatling gun.

But they were decided, agreed. This was how they were going to do it. The afternoon had just kicked in; there was good cloud cover, and still the drizzle filled the air, the day, a drifting haze of water that never let up. Quaid disappeared, heading out to the car and awaiting a prearranged time. Hassell and Roxy disappeared together, preparing to carry out their part of the plan. Mason would head down to the front shortly. Which left Luciane and Sally to scope out the rear of the other house.

It was several plans in one. Mason only saw more chance of failure, more chances for the SED to cause them problems. But it was the best he could come up with, their only chance of success.

The appointed time arrived.

Mason headed down to the lobby, close to the front doors. He phoned Quaid, who was all set. He then phoned Roxy, who needed another five minutes. Sally and Luciane were alongside him. Mason took several deep breaths.

This was it.

*　　*　　*

Roxy waited for Hassell to fully prepare himself. They were going in over the top, somehow. Roxy didn't know how Hassell expected to manage it, didn't really care so long as he did it. She trusted his abilities and would do whatever she needed to do to succeed.

Together, they hurried through the drizzle and the cloudy day to the last house in the row. They walked down the side of it. Hassell looked left, right and then behind, took stock of people and their positions. He waited.

'Trickiest part,' he whispered. 'Getting up top unseen.'

It wasn't as tricky as Roxy might have imagined. The last house had an alley running alongside it, and the back of a row of restaurants to the right, running at a right angle to it. The wall that formed the rear of the restaurants gave them cover. Hassell grabbed hold of the sturdy black iron downpipe, and climbed. He scurried up the wall like an ant, reaching the roof in a matter of seconds. He was used to this shit, Roxy reflected. She tried to ape him, almost managed it, but slipped twice and didn't look anywhere near as graceful climbing up. Soon, though, she was crouched alongside him in the roof's lee.

'Stay as low as you can,' he said.

They scrambled across the slick, tiled roof. Roxy stepped across piles of rubbish and gravel, through plastic bags that had accumulated in one corner. They counted the houses, came to the roof of the one in question, and hunkered down. Now, as observed from the hotel across the way, they had come to a skylight.

Hassell removed his smaller pack of tricks from his rucksack and got to work. Of course, they were visible now, not from the ground because they stayed low, but from anyone who wanted to look out from the hotel's higher floors. But it was daytime, it was raining and the view wasn't exactly enticing. The hope was that they wouldn't be seen.

Roxy counted the minutes. Quaid would arrive soon.

'You nearly there?' she asked.

'Two minutes.'

It was risky work. Hassell cut a hole in the glass and worked his hand through. He picked the inner lock, lifted the outer frame and then grabbed the inner one, holding on as he let himself into the house. He landed soundlessly, looked up and beckoned to Roxy.

Put his fingers to his lips and gestured at the floor. Their enemies were below them.

Roxy let herself into the house, landing lightly. Together, they crouched in a dusty attic. They used the four-by-two beams to walk along and reach the attic hatch. Hassell steadied himself, then reached down to lift it up.

It came easily. Below them now was a view of a carpeted landing and a staircase. Hassell held on to the rim and let himself down once more, now standing on the carpet, crouching. Roxy soon followed.

They left the attic door open.

Now, they had to listen, hope the SED took the bait and then get downstairs amid the furore.

Chapter 20

Mason waited for Roxy's call. His phone bleeped three times and then cut off. That was the signal. They were in place. Next, he called Quaid, who was sitting a short way off in the car.

'Go time,' he said.

'On it.'

Quaid hung up and then there was silence. Mason counted down the seconds. He knew exactly where he needed to be at the exact time. It was now that Luciane and Sally left the hotel and started walking along the street, waiting until they'd passed the SED house before they crossed the road and ran around to the back of the white-walled row.

Mason waited.

The seconds ticked down. His attention was solely focused out the window. When he saw the car in the distance, he gathered himself, took a deep breath and stood up. He left the hotel, loitered outside the front glass doors and pretended to be looking at his mobile phone but mostly just hid behind one of the marble-effect pillars. He was watching the car approach.

It came slowly along the road, pulled up outside the house Tanaka was supposed to be visiting, and turned its engine off. The occupant waited a while. He wore a low-fitting brimmed hat and a roomy raincoat, and carried a briefcase. Now, he cracked open the door and swung his legs out, taking his time.

Mason could only imagine the sudden commotion Quaid's appearance would have provoked. The SED would have gone immediately into mission mode, dividing and rushing into formation. He expected them to appear at any moment.

And now would be the perfect time for Hassell and Roxy – their silent assassin – to attack.

Mason strolled away from the hotel as Quaid stood up and started walking down the path to the front of the house.

The SED's door opened. Mason saw two figures push their way out. Of course, in the middle of the day, they didn't show their weapons. Mason didn't doubt they were armed to some degree, but not openly at least. He crossed to the car, saw Quaid walk up to the front door, saw the SED flying along the front of the houses, staying silent and low, saw Quaid raise his hand to knock.

And he started running. Sprinted straight towards the SED guys. Quaid whirled, too. As the SED men closed in, Quaid swung his briefcase, catching one of them across the face with a mighty swing that sent the man sprawling. Mason flew at the other one, using a jumping kick to send him smashing into the wall, from which he rebounded and gave Mason another chance. This time, Mason ducked low, swung at the ribs and then came up with an uppercut, catching the guy under the jawline.

Both SED soldiers were out cold.

Mason looked around. So far, so good. Nobody had seen them. The traffic splashing by hadn't slowed. Now they had to get rid of the unconscious men.

Now was the time to trust Hassell and Roxy.

* * *

As soon as they heard the shout from below, Roxy and then Hassell started slowly down the staircase. They didn't rush, but they were in a hurry. Roxy stayed low, creeping from one step to the next, reaching the bottom in a matter of seconds. She crouched, peering through the railings.

The SED were mostly gathered in the front room, as expected, but as she waited she saw a lone man make his way along the hallway.

She pounced, grabbed him around the throat, lifted and squeezed. She patted his body for weapons, found a gun, a knife and a cattle prod. Ordinarily, in warfare, she would have used the knife but, today, they wanted their enemies trussed up in a living bundle. Roxy used the prod. Her captive slithered through her hands.

Hassell came up close behind her. They advanced through the hallway to the kitchen. Roxy saw two men in there, preparing to leave through the back door.

She leapt at one; Hassell took the other. She led with the cattle prod, jamming it into the man's back just as he sensed the attack and tried to turn. He went down like a sack of spanners, slamming to the floor. Hassell struck his opponent across the back of the neck, making his forehead jerk forward into a kitchen unit. The man staggered, but he was tough and didn't go down. He whirled, leading with an elbow that struck Hassell viciously across the left ear and made him stumble to his knees. Then the man ripped a weapon from his waistband.

A handgun.

Roxy leapt at it and slammed the man's hand down just as he fired. The sound of the shot was loud in the kitchen. She continued to lean on the gun arm, forcing it down. With her free hand, she exchanged blows with her enemy. She didn't know where all the other men were. At any moment, one of them could come up behind her. Just then, the kitchen door flew open.

Roxy gasped and looked up.

Luciane and Sally stood there. They'd been waiting to see if anyone would emerge to ambush them and, when they didn't, came in through the back way.

Roxy smiled grimly. Luciane was staring beyond her at the kitchen door, and showed no signs of alarm. She concentrated on her own opponent, deflecting the gun. She looked up at Luciane and nodded at the fallen cattle prod.

'Use it,' she gasped.

With a lunge, Luciane shoved the prod into the man's neck. Even Roxy winced as he jerked upright and started shaking through his entire frame. His body went rigid and then, when Luciane removed the prod, he collapsed limply to the floor.

'Bit much,' Roxy said. 'But I like your style.'

There was a commotion behind them. Roxy whirled, but it was just Mason dragging two of the SED guys through the front door with Quaid. Roxy took a quick moment to count their opponents.

Crap.

We've only taken out five.

She shot to her feet and ran towards Mason, assuming the last remaining SED member would be in the front room. She hit the door hard, slamming it back, and rolled inside. There he was, standing at the back of the room with a radio in hand, maybe calling the two men Mason and Quaid had neutralised.

He was too far away.

Roxy despaired at the gap. She stood no chance of reaching him before he drew his gun. But there was no option. She ran anyway. She set off like an Olympic sprinter, threw her arms out, and roared at him. Anything to put him off. The man stared for half a second, then dropped his radio and reached for his gun.

Whipped it out and aimed in less than a second.

Roxy was still four steps away.

He aimed it at her centre mass, frowned and fired. But not before Mason, behind him, snatched out the gun he'd taken from one of his captives and opened fire first. His bullet struck the man's gun hand, severing a finger and making him scream and drop his weapon. Roxy struck him a second later, bouncing him off the far wall.

Still screaming, he fell to the ground.

Roxy was quick to cover his mouth, to shut him the hell up. The gunshot was bad enough in this row of houses, never mind the yelling. His grunts became muffled behind her hand. Hassell brought bedding and towels they could use to gag and bind the captured men. Sally kept the cattle prod handy. Soon they were all in the front room, a team again.

Mason glanced up at Quaid. 'Keep a watch,' he said. 'The last thing we want is to miss Tanaka now.'

Quaid smiled, seeing the irony in that. He left by the front door, drifting back across to the hotel. Soon, he was calling Mason.

'See anything?' Mason asked. He meant after the gunshot and the screaming.

'All clear. You know how it is. So long as it's brief, people tend to dismiss it. Blame it on the telly, a car backfire, a video game.'

'That works,' Mason said, and ended the call.

They spent some time trussing up their enemy. There was a lot of resistance, which Roxy soon put an end to with the cattle prod. The fifth time she used it, Mason glanced at her.

'I believe you're enjoying yourself.'

'Hey, they brought it to the party, not me.'

It was a good point, not to be argued with, especially since she still had some juice in her prod. Mason finished tying up the SED with the others' help and then rose and backed away, viewing his handiwork.

The six men lay trussed in a corner, side by side, gagged, tied at the wrists and ankles, able to struggle but not to slither around much. They had been relieved of their weapons, a cache of knives, cattle prods and handguns, which Mason and the others now held and were grateful for. Mason had already checked the guns and had found that only one had been fired. They also secured three extra mags each.

'Leave them,' Roxy said.

'That's the idea,' Mason said. 'We can check on them every day, or maybe leave someone here to keep an eye on them?'

'Do you fancy that job?' Roxy asked, with distaste in her voice.

He didn't. And he'd never ask anyone else to do something he wouldn't. The bonds were good. They would hold, at least for a while.

He looked around at his team. 'Good job,' he said, amazed that they'd done it with little to no injuries. Hassell had a substantial bruise developing across his face, and

153

Roxy was a little banged up. But, apart from that, they were fine.

'Let's hope it's all worth it,' Sally said.

'We negated half an SED team,' Mason said. 'That actually makes me wonder where the other half are.'

'Another quarry,' Sally said. 'Another outlet for those coins.'

Mason nodded. It made sense. It was unfortunate that the SED could track the coins in other ways but, hey, he thought, they could only do their best here.

Together, they left the house and returned to the hotel.

Chapter 21

After the excitement, distraction and pressure of capturing the SED team, the act of surveillance was a yawning bore. The rest of that day went by steadily, mind-numbingly, and the only relief they felt was when no police turned up at the SED house, confirming that the operation had gone off without a hitch.

Every few hours, they sent one person back to the house to check on the captives and tighten their bonds. They didn't want them to escape, but they didn't want them to die either.

The rest of the day passed wearily. The next night passed slowly, a non-event. Mason slept fitfully, waking every hour and wondering where the hell he was. When the answer dawned on him, he yawned and went back to sleep.

But, finally, their patience paid off.

The morning sidled by, taking its time. They ate in their rooms, took mugfuls of coffee and tea and tried to stay upbeat. This could take days, more days than they could afford to spend. Mason slumped in his chair.

Outside, a car pulled up to the kerb.

At first, it didn't quite register. Mason saw the car, saw the occupant, but he was so bored and acclimatised to the ennui of the day that he didn't react straightaway.

Then he sat forward.

And then he started fumbling for his phone as he leapt to his feet. He knocked his mug off the table and sent the contents spilling to the floor. Swearing to himself, he put a keyword message in a group chat that all the others had been told to monitor.

'Action,' it read.

He imagined the others scrambling to their feet, rushing to the front of the hotel. He was racing for the door, yanking it open and charging out into the corridor. He went straight for the stairs, not trusting the elevators to be any quicker, and pounded down them two at a time. Passing a couple on the way down, he didn't slow, just dashed past them, much to their visible surprise.

Mason hit the bottom of the stairs and pushed the door that led out to the lobby. It flew open, cracking into its stopper and bouncing back, striking his right bicep. He ran out into the lobby and saw Roxy and Hassell already at the glass doors that led to the street. On seeing him, they turned and waited.

Mason rushed past, gaining the street and then running to the kerb. He waited impatiently for traffic to pass, Roxy and Hassell at his side. The man had already got out of his car and was ambling down the path to the house. Mason wanted to reach him before he knocked. He hurried across the road, weaving between cars and getting some furious looks, but no honks. Maybe they were too civilised here for honks. He reached the opposite kerb and let out a shout.

'Tanaka!'

It was a loaded shout. If the guy turned, they were in business. If he didn't, they were back to square one.

But the man turned, surprise on his face. He carried a large briefcase and wore a long black coat, shiny black boots, and a hat with a wide brim. He looked thin, pale, and carried himself erect, his spine as straight as a girder. When he saw Mason and the others rushing at him, he stepped back and flinched.

'Please,' he said in English. 'I don't want any trouble.'

Mason slowed immediately, wanting to pose as little threat as possible. 'We're here to assist you, to warn you and get your help.'

By now, the entire team had assembled and stood around Mason, collected on the narrow path to the house. Worried about standing around in the open, Mason led them all into the more private, more shadowy lee of the house.

'Who are you?' the man asked warily.

'You speak good English,' Roxy complimented him.

'I am a traveller. I sell all over the country and further afield. I speak many languages, but mostly the languages of trade and commerce.'

Mason cleared his throat. 'Listen,' he said. 'You're in danger. A man named Kenji, a gambler from Tokyo, has named you as the man he exchanged some bags of old coins with. Is this true?'

An expression of wariness came into Tanaka's face. 'What is this?'

Sally stepped forward. 'Don't worry. We're not here to rob you. The bags of coins you gave Kenji have aroused a good deal of attention. That's all.'

Tanaka frowned. 'Yes, I worried that they might cause a

bit of a stir and asked him to be as unobtrusive as possible. I see that advice wasn't taken.'

'Well, they weren't exactly collectors' items,' Mason said, wondering just how much the man actually knew and deciding to plunge ahead. 'They came from an old Chinese casino, which you no doubt know. Now, whoever originally found the coins knows exactly where it is. We're trying to track that person down and find the casino.'

'But there's a complication,' Luciane added.

'What kind of complication?' Tanaka asked.

Mason watched the houses to either side and especially the house inside which the SED team was bound. He saw no movement anywhere and ploughed on.

'The Shadow Kings and the SED want the same thing,' he said. 'And they're being very aggressive about finding it. *Very* aggressive.'

If possible, Tanaka's face went even paler. 'Who are the Shadow Kings?'

'Guns. Knives. Tasers,' Roxy said deadpan. 'Just a few houses down from here. They were on the lookout for you, but we got to them first. We're trying to save as many people as we can from them.'

'You killed them?' Tanaka looked aghast.

'No, we neutralised them. But, believe me, they would have had no qualms about killing you.'

'So the threat is over?'

'Only got half the team,' Quaid said. 'And we're gonna have to let them go, eventually.'

Tanaka shuddered. 'What can I do?' He switched the heavy-looking briefcase to his other hand.

Mason stepped closer. 'Help us,' he said. 'And then go into hiding. Just for a few weeks, maybe. It will be all over

158

by then.'

'Hiding?' Tanaka was visibly shaking.

'We got them off your back,' Hassell said. 'It's up to you to help yourself from here.'

'Don't be so predictable,' Roxy told him.

Tanaka stared at her. 'Are you joking with me? Predictability is how I make my living. My customers know when and where I will turn up. They are ready for me. They know to expect me. It is all about building the foundations and then sticking to the schedule.'

'It's simple,' Roxy said, typically blunt. 'Stay predictable and die. Or you could take a vacation and live.'

Tanaka hung his head. Standing there, in his long coat and his wide-brimmed hat, he looked quite forlorn, a character out of time who'd just had all the wind taken out of him.

'I could go somewhere,' he said.

'You should,' Roxy said. 'But first tell us all about the coins.'

Tanaka glanced up. 'Yes, the coins. I certainly didn't find them, if that's what you're asking. I'm no explorer, and I know very little about casinos in the desert beyond Las Vegas.' He managed a grin. 'Is this the Las Vegas of old?'

Mason shrugged. 'Could be. We don't know that much about it.'

'Maybe you should do some research?' Tanaka suggested.

'Hey, I've done my research,' Sally said. 'I just haven't shared it yet.'

Tanaka looked from them to the house he was visiting. He bit his lip. 'All right,' he said. 'I have no bags of coins left now. I won them in an underground gambling game.

Right here in Japan. I have lots of friends, an assorted bunch. Criminals run the underground gambling scene—'

'Yakuza,' Hassell sighed.

'No not the Yakuza,' Tanaka said. 'The Japanese Cranes. They are a rival of the Yakuza. As you probably know, during the last thirty years, other criminal groups have been infiltrating the Japanese criminal underworld that was once fully controlled by the native mafia, the Yakuza. The Cranes originated in the late Eighties, and see themselves as hard-done-by children, cast-offs, loners sick of persecution, a real family united by adversity and opposed to the coalition of criminal syndicates that make up the Yakuza. Of course, the authorities have overlooked the Yakuza presence in many cities in the past, since they helped restrain the extravagances of the lesser gangs, but recently they have been forced underground.' Tanaka looked unhappy. 'All I'm saying is, the Cranes are not the Yakuza. I wouldn't associate with them if they were.'

'We understand,' Sally said. 'You're not a bad guy, not a criminal. We get it.'

'It doesn't matter to us who you associate with,' Roxy said. 'It's the information we need.'

Tanaka nodded. 'Yes, I see. Like I explained, I won the bags in an underground gambling game. I won them off a man named Saito, a notorious gambler, part of the gang. But Saito…he is a rarely seen creature.'

Mason frowned. 'What are you saying?'

'That Saito only surfaces to play in these underground gambling games. That, as I explained, he's a loner, a reject. Gambling is his love. He's considered a major player, a crazy character, a standout personality. If you can play with Saito, you've made it.'

'And you've played against Saito?' Quaid asked.

'I have. Not only that, I beat him. Hence the bags of gold coins.'

'And how do you get an audience with Saito?' Mason asked.

Tanaka smiled. 'You play against him, of course. If you are good enough, he will talk to you. If not...' he shrugged. 'Bye, bye.'

'He won't just...have a chat?' Roxy asked. 'Shoot the shit?'

Tanaka looked confused. 'A chat? A shit? No. As I explained, he is a cult figure. An icon. Get Saito at a table and the night is yours, most of the takings as well. They afford him a certain protection.' Tanaka went on to give them a short physical description of the man.

'But around the gaming table...' Mason saw it.

'Exactly. He is yours to talk to.'

'Can *you* help us?' Quaid asked.

'I can't go with you. As you said, I have to run. I can't be involved in this.' Tanaka already looked antsy. 'But I can make a few calls. I can probably get you an invitation to the game.'

'What game, and where?' Sally asked.

'Saito plays in Osaka. I can give you a suburb. The games move about.'

Mason exchanged information with the man. 'We'll go to Osaka,' he said. 'Let me know an address.'

Tanaka nodded. 'I can do that. There is only one problem.'

Mason frowned at him. 'Which is?'

'You don't look like gamblers. How good are you at gambling?'

161

'Oh, I've gambled a fair bit in my time,' Roxy said. 'Mostly with my life.'

'Don't make me look bad,' Tanaka said. 'You're my recommendation. If you fuck up, I'll never get an invitation again.'

'Don't worry,' Mason said, managing a smile. 'We're gambling gods.'

Chapter 22

Osaka, known as the Nation's Kitchen, is famous for its mouth-watering food, its glittery nightlife and its modern architecture. On the surface, at least, it is a friendly city, full of light and warmth and pleasantries. From its bustling outskirts to its metropolitan heart, Osaka wields a tremendous influence on Japan's economy and boasts everything from Universal Studios to the Museum of History and the ancient Osaka Castle.

Mason shared the drive with Quaid. It took them six hours to drive from Ueda to Osaka, a journey in which nobody spoke much and Sally, in the passenger seat, brushed up on everything from ancient Chinese casinos to how to play a hand of poker.

'Are we really all that great at gambling?' Roxy had asked when they started their journey around midday.

'No,' Mason had said. 'So get Googling.'

'Oh, that's gonna help,' Hassell groaned. 'I have a grounding in gambling. I used to be in a gang, remember? It's how we used to pass our nights.'

'Tanaka said Saito's game was poker,' Sally said.

'Yeah, I heard. I can hold my own.'

Roxy nudged him. 'But can you play poker?' she asked with a smirk.

'Yeah, I can do that too.'

'How good are you?' Quaid asked. 'It sounds like this Saito is an expert.'

'I'm no expert,' Hassell admitted. 'But I have the face for it and I can make a good bluff. Sometimes, that's all you need.'

'I used to play with the officers,' Quaid told them. 'Back in my army days. The talk on those nights was frank and to the point. No one was content with following many of the orders we were given, but they all capitulated with a shrug and a shake of the head. If only more of us had spoken out.'

'I didn't know you'd spoken out,' Luciane said, turning to him.

'Oh, I spoke out. I laced right into them. It didn't do any good. Three months later, I quit before they could make me. And don't forget, I have spoken out about this quest too. I'm not totally against it, but I'm not all for it.'

Luciane reached out a hand and clasped Quaid's left wrist. 'I'm sorry.'

'What can you do?' Quaid seemed not to notice. 'In the army, you're up against the establishment. The old guard. They'll just close ranks and squeeze you out. I was never very good with stupid orders.' He smiled.

Roxy pursed her lips. 'For twelve years, I was good with it. I was thirty before I saw the light and quit. Lost a lot of life that way.'

'Which you're seeking to recover now,' Mason said, trying to gee her up a bit, sensing her dejected mood.

164

Roxy sat up. 'Yeah, and I'm doin' a damn good job of it,' she said. 'Building those barriers. I'm almost there.'

Mason was glad to hear it. Helping Roxy free herself from her demons also helped him climb his own conflicted ladder.

'I didn't have any of that.' Hassell spoke up unexpectedly. Maybe because he'd earlier mentioned the criminal gang he used to work for. 'I didn't even know I was working for that bastard.' He shook his head. 'The bastard that murdered Chloe and blamed his rivals, making me take revenge on them, along with the murderer. I was caught then, a fish in a net. How do you get over something like that?'

Mason didn't know. Hassell might have killed Gido in the end, but Gido would always be Hassell's disgrace. *How do you get over something like that...?*

...you don't.

'I'm a firm believer in moving forward,' Roxy said. 'Raising barriers between the present and the past.'

'You learn to live with it, accept it, even if it was your fault,' Mason knew he was talking about himself. 'You atone by helping others. Make up for the men you lost. Protect people. That's why I initially took the protection job and now run around with you guys, protecting inanimate objects and the weak. Today, see, we're protecting Kenji and Tanaka. We're protecting whomever else the SED might attack. That's me, now. That's what I do.'

After that, there wasn't much talk. They stopped halfway for food and drink, finding a service station that sold a few recognisable items. By the time they arrived in Osaka, it was past six p.m.

'Has Tanaka contacted you?' Roxy asked, as Mason stalled in traffic along a colourful street.

'Not yet.'

165

'We're kinda reliant on him.'

'I know.'

Mason drove down a narrow street lined by six- and seven-storey buildings all fronted by multicoloured signs with Japanese lettering running vertically down their lengths. It was raining, the slick city streets lit up by the gaudy lighting, the black roads reflecting a myriad vivid lights. The shopfronts were bright too, shedding their illumination onto the pavements.

'Should we find a hotel?' Quaid asked.

'Osaka's a big place,' said Mason, sounding worried. 'We need Tanaka to narrow it down first.'

They drove on, going effectively nowhere. Through the steady sweep of the windscreen wipers Mason saw pavements packed with wet, hastening citizens. He slowed to let a bunch of them cross the road and saw an assortment of life: people with their jackets pulled up over their heads, people struggling with soggy bags, people politely letting others take the path in front of them. It was a hodge-podge of humanity, a snapshot of life in Osaka, a procession of strangers he would never set eyes on again.

His phone buzzed. Stuck in traffic, he looked down to where he had it trapped between his legs. A message flashed up.

'Go to Nishinari-ku. Red-light district. Be careful. Go to Kuma Chao "Japanese-style restaurant" at 9. They will expect six foreigners under my approval. Don't fuck it up for me.'

Mason read it aloud three times. 'I wonder why he stressed a Japanese-style restaurant?'

'I know why,' Sally said. 'I've been researching underground gambling in Osaka and other big cities. It's a front. These places operate as restaurants, traditional places, to avoid getting sanctioned by the anti-prostitution and gambling laws. I guess that's why it's classed as "underground".'

'And dangerous as hell,' Roxy said. 'Check your weapons.'

It was a favourite and necessary pastime of hers, and Mason's and, of course, of anyone who knew the military. It was engrained in her. They still had the guns they'd confiscated from the SED team and all took them out now.

'Let's hope we don't get pulled over,' Mason muttered. 'We'll be spending the next week in jail.'

Steadily, he made his way over to Nishinari-ku. The rain let up after a short while, leaving the streets gleaming and smooth, the lights all around them glossy and sparkling. More people came out after the rain stopped, practically throttling the pavements. Mason lost count of the number of pedestrian crossings that stopped them.

'How do we look?' Sally said suddenly.

'Mason's looking pretty rough,' Roxy said.

'We fought in these clothes,' Quaid said.

'Yeah, if we're going into a gambling den, we need new rags,' Sally said.

Mason didn't slow, didn't veer off track. Sally looked up the nearest department store on her phone and soon they had stopped close by and were walking in through the revolving doors, now part of the flow of humanity. They quickly made purchases, stowed their old clothes in their rucksacks and were back in the car twenty-five minutes later. Mason wore black trousers, a white shirt and a roomy jacket, as did Hassell. Quaid had gone for a dark grey suit. The women all wore trousers and blouses with jackets that fit their different personalities. Roxy's was a small leather jacket, tight-fitting. Sally had bought a loose denim jacket of a standard sort, and Luciane a light-blue, padded non-brand. What was important was that they looked smart and well-kept – better than they had half an hour ago.

Mason made the rest of the drive to the Kuma Chao restaurant in about thirty minutes. They were a tad early, so sat in the car waiting, getting the lie of the land. Osaka's red-light district was a huddle of murky back streets, illuminated only by a series of globes strung above the street that gave off a yellowish glow. There were graffiti everywhere. The buildings were stark block work and much darker than what they'd seen so far. From their vantage point, they could see several brothels, identified by the half-clad women standing in the windows.

Sally gave them all a crash course in playing poker. It wasn't going to win them a lot of money, but it would get them by. Their cover was bored tourists, looking to live a little on the wild side, feel a little real danger. At this point, they did not know who Saito was or what he looked like beyond a vague description. That was going to take work.

The Kuma Chao restaurant sat up the street a short way. Like everything else along this street, it was understated, badly lit and the single sign above the windows was almost too small to read.

'Shall we take the guns?' Quaid asked, as nine o'clock ticked closer.

'Good question,' Mason said. 'Probably not, since we're heading into a den of thieves.'

'All the more reason to take them,' Roxy said. 'They can always take them off us if they have rules.'

Mason was sure they would have rules, and he was also sure anyone wanting to enter the gambling establishment would know them. Still, they were foreigners. They always had that excuse.

'Obviously,' Sally said, 'the guns will be taken away from us at the door. We might not even get them back.'

It was a good point, and since it was time to go, Mason made a snap decision. 'Leave them,' he said. 'We have no reason to expect a firefight.'

Roxy huffed a little as she climbed out of the car. The night was cool but clear. Stars littered the vault of the sky that stretched above the dingy street. Their new shoes echoed off the concrete as they walked the short way to the restaurant. There were other people around, mostly men, a few couples. Nobody spoke much. It was as if the foreboding atmosphere that hung over the place had stilled everyone's tongue. Mason led the way to the front of the restaurant.

He placed a hand on the door. 'Are we ready?'

'Since we don't know what to expect – no,' Roxy said.

'Always ready,' Quaid said, to an eye-roll from Luciane.

Mason pushed his way into the restaurant. There was faint music playing, something Japanese and traditional, and the low hum of conversation. About half of the tables were occupied, giving the 'front' business some authenticity. Several of the diners looked up as Mason and his team entered.

Mason made his way to the counter that stretched across the back of the place, leaned over and attracted the attention of a tall man with a lot of hair and a wizened face who was bending over with a mop in his hand.

'Hey,' he breathed. 'We've come to play.'

The old guy looked up. 'Play?' he said in passable English.

'Play games,' Sally leaned over too. 'Six foreigners,' she pointed them all out. 'Tanaka sent us.'

The old man studied them, counted them with the end of his mop and then smiled. 'Come with me,' he said.

Chapter 23

Without ceremony, they were all quickly searched.

They had been ushered down a short, cluttered corridor to a small room where two men wearing suits stood with their backs straight. These men didn't speak English, but mimed them holding their arms out and getting searched. The search was quick and perfunctory. When it was done, the men opened the door behind them and waved the team through.

Mason traversed another corridor, this one painted black with golden dragon wings down its entire length. There were boxes and shelves to negotiate, and piles of crockery. Mason wondered if they were still in the 'front', if this was all show to deter any would-be investigators. At the end of the corridor, they came to a set of double doors, also painted black.

Alone, they weren't sure what to do, but Mason just shrugged, grabbed the handles and opened the doors.

Immediately, a wall of sound hit him.

He stood for a moment, shocked. A vast room opened out, well lit by spotlights in the ceiling. Tall plumes of smoke wreathed their way through the air and among the rafters.

There were people everywhere, mostly Japanese but some Europeans too, strolling back and forth, sitting at a vast array of gaming tables or playing the coin-operated slot machines that lined the walls. Among the patrons walked waiters and waitresses wearing tight-fitting emerald green trousers and tops, carrying silver platters full of umbrella-heavy cocktails or frosted glasses of beer. Dealers and pit bosses stood upright at dozens of different tables, their black suits making them stand out in the crowds. There were people standing apart, smooching; couples standing at the tables, cursing their luck; and others, watching like unsociable voyeurs. And still more…a man waving a wad of notes above his head, a man striking a gaming machine with his bare knuckles and being visited by a guard, a woman wearing a slit skirt and enough jewellery to bury her under sidling up to a dealer with a wry smile on her face, a man lifting his girlfriend onto his shoulders to get a better look at a game of blackjack. It was organised bedlam, orderly chaos, an array of humanity that should be uncontrollable, and yet everything seemed to be going smoothly.

Mason stepped into it all. Already he knew they would be hard pressed to find a particular man in here, but then Tanaka was supposed to have arranged something. They should face off with Saito. That should help narrow it down a tad.

They entered the fray, walked among the tables. When Mason looked up, he saw a balcony running around the top of the gaming area and several men leaning over it, watching what was going on. A set of stairs ran up to the balcony. It was roped off, but he walked over to it anyway.

'We have a game at nine,' he told the guard stationed there. 'With Saito.'

The man remained stony-faced. He beckoned to another, a stocky guy standing a short way off. He gestured for Mason to repeat his words.

Mason did so.

'English is not so good,' the new man said. 'You say Saito?' he was shouting above the general commotion.

'Yeah!' Mason yelled back. 'Saito! Arranged by Tanaka.'

The man nodded and wandered off. Mason and the others stayed where they were, watching the underground casino work. Mason guessed the only difference between this place and, say, a legal Las Vegas casino was the size. Here, they had to fit everything in one room.

Time passed. People on the floor yelled their woes, backing away from tables so hurriedly that they struck other people. The guards came in and calmed them down. Another man started yelling when he won at roulette, jumping up and down until someone shouted at him to shut the hell up. Mason heard all kinds of languages, from the obvious Japanese to English and French and Russian. It was a clutter of humanity, a jumble of like-minded civilians enjoying a night on the wild side. Mason saw several of the guards carried guns and Tasers at their belts.

Finally, their guard returned. He bent over so that he could yell in Mason's ear.

'You...follow.'

Mason nodded at the others. He followed the guard, winding through the outskirts of the throng until he came to a wide niche in the back of the room. A red rope had been drawn across, separating the niche from the rest of the room.

Beyond the rope was a poker table and, around it, eight seats. Seven were occupied. Mason looked at the free seat. The guard gestured to it.

'Oh,' he said. 'I thought it was all six of us.'

The guard frowned and gestured again. 'One seat,' he said. 'You go.'

Mason wasn't close to being the poker player of the team. That honour would go to Sally and her research. He turned quickly towards her.

'It's going to have to be you,' he said. 'At least you can hold your own in there.'

Sally looked nervous. 'Me?'

'Can we watch?' Roxy asked.

The guard looked confused and was growing impatient. He unhooked the red rope and gestured that one of them should go through. Roxy didn't back down but put her hands to her eyes like she was looking through binoculars and inclined her head towards the guard.

He nodded. 'Watch,' he said.

They all went through, standing a respectful distance from the table so that they couldn't see any of the cards that would soon be in play. Sally kept walking, but Mason pulled her back.

'Don't forget,' he said. 'This is all about Saito.'

She nodded, carried on to her seat and sidled into it. Mason watched. Now there were eight gathered around the table, six men and two women. Apart from Sally, everyone was Asian, and they were quite an assortment of ages and sizes. One enormous man took up two spaces and had arms like tree trunks. One tall thin man wearing black hunched over like a praying mantis. Others were younger, some in their twenties, whilst the other woman was middle-aged and sported a studded choker necklace and studded bracelets. Her hair was black, and she had a large spider web tattoo on her right cheek. One hand was resting gently across her stacks of chips, and Mason saw it had a tiny tattoo on every knuckle.

'Which one is Saito?' Roxy asked, yelling in his ear.

Mason shrugged. 'Fucked if I know.'

* * *

Sally placed her hand on the dozens of ceramic poker chips that the dealer had set before her. They were of intricate design, featuring full-colour graphics and custom denomination. Sally separated them into piles, mentally translating the yen to pounds in her head. A thick layer of tension hung over the table, curdling just a few metres above their heads. Sally kept her face impassive and studied every one of her opponents.

Saito couldn't be the woman or the massive guy. That left five smartly dressed, thin opponents who might or might not be the man in question. Should she mention his name, maybe drop Tanaka's name at the same time? It seemed the right way to go.

But before she could put her plan into action, the dealer called for their attention. He ratified they were playing Texas Hold 'Em, dealt each player two cards and then called out the small and big blind, speaking both in Japanese and English. Sally studied her hand, a three of clubs and a jack of spades. It wasn't great, but she didn't change her facial expression, just sat stoically after folding her cards and studying the other faces. Eyes flicked left and right. Jaws and cheeks twitched. The tattooed woman made a deep sigh that might signify a good hand or a bluff. Next came the first round of betting. Sally wasn't confident in her hand but didn't show it, betting well. Then the dealer placed three community cards face up.

Sally stared at them, her face expressionless.

The second round of betting began. There was complete silence at the table. Of course, the room at their backs was a veritable melee of raucous vice. The noise came in waves. Sally did her best to block it out, but found that she couldn't. It was just too loud and unpredictable, every moment someone new shouting or laughing or expressing their anger. She made a show of turning around and studying the crowd – more than once, in an effort to draw her opponents' attention towards it, too. Maybe she could even the odds that way.

The dealer turned the fourth community card face up.

Another round of betting began. Sally stayed in, always calling, never raising. The tattooed woman had folded; the big guy with the trunk-like arms was sweating profusely, but still in the game. Out of the five others, two had folded and three were sitting as if they were playing for beans, not cash.

Sally knew she was beaten when the dealer dealt the fifth community card, known as the river. She couldn't advance with the cards in her hand. This was the final round of betting and, since three players hadn't yet folded, all players had to show their hands. Tree trunk won.

Who'd have thought it?

Sally stayed in for the second hand. Turned to a passing waitress.

'Singapore Sling,' she said.

The woman nodded. Two other players ordered drinks. Sally saw Mason and the others standing near the rope at her back, encouraging expressions on their faces.

Saito, Mason mouthed.

Sally turned back to the table, picked up her new cards. A jack and a ten, same suit. Nice. She waited for the community cards and didn't change her strategy of calling, not raising.

She was more into the game now, enjoying it. She sat back, crossed her legs, felt relaxed. She slid her chips into the main pile, watched the community cards grow. This time she was in the final round, but still lost. One of the younger guys with black hair and green eyes scooped the prize and slid all the chips to his side of the table. He grinned. He told them all how great he was. They ignored him and waited for the dealer to start the next hand.

Sally uncrossed her legs and leaned forward. She hadn't wanted to show her hand until now, but it felt like she was getting nowhere. Time to gamble with more than just cards. 'Saito,' she said.

They might be playing poker, but the man who started and then blinked at her gave himself away immediately. Saito was the younger man opposite her, maybe early thirties, with short-cropped hair, blue eyes, thin, and wearing a snazzy black Armani suit that clung to him. He frowned at her and licked his lips nervously.

'Yes?' he said shortly.

'Hi, I'm Sally. You speak English?'

'Some.'

'Tanaka sends his salutations.' Sally made sure the others could see who she was talking to by turning around and nodding.

'Tanaka?'

'Travelling salesman. Your friend.'

'Can we get on with it?' the immense man growled, also in English.

'Ah, Tanaka,' Saito said, ignoring the man. 'Yes, a friend. How do you know him?'

Sally shrugged. 'He sold us some wares.'

Saito shook his head as if not understanding. Right then,

the dealer started the third hand and Sally went quiet, not wanting to spook Saito with too much conversation. It was enough that she'd identified the man. You couldn't go beyond that and hold a full-on conversation in the middle of a poker game.

She played out a third hand, won the fourth. By then, some players were getting restless and departed the table. Saito stayed where he was, and so did Sally. She took a break from one hand and wandered back to her friends with her Singapore Sling in one hand.

'You see him?' she asked Mason.

'Got him in my sights and on camera,' came the reply, shouted, but still lost underneath the overall uproar.

'We can't approach him at the table.'

'Agreed, but he can't stay there for ever.'

The night turned. Nine o'clock soon became ten and then eleven. The gambling den only grew busier, louder, filled with more tumult. Sally played Texas Hold 'Em hands with Saito and the big guy and the tattooed woman for most of the night.

As Sally's watch showed midnight, Saito rose to his feet.

Her brain was electrified, her chest thumped. Finally, they would have their chance.

Saito nodded to her as he left the table. Sally cashed her own chips in, leaving the others to follow Saito.

When she was ready, she turned and dashed away from the table, stuffing her cash into her bag and trying to stay on the fringes of the madness that filled the room.

Ahead, Saito was heading for the exit.

Chapter 24

Mason was ten steps behind Saito as the man exited the underground casino and headed for the front door. The guy paused to collect his coat from a cloakroom Mason hadn't even noticed on the way in. He slowed, checked behind him, saw the others close by and Sally just a few steps behind. The casino itself was still humming; it probably went on like this all night, maybe emptying in the later morning hours.

Soon, Saito was on the move again.

They didn't want to stop him inside the casino. There was entirely too much security, and if Saito caused a scene, enough guards to shield him. Saito grabbed his coat, shrugged it on, and they continued through the restaurant, into the street.

When Mason stepped out, he found that more and more people were out on the streets. The red-light area overflowed with foot traffic and voices both loud and quiet. He saw a little more light now; square and rectangular signs were lit up with Japanese writing and the faces of women, while other establishments promised pizza and pasta in English. The flow of humanity rushed by in all directions.

Sato inserted himself into it. He wasn't exactly tall, and soon vanished into the flood. Mason hurried. It was through Saito's red padded jacket over his Armani suit that Mason and the others could keep him in sight.

Roxy cut through the crowd hard, ranging ahead. She would stay in front of Saito. Quaid and Hassell drifted to the sides. Mason stayed behind with Luciane and Sally. They followed the guy up the street.

'Should we drag him into an alley?' Sally yelled in his ear.

'Love the idea, but it has to be a last resort,' Mason replied. 'Too many people about.'

A fried-food smell filled the air, reminding Mason that he hadn't eaten anything except a quick sandwich today. Small takeaways stood on either side of the street, doing a brisk business. Mason saw people with cardboard boxes and chopsticks eating in the street. He slowed as Saito angled towards one and entered a queue, finally coming away with a box and some utensils clasped in one hand.

Mason's stomach grumbled. 'That's just taking the piss,' he said.

'I want to mug him just for the food,' Roxy said.

Saito didn't linger long. He shovelled the noodles and fried chicken into his mouth in about two minutes flat, slurped a drink and then started off again. Mason was close by. Saito walked up the street for a while and then slowed. He turned to his right. Mason frowned.

'Bollocks,' he said. 'That's not good.'

Sally, to his left, squinted. 'What is that place?'

It was three storeys high, its front window long and low and topped by a red sign and a stringline of white Japanese writing. There was a single front door, manned by a broad guy in a suit.

'An unexpected turn,' Roxy said, grinning at them. 'Who's up for it?'

The American was standing in front of the window, sizing up the wares on offer. A tall woman clad in suspenders and a bra stood next to a shorter woman wearing a negligee and high heels, and a bare-chested man flexing his pecs.

'Oh,' Sally said when she saw.

'It's a house of ill repute,' Quaid said.

Saito squeezed between the guard and the open door, disappearing inside.

'Quickly,' Roxy said.

Mason knew they could wait for him to emerge, but there was no telling if the place had a back door. And the chances were, considering what it was, that it probably had several. This was their only chance to question Saito.

'Me and Roxy,' he said. 'The rest of you try to look busy. We'll be back as soon as we can.'

He grabbed Roxy by the arm and headed for the open door. The guard eyed them closely, then nodded. Mason nodded back and pulled Roxy inside.

'At least it's an equal opportunity whorehouse,' she whispered.

Mason let himself smile briefly. Inside was a lobby, gaudily lit in dark red, and several sofas arranged around the periphery of the room. There was a bar to the left, a cloakroom to the right, and a set of big double doors to the front. Mason headed for the bar.

'Two,' he said.

The barkeep handed him two tokens and took a wad of cash. Mason saw Saito now standing before the cloakroom counter, shedding his padded jacket so that his Armani suit was visible. The man was taking his time, looking like a regular.

'How did you know what to do?' Roxy leaned in to whisper, her voice laced with irony.

Mason made a face. 'Just a guess.'

'Yeah, right.'

Mason took his time. He wanted Saito to breach the double doors before he did, wanted Saito in front of him. The Japanese man shed his jacket, took a token, and then spun on one heel, heading for the doors. He grabbed one, twisted the handle and went into the next room.

Mason followed with Roxy alongside, and they found themselves in another foyer, this one large and round, lined with chairs and sofas in red plush. The lights in here were a little less gaudy than those outside, but still deep red and gold. The room was probably supposed to feel reassuring, relaxing, but it set Mason's nerves on edge.

Around the room, on the sofas, sat countless males and females. Most of the women wore negligees and basques of varying colours and sat with their legs crossed, their faces turned away. The men were bare-chested and wore shorts. Mason guessed this was where you made your choice.

Ahead, Saito didn't even slow down to take in the surroundings. He veered towards a woman with long bleached blond hair, pink highlights and slender legs, wearing a miniskirt and a small silver jacket.

Mason looked at Roxy. 'This just got harder than it should.'

'Do I really need to know that?' Roxy reacted seamlessly to the situation, peeled away from Mason and approached the group of men. She had half an eye on Saito, half an eye on the assembled hunks. Mason swallowed, sighed and made a beeline for the collection of women.

It didn't matter who he chose. Nothing was going to happen. He, too, monitored Saito. The Japanese man held out a hand and waited for his chosen woman to accept it, then clasped hers tightly and led her towards another set of double doors in the back wall. Mason didn't want to lose him.

The women smiled as he approached, holding their hands out towards him. He hadn't expected that. He pulled up short, glanced over at Roxy. She already had a wide-chested man by the hand and was pulling him to his feet.

Mason, feeling self-conscious, grabbed a hand and pulled. The woman who came with it was about five foot tall with silver hair and flashing blue eyes. Mason ignored her radiant smile, his eyes following Saito.

The guy was already at the doors. Roxy was ten steps behind. Mason pulled his woman by the hand and rushed to catch up, leaving all the women giggling at his hurry. He reached the doors just behind Roxy.

They all pushed through, Saito about five steps ahead. Beyond the doors stood a wide marble-floored corridor, with closed doors on each side. Some doors had a red flag attached to their handles, others green. Saito didn't go for the first green door, but led his woman to a room three from the far end, opened it and pulled her inside. Mason and Roxy went to the adjacent doors, stopped outside them and turned to each other.

'The moment of no return,' Roxy said with a grin, and then eyed her chosen guy. 'I'm happy to give it five minutes.'

Mason was trying to fend his choice off. 'Restroom,' he said suddenly to her. 'Toilet?'

The woman looked disappointed and then pointed to a room at the far end. Mason opened a green-flagged door and ushered her inside, then held five fingers up.

'Soon,' he said.

'Be quick,' she said, to his surprise. He'd just assumed she wouldn't speak English, a silly assumption.

Roxy bundled her own guy into a room with the same pretence. Then, they went to Saito's door, looked left and right down the passage, saw nothing untoward, and turned the handle.

Mason rushed in first.

'Bloody hell,' he said.

Roxy flew in after him but pushed her way past him to see where Saito and his woman were. Then she and Mason pulled up short. Saito hadn't wasted any time, and neither had the woman – they were lying on the bed, naked, wrapped around each other and laughing. They were so engrossed that they didn't notice Mason and Roxy at first.

It was Saito who saw them. He looked shocked, then angry, and quickly stood up. He shouted at them in Japanese, the anger belying the fact that he appeared to be a very happy man.

Roxy made a pretence of covering her eyes. 'Put it away, man.'

Saito quickly realised they were English and tried his hand at the language, 'You are in wrong room. Go away, now.'

Mason waved at him. 'Put on some clothes,' he said as he moved forward. The woman shrugged herself into a basque. Saito didn't seem at all bothered by his own nudity. Mason slowed as he reached Saito, not wanting to touch the naked man, but Roxy pushed past, grabbed his throat and forced him back on the bed.

'Now,' she said. 'We have a few questions.'

Mason shook his head at her. He was hyper aware they had to be quick.

'Saito,' he said, holding the guy's gaze. 'We know who you are. Your gambling habit. The company you keep. Now, we don't have a lot of time here, so I want your answers quickly. Got it?'

Saito gasped as Roxy eased her grip on his throat. 'What you want?'

'Information,' Mason said. As he spoke, the young woman slipped off the bed, but Mason held up a hand to stop her.

'Wait,' he said. 'This won't take long.'

The situation was beyond difficult. He didn't want to threaten her, but knew he couldn't let her leave the room. Their own companions would soon start growing suspicious. Saito himself didn't look the talkative type.

Mason fixed Saito with a glare. 'You gambled a few bags of old coins recently,' he said. 'Gave them to a man named Tanaka. We want to know where those old coins came from.'

Something shifted behind Saito's eyes. The man shook his head. 'I don't know,' he said. 'Don't know what you are talking about.'

About a minute had passed since they had entered the room.

'Don't give me that crap.' Roxy shook Saito by the throat like an Alsatian would shake a chew toy. 'Tell us now, or you're toast.'

Mason blinked, glanced at her. *Tell us or you're toast?* Where the hell did the American get her threats from? The back of cereal packets?

Saito himself just looked confused.

Mason, conscious of the clock ticking, gave him a last chance. 'Tanaka told us you gave him the coins,' he said. 'All we want to know is where you got them from.'

'Don't lie to us.' Roxy shook him again.

Saito gasped, going bright red in the face. Mason laid a hand on Roxy's arm to get her to ease up. Saito's woman friend was looking at him closely, as if fascinated by the colour change.

'I...don't...know who Tanaka is.'

Mason reacted fast. He knew Saito was in with the criminal underworld, knew he was a consummate gambler, knew he at least trod the dark byways between legal and illegal even if he wasn't fully committed to them. He wasn't a stranger to violence.

Mason punched him in the gut. Roxy let go of his throat for just a second, letting the breath whistle out through his teeth. Saito's chest heaved. Before he could recover, Roxy had him by the throat again.

'Tell us,' Mason whispered.

'I...don't...know...'

Roxy covered his mouth and then pinched his nose shut. Mason punched him in the ribs, heard a crack. Saito's eyes flew wide open, but he didn't make a sound.

'We want you to talk,' Roxy said evenly. 'We want you to make noise. But the right noise. You know what I mean, bud?' She didn't allow the man to draw even an ounce of air.

Mason leaned close to his ear. 'Coins,' he said. 'Where did they come from?'

Saito abruptly stood up. 'There's a special room upstairs,' he said. 'And a roulette table. I say we have a high stakes game. If you win, I tell you what you want to know. If I win, *when* I win, you go away.'

Mason stood back, surprised. 'Are you kidding?'

'No. We go now. Follow me.'

And Saito rose abruptly, dressed, and led the way out of the room and headed for a rear staircase. He walked quickly, purposefully, the woman at his side. Mason exchanged a sidelong glance with Roxy and then shrugged. What choice did they have?

Saito reached the top of the stairs where a suited guard stood, holding a hand out. Saito went forward, pressed a note into it and then pushed through the door. Mason followed. On the other side of the door there was a wide room with golden light fittings, sconces that glowed and several gaming tables. The roulette table stood at the centre, and there were dozens of smartly dressed people standing around. The buzz of low chatter hung over the room, along with the heady scent of expensive cologne and perfume.

Saito went straight to the roulette table and bent to whisper in someone's ear. The man straightened and nodded and announced that the table would close for five minutes after the next round.

Saito turned to Mason. 'Get ready.'

Mason felt the tension start to rise. An awful lot was riding on this. His hands were clenched into fists and he deliberately opened them, trying to relax. The current game soon finished and then Saito stepped in. Both he and Mason were given one chip each to play, but it was Saito who put his down first, on all the reds. Mason had no choice but to place his chip on all the blacks.

'One roll,' Saito said huskily, eyes shining. 'It all rests on this.'

Mason breathed deeply, his body knotted with tension. He watched the croupier take a white ball out of a case and then set the wheel spinning.

'All bets finished,' he said in English.

Mason leaned over. At his side, Roxy was breathing deeply. With a swift movement, the croupier placed the white ball on the spinning wheel. The ball bounced a little, settled and then started whizzing around. It was a blur, a fast-moving, entrancing blur. Mason held his breath.

Soon, the wheel started to slow. The ball began to bounce and clack from one hole to the next, starting in red five and then bouncing over to eight black. It kept bouncing, hitting both reds and blacks and making Mason gasp. Roxy grabbed his hand and held it in a death-grip, practically bruising the knuckles.

The wheel still spun, slowing, slowing. The numbers became clearer. The white ball skipped between them one by one, not settling, still bouncing. Saito leaned forward, nose close to the table, whispering to it, cajoling it. The moment was laden with the deepest tension.

'I can't stand any more,' Roxy breathed.

Mason gripped her hand, holding it as tightly as she was holding his. The fact that they were holding hands in the moment didn't occur to either of them.

'Yes,' Saito breathed.

The white ball came down in three red and seemed to settle, but then it gave one last skip and bounced over into thirty-five black. Mason felt his heart skip a beat. He grinned at Saito triumphantly.

'We win,' he said.

'*Kobayashi,*' came a frightened whisper from Mason's left. '*They came from Kobayashi.*'

It was Saito's companion, the woman with the bleached blond hair. She leaned in closer. 'Saito is too scared. Please don't hurt him. I will tell you.'

Mason turned to the woman. 'Tell us.'

'Could you please let us go?' she said, nodding at Saito.

'Of course. After you tell us.' Mason kept his eyes on the woman.

'How do you know?' he asked.

'Saito…' She grinned. 'He is my man. We share everything.'

Roxy narrowed her eyes. 'But he has to come here to get a date with you?'

The woman shrugged. 'It is a game,' she said, as if expecting them to understand.

Mason didn't pretend to get it, nor was he interested. He guessed at least ten minutes had passed since they'd entered the first room and then the gaming room. It was getting desperate.

'Tell us about Kobayashi,' he said.

The woman opened her mouth, but Saito chose that moment to lunge forward. He didn't attack Mason or Roxy, though. Instead, he grabbed the woman's hands beseechingly.

'*Lisa,*' he said hoarsely in Japanese. '*No. You can't. It's Kobayashi.*'

Mason understood nothing except the names.

The woman, Lisa, shrugged. 'You take one danger at a time,' she said in English. 'We deal with this.' Then she turned to Mason. 'You can't tell him we told you. Please. You *can't.*'

'He sounds like a really bad guy.'

'He is a demon. Kobayashi is terror.'

'He is my master,' Saito said.

Mason frowned. 'Hurry it up, please. Your master?'

'He means he works for Kobayashi,' Lisa said. 'Many do.

189

Saito showed me the coins. I told him he would get himself killed.'

Mason understood. 'Saito stole the coins from Kobayashi?'

Lisa nodded as Saito hissed, 'Kobayashi is a boss of bosses, a big man. He lives in a big house surrounded by guards. He has *collections,* secret stashes of many treasures that he protects jealously. I plundered one of them.'

'Why the hell would you steal from a man like that?' Roxy asked.

'My Saito is a gambler,' Lisa shrugged. 'He can't help it. He gambles…with everything, including his life.' She shook her head.

'Tell us more about this man Kobayashi,' Mason said. 'Quickly.'

'He is very wealthy and lazy. Fat like a whale. Jealous of everything, including his wife. He is a hoarder of treasures, and enjoys flaunting it, though he doesn't allow anyone to see what he's got. Evil man.' She shook her head. 'Very bad man with much power.'

Mason knew they'd exceeded their allotted time. Their companions would be beyond suspicious now, wondering where they were. He rose, asked Saito for an exact location for Kobayashi, and then turned to leave the room.

'Thank you,' he said. 'Hope it all works out for you two.'

Roxy patted Saito on the head as she backed away. 'Hope we didn't break you,' she said. 'And thanks for the game.'

They left the gaming room quickly and then made their way back downstairs where they sought out their own rooms. Roxy paused at the door and gave Mason a look.

'Ten minutes?' she said in a pretend, whiny voice.

'Don't be an arse.'

190

'Five minutes? I can get it down to three.'

'Just meet me back here in ten seconds. All right?'

'Damn, you're a fun spoiler.'

Mason pushed through his own door. His companion sat on the bed, legs crossed, scrolling through her phone, and looked up uninterestedly.

'You choose other woman, yes?' she asked.

'What?' Mason stopped.

'That why you went to toilet with her. You choose her?'

Mason saw an easy way out. 'Yeah,' he said, trying to look downcast. 'Sorry.'

'It is okay,' the woman sighed, put down her phone and looked expectantly at him. 'You do me now?'

Mason tried to look embarrassed. 'Can't,' he said. 'Sorry.'

The woman nodded, rose to her feet and came over to him. She grabbed hold of his hand and led him out the door. Roxy and her companion were already standing in the hallway, both looking sheepish and embarrassed. Roxy's eyes glinted.

'We all good?' Mason winced at the inadequacy of his words.

'Ready for round two,' Roxy said.

The Japanese woman shook her head as if to say, *weirdos*.

Mason walked the length of the corridor, pushed back through the double doors and once again found himself in the circular room. It was a walk of shame like no other, passing among the men and women as his would-be companion ran back to her group and spilled the beans. Roxy was to his left and gave her man a pat on the six-pack to say goodbye.

'Look after them for me,' she said.

Together, they left the house of sin.

Chapter 25

It was late. Mason and the others met outside the whorehouse and decided it was time to retire to a hotel, armed with their new information. As they walked, Mason and Roxy explained it all to the others. Sally found them a four-star hotel about a twenty-minute drive away.

Once there, they split up for the night and retired to their rooms, determined to get a good rest and then resume in the morning. It had been a long day and tomorrow was already shaping up to be just as long. Mason showered and climbed into bed, drank a bottle of water and lay in the dark with his head on the pillow, staring at the ceiling. The paper-thin, yellowy curtains were closed against the night, but he could see the darkness pressing in around the edges of the window. Cars passed along the road. He could hear their rolling tyres, their exhausts. People still walked down the street, some of them shouting in languages he couldn't understand. Somewhere, a horn honked. Further away, a siren split the night, wailing. Mason lay in the dark, listening.

These were the moments when the past intruded. These

moments used to be more frequent – hourly, in fact – but ever since he'd started working with Roxy and then the others, the dreadful memories had receded. It wasn't that he wanted them to go away for ever, to die; he just needed to be able to control them.

His friends Zach and Harry had been killed in Mosul in the war, when they'd entered a house that Mason, their captain, had already checked, and were blown up by an IED. The event had practically destroyed him; changed the entire course of his life, turned him from a soldier to practically nothing – a man who couldn't even talk to his wife. Mason hadn't turned to drink. He had turned introspective. The new gulf between him and his wife eventually led to an amicable divorce. Luckily, there were no children involved.

Mason ended up working for a private security firm, taking a job offered to him by an old friend, Patricia Wilde, who later sacked him and Roxy for their insubordination during the Vatican secret escapade. As Mason worked with Roxy, and later Sally, Quaid and Hassell, he'd been able to tune the old memories out, to go beyond them and focus on the job at hand. What happened to Zach and Harry made Mason believe he had to help everyone, to help atone. That was part of the reason he'd accepted the current quest – to help Luciane, and now to stop the Shadow Kings' SED from coming after his friends after their encounters.

Mason knew he needed to accept the blame for what happened to Zach and Harry and move on, to admit that it might have been his fault, but he never meant it to happen. It was war. He had to forgive himself. At first, he'd wanted to be left alone to work by himself, but after Roxy came into his life, try as much as he could to prove otherwise, he'd realised that he needed companionship.

I'm not to blame, he said silently to the darkness that enveloped him, knowing it wasn't just a physical thing. *I am not to blame.*

He would fight on. For himself. For his friends. For Zach and Harry, who couldn't. Every step forward was a step of atonement. Somehow, he'd found himself working among friends who could help drag him through the mire, who made every day worth the effort it took to live. He'd found... something.

I am not to blame.

It felt good hearing those words inside his head. It felt like release. Mason lay in the dark, staring at the ceiling, not chasing sleep or dreams or rest, but feeling happier than he'd felt in a long time.

* * *

The next morning found them gathered around the breakfast table, coffee and tea to hand, wondering what the day would bring. Sally had toast, muffins and fruit in front of her, but didn't look interested in any of it. Instead, she flicked at her mobile phone, in full research mode.

Mason sat drinking coffee, in a good mood. The room was crowded, twenty small round tables pushed so close together that the backs of all the chairs touched each other. The double windows to the right ran with rain, droplets streaming down the glass. He could hear the wind gusting outside and was thankful for the warmth that permeated the breakfast room. He buttered a slice of toast.

Besides the toast and coffee, they had elements of a traditional Japanese breakfast arrayed around them: some steamed rice, miso soup, a little grilled fish. There were side dishes of pickles, seaweed and soy beans too. Mason picked from the dishes.

'What do you have?' he asked.

Sally looked up. 'Just what's in the press. This man Kobayashi is a bit of a criminal celebrity. He lives large, he *is* large, and likes to flaunt it all. He's well protected, has a humongous house, and there's not a jot of information relating to any treasure collection.'

'There won't be,' Roxy said. 'Lisa said he hoards it jealously.'

'Is he married?' Mason thought it was a good idea to test the information that Lisa had given them.

Sally flicked her phone a little more. 'Yep,' she said after a while. 'To an ex Japanese supermodel named Rose Li. She looks quite the part. He, on the other hand, looks like he doesn't care too much.'

She turned her phone around, showing them pictures of Kobayashi and his wife. Mason saw an immensely fat man wearing shorts and a baseball cap standing by the edge of a blue pool. The woman was a skinny model with black hair and long legs, seated in a deckchair and ignoring him.

Mason inspected the man. 'Address confirmed?'

Again, he was testing Lisa's information.

Sally shrugged. 'It doesn't say exactly where he lives, but it mentions he has a home in Osaka.'

That gelled nicely. Mason was increasingly confident that Lisa had been truthful, and why wouldn't she? She clearly wanted her boyfriend out from under Kobayashi's thrall.

'Far?'

Sally shook her head. 'We could be there in forty-five minutes.'

'What else do we know about this Kobayashi?' Quaid asked.

'He runs a drug enterprise, deals in arms, manages a

prostitution ring, a human trafficking organisation, and dabbles in cyber attacks.'

Quaid nodded with pursed lips. 'So your regular salt of the earth then.'

'A regular asshole,' Roxy growled. 'Who I want to fuck up.'

Mason could understand her reasons. She rallied just as much for the normal, everyday civilian as he did. It was part of her makeup, and her calling.

'The cops have a lot of dirt on him. He's been in the papers many times,' Sally went on. 'Nothing ever seems to stick. According to the *Japan Times* he's been arrested multiple times only to see the cases against him collapse. Lots of info about lack of witnesses, disappearance of witnesses, intimidation. Even cops have been fired, discredited, removed from the force. The press quoted one of them as saying, *"There's no point gunning for him. The guy's just too slippery."* Kobayashi seems to have garnered himself a reputation for being, umm, *slippery* as well as monstrous. Nobody wants a part of him.'

Roxy sat forward. 'We do.'

Mason ate his toast. 'I don't suppose we're gonna get real lucky?' he asked. 'Like it mentions something about coins or casinos?'

Sally smiled without humour. 'Not a bloody thing.'

Luciane sat forward now. 'Here's one for you, just to put the cat among the pigeons,' she said. 'How do we know the ancient casino even exists? It's supposed to date back to the fifteenth century. Does that seem right to you?'

Sally stared at her, eyes narrowed. 'Are you testing me? You've been chasing it for months. But gambling has always played an important part in human history. It doesn't matter how far back you go. Gambling is not a recent creation. It's tens of thousands of years old. Our modern games are only descendants of games played for goods long ago in Europe, the Middle East and Asia. They found stones in China dating back to 3000 BC, ivory dice in Egypt, gambling paraphernalia used by ancient soldiers. There's proof that China invented games of chance. Many used animal bones to play with. Gambling may well have evolved out of people's interest in good luck.'

'Or warped curiosity about random chance,' Luciane said.

'That too. The ancients believed in the supernatural and that the outcome of games of chance was controlled by supernatural powers. They may have banned it in China for a while, but that doesn't mean it still wasn't very popular. It was around when the Shang dynasty was flourishing. It wasn't until the seventeenth century that Europe thought to run a gambling establishment.'

'The Ridotto,' Luciane said.

'Exactly. A gambling house run by the government in Venice, primarily built to control the activity of gambling but also to make money. People could play dice and card games, find something to eat and drink, all of which kept them inside, under the roof. You think the labyrinthine casinos of Las Vegas with their dozens of restaurants, shops and dimly lit hallways are clever? They're old hat. It was all done in the seventeenth century.'

Luciane sat back, as if satisfied. She *had* been testing Sally. Sally stared at her for a moment, and then went back to her mobile, scrolling. She hadn't touched a thing on the plate in front of her.

'So what next?' Hassell asked. 'Kobayashi, the demon?'

'Kobayashi,' Mason said, nodding.

Chapter 26

Kobayashi's residence was vast, sprawling, set behind white gates and a tall white wall that bordered a wide street. Through the gates, Mason couldn't see a lot, no matter how slowly they drove. There was a frontage with marble pillars and steps and a fountain, and a wide, grassy lawn. There were men inside the grounds, clearly guards, though they carried no obvious weapons.

They dared not pass the property more than twice, but found a winding, hilly road that switched back on itself several times before continuing on through another wide street. Halfway up this street, they were able to pull off the road into a lay-by and overlook Kobayashi's mansion about a hundred feet below.

Two storeys high, it stretched back several hundred feet and was clearly composed of many rooms. It shone in the sunlight. There was a stand of trees in the back garden, a blue pool and a hot tub. There were guards everywhere, strolling along in their black suits and keeping watch.

They saw no sign of Kobayashi or his wife, Rose.

'Can't stay up here too long,' Mason said. 'They'll make us.'

'Just a few more photos,' Quaid said, using his camera phone.

'Do you see a way in?' Mason asked Hassell.

'I see danger at every level,' Hassell said. 'Do you see the gates? How about the guard towers to left and right? No... they're long and narrow like a Beefeater's sentry box. See the roof security? No? At least two snipers lying flat out in the gables. Look at the way they patrol. They're well rehearsed, well trained. They carry Uzis under their suit jackets – that's why they wear suit jackets. To conceal the lumps. To be honest,' Hassell peered left and right, 'they can see every inch of that compound.'

Mason sighed. 'Not much luck then.'

'None at all.'

'Plan B?' Roxy ventured.

'There is no plan B. There isn't even a plan A yet.'

'How do you infiltrate a highly secure building, under the noses of its guards, and interrogate the man they're protecting?' Mason asked. 'How do you do that?'

'Aren't you all ex-army or something?' Luciane said. 'Isn't that what you're good at?'

'With intel. With backup. With a battery of CCTV cameras and listening devices and inside men and long-lens cameras, maybe,' Roxy told her. 'With a week of prep.'

'There's always a way,' Quaid said.

Sally started the car and drove them away, just in case they themselves were being watched. She drove them along the next street to another lay-by that couldn't be seen from the house and pulled in there. The team sat staring at each other as Quaid showed his phone around, flicking through the photos he'd taken.

'No easy days,' Mason said.

'Let's start thinking outside the box,' Roxy said.

'You think we can return to that lay-by?' Sally asked. 'What we really need to do is more surveillance.'

Mason chewed on his lip. 'Not a chance,' he said. 'If they're that well trained, they'll see us.'

'But there is another way,' Roxy said. 'We take a leaf out of the SED's book.'

Mason frowned. 'What do you mean by that?'

'Back in Dublin, they broke into that sweet shop, right? To keep a low profile. They essentially used an abandoned building.'

Mason stared at her. 'Are you saying you want to break into a house? An empty one, and surveil that way?'

'Best way to do it,' Roxy said.

'And did you happen to see any abandoned houses?' Mason asked.

'I saw a blue and yellow flag sign outside one of the rows of houses,' Sally said. 'Let me check if that's basically a For Sale sign.' She clicked around her phone.

'I saw that too,' Roxy said.

'All right,' Sally said eventually. 'The house is up for sale. What say we try it, make sure the owners aren't at home, and then move in?'

'Worth a try,' Mason said.

They decided not to go as a group. That might be too obvious. Instead, Mason and Hassell donned their backpacks and went first, walking back down the street to the winding hill and the house with the blue and yellow flag outside it.

It was barely 9.30 a.m. There were few cars parked outside driveways and no people around. With luck, most would have left for work already. Mason followed Hassell down a little path that led to the house's front door.

They knocked. Waited. Nothing happened. They knocked again and looked around. Mason saw nobody watching, no passers-by, no cars. Hassell bent his head to the lock and worked at it with lock picks. As he worked, he grumbled.

'If there's an alarm, we're done,' he said. 'I didn't bring my code reader.'

Mason made a face. 'I know that, mate. Very silly.'

'We left in a hurry, remember? Chasing Quaid to Dublin.'

'I remember. Don't you have a go-pack?'

'This is my go-pack.'

He twisted the handle and pushed the door open. There was no alarm. Together they entered the house, a basic abode with threadbare carpets and peeling walls. It wasn't the best advert for its own sale, but Mason assumed it was typical of the area. They hurried through the house, verifying that nobody was at home.

Mason went into the front bedroom, approached the window and took a good look outside. Kobayashi's mansion was sprawled out below, the white walls glaring under the sun. He used his binoculars – part of *his* go-pack – and nodded briefly.

'This'll do,' he said.

Two by two, the rest of them entered the house. It wasn't a pretty plan, it wasn't perfect, but it was the best they could do under the circumstances. Leaving the car in the lay-by was a risk. Entering the house was a risk. Even standing close to the window was a risk. But right here, right now, in the thick of it, this was their only choice.

They split up the watch. They used their phones' 'notes' app to record various activities going on below – the change of the guard, the appearances of certain people from the house, the arrival of a delivery van, different cars pulling up to the gate and being let through, the first time they saw Kobayashi and Rose.

Kobayashi was indeed an outsize human, a fleshy walking mound with broad shoulders and an enormous bald head. Mason watched him walk from the house to the pool ,where he stripped off to trunks and then manoeuvred himself into a chaise longue. It took some time and, at one point, one of his men had to come over and lend a hand. Mason checked the time. Kobayashi had left the safety of his mansion for his pool at 10.33 a.m. Mason noted it down. Soon after, his wife appeared. She wore a sheer white kimono, which she soon took off, and then slipped into the pool. Her husband watched her do a few laps before she climbed out and retreated into the mansion.

All the while, the guards strolled around on their preordained paths, hands always close to their concealed guns.

Mason kept watching. At eleven a.m. he saw a beaten-up old car drive through the gates and deliver a pizza to the front door. Two minutes later, that steaming pizza was in Kobayashi's hands. Twenty minutes later, a white van pulled up with a delivery – three small boxes. At midday, a postal worker called the guards over and talked shit with them for a few minutes, leaning against the gate. At 12.39, there was another pizza delivery, this time brought by a different car. Mason kept watching. The activity didn't let up. He changed shifts with Roxy, relating what he'd seen. They had a few rations in the backpacks, which he nibbled at now, and he drank a bottle of water. They tried to stay away from the window as much as possible. The sun moved gradually across the sky. Three p.m. turned into four and then five. There wasn't much activity on the road outside, and thankfully no houses opposite, but when they saw something happening, they shrank back into the room, taking no chances. They'd been fortunate to find this place and didn't want to push their luck.

'That's nearly a full day,' Mason said finally. 'What have we learned?'

They sat sprawled around the room, which was unfurnished apart from an incongruous bedside table that was currently full of empty plastic bottles. They'd found out that the toilets worked, that there was running water, but no heating. Tonight could be cold. No visitors approached the house. Not even a postal worker. Maybe the mail had been stopped. Whoever hurried along on the street below kept their eyes ahead or down on the ground, looking neither left nor right.

'Seven pizzas,' Roxy read her notes after consulting with the others. 'Each time a different car, right up to the front door.'

'Two white van deliveries,' Quaid said.

'He's outside in the warmer hours of the day,' Sally said. 'Doesn't walk. Just sits in that chaise longue. Eats. Drinks. Wanders off for a while. Always wears the same clothes.'

'The wife has made five appearances,' Hassell said. 'Swimming and sunbathing. She reads. She slathers suncream on. She distracts the guards, but not for long.'

'I saw no sign of any weapons,' Mason said. 'Beyond the obvious Uzis.'

All the others shook their heads in agreement.

'Anything else?' Mason asked.

'The postal worker is on good terms with some guards.'

Roxy shrugged. 'There are no dogs, a good thing. Those roof snipers change three times during the day.'

Hassell spoke up. 'I've been looking at the transport and the gates,' he said. 'And external security. The windows never open and are *not* guarded by bars. The front door is solid and steel, formidable. The garage is always open and contains at least three vehicles, a big Nissan SUV, a Range Rover and a sporty Mazda. The keys hang inside, on a corkboard beside the cars. The guards go to the garage often. I believe there's a tea and coffee machine in there and maybe a toilet. There's a beach buggy type thing,' he shrugged, 'for getting about the grounds, I guess, though nobody seems to use it. Now... the gates. They're high and unscalable, with their thin rails and speared tips, but they're relatively flimsy. When the postal worker leaned against them, they bent slightly. The walls are high, nine feet roughly, but surround the entire property. They have a few vulnerable points. You see where the trees grow?' He pointed at his phone rather than risk all of them standing at the window. 'You could probably hop over there.'

Mason nodded. 'I like it,' he said. 'But getting close to Kobayashi isn't gonna be easy.'

Roxy shrugged. 'We've done difficult before. There comes a time when it's just another mission.'

Mason nodded. 'Agreed, and it's not the getting close that worries me. It's the Uzis.'

'I defer to you,' Luciane said. 'I admit I am out of my element on this. My Garda training didn't include staking out gangsters' mansions.'

'Neither did mine, to be fair,' Mason said.

'Mine did,' Roxy murmured.

'So what do we do next?' Luciane asked her.

Roxy turned quickly, too quickly, her expression haunted. 'Isolate,' she said. 'Isolate and kill.'

Mason moved in before she could regress any further into her troubled past. 'We watch through the night,' he said. 'See – they've already turned on the floodlights for us.'

Roxy turned towards the window. 'I'll take first watch. Can't sleep anyway.'

Mason moved to her side. 'I'll help,' he said.

Chapter 27

Throughout the night and the next morning, they watched. They needed to see a pattern, a way in, a vulnerability. All they saw was Kobayashi lumber about, sunbathe, eat pizza and watch his wife swim. Rose creamed up and stretched out and read for a while, heading inside when the clouds came. Kobayashi yelled at a few guards who went the wrong way, spoke to a gardener and went inside when a van full of hoodlums pulled up. Mason watched the exchanges carefully, seeing little as they all went inside the house and then, ten minutes later, reappeared. Whatever Kobayashi had ordered them to do would remain between them. Ten minutes after that, Kobayashi was outside again, struggling into his chaise longue.

'What do we have?' Mason asked that afternoon.

'Six pizzas,' Roxy said.

'Two rounds of post,' Hassell said. 'The Range Rover and the Nissan both went out today and came back within half an hour. Probably errands.'

'Usual guard routine,' Quaid said. 'No modifications.'

'Rose's routine didn't vary,' Sally said. 'Neither did Kobayashi's really.'

'I saw the cops drive by twice,' Luciane said, and then shrugged. 'Could have been routine.'

Mason leaned forward. 'So,' he said. 'What's our way in?'

'Already?' Roxy said. 'This type of surveillance should take weeks.'

'We don't have that kind of time.'

'Because of the SED?' Quaid said. 'Agreed.'

'Miura,' Luciane said, remembering the man with a shudder. 'He's driven. The Shadow Kings' secret plan to find that ancient casino at all costs, even murder, is everything to him. Nothing else matters.'

'I can get us to the door,' Roxy said. 'Maybe two of us, tops.'

'The door is steel,' Hassell reminded her. 'It'll take a bomb to get through it.'

'I can get it open,' she said. 'Easily.'

Hassell made a face. 'Really?'

Mason looked across at her. 'How?'

'Leave that with me. The problem will come after that. We have to make sure Kobayashi's in the house, not out by the pool. It has to be timed just right.'

'He goes inside in the afternoon, when it gets colder,' Sally said.

'That's good intel. Do the guards then change their routines?'

'No,' Hassell said.

'Do we have any idea about the guard numbers inside the house?' Mason asked. He already knew the answer.

There were several shakes of several heads.

'He has at least two housekeepers,' Hassell said. 'I've seen them answering the door.'

207

'That's gonna help,' Roxy said.

'Care to enlighten us?' Mason asked.

'I can get two of us inside that house,' she said. 'But which two? We need to be mean, ready to kill or be killed, ready to kidnap. We will have to move ultra fast and with as much stealth as possible.' She looked at Mason. 'You up for it?'

He wanted to help. 'Always.'

Roxy checked the time. 'We go at three-thirty. Be ready. And you?' She turned to the others. 'We'll need backup just outside. There could be a chase. I need you in place to cut it off before it starts.'

'We only have one car,' Quaid pointed out.

'Yeah.' Roxy scrunched her face up. 'But inside that compound, we can change that.'

Chapter 28

Mason found that high-risk missions such as this held all his attention, much of Roxy's attention, and insulated them from whatever memories might rear up during the day. For his own part, he was feeling much better now, able to force the worst memories into remission, but Roxy seemed to struggle as much as ever.

They left the house carefully at 3.30 p.m., walked up to their car and got inside. They drove a short distance to an establishment they'd pinpointed on the map, got out and placed an order. They came out ten minutes later with fourteen inches of pepperoni, onion, and extra cheese and put it on the back seat. Roxy gave Mason a look before she set off.

'You ready? This time we're really walking into the lion's den.'

'Danger is my middle name.'

She held his eyes. 'Really?'

'Yeah, sorry. It sounded better in my head. I think I heard it on TV once.'

'After hearing that, I'd say *dickhead* is your middle name.'

Mason took it on the chin, hanging his head. Roxy started the car and set off on the five-minute drive that would lead them to the front gates of Kobayashi's mansion. Mason flexed his fingers, rolled his shoulders and massaged his knuckles. One way or another, this would end up in a fight.

Time ticked by. Mason knew the others would have made their way down the hill by now and would be waiting somewhere by the road, trying to remain inconspicuous. Would Roxy's plan get them inside the house? *Sure,* he thought. *This guy gets eight pizza deliveries a day.*

They came around a bend and pulled up to the gates. Roxy got out and put her hand on the buzzer, keeping her head down, shielded from any watching guards. Mason looked out for her, but saw no one approaching.

'*Konnichiwa?*' a tinny voice came through the intercom.

'Pizza,' Roxy said simply.

And all Kobayashi's impressive and extensive security was circumvented as the gate rattled open.

Roxy got back in the car and turned it into the driveway. She drove through the mansion's grounds, past the burbling fountain, and pulled up outside the front door. She turned the car around to facilitate a fast getaway. Then she turned to Mason.

'Game time.'

She cracked open the door, got out and reached into the back seat for the pizza, making a great show of holding it out in front of her. Nonchalantly, Mason joined her. Together, they walked up five marble steps to the front door.

Roxy knocked and waited.

Mason's spine itched. Maybe they were being watched, maybe they weren't, but it certainly felt that way. He kept his head down, gazing at the ground. He slouched, not wanting to appear threatening.

Minutes passed. Roxy knocked again. Finally, the front door swung inwards to reveal a man wearing a suit, a hard expression on his face. His left hand hovered close to his concealed gun.

'Pizza.' Roxy offered it up.

The man barely looked at her before grunting and reaching out for the offering. Both hands grabbed the box, and he moved backwards. That was when Roxy stepped into the house after him and attacked mercilessly. With his hands full, he couldn't react or protect himself. Roxy's first punch was in the centre of his throat, stopping him from making a noise. Her second was to his sternum and then two more to his temples rendered him unconscious. The man fell to the floor, the pizza box slithering out of his grip.

Mason picked it up, seeing that it might provide them with further cover. Roxy dragged her comatose opponent into a nearby cloakroom. She frisked him for weapons, came up with the black lightweight Uzi compact automatic pistol, and shrugged.

'Now we're talking,' she said and thrust it into her waistband.

They loitered for a moment in the cloakroom.

'Where to?' Mason asked.

'How the hell should I know?'

'It was your plan.'

'I got us inside. The rest is up to you.' She smiled.

Mason grinned back. 'I know where he'll be,' he said.

After a few seconds, Roxy's half-smile turned into a grin. 'So do I,' she said.

They left the cloakroom, closed the door firmly and made

211

their way through the house. They passed under a wide staircase that curved up to the second floor, where a balcony overlooked the lower hall. Mason saw a housekeeper moving up there and ran lightly into cover, passing out of sight. They were aiming for the rear.

They reached the kitchen two minutes later. The door was open, revealing a six-person peninsula counter top, leather stools and a row of windows beyond. Through the door, they could see one half of Kobayashi slumped over a bowl of steaming rice, the thick vapour making a cloud around his head. The big man lifted a spoon to his lips.

Roxy moved behind him, slipping through the doorway into the kitchen. Mason was a step behind.

Inside, they had a surprise. Kobayashi wasn't alone. A guard stood at the sink, tap running, grabbing a glass of water. Some sixth sense must have warned him for, as soon as Mason revealed himself, the guy turned around.

Stared at them open-mouthed.

Kobayashi stared at his guard, oblivious to Roxy and Mason.

'*Nande?*' he asked.

The guard let the glass drop. It hit the floor and shattered, spilling water. By then, Mason was dashing past Kobayashi's tree-trunk-like arm, vaulting the countertop and hitting the guard in the chest with his legs outstretched. Mason landed in the water, boots grating against the chunks of glass. The guard staggered back several steps into the sink and smacked his right hip against it.

Roxy looped an arm around Kobayashi's thick neck.

'Stay calm,' she said. 'We know you're an evil little bastard and we won't hesitate to use force on you.'

Mason sprang to his feet, struck out. He caught the

212

guard in the face, made him flinch, but the man ignored it and reached for his Uzi. That was his downfall. As his hand slipped inside his jacket, Mason elbowed him across the nose, breaking it, and then kicked him in the groin. The guard went down hard. Mason smacked him in the head and he knew no more. He jerked the Uzi from the guy's inside holster and turned it on Kobayashi.

'How's it going?' he said.

Quickly, he paced back into the depths of the kitchen. The windows overlooked the garden and it would be quite easy for a patrolling guard to see him if he strayed near a window.

Kobayashi stared, the hot rice blooming around his face.

Roxy let go of his neck and tapped him on the head with the barrel of her Uzi. 'Are you Kobayashi?' Mason knew she didn't want to ask the guy if he spoke English because it was too easy to deny the question. It was better to appear as though you'd done your homework and already knew he did.

Kobayashi nodded, the flesh underneath his chin wobbling.

Mason looked around the kitchen for dangers, seeing only piles of pizza boxes, crates of lager and an open dishwasher full of plates. He could smell meat lingering in the air, the aroma of pepperoni and ham. There wasn't another sound in the place, save for Roxy's questioning.

Mason lifted a carving knife from a holder on the kitchen counter and took it over to Roxy. 'Use this,' he said ominously.

Kobayashi's eyes flicked from the window to the doors and then back to Roxy. He was gauging his chances.

'Shout and you're dead,' Roxy said. 'I'll jam this knife in your brain pan faster than you can blink.'

Kobayashi didn't look in the least scared, but he did lock eyes with her.

'What do you want?' he said in heavily accented English.

'Among your secret treasures, your private collection,' Roxy said, 'are several bags of coins that came from an old Chinese casino. We want to know if—'

'No!' Kobayashi yelled out and swung his arms from side to side.

Roxy, surprised, backed away and only just held on to her weapon. Kobayashi's size made him a formidable opponent. Quickly, she smashed him across the back of the neck; not too hard, just enough to let him know she was prepared to hurt him.

But Kobayashi hadn't been trying to escape.

He'd been trying to give himself enough time to reach out, snap back the cover of a black box that was fixed to the counter and press the small round button inside.

As soon as he did so, an alarm sounded. The blaring wail filled the entire house, probably the whole grounds. Kobayashi sat back, crossed his arms and stared at them with satisfaction.

'Now, we will see how well you die,' he said.

Mason and Roxy wasted no time. The game was up. They forced Kobayashi to his feet, turned him around, and then prodded him out of the kitchen. They held their Uzis in front of them, swaying from side to side. Kobayashi lumbered ahead, filling the corridor.

'Front doors, now,' Mason said.

They pushed and prodded Kobayashi, making the man-mountain move as fast as he could. The guy's head was on a constant swivel, looking for help, but all Mason saw was a maid wearing black and white, a bundle of towels in her hand, a shocked expression on her face, retreating down another passageway.

They came into the front hallway. Kobayashi clumped to a halt. Mason checked the balcony above, found it empty. Roxy ran forwards. Both of them were ready with their Uzis.

'Straight to the car,' Roxy said. 'Then we get the hell out of here.'

Mason nodded. He was worried about their companions somewhere outside the mansion, but knew they could always retrieve them later. This plan had never been perfect. They'd done well to get the Japanese criminal this far.

'You will never escape,' Kobayashi said. 'Not with me.'

'Tell us what we want to know, and we'll leave you alone,' Roxy countered.

'I don't know what you're talking about. I have no private collection.'

Mason punched him in the face, feeling the flesh give way and then spring back under his fist. It was like punching a jelly. 'We know you do,' he said.

'My men will kill you.'

'Better men have tried.' Roxy dashed for the front door, the alarm wailing all around them, opened it and jumped out into hell.

Chapter 29

Leaping outside, Roxy jumped into a hail of gunfire. Bullets smashed into the pillars and the walls by the door. Then Mason shoved Kobayashi out and the shooting abruptly stopped.

'Get behind us,' Mason shouted at Roxy.

'Damn pleased you're such a big target,' Roxy said to Kobayashi.

'Don't shoot!' Kobayashi yelled in Japanese, holding his arms out.

Mason stayed behind the man, prodding him forward with the barrel of the Uzi. Kobayashi's own men wouldn't risk shooting him. Plus, the guy was an evil criminal. He didn't deserve to be safe. Roxy slipped behind him. Together, they passed from the shadows offered by the pillared portico into the sunshine. Their car was parked just a few metres away.

Mason counted four guards scattered across the grounds, facing them with more arriving. Two were standing beside the fountain, two on the driveway. Another came around the side of the house. In the distance, he could see the two gate guards had emerged from their sentry boxes and were shielding their eyes against the glare of the sun, trying to figure out what was happening.

Mason waved the Uzi to show he meant business, then prodded Kobayashi forward once more. The man was panting angrily, shrugging his shoulder every time Mason touched him. He was putting on a show for his guards, trying to look courageous, but Mason could sense the fear in him.

'One wrong move…' he said ominously.

'The car,' Roxy said.

They descended the steps in front of the house one at a time. The day stretched before them like a taut line stretched to breaking point. Mason had hold of the back of Kobayashi's shirt. When they reached the car, Roxy slipped past them, crouching and moving swiftly. Mason monitored the guards, seeing more now coming from the right, all with their guns raised and aimed.

'Hurry,' he said.

Roxy swung open the rear door and beckoned to Kobayashi.

'Get in!'

'*Stay back,*' Mason shouted, seeing the guards on the right creeping forward.

Roxy grabbed Kobayashi's arm as the man approached the car and shoved him towards the back seat.

Mason was having trouble with the guards on the right. They wouldn't stay still. They kept coming, just a step at a time, but advancing nonetheless. He made sure that Roxy was covering the big man, then moved his Uzi in their direction and opened fire, spraying above their heads.

'I said stay back,' he yelled.

Even if they didn't speak English, his action with the gun got his message across. The men kept their weapons trained, but stopped moving. Mason, close to Kobayashi, could feel the man struggling. He still wasn't in the back of the car.

'What's happening?'

'He won't fit!' Roxy yelled in shock. 'The bastard won't fit in the back of the car.'

Such a scenario hadn't crossed Mason's mind. 'You're fucking kidding me.'

He glanced around Kobayashi's bulk. The guy had one leg, one thigh in the car but couldn't fit the rest of him inside. The space was too small for his ample shoulders and stomach. Roxy was trying to force him inside and the guy wasn't protesting, but there just wasn't enough space for the manoeuvre.

'Shit,' Roxy cried, then grabbed hold of Kobayashi and looked around. 'What the hell do we do now?'

Mason, staying low and close to Kobayashi, looked around once more. Their means of a getaway had been thwarted. Three guards stood to the right, two to the left, and at least four in front. Uzis were primed and aimed. They still had Kobayashi, but they were in a terrible stalemate.

The guards had seen that something was amiss. They were communicating with each other through earbud comms. As one now, they took a step forward and then another. Mason saw the noose tightening, the severe faces coming closer, the guns held eagerly.

'You are dead,' Kobayashi spat at them.

Mason didn't fancy their chances. The mini Uzi he was holding didn't have an extended mag; it was the standard twenty-round weapon. He'd already squeezed off five. With a flick of his finger, he switched the Uzi from semi-automatic to single shot. It had limited long-range accuracy, anyway. Roxy did the same.

Then there came another tightening of the noose. The guards were all stepping in now; they couldn't cover all of them. Kobayashi was upright again, leaning on the car and panting. Mason and Roxy were inches away.

'Dead,' Kobayashi whispered.

'Call your men off.' Mason grabbed hold of his collar and hefted him upright. 'Call them off right now or I'll break your neck.'

Kobayashi struggled, tried to keep his head low and his shoulders hunched. He was harder to handle that way and knew it. Mason jabbed him with the Uzi.

'Tell them!'

Kobayashi refused. The men advanced another step. Mason saw he was going to have to perforate some of them, but there was a high risk that once one person opened fire, everyone would open fire.

He looked at Roxy. Sunlight surrounded them, but the situation was anything but balmy.

'There's no way out of this one,' Roxy said quietly. 'The Devil is definitely calling.'

Mason watched her closely. There had been a time, not so long ago, when Roxy's own severe self-analysis had put her off her game. She'd shut down, unable to operate. That had only been for a few minutes, but Mason needed her at the top of her game now.

'Don't listen,' he said. 'You know what to do. You always have. You *don't* listen.'

She looked at him. 'I'm okay,' she said.

Mason saw the guards move closer. He wondered how many steel sights had him lined up. The number of guards

219

was ridiculous – and there were also the snipers on the roof, out of sight and range for now. But once he and Roxy came out from under the house's shadow…started heading towards that gate…

Mason jabbed his Uzi under Kobayashi's ribs. 'Tell them to fall back.'

'Fuck you.'

And still they came, one step at a time. Mason could see them communicating with each other. The situation was severe, and Mason and Roxy were going to have to become equally harsh if they were going to survive it.

Now, he jammed the Uzi into Kobayashi's elbow joint. 'Last chance,' he said. 'I will shoot.'

Kobayashi panted hard. He raised his free hand, took a deep breath and was about to say something when it all went a little crazy. He opened his mouth, looking towards the gates – which suddenly smashed apart as a four-wheel-drive vehicle broke through, followed by another. The vehicles were black, big and meant business. As they crashed through the gates, men leaned out of the windows and fired at the sentry guards.

Mason stared, shaking his head. 'What the fu—'

The guards whirled towards the new threat.

Mason didn't need to take cover. The car and Kobayashi were enough. Together, the three of them hunkered down behind the car, Mason peering through the windows.

'The house,' Kobayashi moaned. 'We need to get back inside the house.'

But that would be cornering themselves. The safe assumption here was that the newcomers were here for Kobayashi. Unfortunately, Mason and Roxy were right where they wanted to be.

The four-wheel-drives had screeched to a halt. Doors flung open. Men leapt out, all carrying automatic weapons, which they unleashed with impunity. Bullets laced the air, pinging everywhere.

Mason stared at them. 'SED,' he said. 'Who else?'

'And the gloves are fucking *off*,' Roxy said. 'They've been holding back until now.'

The Shadow Kings' mercenaries piled out of their vehicles, thirteen of them including their leader, Mason thought. They latched on to their targets, using the vehicles as cover or running to the nearest statue or fountain. At first, Kobayashi's guards were caught out in the open, but then started scuttling for cover or flinging themselves to the ground. All of a sudden, Kobayashi's plight was secondary.

The SED advanced. A guard twisted and fell, spouting blood. The sentry guards had been blown to bits and lay twisted on the ground. The SED clearly hadn't reconnoitred properly – they didn't know about the snipers on the roof, who now opened fire. An SED trooper was struck in the chest and then another, their lives saved by their bulletproof jackets. The high-powered gunfire sent the SED into hiding.

Mason gripped Kobayashi tightly. 'We may have an opportunity here.'

Roxy glared at him, at the scenario before them. 'I'm all ears.'

'He has his own cars. Clearly, he can fit into them. All we have to do is get to the garage.'

Roxy looked like she was trying to stay optimistic. Mason imagined the struggle going on inside her brain. 'Trust me,' he said.

'You're the boss.'

Another title he didn't like. Mason didn't care to be

thought of as a leader, not since Mosul, but he found that now, after that resolution in the hotel room the other night, he wasn't as affected as he used to be.

'Kobayashi,' he said. 'You're the meat barrier.'

'He means *protection*,' Roxy said. 'You're our protection.'

'Same thing.'

Mason was about to drag them in the garage's direction when gunfire burst all around them. Bullets struck their car, glancing off the bodywork and the roof and shattering the windows. Mason flung himself to the ground, dragging Kobayashi down with him. Roxy hit the deck at their sides.

'You all right?' Mason yelled.

Bullets still peppered their car, breaking through the bodywork. Mason felt a round whistle by just above his head and heard it smash into the brickwork of the house at his back.

'Fine,' Roxy whispered back.

Kobayashi rolled in between them and gave them the thumbs-up. Somehow, they were going to have to get the big man back to his feet.

When the fusillade died down, Mason jumped to his feet, bent over and, with Roxy's help, hauled Kobayashi upright.

Soon, they were ready again.

'We don't stop running until we hit the garage,' Mason said.

'Just wait,' Kobayashi held up a hand, clearly seeing his own mortality. 'It's safer if we run through the house. There's a side exit to the garage.'

Mason eyed Roxy. 'Of course there is.'

'We should have known that.'

Mason grabbed Kobayashi's shirt. 'Move.'

Chapter 30

Mason ran up the steps, hauling Kobayashi along with Roxy at his side. They hit the front door, crashed through it and turned right. Kobayashi was lumbering, breathing heavily, but seemed up for the run. He knew this was pure life or death.

'Who are those people?' he asked. 'The ones disrespecting my house?'

'Covert special forces,' Roxy told him. 'Working for an entity called the Shadow Kings. They're here for the same thing we are. I suggest you give it to us first.'

'I don't know what you mean.'

Mason somehow refrained from tapping him on the head with the Uzi. 'You know exactly what we mean, arsehole.'

'The reckoning is coming,' Roxy said threateningly.

They raced up a shiny corridor, through a library furnished with floor-to-ceiling shelves and a thousand hardback books that Kobayashi probably didn't even know the titles of, through a study with a leather desk and a painting of Macau at night, and finally through a games room that contained a pool table, darts and a video game corner. Kobayashi couldn't speak by the time they got there, but he raised his hand and pointed to a door.

Mason turned the handle, found it unlocked. The door opened inwards. He let it swing and then took in the lie of the land. They were on the garage side of the house. A gravel path six feet wide separated them from the brick structure.

The sounds of gunfire continued outside as the SED fought Kobayashi's guards for control of the grounds.

Mason let Kobayashi have about thirty seconds, then grabbed him again. 'The Range Rover,' he said, 'should be the biggest. I assume you fit into it?'

Kobayashi nodded.

'Right, let's go.'

They slipped out of the doorway. To the right Mason saw a sliver of the grounds, the far broken gates and the SED fighters running forwards. Together, the three of them ran to the front of the garage and slipped inside. Three vehicles stood before them, one a large black Range Rover.

A burst of bullets smashed into the brick wall at their sides, sending flaked-off mortar debris all over their shoulders. Mason ducked, then looked out the garage door.

Two SED fighters had spotted them and had lined them up. As he watched, they let off another few rounds that clattered around inside the garage.

Roxy ran to the corkboard set in the far wall, cast her eye along the rows of hooks. Soon, she gave a shout of triumph and plucked one of the key fobs. Then she turned, aimed it at the big vehicle and clicked it.

There was the sound of chunky locks opening.

Mason flung scenarios through his brain. The most dangerous option could be the best, he thought. Kobayashi had already proven uncooperative.

Roughly, he dragged Kobayashi to the most open part of the garage, in full view of the SED and his own guards.

'Now,' he said. 'Tell us what we want to know or you stay right here. And you will die.'

As if to emphasise his point, a couple of bullets zinged through the opening and hit the rear of the garage, passing a few feet away from Kobayashi's bulk.

'I can't remember what you said.' Kobayashi, standing in the open, had started to tremble.

'The coins from the ancient casino. Where did you get them?'

'How do you even know about them?'

Mason didn't reveal Saito's role in it. He said, 'The coins have been spread across half of Japan.'

Kobayashi hissed between closed teeth and then started cursing in Japanese. He kicked the air in front of him.

Mason, sheltered behind the man, let him have a few seconds.

Roxy ran to the vehicle and opened the side and rear doors to prepare for their getaway.

Kobayashi spat in disgust. His face had turned red. Mason let him have his anger, but prodded him with the gun.

'Answer the damn question.'

'My treasures…are sacred,' Kobayashi whispered. 'They cannot be plundered. They exist just for me, for my eyes. Your…your revelation is…shocking.'

'I don't care,' Mason said. As he spoke, another burst of bullets zinged in their direction, this time splattering the front of the Mazda. The front grille was blown off, the engine hammered by lead. Kobayashi shook.

'Please,' he said.

'You give us answers or you get perforated,' Roxy

growled at him. 'That's the deal.' She too was now sheltering behind the man, though further back than Mason.

'Damn it.' Kobayashi, in dire fear of his life, knew he was cornered. He spoke very quickly. 'I got them from the casino, of course. From the ground. From somewhere. Seven years ago.'

Mason poked him. This was just the kind of knowledge they were looking for. 'Go on.'

'Seven years ago these…I guess you would call them treasure hunters…came to my door and offered to sell me the bags of coins. They knew I was a collector. Everyone knows I am a collector.'

'Probably not wise to let everyone know,' Roxy said.

'Why? They all fear me.'

Mason waved it away. 'Get back to the question,' he said.

'I told you. Seven years ago these men came to my door, sold me the old coins. Said they came from some lost casino in the Gobi. Part of the deal was to tell me where it was.'

'You went there?' Mason pressed.

'No. Later, when I found out that it was in China, I couldn't be…umm, I decided not to pursue the find.'

'You're a lazy bastard,' Roxy said.

'No, no. It was just too risky,' Kobayashi blustered. 'These men unearthed the coins at substantial cost to themselves. I spoke to them at length, learned something about them. Anyone offering me treasure is my friend.'

'So that's all we had to do?' Roxy said archly. 'Bring along a Rembrandt with us?'

'It's called "greasing the wheels".'

'How many coins did they give you?'

'Just three bags. But they had many more. For other collectors, I imagine.'

'Where did they get the coins from?' Mason asked.

'I told you. The Gobi,' the man said. 'You know about the Silk Road?'

Mason nodded briefly. Just as he did so, a stray bullet flew through the garage, narrowly missing Kobayashi and slamming into the Nissan. The big Japanese collector started visibly shaking.

'You have to protect me.'

'We don't have to do anything,' Mason said. 'Now, go on.'

'The Silk Road is an ancient trade route between the East and the West. There's an ancient city along that route, even now, called Dunhuang. Near Dunhuang, are some famous caves called the Mogao Caves, located at a religious and cultural junction on the Silk Road. It would make sense to position the old casino along the Silk Road, yes?'

Mason nodded. 'Yes.'

'I can give you directions from a point in Dunhuang, the caves. That is what the treasure hunters gave me seven years ago.'

Mason flinched then as their luck ran out. A bullet flew through the garage door, struck Kobayashi in the right shoulder and spun him around. He fell to his knees, blood spurting over Mason's shoes. Roxy dived into the Range Rover and stabbed a button to start it up.

Mason reached around Kobayashi, trying to help him up, but the man was bleating to himself and crying heavily. Half his weight was on his injured arm, but still he couldn't seem to move.

Another bullet streaked through the air at the top of the garage. Mason saw a gun appear in the doorway, saw one of Kobayashi's guards follow it. He had little time to react.

He fell to the floor behind Kobayashi's bulk, barely escaping the strafing stitch-marks of bullets that flew across the garage floor in his wake. He raised his Uzi and fired twice at the man.

The shots knocked the guy's gun from his hand, but he didn't stop. He came through the opening at speed, rushing towards Kobayashi and Mason. A knife flashed in his right hand.

Mason didn't wait for a fight. He fired twice more and took the guy out, saw him stumble to the floor right in front of Kobayashi. The big guy barely gave him a second glance.

Roxy inched the Range Rover forward.

Mason got the hint. He bent down and hauled Kobayashi to his feet, using every ounce of his strength. He shoved the stumbling man to the car's back door, prodding and poking, directing him. Kobayashi lumbered first one way and then the other, hand clapped to his shoulder, head down, sobbing. Blood leaked down his arm and dripped to the floor.

Mason spun once more. Another one of Kobayashi's guards had made it to the garage door. This one already had his Uzi up and aimed at Mason's heart. Mason felt a surge of bitter regret, annoyed at not being careful or fast enough. He could raise his own Uzi, but he'd be about one second too late.

Bullets ripped through the air, only they didn't come from the guard but from behind him. An SED fighter had targeted the guard and sent a burst of ammo slashing into him. The bullets ripped through his ribcage, making him jerk spasmodically and then fall dead to the floor.

Mason took a breath. Kobayashi was at the vehicle's back door. Mason backed up this time, keeping his eyes peeled in all directions. The SED fighter was staring at them, probably wondering if he should make a move towards them, but became distracted by a flash of bullets in his own direction. He flung himself to the ground.

'I think the SED have taken the gloves off,' Roxy yelled.

'They're gonna be pissed when they find out we've beaten them to the main prize,' Mason said.

Kobayashi squeezed his bulk through the back door, pushing and struggling, filling half of the rear of the car.

Mason slammed the door shut, felt it rebound off the guy's massive shoulder and waited a few seconds more for him to shuffle along the leather.

Moments later, he was in the front seat.

Raising his weapon, he turned to Roxy. 'Gun it.'

Chapter 31

Roxy slammed her foot to the floorboards.

The big vehicle spurted forward, sped out of the garage and emerged into the sunshine. Mason took a moment to think. He didn't believe they'd be shot at by Kobayashi's guards, nor by the snipers on the roof. None of them could know exactly what was happening inside the car. Their only danger was the SED.

The driveway lay in front of them, curving around the fountain, past a couple of statues and the SED's two four-wheel-drive vehicles. Roxy didn't let up; she kept her foot down and both hands firmly on the wheel. The tyres slewed across the crunching gravel, tiny stones flicking up in their wake.

Now half the SED's attention turned towards them.

Mason ducked into the passenger footwell. Kobayashi screamed to see the weapons pointed at them. Roxy put her head down to wheel level, just able to see over its leather upper.

There was an outburst of gunfire, but it didn't come from

the SED. It came from Kobayashi's guards, and their bullets pinned the SED down for several crucial seconds. The vehicle raced towards them. Mason raised his head a little, saw several of them scrambling out of the way, one man even jumping into the fountain.

It was then he realised how close Roxy was getting to the large concrete obstacle.

Her head was below the steering wheel. She couldn't see properly, couldn't see the impediments before them.

'Look out!' he cried.

Roxy twisted the wheel savagely, but not fast enough. The vehicle struck the fountain side-on, smashing the passenger-side headlights and buckling the metal, bringing it to an abrupt stop. Everyone inside was jerked forward, slamming their heads on the bulkheads. Roxy struck the steering wheel with some force, dazing her. Mason was momentarily stunned.

The engine roared. Kobayashi was yelling. Mason put a hand to his head; his fingers came away slick with blood. No wonder the world was spinning. But he couldn't let the shock overcome him now. He stretched his neck, rolled his shoulders, turned to Roxy and shook her.

'You okay? Get us moving.'

The car was wedged against the side of the fountain. Mason saw figures. It had to be the SED; they were closest. Did they know Kobayashi was in the car? It would explain why they weren't firing at it. He pressed the electric window button, felt a little absurd as he waited for it to slide down, then poked his Uzi out and fired randomly.

Instantly, the approaching figures backed off.

Kobayashi was still yelling in the back seat. Mason paid no attention to him. The Japanese man tried pulling on the

231

door handles but the car's electronic locking mechanism had engaged when they set off and now wouldn't let him out. Something you could change in the settings of the car. Mason was thankful for it.

He turned quickly now. 'Calm down,' he said. 'If you leave the car now, you're running straight into the hands of your enemy. They came here to grab and kill you.'

'Just look at it this way,' Roxy's slurred voice said. 'Now, we're your saviours.'

'You got me into this mess,' Kobayashi screamed at them.

'No, they'd have come for you anyway, and they *would* have killed you after interrogation.'

Kobayashi suddenly went quiet. 'Interrogation?'

'These are a secret group of special forces soldiers,' Mason said. 'In the country secretly and plotting to murder anyone who's had a hand in uncovering their casino. They don't give a shit about you.'

Kobayashi clammed up. Mason turned to Roxy. 'You okay?'

A figure appeared next to his window, body clad in black. The man reached in and tried to grab Mason's Uzi. Mason jerked his weapon away with two hands, which left him vulnerable to attack. He took an elbow to the face and then one to the forehead. The attacker reached in through the window.

Mason let go of the Uzi, saw it clatter into the footwell, took hold of his opponent around the neck and dragged him in through the window. The man struggled, arms trapped. Mason found he could barely manoeuvre despite the vehicle's generous cabin space. He had the man in a headlock and forced him down.

It was Roxy who leaned forward, her gun reversed, and

smashed it into the man's head. Once, twice, three vicious strikes. Finally, the SED guy went limp. Mason heaved him back through the window and watched his body slump outside.

'You okay?' he asked Roxy.

'I'll live, I think.'

'Good enough for me. Now, do you think you could get us moving before these SED bastards decide to swarm us?'

Roxy smacked the car into reverse and put her foot down. The engine screamed. In the rear-view, she saw a dark figure lurking behind her and yelled. Mason looked back. The vehicle slammed into the figure, sending it flying to the right. Mason jerked forward as he felt the impact.

There were figures in the side mirrors, someone trying to wrench open both back doors. A gun was reversed and struck one of the back windows, shattering it. Kobayashi scooted away from the falling glass, screaming. Roxy engaged Drive and put her foot down.

The car leapt forward, tyres slewing across the gravel, spitting stones into the faces of their pursuers. This time they scraped by the fountain, the concrete scarring the vehicle's entire right side. Mason flinched.

'Bloody hell,' he said.

'Sue me, bitch,' Roxy murmured.

They picked up speed, hurtling beyond the fountain now and angling for the gates. They threaded a gap between the SED's two vehicles, only snapping off a wing mirror, which Mason reckoned was quite a feat for Roxy under the circumstances. He swivelled in his seat to look behind, saw several SED figures racing after them on foot, then heard the gunfire resume.

'Your men are bright,' he told Kobayashi. 'They knew you

were in the car. They stopped shooting. Now they're trying to pick off the SED again.'

The gunfire was unnerving. They sped closer to the gates. Gravel flew from under their tyres. A howling wind swept in through the broken window. Mason reached over to check Roxy's forehead as she drove.

'You're bleeding.'

'I know. So are you.'

It was running into her right eye. Mason used his sleeve to staunch it, wiped it clear. Roxy nodded as she drove.

'Better.'

They were nearing the gates. Mason turned again to look through the back window. Ideally, they should let Kobayashi go now. He'd told them all he could. But if they let him go now, they were condemning him to certain death. The SED would nab him and do what they did best. Of course, Kobayashi was a criminal, and a nasty one at that. Should Mason worry about his ultimate plight?

He wouldn't send Kobayashi out to his death. He turned forward, saw the gates looming ahead. Roxy was aiming for the gap that the SED had made on entry.

A barrage of bullets smashed into the Range Rover. This was no idle machine-gun sweep; this was a concerted attack. Mason swore, hunkering down. The SED clearly didn't want them to leave the compound. The rear window smashed in. The windscreen too. Glass flew everywhere. At least two bullets smashed into the centre console, shattering instrument panels and switches. In the back, Kobayashi was on his knees, hands to his ears, head down.

Roxy lost control of the vehicle as she neared the gates. The front end slewed around, ended up facing the way they'd come. Now they were looking at the SED team bearing down on them. They were facing a hail of bullets.

Which abruptly stopped. Mason knew they still wanted Kobayashi alive…if possible. The purpose of their gunfire was to stop the car, not kill the criminal, and they had succeeded. He raised his Uzi now and sprayed through the broken front window.

Five bullets were expelled, then the gun clicked on empty. Mason cursed. Roxy still had her weapon. Ahead, four dark-clad figures were closing in on the car.

What's our next move? he thought.

For now, they couldn't stay in the car. They were sitting ducks. He motioned to Roxy, then grabbed the door handle.

'Kobayashi,' he yelled. 'Out.'

He clicked the lock release button as he flung his door open and leapt down from the car, boots crunching in the gravel. He had an idea. Roxy jumped out the other side. Kobayashi followed Mason.

The sound of gunfire increased. Bullets strafed from in front of the house, across the grounds, and flew among the SED mercenaries. Several of them went down, not killed, just hit in their bulletproof vests, groaning. One man took a bullet to the arm. Mason was in the thick of it, keeping Kobayashi low, wincing as bullets whined past him.

'Your men are getting desperate,' he said.

'They are idiots.'

'No, they are fighting for you.'

Mason stayed low, scooting over to one of the fallen sentry guards. As he'd hoped, the dead man had been carrying an Uzi. Mason now scooped it up and checked the mag.

Full.

He glanced over to Roxy, saw that she'd dashed over to

the other sentry guard and grabbed his weapon too. Mason ducked behind the sentry box as two more bullets skimmed past.

'It's fucking crazy,' Kobayashi said.

Mason had to agree. Gunfire swept the grounds, smashing through the air, peppering the fountain, the Range Rover, the gates and the sentry boxes. It was a deadly hail. The SED had hit the ground and were covering up; those behind the fountain were taking cover. Mason saw one man caught behind a statue, the concrete figure barely wide enough to cover him. The SED's only recourse was to fire back, to take the attackers out of play. They lay low and opened fire, making Kobayashi's men duck and cover.

Mason was desperate to move. They weren't done with the vehicle yet. It was their only way out of here. Every time a bullet struck it, he winced. But, as the SED's attention was caught by Kobayashi's men, and they started returning fire, the bullets flying past him decreased.

He peered out from behind the sentry box.

Ahead, three SED fighters were prone on the ground, about two hundred yards distant. To left and right, others were lying flat or concealed behind statues and the fountain. Their attention was fully focused on Kobayashi's men, who were firing from the house, from windows, from the garage and from behind two large plant pots.

It was now or never. He signalled to Roxy.

They broke cover, raced back for the Range Rover. Two hundred yards in front of them, the SED fought in the face of a barrage of bullets. Mason reached the car and dived inside, remembered Kobayashi's earlier struggles, turned, and helped shove the man in through the back doors. Kobayashi's panic helped, but he still groaned in pain as he forced himself through the gap.

Roxy leapt in through the other door, again behind the wheel. 'Engine's still running,' she said. 'You ready?'

'Hit it.'

Roxy put the car into reverse, backed up, then flung it into Drive and twisted the wheel to the right. The car flew over the gravel, turning towards the broken gates. Mason aimed his weapon and, when the SED turned their attention to the fleeing vehicle, let off a couple of bursts. The bullets kept the situation contained.

Roxy aimed the car at the gap in the gates and put her foot down. The vehicle spurted forward, scraping the broken metal as it went through, then bounced down a kerb onto the road outside. Roxy sawed at the wheel. The car veered to the right, Kobayashi rolling around the back and smacking into various bulkheads and the back seat.

Mason didn't look back as Roxy put her foot down.

Chapter 32

Captain Miura stamped out his cigarette and lit another, furious. His men were incompetent, unable even to take down a bunch of low-brow criminal scum. They had completely botched the mansion attack, letting themselves get pinned down under fire, and allowed that damn car to escape from the compound. Of course, that *damned* car had the criminal Kobayashi inside it. The fat man, as Miura thought of him.

Miura sat in a large SUV, the interior filled with smoke from his cigarettes. Some of his men were there too, wreathed in smoke, and he didn't care. He puffed on his second and was already contemplating a third. He was trying to calm himself, trying, although surrounded by smoke, to see a clearer picture.

They had been lucky to stumble across Kobayashi's name. It had come in the middle of an interrogation, some despicable man named Endo, who had handled the coins in question. The guy had spilled the beans pretty quickly, giving them Kobayashi's name and then begging them not to tell him who gave them the information. Miura had taken his knife out, handed it to one of his men and watched in pleasure as the idiot's throat was slit. Miura had then made a few enquiries through his secretive organisation back home and, three hours later, had been rewarded with Kobayashi's address.

And now, this rival team was really getting on his nerves.

Again, they were there first. Again, they had thwarted his plans. These barbaric, brutal adversaries had got the drop on him and sped off with the criminal in question. This put Miura in a difficult position with his bosses.

Admitting failure to them wasn't possible. Such a stupid move would spell his doom. At the same time, he needed to move forward.

What next?

They were a secret group with orders to harm if they had to, to kill if they needed to, to conspire to safeguard the Shadow Kings' agenda at all costs. Miura was determined that he wouldn't fail in the attempt. His team was a little bedraggled, but they were still thirteen strong. Despite everything, he hadn't lost a man yet. Yes, one man had been shot in the arm, others were banged up, but they were all still in working order. That was a plus.

But how to best the stupid enemy?

All they really needed was the location of the casino. That was it. If they had that, then the enemy would eventually come to them. Did he really need to run around like an entitled fool, mad for materialistic gain, chasing across a country that was becoming lost in its own greed? Or was there a better way?

Miura was sure he had time. He finished the second cigarette, ground it beneath his boot and lit up a third.

Someone coughed in the back seat. Miura turned to stare at the man, giving him hard eyes.

'Kobayashi,' he said, 'is the key.'

And then he struck the back of the leather seat again and again. 'Where is he?' he screamed, punctuating the strikes. 'Where is he?'

He drew down hard on the third cigarette.

A brave man spoke up, the driver. 'We will get him,' he said confidently. 'Don't forget, normal soldiers are indolent, unfocused. Not like us. We are relentless with laser-guided focus. We are better because we work for the Shadow Kings. Normal soldiers think they have a democracy, believe they are masters of their own destiny. But they are slaves, slaves to a government that cares little for them as long as it can line its own pockets. They simply do not learn. The world and its governments do not deserve this casino. We are working for a greater good.'

Miura agreed with the man, but backhanded him across the face anyway, just to let out a little more anger.

'They are all undisciplined,' he said. 'We know that. Even so, they stumble through, they get things done. Perhaps they are well trained. But we are a better team. Though the Shadow Kings are young as a world presence, we are *strong*. We grow, we fortify, we consolidate our power.' He went silent, thinking. There had to be a way to get to Kobayashi.

And there was.

Miura believed he was doing a good job. They should praise him, promote him maybe. He was fighting in a flawed country, against men and women who embraced all the world's vices, fighting for his country, his home. The boss knew that; the boss would see the good in him.

Even so, failure would not be tolerated.

Miura hadn't failed yet. Yes, they had lost the fat criminal, lost the other team, made a mess inside the compound. They had killed men more or less openly.

But all this wasn't the reason for Miura's chain-smoking and general mood. Right now, Miura had to call his boss.

He stepped out of the car, crushed out the cigarette and dialled a number. The call was answered on the third ring.

'Yes?'

'We are moving closer to our goal.'

'Then you have nothing new?'

Miura ground his teeth. 'The operation is ongoing.'

'I hate speaking in these general terms, but understand it is necessary. Tell me, captain, what is new?'

'We have tracked down the ultimate source.'

'Are you sure it is the ultimate source?'

Miura hesitated. *Was* Kobayashi the ultimate source? Had he taken the coins from the ancient casino? Did he know its location? Miura realised all he had were a few tentative leads.

'It's not positive, but it is promising.'

'Then you have *nothing new*.'

Miura stiffened at the angry tone. He wanted this man's job. No, he wanted something loftier. The boss sat in a windowless office, in a sweaty, dark basement, in a concrete-shrouded, funereal building in the heart of busy Paris. Miura wanted much more than that.

The man said, 'You have an aptitude for this kind of thing. Show me.'

Miura knew he had more than an *aptitude*. He lived and breathed war and death. The weasel snapping at him couldn't hope to comprehend how powerful and lofty Miura's aspirations went.

'We are under cover. We creep from place to place. This

country, it is turning into a European cousin. Difficult to negotiate, to talk to people, to make them understand, even though we share similar ideals. I do not make excuses.'

'Do you have another move?'

'Yes, I am working on it.'

'Do you need more men?'

'No, that is good to report.'

'I don't care. I only care about results. Do you understand?'

'Yes, and I will have them soon.' Miura held his breath then, hoping the boss wouldn't just summon him home and get someone else to take his place. That would sound a terrible death knell for his career. He thought briefly about his wife, visiting her sick mother in Paris, pregnant. Amelie would be feeling the pregnancy now. Miura wanted to be back for the birth. Again, was her pregnancy changing him?

The boss sighed down the line, seemingly at the end of his tether. 'Captain,' he said. 'You have failed so far. On many levels. I should reassign you and your men, bring you back here in shame.'

Miura had expected this speech. He only hoped that he wasn't about to be humiliated before his own men and reduced in rank.

'Captain,' the boss said again. 'I will give you one more chance. Do not fail in this.'

'I will not fail,' Miura said.

'You will stay in the country. You will perform the task we sent you to carry out. This relic – if the enemy find it, if they get away with video footage, it will humiliate the Shadow Kings. It will seem as though we cannot hold on to our treasures, that we are always a step behind. Do you understand me?'

242

'Yes, sir, I do.'

'You are one secret group with a plan. I would wholly recommend that you do not fail.'

Miura knew exactly what the boss was saying. 'Thank you.' Would the boss spring a trap now, cover him in shit, cut off his legs from under him? This was how they worked. They lulled you…and then they destroyed you.

'You are on your last chance,' the boss said.

Miura sought to put confidence in his voice. 'I will not fail.'

'Do not tarry. Make your next plan your best plan. You will find this ultimate source and make it work for you, for us. Understand? Do whatever you have to do.'

The boss signed off. Miura stood out in the sun for a while, thinking. *Do whatever you have to do.* It was a blanket command, free rein. It allowed him to kill indiscriminately, to commit mayhem and then just vanish like a black cloud in a dark sky. Miura would be unstoppable.

And the imbecile enemy would wish they'd never crossed him.

Miura climbed back into the car.

Chapter 33

Mason had sat in silence as Roxy stopped the Range Rover just up the road, allowed the rest of the team to climb in the back seats and the large rear compartment, and then taken off at speed. At first, she did not know where she was going, but then Sally suggested they simply return to the safe house.

It made sense, Mason thought. They didn't want to take Kobayashi too far; they needed time and space to think. Kobayashi, listening to their conversation, agreed that the safe house was the right move.

'Shut up,' Roxy told him, tending to his wound.

But soon they had parked the broken vehicle some way up the winding hill, then walked back to the house with Kobayashi. It was getting on for six p.m. They scarfed down what few rations they had left, drank water and gathered in an upstairs room behind net curtains to hash out a plan. Mason sat on the floor and explained what little Kobayashi had told them about the three men who'd come to his door seven years ago, the bags of coins, the lost gambling den in the Gobi, the apparent location of the casino. As he spoke, it surprised him to hear Kobayashi interrupting.

'You did save my life,' the big man said, his tone incredulous. 'I thought you were here to kill me, yet you were here to save me.'

Mason shrugged. He didn't care about the criminal one way or the other.

'The SED won't stop hunting you,' Sally told him.

'Thank you,' Kobayashi said, nodding, his flesh wobbling, his bald head catching the light as it dipped. 'I have told you everything *I* was told about the coins and the location of the casino. But there is one thing I haven't mentioned.'

Mason raised an expectant eyebrow. 'There is?'

'You never asked about the three men who came to visit me, the three men who *really* found the casino. Do you not want to know about them?'

Mason coughed. They'd been in a hurry. Was he expected to remember everything? 'Anything you can tell us will be useful,' he said.

'They were treasure hunters, nothing more, nothing less. They wore dusty, torn clothes and had much facial hair,' Kobayashi said with distaste. 'Beards. Moustaches. They carried old guns and backpacks, from which they produced the coins. I believe they had far more than they gave me.'

'Why?' Quaid asked.

'Because of the backpacks. They were all full, and through the gaps, I glimpsed more of the same bags. I believe they visited more collectors than just me. But that is not what I am saying. I dealt with one man, the leader. He was the only one that spoke to me at length.'

'Can you describe him?' Luciane asked. 'Did you get a name?'

Kobayashi nodded. 'The man's name was Phoenix Basso,

245

an American. He spoke a lot about the casino in the desert. I don't think he understood the significance it may have to China. He was a tall man with long, wiry blond hair held up in a bun. The little finger on his left hand was missing. His teeth were yellow.' Kobayashi pulled a face. 'Blue eyes. A… what do you call it…a winning smile? The kind that makes you believe a man is trustworthy. And his manner, too. That came across the same. All three spoke in American accents.'

Mason could hardly believe Kobayashi had furnished them with such an excellent description of the leader of the treasure hunters. The man must be really grateful for his life. He spoke up. 'As Sally said, they won't stop coming after you. Go somewhere. Lie low for a while. Stay with someone you trust. Okay?' He didn't know why he was helping the criminal, but it felt like the right thing to do.

Kobayashi nodded. 'I can do that.'

'We'll drive you somewhere when it gets darker,' Roxy told him. 'No point in pushing our luck.'

Kobayashi nodded and sat back, silent. Mason checked the time, saw that it was now seven o'clock in the evening. He thought about the directions the criminal had given them, from Dunhuang to the Mogao Caves and onward. He knew that Phoenix Basso had furnished him with those directions. He felt happiness, not elation. They had come a long way and now, despite knowing the casino's location, he felt they still had a long way to go.

'It would appear we're headed to China,' Quaid said. 'Into the mouth of the dragon, as it were.'

Mason looked up at him. 'How're your contacts there?'

'Practically non-existent, I'm afraid.'

'Practically?'

'I mean only that I have contacts who can help facilitate

our entry. Direct flights. Travel visas, that kind of thing. In China itself...' He shook his head.

'A travel visa to China takes four days,' Sally told them, researching. 'Which is far too long. If the SED finds another way to locate that casino, they can be there almost immediately. Now, we're hopefully several steps ahead of them because they don't have Kobayashi's information, I'd like to think. Let's not waste that.'

'How would you suggest we expedite a visa?' Hassell asked.

'Rush service. Express service,' Sally said, tapping away. 'It can be done. You can get same day service, actually, for a very reasonable thirty dollars.'

Sally set about the unenviable task of getting an L Visa, a Chinese tourist visa, for all of them. The process was interrupted when she found out they needed to present an itinerary for their trip, and hotel bookings, but she soon overcame that by booking them all several nights in the tourist city of Dunhuang.

With Sally wholly occupied, Mason and Hassell set about using their old car to drive Kobayashi further towards the centre of Osaka, letting the man out into the night and watching him walk off.

'You think he'll survive?' Hassell asked.

'He seems to be a survivor,' Mason said. 'But he's a criminal. I hope that's the last we see of Kobayashi.'

It wasn't too late to pick up some takeaway food, a few bottles of alcohol and some bland clothes for everyone. Mason grabbed an assortment of jeans and T-shirts, checked the sizes (which he knew by heart), slapped several jackets on the pile, and bought socks and underwear. It was oddly surreal, shopping for everyone mere hours after being in one of the fights of his life. Actually, just shopping for Roxy and Sally and even Luciane was surreal. He didn't know what to make of it, so he just stepped up and did it. It didn't take long. There was no browsing, no sorting between garments. If a desired item fell before Mason's nose, it was quickly scooped up and purchased.

'Do we need suitcases?' Hassell asked at one point.

'Backpacks will have to do,' Mason said. 'Suitcases won't all fit in the car.'

'But all the clothes will wrinkle.'

Mason gave him a dead-eye smile. 'Did you really just say that?'

Hassell looked suitably embarrassed and closed his mouth. Mason carried the bags back to the car, which was smelling wonderfully of takeaway food. They climbed in and drove back to the lay-by and then walked the few hundred yards to the house. Soon, they were inside and the others were crowding around for their takeaways.

'Absolutely freakin' starving.' Roxy was first at the cartons and the chopsticks. 'What have you got?'

'Chicken, chicken and for an alternative – slightly burned chicken,' Mason said.

'Perfect.'

They sat and ate ravenously. Mason had over-ordered by far, but somehow they managed to polish off all the food. Hours had passed since Sally started her visa process and she was still at it, crossing all the Ts and dotting all the Is, but she paused for dinner, her mouth watering. They sat in the dark, on a carpet in the living room, eating their food.

Later, Mason broke out the alcohol, two bottles of Nihonshu rice wine, or sake for short. Since it was the most famous drink in Japan, Mason had thought, what the hell, and decided to partake. He had bought plastic cups too. When he put the sake to his lips, it tasted and smelled rather sweet. It was colourless and clear. Not sure at first taste, he swallowed some more. By the eighth or twelfth swallow, he was okay with it.

They sat around the darkened room, eating and drinking and wondering what tomorrow would bring. Mason, sitting beside Quaid, turned the conversation around to Luciane.

'She seems capable,' he said, wondering if the sake would loosen Quaid's tongue.

'Oh, believe me, she is,' Quaid said. 'Garda cop at heart. Always was and still is, in my opinion. When she sets her eyes on something, like this casino, there's no stopping her. Unfortunately.'

'You two know each other well, then.'

'Once we were soulmates.'

'Aren't soulmates supposed to be together for ever? I thought Anya was your soulmate?'

'That crazy person?' Quaid laughed and then stopped, and Mason felt he was looking inward, evaluating his life.

'Sorry,' Mason said, taking another drink. 'Didn't mean to make you think too hard.'

'No, you're right, you're right,' Quaid said. 'I have more than one soulmate. I was thinking...maybe it's *me* who's the problem.'

'Do you make Anya crazy? Did you make Luciane leave?'

Quaid shrugged. 'Probably.'

'Then there you have it.' Mason clinked plastic cups with the man. 'Problem solved.'

They laughed. The darkness thickened, relieved only by the slivers of moonlight slanting in through the windows, and the faint glow of Sally's laptop. Sally finally announced that she'd finished the visa application process and was just waiting for return emails. She'd applied for the fast-track documents. She sat back and relaxed, still toying with her food. Roxy offered her a drink, and she took it.

Quaid leaned closer to Mason. 'With Anya,' he said, 'it's the excitement, the danger, hell, even the arguments are fun. But with Luciane, it's the passion she has for her projects, the love of entertainment, all the way to the way she calls me "honey" in that accent.'

'Do you have other...soulmates?' Mason ventured.

'A few.'

Mason shook his head, wondering if Quaid was the 'girl in every port' kind of guy. He didn't seem it. To Mason, it felt that Quaid was torn between the women, fighting inwardly with himself. Maybe he was just the kind that could never settle down. Perhaps it had something to do with being in the army.

'The military spoils you,' he said of his own experiences. 'It offers you a home, a family, right until it rips it all away.'

Quaid thought for a moment and then said, 'I couldn't agree more. Kind of makes it hard to settle down afterwards, don't you think?'

Mason nodded. Satisfied they'd put all that to rest, the two men fell into a slightly inebriated silence and listened to the others talk as the moon passed across their windows and the winds battered the glass. Mason had bought enough food so that they all managed seconds, but the alcohol didn't last long. The conversation turned, centring on the SED and their leader, Miura, whom Luciane had encountered, and then the lost casino and the three Americans who had discovered it seven years ago. Finally, it turned to the Gobi Desert, and China, and what they might find tomorrow.

In Mason's mind, there was no doubt the SED would have killed Luciane. That put them firmly on his shit list. It made him want to beat them at their own game, tear them down, defeat them utterly.

'We'll find that casino,' he said. 'Make it universally known that *we* found it, and cause some chaos around the archaeological world. The Shadow Kings should never have sent killers to protect a jewel.'

Sally looked over at him, grinning. Her face lit up. Archaeological discoveries were what she lived for, what they were basing their new careers on. This would be epic for them, put them even more firmly on the map and bring them bigger clients.

'Roll on tomorrow,' she said.

'Are you ready to go find an ancient casino?' Mason asked.

'I've been ready for months,' Luciane put in.

Sally nodded. 'They can't stop us. We're a step ahead. I don't see how the SED can beat us now.'

'That was pretty close back at the compound,' Roxy said with a shudder. 'I came close to losing it at least twice.'

Mason wondered if she meant being hit by a bullet or losing it in her head. He didn't ask out loud; the answer was private.

'Did it build more barriers?' he asked instead.

'I'm there,' she said.

He latched on to that, stared deeply into her eyes, suddenly rapt with attention. 'Honestly?'

'I think so,' she said with meaning. 'I think there's a little of the woman I might have been coming through now.'

For Roxy, it was a revelation. For Mason, it was credibility, acceptance. It galvanised him and made him rise to his feet, walk over and give Roxy a hug.

'I'm so glad to hear it,' he said.

'You and me both,' Roxy said. 'It's a start, at least. And it clears the way for more angst and anguish to form.'

Mason shook his head. He knew she was joking, but the words bothered him. He'd never hoped to fully cure Roxy of her sorrows, but he liked to think he'd helped her get through the worst of them.

'Like Sally said,' he intoned. 'Roll on tomorrow.'

Chapter 34

On the borders of the Gobi Desert in Central China lies the
town of Dunhuang. It is ancient – with evidence of habitation
as early as 2000 BC – and historic, and was once of military
importance. The Great Wall stretched to Dunhuang, a string
of garrisoned beacon towers extending into the desert.
The very name, Dunhuang, means 'blazing beacons'. Most
famously, it was a major stop along the Silk Road, a centre
of commerce. It is surrounded by mountain-high sand dunes,
mysterious statues, ancient watchtowers, the Crescent Lake
and a fierce heat that scours the land. Close by, the Mogao
Caves, or the Caves of a Thousand Buddhas, can be found,
735 manmade grottoes formed for worship and meditation.
The caves defy the transience of the desert, of the drifting
dunes, showing permanency, their construction having
spanned more than a thousand years, beginning in AD 366.

The Gobi Desert itself is well known for its enormous
sand dunes, rising like immense tidal waves across its vast
expanse. Winding between are camels carrying tourists on
desert tours. The crescent-shaped lake oasis in Dunhuang

is a spot of tropical beauty amid the fierce and unrelenting landscape.

Mason and his team landed at Dunhuang Mogao International Airport at night, negotiated its customs and exited the arrivals area. Sally had already told them that there was an airport commuter bus that ran three times a day, which took about twenty minutes to reach the city, but they needed to be more flexible than that. The other problem was that, with most of the tourist attractions not being downtown, the authorities had not developed the urban public transport system, thus leaving them only two modes of transport: buses and taxis.

So a taxi it was.

Mason climbed into the outsize minivan, along with his five colleagues, and settled in for a short, dark drive. At this time of day, it made sense to drop their main gear off at the hotel before scouting the area. Mason saw many domestic and foreign tourists as they wound along the busy, dusty roads, coming finally to their hotel off Mingshan Road. It was a four-storey affair with pagoda-like towers on both sides and at the centre, painted to match the colour of the desert, and with a silver-hued metal entryway supported by four stanchions. Soon they had pushed their way through the doors into the well-lit, air-conditioned lobby and were wiping the sweat from their faces. Sally booked them in and then they were heading up to their rooms, agreeing to meet downstairs half an hour later.

It had been a long flight on China Eastern, involving two stops and a duration of over thirteen hours. The time in Dunhuang now was eleven p.m. Mason took a quick shower and then headed down to the lobby, grabbed a drink at the bar and ordered some food by pointing at items. Several minutes later, his colleagues appeared and did the same, sitting close to him and moaning about losing the entire day to travel. It wasn't ideal, but it was unavoidable.

They were all tired and soon dispersed to return to their rooms to get some sleep. Tomorrow would be a major day. Mason was asleep the moment his head hit the pillow and, despite the creaking of the ceiling fan, the laboured purr of the air conditioning and the ambient hum of cars passing along the road outside, slept well. He woke feeling refreshed when his alarm went off the next morning.

The team gathered together around the breakfast table. It was only eight a.m., but already the sun was glaring from a cloudless sky and the people who passed the windows that looked out on the street outside were sweating, the tourists at least. The few locals Mason saw ambled along dressed in loose clothes and didn't look at all bothered.

Sally led the conversation. 'Right,' she said. 'Are we ready for some proper treasure hunting? We have to hope we're still well ahead of the SED. Clearly, they do not know where this casino actually was, which kind of makes sense. They outlawed the casinos at the time, and they didn't stay in one place for too long. Even if they used walled structures, the occupants flitted from place to place. So.' She laid her hands on the table. 'What do we have? Kobayashi told us that the Americans told *him* they found the coins and the entrance to the casino in the Mogao Caves. Now we know the Caves were first constructed in the fourth century and used as a place of pilgrimage. The caves are recognised by their numbers. For instance, caves 268, 272 and 275 were built in the fifth century and share common characteristics with other cave systems such as the Kizil Caves in Xinjiang. The Buddhist beliefs and stories are the common denominator.

Inside the Caves are over half a million square feet of religious murals and, once, a vast cache of manuscripts, a fantastic archaeological find in what has come to be known as the Library Cave. The Mogao Caves are now a UNESCO World Heritage Site.'

'So we're gonna have to be careful,' Roxy said. 'Got it.'

'Not careful,' Sally said. 'Practically invisible.'

'Do you have a map of the caves?' Luciane asked.

Sally nodded. 'There are several available. I just got the most recent.'

'What exactly are we looking for?' Quaid asked.

Sally took a deep breath, thought about her answer and then took a long gulp of coffee. She said, 'There's a lot of art in there. Stucco sculpture. Wall and silk paintings. Calligraphy. Embroidery. Literature. The list goes on. Most of the caves had wooden fore-temples that once stood out from the cliff, but all save five have now decayed. Over two thousand clay sculptures. Crucially, a book called the *Diamond Sutra*, the oldest known printed book in the world, was found in the Library Cave. It's dated back to AD 868, or CE for the common era.'

'Time's ticking,' Hassell said, to hurry her along a little.

'Yes, well, I guess it is.' Sally sounded chagrined to be diverted from her subject. 'The American leader, Phoenix Basso, told Kobayashi that he could find the entrance to the casino through a tiny niche at the back of one of the fourteenth-century caves. Now, we know there are fewer than ten caves attributed to the fourteenth century, but it's complicated. The numbering is all over the place. For example, caves 329 and 45 are on either side of the entrance, flanked by caves 335 and 275, also 61. We will head inside and climb towards the fourteenth-century grottoes.'

'Sounds like a plan.' Mason rose to his feet and took a last gulp from his coffee cup. 'Shall we put it into motion?'

They left the hotel. As they passed through the doors, sunlight struck them, blinding, making Mason wish he'd remembered to grab a handful of sunglasses during his shop the other night. Outside, it was mild, the sun not having burned off the chill of the night yet. They found a taxi idling in front of the hotel, squeezed inside and asked to be taken to the Mogao Caves complex via a hardware store. The driver nodded, recognising only the destination in their words, probably because he'd made the journey a thousand times. The car set off and joined the traffic. Mason did his best to relax in the back. They had no idea what they were walking into, what they would find, if perhaps the SED were already here. Of course, the latter possibility was unlikely, unless somehow the SED had nabbed Kobayashi after all.

The taxi dropped them off outside the cave complex. Rearing before them, it looked impressive, a tall, wide, rugged, sandy-coloured edifice of rock with craggy cave entrances stretching across its length. Mason and the others gathered together to shield their eyes and look upwards.

Sally headed for the manmade entrance. She led them into the cooler, darker building and then consulted a local map to make sure they were going in the right direction. They had two backpacks between them, torches, small shovels they'd got from a hardware store on the way, chisels, pen and paper, hefty bags, bottles of water, spare batteries, a disposable camera for documenting evidence besides those on their mobile phones, gloves and other useful items.

Sally set off steadily, slowly, threading them through the throng of tourists that lined the way. It took them more than an hour to reach the caves that had been developed in the fourteenth century. All the while, Mason and the others were on the lookout for their enemies, for anyone looking suspicious. They did their best to blend in, stopping along the way to look at other complexes, the Library Cave and the Lower Temple, going with the flow of tourists for long minutes.

Inside the caves, it was both busy and hot. There was a wind flow, but it didn't do much to alleviate the heat. They stopped for refreshments and then, a short time later, slowed down as Sally pointed off to the left.

'The fourteenth-century caves,' she said.

Mason scanned them carefully. They were temple grottoes, carved deep into the rock, rounded at the ceiling and smooth-walled. Most of them stretched back into a well of darkness.

'What are we waiting for?' Roxy crossed a narrow expanse of sand to the first cave that presented itself.

Mason felt a surge of excitement. It had occurred to him to wonder how, with so many tourists and scholars and archaeologists at the caves, nobody but the Americans had located the casino yet, how it had remained a secret for so long, but there were plausible explanations for that too. Maybe the niche was small, hard to negotiate, and attracted little attention. Maybe it was hard to gain access to. Perhaps it was well hidden at the end of a passageway or sunk into the ground. Maybe, he thought, someone had properly resealed it.

They split up, taking two caves at a time. The first cave was blissfully empty of tourists, giving them ample opportunity to delve around at its rear, Hassell and Quaid doing the work as the others blocked them from view. They rooted around the floor and walls, dug at a few seams, used their chisels to test for hollow walls, checked dimensions to test for hidden rooms, effectively coming up with every scenario they could think of that might lead to a hidden passageway and trying it out. They took their time, spending half an hour in the first cave alone. They kept in contact using their mobile phones. Sally and Roxy foraged in the second cave whilst the others stood guard.

The first and second caves yielded nothing. Undaunted, the split team moved on to the third and fourth. It was here they encountered a problem: several people were hanging around inside staring at the murals or studying the interior designs. When those people left, others came in. If it wasn't for the team members covering the actions of the searchers, they could never have succeeded. At one point, Mason froze as a curator entered, looking around. At first, he thought someone had complained about them, but then the man left, none the wiser. After that, they took extra care.

They finished with the third and fourth caves, finding nothing. By now, it was past midday, and the temperature was rising. They had been at the cave complex for hours and had no results to show for their efforts. Now, they entered the fifth and sixth caves. Mason switched places with Quaid and the search went on. They waited until they could access the rear of the caves, squeezed in, and then let the others mask their actions. They tapped lightly, felt gingerly, measured carefully. The walls and the floors were sheer rock, ungiving and dusty and chipped with the efforts of previous archaeologists. It seemed unlikely to Mason that such a secret could exist inside here.

He backed out of the fifth cave when they were done and called Sally on the phone, voicing his frustrations.

'I know,' she replied. 'But it *is* possible. Any archaeologist could miss something. The Americans might have left a suitable cover or seal behind. The passage might be so obscure it defies normal investigation. Try everything.'

Mason had – and continued to do so. Hours passed. They reached the seventh and eighth caves, searched those and came up empty-handed. Finally, they met up and conferred. Mason felt despondency hanging over him like a thick shroud.

'Do you think the three Americans were lying to Kobayashi?' Quaid asked. 'Did this Phoenix Basso feed him a load of bullshit?'

Mason felt that statement settle like a heavy weight across his shoulders.

'We didn't find anything yet,' Sally told them. 'Shrug it off. We go again.'

Mason groaned.

Chapter 35

Kobayashi was not a healthy man; he was grossly overweight, unfit and impossible to hide. Everyone knew who he was; everyone who mattered, at least. When Joe Mason dropped him off in downtown Osaka, Kobayashi considered calling his men at the mansion and ordering them to pick him up. It was the easiest, most logical, simplest thing to do. *Easiest* being the operative word. Kobayashi was nothing if not lazy, always taking the comfortable route. He paused in the street with his mobile phone in his hand, his large fingers hovering over a speed dial number, his bald head flashing with reflections from the gaudy, blinking signs around him.

He'd seen several of his own men murdered today. Gunned down in cold blood.

He considered himself lucky. Firstly, the wound Roxy had tended to had all but stopped hurting. And yes, he knew Mason hadn't exactly come to save him. Mason had come for information and had been intent on working it out of him. But they *had* saved him from the organisation they called the SED, some kind of clandestine special forces division. They had risked their lives to save him rather than leaving him as prey.

Should he heed their warning?

Kobayashi decided he was too valuable not to. He held information much more delicate than the whereabouts of some stupid casino. He knew things, knew names and drop-off details, meeting places, the places where dead men were buried, and some not so dead.

He hesitated, surrounded by the blinking Osaka lights, the darkness, the buzzing, flashing signs. Some passers-by were staring at him. One of them laughed. Kobayashi wished he had his gun with him.

He made a call.

'It is me,' he said when a tentative voice answered. 'Is that Ito? Do you know my voice?'

'Yes, boss.' The answer was rushed, scared.

'Come pick me up now.' He reeled off the name of the street he was on and the business establishment at his back. 'Come immediately.'

'Yes, boss.'

Ten minutes later, he was bundled with difficulty into the passenger seat of Ito's van. The underling had tentatively suggested Kobayashi climb into the back, but had been backhanded across the face for his insubordination. In truth, Kobayashi was actually considering it as a way to get the hell off the street in a hurry before, finally, he popped into the front of the van and managed to perch on the plastic-covered seat.

'Go quickly,' he said.

As they drove, the underling ventured a question. 'Why are you here, boss?'

Kobayashi could understand his confusion.

'There was an attack at my compound today. Men are searching for me, looking for information that only I can impart. My only option is to lie low for a few days.'

'Men are looking for you?' The underling looked interested. 'Which men?'

Kobayashi felt the need to shut the underling up. 'Special forces,' he said. 'Unfortunately, they are in town.'

'And they attacked the mansion?'

'Yes, killed some of my men.'

'Is my brother okay?'

Kobayashi pulled a face and shook his head. 'How the hell would I know? If he's dead, he died for a good cause.'

The other man, Ito, was silent for a while.

'Take me to the fleapit you call home,' Kobayashi ordered the man. 'And we shall see about accommodation.'

'My home?' Ito looked shocked. 'I have a small one-bedroom flat, boss. It is not suitable—'

'It is shit, I know. I get the idea. But I will have to make do for a few days.'

'What will you do?' Ito looked to be in shock. 'Can you check on my brother?'

'Do? I will do nothing. That's what you will be there for. To fetch and carry for me. To do my bidding.' He made no mention of the brother. He barely knew Ito and couldn't care less about some brother.

'You can't contact the mansion at all?' Ito asked.

'Are you not listening? It was and may well still be under attack. There were Shadow King soldiers everywhere.'

'And cops?'

'We can deal with the cops when the time comes. I am sure when they see it was my mansion that was attacked and my men killed, they will be less interested.'

Ito found a parking area, switched the van off and then glanced sideways at his boss. He had a speculative look on his face. 'There is a stairway,' he said. 'A steep one.'

'Oh, I am sure you will find a way. Now help me out.'

Ito tugged and pulled until Kobayashi levered himself out of the van. At Kobayashi's urging he led the way to his front door, a small, flecked blue affair flanked by restaurants, electronics and manga shops, cheap food and kitchenware establishments and an elegant place that sold kimonos. Ito unlocked his door, asked Kobayashi to turn sideways, and dragged the man through the gap.

'The stairs,' he said ominously.

Kobayashi eyed them, licked his lips. They were indeed steep and dark. From down here, it looked like they led to Hell. He couldn't do this, couldn't bear the ignominy of it. His heart was already racing at double speed. But Kobayashi knew they had been lucky so far. Nobody had seen them, at least nobody important. All he had to cross was this last hurdle, and he'd be safe.

'Stay behind me,' he blustered. 'If I start to fall, catch me.'

Ito's eyes widened. Clearly, he didn't know what to say, so he said nothing but positioned himself behind Kobayashi, who started up the stairs a riser at a time. He moved as fast as he could, groaning, unbalanced most of the time, swaying. Twice, Ito had to bury his hand in Kobayashi's back and push him forward so that he didn't topple backwards. Bit by bit, they made it up the stairs and then paused for Kobayashi to get his breath on the landing of the first floor.

'Hurry,' Kobayashi said between pants. 'I don't want anyone to see me.'

Ito ran to his door, flung it open. Kobayashi squeezed inside. Finally, he could relax. He sighed, looked around the flat and stiffened.

'This is actual shit,' he said.

Ito squeezed past him, tidying up quickly. His front room contained a two-seat sofa, dipping precariously at one end, a small TV perched on a stand held together with duct tape, a pair of grey curtains and Ito's only luxury, a mini-fridge that held cans of beer. Kobayashi went straight for the sofa, kicking the fridge out of the way, and lowered himself into it. Immediately, the good end collapsed. Kobayashi seemed not to notice.

'Beer,' he said. 'And noodles. And none of your crap. I want thick Ramen with *menma*. Don't return without the good stuff.'

'I don't have much money, boss,' Ito said subserviently.

'Then dip into your savings,' Kobayashi dismissed him. 'You know I am worth it.'

Dismissing Ito from his own home, Kobayashi sat back. He was in quite a bind. Perhaps he wouldn't have to stay here for too long. He could contact his men at the mansion soon, get the lie of the land. But Kobayashi didn't want to walk into a massacre. The special forces soldiers might be watching and waiting.

Better to hide out here for a few days.

He stretched out, sighed. What a shithole this place was. Ito certainly lived like a bum. Kobayashi then realised Ito hadn't furnished him with any beer before leaving. The mini-fridge was at least twelve steps away and too far to reach from a sitting position. Had Ito done that on purpose? Never mind, Kobayashi would reprimand him later.

Where the hell was he, anyway? The little shit better not have run off.

Time passed. Kobayashi wanted to check outside the

window, but couldn't be bothered to move. Finally, he heard the door behind him rattle and Ito reappeared. The guy had his arms full of noodles and a funny look on his face. Kobayashi didn't even speak to him, just held his arms out for the noodles. They were laid out before him, chopsticks handed over, and then he dug in, not caring that the boxes leaked on Ito's furniture or that the thick liquid dribbled down his chin onto Ito's floor.

The night was hell for Kobayashi. He had to sleep in the peasant's bed and there were no clean sheets. Several times he heard Ito shuffling about, once on his phone. Kobayashi was left wondering about his own business empire, the various deals he had going. Would they survive a day or two of inattention? It wasn't an ideal situation – the men he dealt with were fast-acting and ruthless. Kobayashi might be able to broker an extra few days, though. He was good for it.

Morning came and went. Kobayashi slouched and complained. This was not the luxury he was used to. Ito was a waster. He disappeared at breakfast, came back with rice porridge, grilled fish and several side dishes. Not a terrible start to the day, Kobayashi decided, but he still turned his nose up at Ito's efforts.

Kobayashi had never been so bored. His thoughts turned to his wife. She wasn't often the first thing he thought of, nor the tenth or the twelfth. She was part of his life, sure, but she didn't figure much in his plans. He wondered if she'd survived.

He shrugged and thought about something else.

Ito came and went. Often, he brought snacks, which kept Kobayashi quietly comforted. The afternoon passed in a kind of peace. It occurred to Kobayashi that he'd soon have spent twenty-four hours in the hovel and, despite everything, was doing well. He was pleased with himself. He found the TV remote in the late afternoon, ignored the sticky keys and tried to find something suitable to watch. Ito only had a few channels, nothing like Kobayashi's satellite setup, and he soon grew bored, launching the plastic remote at a nearby wall and breaking it, leaving a dent in the plaster. That, at least, was satisfying.

And in the early evening, Ito brought Kobayashi something extra special.

The flat's door opened. Kobayashi heard it, didn't turn around, just growled at the idiot to bring him some food and another crate of beer. There were footsteps…several of them.

Kobayashi tried to turn. He couldn't. A figure came around the sofa from the left, another from the right. Kobayashi got a better look at them. His mouth fell open, his blood froze.

How…?

More figures appeared. Eight of them in total, carrying handguns and wearing black combat gear. Kobayashi swivelled left and right as best he could but found that, even if he wanted to get up, his legs were just too weak and shaky to allow it.

The men filled the room. Ito entered last, a smirk on his face and a wad of cash in his hands.

'I'll leave you alone,' he said, backed out and shut the door.

That left Kobayashi with the eight black-clad men, staring up at their angry faces, casting glances at their weapons, their guns and their wicked military knives.

'Please,' he said immediately. 'I can help you.'

A man stepped forward. He was tall, blocky, bald, a powerful-looking figure. 'I am Captain Miura of the Special

Exercise Division,' he said, prompting Kobayashi to wonder why the hell he'd just identified himself.

'We have questions for you,' the man said.

'How…how did you find me?' Kobayashi's asked, though he already knew the answer. His mouth was as dry as if he'd just licked dusty gravel.

'Your *friend*, Ito. He has connections. You should pay more attention to your men. He knew a man who knew a man who knew how to contact the Shadow Kings through the Dark Web. From there, it is merely a matter of phone calls.'

Kobayashi wanted to spit, but didn't dare. It was all he could do not to curl up into a ball. The men stood menacingly all around him.

'What do you want to know?'

'The name and location of the man who brought you the casino coins.'

Kobayashi swallowed heavily. That was a pretty succinct and simple question. Miura clearly wasted no time. Again, he berated himself. How could Ito have betrayed him this way? One of his own men? A man he'd called upon in a time of need, blessed his home with his presence. Kobayashi vowed that once he was out of this, Ito would meet a violent and sticky end.

'It was seven years ago,' Kobayashi said. 'I do not know where he will be now.'

'Name?'

'He was an American. There were three of them. The leader was named Phoenix Basso.'

Miura drew the knife from its sheath with the faint whisper of leather and stepped forward. 'Tell me everything he said to you.'

The man's voice, so close, was worse than any nightmare.

268

Chapter 36

Mason threw his crowbar down with a heavy sigh. It made a clunk and a rattle that drew the attention of several tourists. Roxy just smiled at them and waved. The rest of the team was gathered around the top of a set of narrow steps outside the eighth and final cave.

'Nothing,' Mason said in disgust. 'We've made three passes now and I'm pretty sure we're drawing attention. There is *nothing here.*'

A warm wind flicked and grazed its way across the towering façade of the Mogao Caves, carrying with it flecks of sand. People pressed past them to left and right. There were tourists and there were locals, all chattering to each other. Mason believed they'd stayed in one area, searching, for about as long as they could.

'There's nothing here,' he reiterated.

'Then we're done,' Quaid said, sounding slightly pleased.

'No.' Luciane spoke up. 'It can't end here. Not like this. We're so close.'

Mason shrugged. 'To what? All we know is that the three

Americans told Kobayashi this was the location. One of the fourteenth-century caves, they said. Well, we're here, and there's a fat lot of nothing.'

It felt like an utter failure, especially after coming so far. Mason didn't want to move away from the general area of the fourteenth-century caves; it was disappointing to do so. This was all a massive let-down. He looked at the others, spread his arms.

'We can't keep on searching the same places.'

'Maybe we missed something,' Luciane said urgently.

Sally put a hand on the woman's shoulder. 'Honestly,' she said. 'I don't think so. I personally went over every inch of those caves. There's nothing. We're searching in the wrong place.'

Mason knew that Sally often liked to scrutinise what he and his colleagues had already gone over. It was her way of being thorough, proving to herself that she was on the right track.

The team made their way down the steps and back through the edifice until they were standing in the vast space outside, staring up at the big arches of the tiered tower that formed the main entrance. They paced down the concrete steps and formed up near a statue, hiding their faces as the wind skimmed past them.

'We searched every inch of those caves,' Quaid said. 'Three times. Maybe Kobayashi lied to us.'

Mason nodded. It was possible. It was also possible that the American treasure hunters had lied to Kobayashi to keep their secret.

'We should leave this place.' Sally spoke up suddenly. 'It's doing us no good standing here.'

'We could always revisit the caves,' Luciane said hopefully. 'Maybe just two or three of us. Just to be certain.'

Mason had already seen the staff sending looks their way. Even now, as they stood outside the grand entrance, a couple of employees were monitoring them.

'We've definitely outstayed our welcome, if not our visa,' he said. 'Let's talk about this back at the hotel.'

They walked away, grabbed a large taxi, piled in and drove away. They entered the hotel's lobby, found some plush seating and ordered coffees and teas all round. Mason ordered toast and jam, and then so did Roxy, copying him. Soon, they were all sitting in the air-conditioned comfort, the bones of the mission laid out before them.

'Dead end,' Hassell said. 'That's what we call it.'

'We don't deserve to hit a dead end,' Sally said. 'Not with all the effort we've put in.'

Hassell shrugged as if to say, 'That's life.' Mason considered the problem. The Mogao Caves were clearly not the location of the ancient casino and, when he thought about it, it made total sense.

'I have to say,' he said, 'that the caves are well documented. If there had been an ancient casino attached to one of them, surely they'd have found it by now.'

Sally nodded. 'I didn't want to think that way before,' she said. 'Not with the search in front of us. I was excited, carried away. But you're probably right. I wanted to think there was some way Basso had concealed the entrance, some fancy way. It's not impossible. But my guess is, he was lying.'

'And that makes sense too,' Roxy said, chomping on her toast. 'Because even Kobayashi said Basso didn't deal solely with him. He dealt with several collectors in Japan and probably made a fortune.'

Mason nodded. 'Of course he did. You wouldn't limit yourself to just one collector. This Phoenix Basso guy

271

and his two associates would have used a few in Japan.'

'Speaking of Phoenix Basso,' Sally said. '*He* is the bottom line here. The crux of it all. Can we track him down?'

Mason stared at her. 'We're good,' he said. 'But he was here seven years ago. We're not that good.'

'But only he and his two associates know exactly where the casino is,' Sally said.

'It's been seven years,' Roxy said.

'But we can try,' Sally said.

'I have my contacts,' Quaid said helpfully. 'But I don't know anyone on the inside of an agency. For example, MI5 or the FBI. They're the kind of people who could track Basso down. And do we have any more information on him?'

'What more information do you need?' Luciane said in desperation. 'He's a treasure hunter.'

Mason could see how the failure had affected her. She'd been tracking this casino for months, tracing the various parties involved, had even been kidnapped over it. The woman was fully invested and would accept nothing other than success.

'He's American,' Sally said with little hope in her voice. 'Do we know any Americans who can help?'

Mason turned to Roxy.

'Hey, yeah,' she said sarcastically. 'We Americans all know each other real well. Let me grab his number.'

'I think she meant your former employer,' Mason said.

Roxy's face fell. 'I will never contact them again as long as I live,' she said shortly.

Mason had expected as much from the feisty American. Roxy was trying to escape her past, not reconnect with it.

'There may be another way.' Luciane sat forward, placed her cup of tea on the table and bit her lip. 'As you know, I'm a historian, a treasure hunter myself. I know an awful lot of people in the so-called game. I've been doing this for years, ever since I quit the Garda.'

Quaid eyed her. 'What are you saying?'

'That I know the same people Basso knows,' she went on in her breathy voice. 'I've been at this for more than a decade. The key players don't change much. You get a few new players every now and again, but the beat remains the same, if you know what I mean.'

Mason thought for a moment before saying, 'You know the same people Basso knows?'

'Yeah, that's what I said.'

'So you knew Kobayashi?' Quaid asked.

'Barely,' Luciane said.

'Why haven't you mentioned it earlier?'

'I knew him by reputation as a collector only. He's well known in the community. A connoisseur. Everyone knows *of* him, like me. A man who covets certain treasures that only he can own. You know…the one-offs, the Ming vases, Fabergé eggs and lost paintings that have no pairing, no equal. That's Kobayashi, which is probably how Basso managed to sell him the casino coins.'

'Because they were so rare,' Sally said.

'Exactly. Yes, Kobayashi knew others would get a slice of the pie, but the thought of a Chinese casino centuries old, lost in the Gobi Desert, will have appealed to him. We know Kobayashi wasn't the only recipient.' Luciane fell silent, thinking.

'You'd have thought he'd have made an effort to find the casino,' Mason said.

'You've seen him. He's as lazy as they come. The whole idea would have probably overwhelmed him and, of course, he has a criminal empire to run.'

Mason chewed his toast. 'You're trying to track a treasure hunter from seven years ago by determining which collectors he'd have visited,' he said dubiously. 'It's a stretch.'

'But that's where you're wrong,' Luciane said excitedly. 'As you might imagine, there aren't that many collectors around the world. Give me some time to check my notes and I'll see if there are any close by.'

Luciane worked for some time, using Sally's laptop to check her own uploaded notes, the material she'd been working on for months. She checked through reams of it, it seemed, constantly scrolling. She sighed and sat back and shook her head.

'Any luck?' Quaid asked.

She gave him a hard look and went back to work. After some time had passed she sat forward and raised her eyebrows. 'Of course,' she said.

'Found something?' Mason asked.

'I should have known. Like I said, there aren't that many collectors to choose from, but I didn't realise this man lived so close. In fact, he lives in Kyoto.'

'Are you saying that you know this man?' Quaid asked.

Luciane took a deep breath. 'Of course not. But we have had correspondence,' she said. 'He knows my name, my email, my work ethic. When you talk to these guys, ask for their help, you tend to establish a few protocols.'

'I can understand that,' Hassell said. 'They are cagey, vigilant, and would jealously guard their secrets.'

Luciane nodded. 'They're all that, and more. But the man I'm talking about established a few protocols early on. He wanted to converse with me, but on his terms. You see...even more than most, he's a recluse. This man is definitely what you call off the grid.'

'Yet you know where he lives?' Mason asked.

'I don't know exactly where. He mentioned his home in Kyoto a few times, that's all.'

'And you think this man would have had dealings with Basso?'

'I'm sure of it. This man – the name he goes by is Freddie, by the way – has been around longer than anyone. Longer than me. He's a serious collector and well known in the community. Perhaps infamous. But he's also reclusive, suspicious of everyone, a paranoid man. He's a gambler. He's tried to make bets with me a hundred times in his emails. I guarantee you Basso visited him with some coins.'

'You think he may have more information relating to this Basso?' Hassell asked.

'What can we lose by asking?' Luciane said. 'And Freddie is a level-headed guy, not a Kobayashi who loves to scare people off. I think Basso would have conversed with him. And it gets us past the dead end we're currently experiencing.'

'Email him,' Sally said. 'It can't hurt.'

'Ask for a meeting,' Mason said.

'I really don't think he'll agree to that.'

'Do it anyway,' Mason said. 'Stress the importance, the consequences. Tell him it's about finding an ancient Chinese casino before the Shadow Kings shut access down to everyone else in the world and this archaeological breakthrough is lost for ever. Relics sold on the black market. Explain to him how they've sent a fucking hit team to kill everyone involved, and how we're trying to protect them. The danger he's in. How we can help. Get us that face to face.'

Luciane nodded as she accepted Sally's laptop, opened it up and entered her email address. 'I'll do my best.'

Chapter 37

The team flew back to Japan the next day.

The Shinkansen, known in the West as the bullet train, is a vast network of high-speed railway lines which has been operating for over fifty years. Mason and his team settled back in the plush, white seats for a ninety-minute trip to Kyoto, along with a train full of passengers. The train pulled in to the station in Osaka right on time and left exactly sixty seconds later. It had taken them eleven hours to fly back from Dunhuang, and when they landed in Osaka it was mid-morning. They had then booked immediately onto the bullet train and made their way to the correct station.

Mason was feeling the long travel times and lack of sleep and was determined to grab ninety minutes aboard the bullet train. It was clean, spacious and comfortable. He stretched out, closed his eyes and drifted off for a while.

He woke a little refreshed sixty minutes later to find Roxy staring at him.

'You getting too old for this shit, Joe?'

He narrowed his eyes at her. 'I'm thirty-five, recently

actually. And that reminds me, I don't recall getting a present from you.'

'Oh yeah? What did you have in mind?'

Mason shook his head. 'It doesn't matter.'

'You think this is all a wild goose chase?' Roxy asked more softly.

Mason looked around, saw the others mostly sleeping. 'I don't think it can hurt. And it's the only lead we have. Luciane seems pretty sure.'

Roxy nodded. Despite all the travel and the lack of sleep, Mason thought she looked fresher today, with less weight on her shoulders. 'You seem better,' he said.

'I feel better. I almost feel as though I'm through the worst of it. That I can move forward, maybe take the next step.'

'And is that visiting your family?'

'I don't know.'

Mason nodded as Roxy clammed up. She wasn't there yet, but she was closer than she'd been ever since he'd known her. It was a good sign, and might help negate any issues in the field, or when they were under pressure. He still remembered Roxy's meltdown in London. That lone incident in the London cemetery where she'd well and truly lost it. Her own deep self-analysis had put her off her game, distracted her.

The bullet train sped into Kyoto and slowed rapidly. Mason and the team got to their feet with the other passengers and jumped down onto the platform. It was a cool, clear day. There wasn't a cloud in the sky, but the sun was weak. Pedestrians thronged the platform, the stairs and, later, the pavement. Mason looked around for a good-sized taxi but saw their luck had run out. All the cars he could see were strictly five-seaters.

'Grab a minivan,' Roxy said.

'There aren't any.'

They solved their ridiculous problem by ordering an Uber and asking for a large vehicle. The Uber arrived twelve minutes later and then whisked them off, taking them through the traffic-clogged streets of Kyoto. The beautiful Japanese city perfectly balanced the conservation of its past with ultra-modern services, a peaceful soul in direct contrast to Tokyo's intensity. Mason sat back and enjoyed the ride, listening as Luciane tried to convey the address to the non-English-speaking driver.

It had taken several emails, but Freddie had finally agreed to meet them. At first he was reluctant, but Luciane had begged and cajoled and put her reputation on the line, first to get the full attention of the reclusive collector and then to lean into his emotional side. The man was still unwilling to leave his home, to even step out the front door, so they had agreed to meet him there.

The vehicle deposited them at the side of the road. Mason stepped out onto the pavement and looked around. At first, he couldn't see anything, but then saw a single, tall black gate and a winding path with high hedges. Luciane approached the gate, looked up. Mason now saw the CCTV camera mounted atop one of the brick pillars that held the gate. Luciane gave it a wave.

The gate clicked open. Luciane pushed her way in and Mason followed a second later, just before Quaid, neither man trusting this unknown recluse. The high hedges soon enfolded them in a dark tunnel, making it difficult to pick out the way forward. Mason saw more brick pillars along the way and assumed they were being monitored from those, too. The path turned and wound, once coming back on itself, so that the team felt lost. There was the merest sliver of sky above, sometimes blotted out by the leaning hedges, and they did not know where they were going. Luciane led the way; it was too narrow for anything other than single file.

Mason didn't like it. Plus, of course, they were weaponless, having just come off a flight from China. The path coiled and looped for about five minutes before ending at a set of seven round-edged concrete steps that led up to a silver-coloured metal door.

'Are you kidding me?' Quaid muttered.

Hassell looked carefully at the door and the keypad and nodded grudgingly. 'Very cool setup,' he said. 'Even I would have difficulty breaking into this place. He's the kind of guy who'll have mini magnets on all his valuables. Who uses fibre-optic sensors. Heat detection with AI. Maybe even drones.' He looked up.

Luciane ignored the security system and knocked at the door, again looking up at the camera. There was another click. This time, the front door opened a few inches. Luciane put her hand on the silver metal, pushed and watched it swing wide open. She turned to the others and shrugged.

'We're entering Fort Knox,' Roxy said with a shiver.

'Not Fort Knox,' a voice suddenly boomed out all around them. 'But I like to think, just as secure.'

Mason jumped at the sound of the voice. He hadn't expected audible devices too. He entered the house, finding himself in a narrow dark passage with doors on both sides. Luciane was already halfway down the passage.

'Through the door at the end of the hall,' the booming voice told them.

Mason studied the place as he walked. There wasn't a lot to see right now, but the walls were unadorned, the doors all closed, their handles bright and polished. The polished concrete floor was immaculate. Mason looked up. Even the bloody ceiling was pristine.

They all went through the door at the end of the hall, finding themselves in a spotless, gleaming kitchen. There was a table in the middle of the room with six chairs, all perfectly arrayed; a shiny silver sink and cupboards, a kettle and a toaster, all of which looked unused. As they stood there, the voice boomed out again.

'Onward please.' Another door clicked.

This led them out of the kitchen. Mason himself was becoming a little paranoid. This was beyond ridiculous. Still, CCTV cameras glared down at them from every corner, observing their every move.

Freddie lived a solitary life, Mason thought as he followed a well-lit corridor. A guy suffering such paranoia wouldn't get out much. His own security systems would limit him severely. So, he was a loner, a recluse, someone who liked to surround himself with ancient treasures. He enjoyed cleanliness, craved it. These modern technology systems were more than his security, they were his world.

Another door clicked open. Mason went through it to find himself, finally, in a more human space. The walls were white, the windows that looked out onto a private garden clean. Mason saw three computer desks with PCs, several laptops on coffee tables, a red leather sofa that dominated the room, a television with a PlayStation hook-up and the *Street Fighter* game paused on the big screen, a bowl of fruit and a dirty plate – the only dirty item he'd seen since they entered the place – and walls full of glass cabinets crammed with all manner of items, from those that flashed to those that swallowed the light and those that looked mean and deadly and evil.

Freddie stood at the rear of the room, looking nervous. Mason blinked at the sight of him. He was startling, six-foot-six, cadaverous-looking, skinny, with sunken eyes and long limbs. His face was white in contrast to the dark rings around his eyes; his back stooped because, maybe, he was trying to appear shorter than he actually was. Freddie smiled at them apprehensively.

Luciane walked right over to him and held out a hand. 'Luciane Harlow,' she said. 'Pleased to finally meet you.'

The emaciated man took it and stared at it as though it were something he might eat. 'Freddie,' he said shortly. 'Welcome to my home.'

'Thank you for allowing us to come here. I take it you don't get a lot of guests.'

'Only those I choose to buy from. Other than that, I am alone.'

Luciane nodded and turned to introduce the team. A minute later, Freddie strode to the centre of the room. He wore jeans and a white T-shirt with the Disney logo.

'I live a simple life,' he said. 'I don't like company. But I met you digitally –' he now turned to Luciane '– which is different. We were email buddies before we ever spoke about face to face. I felt I knew you before I ever saw you. For me, that is more important.'

Mason didn't know what to make of that and, judging by her face, neither did Roxy. He contented himself with biting his top lip and motioned that she should do the same.

But Freddie hadn't finished. 'I felt we melded through the internet,' he said. 'Became one. Didn't you feel it too?'

Luciane took a step back. 'Sure,' she said.

'I have more than one digital lady friend,' he said with a wry shake of his head. 'But when you are wealthy, you have

281

to be careful. Keep them at arm's length. The same goes for male friends, of course,' he added quickly. 'They befriend you one day and ask you to buy them a gold Rolex the next.' Again, he shook his head.

Roxy looked interested. 'You have firsthand experience of that?'

Freddie inclined his head. 'Unfortunately, yes. I have always been wealthy, you see. I have seen the worst of human avarice.'

Mason had already decided they should spend as little time in here as possible. 'I believe you bought some coins from a man named Phoenix Basso?'

Freddie took a deep breath, still reminded of covetous days, it seemed, and then smiled at Mason, an act that unsettled him. It was like being smiled at by a corpse. He reminded himself that they were here for this man's help.

'Yes, I remember the American and his two friends. They were full of themselves, hopped up on caffeine, I thought, or something worse. They told me I was the second collector they'd approached, but wouldn't reveal the name of the first.'

'Kobayashi,' Sally said.

'Ah, I thought so. He is the only other serious collector around.'

'And this was what, seven years ago?' Mason wanted to corroborate Freddie's words.

'I can tell you exactly when it was,' Freddie said. He turned around, stalked to a cabinet on the far side of the room and opened it. Luciane moved to his side, craning her neck. Mason walked closer too, feeling protective of her despite what he knew of her career. He saw Freddie pluck something out of a wooden drawer and then deposit the items in his cupped hands.

There was the dull clink of coins.

'Here,' he said, turning.

The man held out his right hand. In it, Mason saw a pile of dull, yellowish coins. They were small with a gnarled edge and the head of a man on one side, the outline of a figure on the other. The head wore a crown; the figure reclined on a seat and had a bow in one hand. Mason saw Freddie had not even attempted to clean the coins, but kept them in their original state.

'Those are the coins?' Luciane asked in a hushed, reverent voice. She looked up at Freddie, who gave her a slight nod. Luciane plucked one coin from the pile and held it between forefinger and thumb, rubbing it and then turning it over and over, examining the surfaces, an expression of happiness on her face.

'They're incredible,' she said.

'The genuine article,' Freddie said. 'Six-hundred-year-old casino coins, dated two hundred years *before* the world's first known casino opened its doors in Venice.' He deposited a few more coins into Luciane's hands.

Luciane held them in awe. 'My investigations led me far and wide,' she said. 'My investigations into the sales of these coins, but I never thought they'd lead me here. Thank you, Freddie, for letting me hold them. I can't imagine how precious they are, how important to the world.'

The lanky man inclined his head before turning to Mason. 'I keep records of those who sell me my treasures, when, how, everything I can think of to ask. Provenance is all. As I'm sure you know, being treasure hunters yourselves. The record attached to these coins tells me I bought them from one Phoenix Basso and his associates, one Rufus Silver and one Rory Thompson.' He opened

283

the cabinet to its maximum extent, peered inside and then reeled off a date.

'Seven years, three months ago,' Quaid said.

'Perfect,' Mason said. 'That slots in nicely. Now, what else can you tell us about these men?'

Freddie raised a single eyebrow, the gesture somehow making him look even more threatening. 'Is that why you're here?'

Since Luciane seemed to be enthralled, her voice lost in the wonder of handling the coins, Sally took over. 'You may be in danger,' she said. 'A secret group called the Shadow Kings has got wind that these coins are out there, that someone found the ancient casino, and has sent a group of mercenaries with a terrible plan, a mission to kill all involved and keep the initial finding of the casino and all its relics to themselves. We're attempting to combat them at the same time as trying to find the casino and catalogue it for the whole world.'

'Danger?' Freddie said. 'I've heard of the Shadow Kings in my various everyday dealings with lost treasures. Their reputation is…evil. What do you want from me?'

Mason could see that Freddie was rattled. He kept his voice steady and low. 'Just please tell us about Phoenix Basso and his associates. Anything you can remember about them.'

Freddie gave them a long frown as he thought about it. 'These Americans,' he reiterated. 'Always talking. Always bragging. They loved their gambling.'

'They were consummate gamblers?' Sally asked.

'Yes, they came at me with every scenario for Texas Hold 'Em. Even wanted me to play a hand, but I brushed them off.'

'In here? Like this?' Mason wouldn't have thought it possible.

'Yes, in my home, behind all the locked doors and the surveillance cameras. Said it reminded them of their home.'

'Their home?' Mason sensed a breakthrough coming.

Freddie nodded rapidly. 'They told me they came from the finest gambling capital of the world. The very best. I don't know that I agree with them.'

Mason latched on to that. 'Did they say where it was?'

'Isn't it obvious?' Freddie asked. 'They told me they lived in Las Vegas.'

Mason felt something akin to an electric shock. 'They *told* you that's where they lived?'

'Several times,' Freddie said. 'Told me they were the ultimate gamblers – treasure hunters. That's what treasure hunting was, they said. An enormous gamble, the biggest gamble of their lives. But then they bragged how they could go back to their favourite casinos and gamble with something other than their lives.'

Mason looked at Quaid, who gave him a small grin. Suddenly, the window wasn't so large; suddenly it seemed rather narrow.

'Las Vegas,' Mason repeated slowly.

'Haven't been for a while,' Roxy told him.

'That's about to change.' Sally turned to look at her.

'It's a crazy, mad, glamorous, glitzy whirlwind of a place,' Roxy warned her.

'Oh, I know,' Sally replied. 'And that's why it's perfect for us.'

Chapter 38

Captain Daichi Miura of the Special Exercise Division tapped ash from his unfiltered cigarette onto Kobayashi's bloody, dripping corpse. He held a military blade in one hand, a steaming iron in the other. The interrogation had gone well; the blistered pile of red flesh in front of him attested to that. Miura grinned, sorry that Kobayashi had expired so early, sorry that he couldn't make the man's eyes bulge and his breath whistle some more.

Around the room, the rest of his team watched impassively.

They weren't bothered, Miura knew. They lived to serve the Shadow Kings, and this was what *they* desired. They deserved to know whatever Kobayashi had known, and Miura had extracted every last delicious morsel out of him.

The living room where he worked was slick with blood. It covered the floor, leaked through the sofa, hung heavy and metallic in the air. There were even whorls of blood on the ceiling. Miura felt happy about that, satisfied. It meant he'd done his job well and placated the hunger that always prowled inside.

He took a long drag on the cigarette, letting the smoke fill his lungs. His men stood stoically, unmoved. The only man in the room with anything other than a gravelly expression on his face was Kobayashi's betrayer – the one called Ito. He was standing in a corner, flanked by two men who held their guns loosely but visibly. Ito looked sick.

'Leave the corpse where it is,' Miura said unnecessarily. 'It will be noted as a gangland killing.'

He then turned a heavy-lidded gaze onto Ito. 'Why did you betray this man? Your boss.'

Ito swallowed heavily, his throat clicking with dryness. 'He disrespected me. My place. He cared nothing for my brother, who gave his life.'

'So he wasn't a good boss?'

'The worst.'

'But we cannot pick our bosses,' Miura went on. 'We can only serve them, trust that they know the bigger picture, that they have our best intentions at heart when they fight the dirty, corrupt enemy. That is a soldier's lot, yes?'

'I am not a soldier.'

'What are you then?' Miura cleaned the knife on the edge of the sofa, wiping the blood away, watching as it came off in thick smears. Kobayashi had bled in copious amounts. It had been wonderful.

'Do you believe the things your boss told me were true?'

'About the Americans? Yes.'

'Why?'

'He…he was so desperate in the end.'

Miura nodded. 'I thought so, too. Like a fat, crying baby. An infant who knows no better. He should have stayed strong.'

Ito stared at him, eyes wide. Miura could tell what he

was thinking. Who could possibly stay strong under that kind of pressure?

'Do you have something else to say?' he asked.

'No, sir. Nothing.'

'We seem to have made a bit of a mess of your apartment.'

'That is okay. It will get cleaned.'

Miura finished his cigarette, flicked the butt at the dripping corpse. Still holding the knife, he approached Ito, pressed the tip of the blade to the man's throat. Ito forced his head back until the wall stopped it.

'You betrayed your betters,' Miura said and shoved the entire blade through the man's throat. Ito's eyes went wide and he choked. Miura stared at him, lowering his bald head so that he could see the man's eyes more clearly. There was an agony there so deep that it filled Miura's heart. He drank in the man's beautiful, profound agony. This man had not expected to die. He thought he'd done the right thing, made new friends, but Miura couldn't let anyone live who went against the will of his leaders.

'Let this be a lesson,' he said. 'We serve the leaders. We will do exactly as they command. There is no alternative.'

Some men nodded, others muttered in agreement. Miura withdrew his knife and let Ito's body slide to the floor. He turned away, dismissing it. Took a phone out of his pocket and dialled his superior.

'Captain.' The man answered the call immediately. 'Have you secured the place?'

Miura knew he meant the casino, that the boss was asking if the mission was over. 'No,' he said, hoping the negative wouldn't put him on an instant kill list. 'But there are developments.'

'Explain.'

Miura peeled drying blood from his fingers. 'We interrogated one of the buyers,' he said, knowing his superior would understand the reference. 'Opened him up good. He told us everything that he knew.'

'Excellent. I am listening.'

'He told me that three Americans approached him with bags of coins. This was seven years ago. He told me the names of the Americans and where they lived. His feelings were…that they would still be there.'

There was a long silence as the boss considered this. 'How would he know that?' he asked.

'The way the Americans talked, how they presented their homes and, frankly, where and how they lived.'

'Go on.'

'The American city of Las Vegas,' Miura said. 'These raiders, these archaeological leeches, are exultant, lifelong gamblers. They feed their habit by locating treasures.'

'You think they will still be there?'

'I think there's a very good chance.'

Another silence, this one profound. The boss knew exactly what he was being asked, and the answer wasn't clear-cut. 'You know what you're asking?'

Miura flicked blood onto the floor. 'It is where the clues lead, sir. We should go immediately.'

'To Las Vegas?' The boss sounded like he was being strangled.

'Are you okay?'

'No, no, not at all. This is a potential career suicide. Well, pure suicide. If you fail…'

Miura knew exactly what the boss was saying. If anything went wrong, they might both end up dead. The Shadow Kings would not tolerate any kind of open failure.

'We won't fail,' Miura said. 'I have come this far without losing a man.'

'You are still thirteen strong?'

'We are.'

'Do you think your men could handle a trip to Las Vegas?'

Miura considered that. The question wasn't as silly as it first sounded. He had twelve highly trained, incredibly capable, vicious men with him, all of whom were perfectly willing to take out any target he set before them at any time. They weren't normal people, not civilians by any means. They were at best animals. Of course, eternally better than the scum they would have to mingle with, but nevertheless animals. Dangerous, savage; they had a different brain-set to the standard, pliable, steady citizen.

How would they mix?

Miura wanted them to mingle, to see what would happen, but he knew that any kind of overt incident might embarrass his boss. That couldn't be allowed to happen. Were his men capable of causing that embarrassment? Absolutely.

'I believe we must make the journey,' Miura said. 'Because, if this Basso reveals the location of the casino to our enemy, then all is lost.'

The boss let out a heavy sigh. 'You are right, I suppose. But I have to warn you – keep your men and yourself under control. If you have to…use your special skills…do it where it can be passed off as something else, something local. Do you understand?'

Miura understood perfectly. What the boss was saying was standard protocol. It was nothing new.

'Can you organise the correct visas and airline tickets?' he asked.

290

'That is easy, the least of our worries. I have people who can do that at the drop of a hat. We got you into Japan with ease, didn't we?'

Miura accepted that. He smiled at all the blood, at the grim faces of his men, at the nightmarish room with its chopped-up corpse, its stench of blood and death, the fallen figure of Ito, the picture of mortality and murder that it represented, and wondered how all this might transfer to Las Vegas.

It could be beautiful.

'Book us on a flight to America,' he said. 'We can handle anything that arises.'

'You can track down this Basso person?'

'No. That is for your phalanx of office workers to do. I know you have hundreds at your disposal.'

'Very well. That is all.'

The phone went dead. Miura continued to revel in the room, not wanting to leave. Finally, he turned to his men.

'We have work to do,' he said, and slipped his knife back into its sheath.

Chapter 39

Mason liked the way Paul Quaid made the best use of his time.

They were inside the Narita International Airport waiting for their fourteen-hour one-stop flight to Las Vegas. They had booked to fly with Air Canada with a stop-off in LAX, not the cheapest but the fastest flight they could find right now, and were keeping an eye on the ever-changing flight information boards. It was evening in Japan, and the terminal was thick with people, most carting their carry-on luggage around, parents and couples and children and security staff all mingling, the air hostesses occasionally forging a path through to their flights in a swathe of colour, the captains in their caps and uniforms smiling as they went. Mason and his team had worked their way through security and past the duty free to find a quiet corner about three hundred yards from their designated gate. They were sitting beside a window, looking out at a runway through the drizzle-coated glass and chatting.

But it was Quaid who was doing the work.

Ever since he'd sat down, he'd been on the phone, calling his contacts in America and then focusing on Nevada, trying to get the ball rolling on Phoenix Basso's current whereabouts. One of Quaid's biggest assets was his worldwide contacts, established when he'd been a British army officer and enhanced later when he'd taken to helping the needy with traded goods from Bethlehem to Birmingham. Quaid had built up an army of connections. Now, they needed him to do his thing.

'Fifth call,' he said aloud, jabbing at his phone. 'So far I've spoken to a cop, a judge, a waitress and a millionaire. You'd be amazed at how much diverse influence you can bring to a problem with a bit of thought.'

Mason listened as someone answered Quaid's call.

'Bill?' he said and then went through the introductions eagerly before landing on the point of his call.

'I'm looking for someone and I think you can help me. A man named Phoenix Basso lives in your town, in your area. He has two associates by the names of Rufus Silver and Rory Thompson. Now, I'm not saying they're criminals, but *may* have files on them. They're gamblers, chronic gamblers, and are probably well known in certain casinos. These people have a connection. I'm guessing the leader at least will be relatively well-off.' For good measure, he gave his friend a description of Basso too. 'Tall with long blond hair tied up in a bun. The little finger on his left hand is missing. His teeth are yellow. He has blue eyes and a winning smile. That should give you something to work on.'

Quaid ended the call after a few more minutes of chit-chat.

'Who's next?' Mason asked.

'Stripper,' Quaid said.

293

'Friend of yours?' Roxy asked, with an arched eyebrow.

'Very much. A lovely girl. And it shouldn't really surprise you to hear strippers know an awful lot of what goes on in the underbelly of a great city.'

Mason passed the time people-watching. He wandered over to the duty free and browsed, absently watching out for anyone who might resemble an SED soldier. He didn't expect anything to stand out – in fact, he felt a little foolish keeping watch in the civilian-heavy airport – but you never could be sure.

Time passed. The hour of their flight grew closer. Mason and the others fought fatigue – they'd been on the go now with little rest for days. The clinical interior of the airport didn't promote relaxation, not for Mason, at least. Quaid called fourteen people, not all in Nevada, and then sat back to await the return calls, stating he'd done all he could.

'You expect anything positive?' Luciane asked him.

Quaid nodded. 'It should be simple enough for the cops. All the other calls are just backup.'

But nobody had called back at all by the time their flight was called. Mason led the way to the desk, passed through the passport checks and walked the length of the jet bridge, finally stepping onto the plane to be greeted by a flight attendant. He then picked his way down the aisle, found his seat and slid his rucksack into the luggage compartment. Now he had time to kill. He wondered if, for a change, he might be able to sleep on board a plane.

It wasn't to be. The plane took off. The flight attendants came around with drinks and snacks. The team had split up, being unable to find adjacent seats because of their late arrival. Meals came and then the stop at LAX where Quaid briefly fired up his phone. His message service bleeped. He'd received seven messages in return, none of them positive, and none of them from any police-based entities. By the time they'd left LAX, Quaid had received one more message, this one also negative.

Mason worried. They were on the last leg to Las Vegas. Time and opportunity were slipping away. He settled back again, wide awake despite his body crying out for rest and relaxation.

It was 3.30 p.m. local time when the plane touched down with a whoosh of air brakes and a squeal of tyres. It slowed and then taxied slowly to its gate where it parked, the journey seeming to take for ever. Finally it stopped. Everyone stood up and went nowhere and, ten minutes later, started filing out. Mason waited for his friends to join him and then went ahead of them, crossing the jet bridge once again and finding himself in the terminal on US soil. This was McCarran Airport and would serve as their entry point to Las Vegas.

Even as they walked through the terminal's interminably polished passageways amid the crowd on their way to check-in, Mason turned to Quaid.

'Switched your phone on?'

'Yeah, it's switched networks again. Just waiting for a connection.'

Mason needn't have hurried. The long walk continued until, eventually, they came into a vast hall where the US Border Patrol were waiting. They joined the long queue, shuffled dutifully down the line, showed their passports, bypassed the baggage carousel and headed straight for the arrivals hall. Once there, surrounded by streams of people, fast-food restaurants, enormous potted plants and high ceilings and a stirring atmosphere of bustle, Quaid's phone rang.

'Bloody typical,' he said, fishing it out.

Mason watched him stick a finger into one ear and yell, 'Hello? Who is this?'

Quaid listened, then looked up. He said, 'Just hold on. We're in arrivals. Let me get to a place where I can hear you.'

Roxy pulled them into a restaurant that wasn't doing brisk business. It was tiny, designed as a takeaway, with just a few plastic seats and chairs inside. Mason ignored the guy behind the counter, who asked him what he wanted the instant he stepped into the joint and looked around. Apart from the server, they were alone.

Quaid put his phone on speaker. 'Go on, Bill,' he said.

'Phoenix Basso isn't his proper name,' the cop told them. 'It's Philip. Probably uses Phoenix because it sounds good, to him at least. Lives on Calico Ridge, Henderson, east of Las Vegas. You won't easily find him there, though.'

'What do you mean?' Quaid asked.

'Like you told me, he's a gambler. Spends most of his time in the city, on the Strip. Yeah, he's loaded, got a few bank accounts we can see and some we can't. No sweat. It's enough to see the guy ain't short of the green stuff.'

'Does he have any favourite haunts?' Quaid asked.

'Yeah, the In-N-Out Burger on the Strip near the Flamingo.'

'No, I didn't mean that. I meant—'

'I know what you meant. Getting this information wasn't easy, Quaid. I had to invent a fake case. I hope you got something for me.'

'Will Captain Morgan Cannon Blast do?'

'You're kidding? Last seen July 2020.'

'They discontinued it, but I recall it's your favourite.'

'You have some?'

296

'A full box just for you.'

Mason knew Quaid still kept a couple of storehouses going in case any of his more precious contacts needed something. In his previous life, it had all been about greasing palms.

'Might take me a few weeks,' Quaid said.

'I can live with that for the good stuff. So...your man, Phoenix Basso. He frequents Caesars.'

'Palace?'

'Yeah, Caesars Palace. What else would it be?'

'That's a pretty big place, if I remember correctly.'

'You can say that again,' the cop drawled on. 'Over 180 gaming tables, 1,300 slot machines. You like poker? You got Pai Gow, Hold 'Em. Let it Ride. Three Card. $500 slots. Christ, I sound like an advert. Oh, it's a big place all right. Six hotel towers. Nearly 4,000 rooms. 166,000 square feet of gaming space. Restaurants. Nightclubs. There's—'

'What game does he play?' Mason asked quietly. 'That should narrow it down a bit.'

Quaid asked the question.

'Blackjack,' came the immediate answer. 'There are fifty tables at Caesars.'

'Any idea of the split?' Quaid asked. 'Where they are.'

'Eight in the high limit saloon. Nineteen eight-decks on the main casino floor. Nine in front of the Nobu nightclub. Others are located in the pit near the sports book and behind the main pit.'

'You say he spends all his time there?' Luciane asked. 'Where's he sleep?'

'Caesars and its sister casinos are well known for establishing good blackjack relationships with their clients,' Bill answered. 'It offers substantial repeat comps. Starts off

297

with free drinks but then, as you return more and more often, that turns into free rooms. Wouldn't surprise me if your man Phoenix didn't have a standing free reservation.'

'There are six of us,' Quaid said. 'We should be able to cover the tables easily.'

'There is one item of news you may not like,' the cop called Bill said.

Mason found that he'd been half listening, half watching the flow of people that passed the open restaurant. Now, he turned towards the phone.

'What news?' he asked.

'You mentioned that Phoenix Basso had two associates. Rufus Silver and Rory Thompson.'

Quaid nodded at the phone. 'He did. They helped him steal the coins from the Chinese casino.'

'Silver and Thompson are both dead. Years ago. Silver died in a vehicle collision on the I15 in 2017. Thompson unfortunately caught cancer and died back in 2019. Neither death was suspicious.'

Quaid looked surprised. 'Ah, thanks for that, Bill. I guess we're lucky Basso is still alive.'

'I guess you are. And, Quaid, don't forget that Cannon Blast.'

Quaid assured the man he had him covered and then ended the call. They all looked at each other. Roxy was the first to walk out of the exit. She looked back as she went.

'What are you waiting for?' she said. 'We just got an excuse to gamble in Vegas. Are you coming with me?'

Mason almost ran after her.

Chapter 40

Las Vegas is a globally famous resort city, celebrated for its no-holds-barred gambling, its world-class shopping, cutting-edge dining, diverse entertainment and glitzy nightlife. The Strip itself resonates with every kind of experience imaginable, a place where a man or woman can be anything they want to be. In Vegas, nobody really knows you. It's an extravagant playground, an all-day buffet where everything is on the table. From the Strip to the landmark casinos to the concert halls, from the buffets and slots and rollercoasters and clubs to the incredible restaurants, there is a magnetic energy in the air, an expectation of the best of times. A hypnotic buzz unavailable anywhere else.

You don't visit Vegas. You live it like it's your last day on Earth.

These thoughts ran through Joe Mason's mind as he climbed into a large taxi with his team and made the brief journey from McCarran to Las Vegas Boulevard, using South University Centre Drive. From red light to red light, they picked their way, sitting back and taking in the sights.

The pavements were full of life, from beggars to dancers to tourists and children, from magicians to cops to partygoers and families. When they stopped at crosswalks, throngs of people strolled by, blocking out all other sights.

As they neared the Strip, Mason made out the themed hotels and casinos. They came to East Flamingo and took a left, followed the road for a while, past congestion where the road branched for Koval. They came up to the Strip near the Flamingo with the Bellagio and its famous fountains to the left, Caesars Palace to the right, then joined the crawling traffic on the wide boulevard. Roxy had her nose to the window, calling out the sights, seemingly quite pleased to be back in her native country.

Mason turned to her as the car inched its way towards Caesars.

'Happy to be home?' he asked. 'In America, I mean.'

'I'm not sure.'

'Where do your parents live?'

'Los Angeles,' she said and, when Mason raised an eyebrow, elaborated slightly. 'An old A-frame in the Hollywood Hills.'

'How hard would it be to go back there now?'

Roxy glanced at him. 'I don't know. I'm growing, I'm raising barriers, but I'm not sure I'm there yet.'

'I think you are.'

'Thank you. We'll see.'

She wasn't any more forthcoming than that. It surprised Mason that she didn't try to turn the conversation back onto him and *his* current situation, but then she seemed entirely too ensnared by the streets of Las Vegas to even think about him. At the next lights, they were the first car, and Mason was treated to the sight of the Bellagio fountains in full flow, the music reverberating across the Strip. More than a thousand illuminated fountains swayed and danced and jetted to the beat of a song, captivating Mason for long minutes. Then they were past the junction and approaching the long road that marked the entrance to Caesars Palace. The taxi driver drove them right up to the front door and let them out into the mid-afternoon sunshine. The day was hot, the sun blasting down from a cloudless sky, reminding Mason that, even here, right now, they were in the middle of a desert. From the Gobi to the Mojave in just a few days.

Stretching above them, the impressive façade of Caesars Palace appeared to touch the very skies.

They didn't stay outside long, but walked quickly through revolving doors into a dim, highly polished interior. The air conditioning was chilly, the circular area inside trimmed with golden lighting, statues and a wide black desk. Mason was immediately lost and turned to the others.

'Anyone know which way to go?'

These places were labyrinths, he knew, designed to keep people at the tables, the shops and the restaurants, spending money. Of course, Sally had a floor plan ready on her phone.

'Turn right,' she said. 'And then follow the casino signs. But listen, these places are a maze, the crowds are big and Vegas itself is a frenzied mess. If we get split up, meet at the old Casino Royale, let's say near the blackjack tables, to be safe.'

Mason liked the idea, and the place where they would meet. He knew Quaid would. The reference to the English super agent would tickle his old-fashioned sense of pride.

They took their time, ambling through the softly lit, gleaming hallways that wound their way through the hotel. Before they'd gone very far, Sally reminded them that it was already four p.m. and wondered if they should book some rooms just to be safe. They took their seats on a plush, studded leather bench and waited for her to reserve the rooms online.

Quaid shook his head at her. 'It isn't right,' he said, ever against the most modern technology. 'We're here, standing inside the damn place, and you're still using that thing to communicate with a bunch of other things like it to book us a bloody room. What happened to face to face?'

This time, Mason knew where Quaid was coming from. After all, they were inside Caesars, booking rooms to stay at Caesars. He watched as Sally lifted her chin and looked up at Quaid.

'Done,' she said. 'It's quicker this way.'

Quaid huffed. 'Nobody enjoys standing at a check-in desk,' he said. 'But there are limits.'

They continued winding along the glossy hallways, threading their way through the crowds. They wandered past Beijing Noodle and the Apostrophe Bar, past the elevators to the Julius Tower, still following signs to the Palace Casino. Roxy saw a sign for Nobu, and then they were inside the gaming area itself, standing under sprawling golden lighting that spread out like an octopus from a central point, and facing hundreds of crowded tables. The noise levels were high, carried around the room and amid the heights of the ceiling.

They stopped halfway along one aisle that led between tables. Mason spoke to them all. 'Split up. Meet back here in twenty. See how many blackjack tables you can cover.'

In his mind, and in all their minds, was the description of Phoenix Basso. Of course, he might have changed his hair, maybe even whitened his teeth, but he couldn't have grown another finger and his eyes would still be blue. If they saw a likely candidate, there was nothing stopping them from asking the man's name.

The casino buzzed all around them. People jostled gently, bent over the tables, most watching. The dealers stood with their backs straight, looking out over the crowd or focusing on their own games. Mason saw a wide cross-section of humanity, from men and women dressed up to the nines to youths wearing jeans and a T-shirt, just as he was. The hub of it all was the gambling, the blackjack and the roulette and the craps. Here, one group cheered. There, another horde gasped. Directly in front of Mason, a man shouted in anger and then flung his chips to the ground. Mason walked around the gaming tables, threading his way between the busy islands. He found one blackjack table and studied the players and those standing close by. The half-round table had a pink rim and pink logos and the words 'Pussycat Dolls' written all over it. Mason wasn't sure what the hell that meant and walked on. The next table had a brown wooden rim, the table all wood. He studied the men all around, looked at them carefully and did a full 360 of the table. He saw no one matching Basso's description.

Mason was flagging now. He couldn't remember the last time he'd slept properly, or even eaten well. He checked the time. It was past five p.m. He checked another five tables and then made his way back to the Caesars rendezvous point.

'Anything?' he asked.

Roxy and Quaid shook their heads. Soon, Sally, Luciane and Hassell arrived, all looking disconsolate.

'No luck,' Sally said, a phrase which made Roxy laugh, considering where they were. 'Listen,' she said. 'We're all knackered. My guess is that Basso, if he comes, will make an appearance later. He'll be a night owl, I'm guessing. How about we go to our rooms, take a break and meet later around seven-thirty?'

Mason liked the plan. It took for ever to walk back to reception, get their key cards and then find their rooms. Mason found himself following endless lustrous marbled floors and walls until he came to a small elevator, took it up to the ninth floor and stepped out into a thickly carpeted corridor. He followed the doors down until he came to his own, used the keycard and let himself inside. Once there, he didn't look around, didn't wash, didn't do anything. He just let himself fall onto the bed, exhausted. He set his alarm for seven and took advantage of some sleep.

When the buzzer went off, he groaned and reached out to switch it off. He sat up, not feeling much better, and drank a cup of water. He looked around. White blinds hung down a far window, a two-seater sofa next to them. The bed was wide and very comfortable, the headboard white leather and plush. He went to the window, looked down, saw the pool area lit with a deep blue hue. People were swimming way down there and sat along the edges, their feet dangling. Mason watched for a minute, then remembered that they were due to meet in the casino at 7.30. He'd better hurry, considering the time it would take him to walk there. Quickly, he changed T-shirts, drank more water and splashed his face, hoping to wake himself up. It helped a little. He left the room.

He paced the long corridor, saw a tall, narrow window at its end, and made his way over. From here, he could see the Paris Casino's Eiffel Tower in all its golden, flashing glory and, to the right, the fountains of the Bellagio swaying and spouting, all wreathed in bright golden light. He leant his forehead on the cold glass, which helped soothe a growing headache. Turning away from the impressive sight, he found the elevators and took one to the ground. Then, walking quickly, barely seeing the surrounding décor of black busts and statues and carvings, elegant shopfronts, stylish restaurants and enormous white Caesar sculpture, he whittled a relatively straight path through the tourists back to the casino, where Roxy and Sally were waiting for him.

'You're late,' Roxy said when she saw him.

'It's the size of this bloody place. You're best booking a taxi to get back to your room.'

'We've already started looking,' Sally said. 'Did you get some sleep?'

'The moment my head hit the pillow,' he said. 'I needed it.'

'A few drinks set me up for the evening,' Roxy told him.

'Standard practice,' he said. 'Now, remember, there are a thousand cameras on us. Look for your man, but try not to look too suspicious.'

Sally nodded. 'Quaid's already at a table, blending in,' she said. 'Hassell's on his way. Luciane is on the prowl.'

Mason nodded, checked his wallet and saw he had enough money to sit for a few hands of blackjack. He started looking for Basso, searched three tables and then hid his intentions by sitting down and playing a hand. After he drew eighteen and the dealer drew twenty, he rose, searched another three tables and played another hand. The other five, he hoped, were doing something similar. That was how they could examine the casino's fifty blackjack tables without much risk of Basso slipping past them unnoticed.

Another thing they expected from the man was that he would linger. He was a face here, a part of the décor, at home, in his element. He would know everyone, and they would know him. No way would Basso be in a hurry.

An hour passed, and then ten p.m. flashed by. Mason ran out of money and had to grab another wad out of the cash machine. The irony of gambling, losing and rushing up to an ATM to gamble and lose some more wasn't lost on him. The crowds thickened as the night deepened, prompting a slight worry: would a seasoned gambler come when the crowds were thickest, during the night, or when they were at their thinnest, in the mornings? The fear ate at him, made him doubt what they were doing. He played another game of blackjack, lost, walked around for a while and then sat down at another table.

Another game played. This time he won, at least a small amount, which he pocketed in triumph. There was something special about beating a Las Vegas casino.

Bang on eleven p.m., Luciane sent them all a message on their group app. Mason heard the chime, fished his phone out and checked it quickly. There were just two words, but they sent a bolt of electricity through him.

Got him.

In her excitement, Luciane had failed to pinpoint her position. Mason spent five minutes looking for her and, even as he approached the table, saw their target sat hunched behind it. Phoenix Basso hadn't changed much at all. The hair was still done up in a bun, the eyes blue, the smiling teeth yellow. And the hand he held the cards with only had four fingers. Mason could clearly see the pinky finger had been severed just below the knuckle.

Mason slowed and took a deep breath. This was the moment they'd come all this way for, the moment of truth. Would Basso even deign to converse with them?

They gathered around him, watching him. They pretended to watch the play, inched closer and closer until they stood to the left and right of him. Basso played the cards like a pro, barely glancing at them most of the time. He doubled his bet when the first two cards totalled eleven, split pairs of aces and eights, and paid attention to the flows in streaks. A winning streak saw him raising his bets, a losing one lowering them. He tipped well, didn't listen to other players' advice and played his own hand.

Basso showed no signs of leaving the table as the night went on. All around, people came and went, players ducked in and out, and Basso stayed put. So far, he was up by several hundred.

Mason ordered a beer and waited, hoping to catch Basso as he flitted between tables. The others waited too, exchanging glances. Roxy downed two rums and then started sipping a third, her eyes bright under the lights. Mason noticed she looked at home here, in this environment, and was reminded of her old job. He guessed she'd had to learn to adapt to any scenario, to appear comfortable with any situation. She smiled and nodded at the admiring glances, brushed an advance away with a slight shake of her head, looked invested in the gaming table and how its customers were doing.

Mason sipped his beer. He waited...

...and he waited.

Chapter 41

Finally, as Basso didn't look like moving, Mason bowed his head until it was close to the man's ear. 'Phoenix Basso?' he asked.

The head turned towards him, the blue eyes flashing. 'Who are you?' he asked sharply. 'What do you want?'

'We need to talk to you. We need your help.'

'I'm busy.'

Mason kept his voice low, under the general hubbub that surrounded the table, but could already see the dealer watching him out of the corner of his eye. He said, 'Sorry, mate, but we really need your help.'

'Go away.'

'It will just take a few minutes.'

Basso spun towards him. 'I don't ask for help. I don't give help. Now, fuck off before I call security.'

Mason straightened, sighed. The others had been listening. Now, it was Sally who bent down so that she could whisper in the man's ear.

'What can we do to get you to help us?'

Now Basso turned a scheming eye on her. 'What can you do?' he asked. 'Look where we are. What do you think you can do?'

Sally frowned. Mason found he was being crowded now, the people to left and right getting closer as the game became more interesting. There was a man's bracelet-covered wrist to his left, a woman leaning over to the right with a golden necklace flashing under the lights. Bodies were close. He accidentally brushed up against Basso.

Sally put her hand on his shoulder. 'You want us to stake you?'

'More than a little.'

Mason understood now. Of course, money motivated Basso. He was a gambler, a treasure hunter, a purveyor of the dollar bill. Nothing would motivate him more than cold, hard cash.

Sally slipped her purse down between them and clipped it open. She showed him the wads of cash inside, then closed it and hugged it to her chest. The blue tips of her hair hung between them.

'Tell me what you want,' she said.

'That depends on how I can help you.'

Sally smiled at him. 'Let me tell you. It won't take long, I promise.'

Phoenix Basso scooped up his chips, took his jacket from the back of the chair and stepped away from the table. His place was filled immediately. He beckoned to Sally and Mason, and then strode across the carpet to one of the marble walkways that wound through the casino. Following it, Basso led them to a dimly lit corner where a black couch filled a wide niche. He waved them to the seat as if he owned the place and then took his place beside them. A member of staff appeared out of nowhere and took Basso's drinks order, allowing Roxy to add a small rum to the total. The gaming tables were still nearby, the conversation washed over them like a wave, but at least they could talk in private now.

'Sorry about that,' Basso said to Mason. 'I have to establish my position first. They love me here.'

'Understood.'

Basso turned to Sally. 'What do you want from me? And make it quick – they'll miss me.'

Mason thought the man might be jaded, self-centred or just oblivious. Sally put a hand on his arm to grab his attention.

'Listen. You are part of a great treasure hunting team, we know that...'

Clearly, Mason thought. She's gone with the jaded option.

'We respect that,' Sally went on. 'Am I right in thinking you haven't done anything for years?'

Basso was frowning and looking unfriendly. 'That's not my fault. My friends...they died. Poor old Rufus lost control at the wheel and the big C got Rory. They were loners, left all their money to me. Now I got this place.' He gestured expansively. 'I come here every day. I'm family.' He sat back, looking exhausted.

Sally tried to revive his enthusiasm. 'Something you did seven years ago has recently come back to light. It's on the world stage.'

Basso's frown deepened. He didn't move.

'And not in a good way,' Roxy added.

Basso watched her with lidded eyes.

Sally went on, 'You found something in the Gobi Desert. An ancient Chinese casino. And then you sold bags of coins to various collectors. Remember?'

Basso now looked uncomfortable. His eyes swept the entire area as if scanning for security. 'I can't admit to that. What of it?'

Sally continued, 'The bags of coins were recently stolen. They're turning up in dribs and drabs all over Japan. This has attracted the attention of a nasty entity called the Shadow Kings, and us. These Shadow Kings know there's the world's oldest casino out there and they know we are on the trail.'

Basso blinked at her. 'I don't like the sound of that.'

'You shouldn't. The Shadow Kings are unadulterated evil. We've tracked down various people who sold or passed on the coins. We've even tracked down two of the collectors you used. But, my friend, you gave them the wrong information. You hid the location of the casino.'

'Which led you straight back to me.' Basso sat up now, looking more interested. 'I knew I should've just been straight.'

'That was silly,' Luciane said.

'We were younger back then. Stupid. High on excitement. We'd made a significant discovery, and we wanted to share the wealth of that discovery, verbally, of course, not physically. Were we too loquacious? Yes. Did we care back then? No. Wait...' he added. 'Wait. Are you saying the Shadow Kings are now looking for me?'

Sally nodded. 'I'm afraid so.'

'But you guys found me...' He hesitated, thinking.

Sally nodded, and Mason leaned in. He said, 'Care to help us?'

'How?'

'We need the location of that casino. And then you need to go to ground until we find it.'

Basso stared at them, scanning their faces. 'It's as simple as that?'

Mason nodded. 'The Shadow Kings want to keep it to themselves. They probably want to sell the artefacts rather than preserve them for historical value. We think the world should see it first, seeing as it's the biggest archaeological breakthrough of our lifetimes. Not only that, they kidnapped and interrogated Luciane here for information. They would have killed her. They've killed others, sent an SED hit team.'

'The Shadow Kings go all in,' Sally said.

Basso looked stunned. 'I get it,' he said. 'We took on a lot of risk back in the day. Some dangerous treasure hunts. We knew what we were up against, searching for caves in the Amazon or tunnels in Iraq. You knew the danger, and you planned for it. But here, in Vegas? Are you kidding? They wouldn't come for me here.'

'They came for me in Dublin,' Luciane said evenly.

'They came for us in Hong Kong,' Hassell said. 'On a tourist-filled gambling boat.'

Basso again searched the room, this time looking for murderous assassins. 'You wanna know where the casino is?'

Sally let the excitement show on her face. 'Yes, we do.'

'And then you're going to find it? Expose it to the world?'

'Yes, we are. We can't allow the Shadow Kings to get away with what they're doing with the SED.'

'All right.' Basso gulped his drink and tried to catch the eye of a passing waitress. Failed. He put the drink on the floor and bit his lip. 'I remember that trip well. It was a good trip. Set us up, really. Set us all up. And you're right. I gave Kobayashi and that other guy a bogus location – the Mogao Caves or something,' he chuckled. 'Wild goose chase.'

'We know that,' Roxy said ironically. 'We found out the hard way.'

'Oh, you went?' Basso laughed now. 'I'm impressed you got that far. Well, I hope you still have your Chinese visas, because you're going to have to go back.'

'We figured out that much,' Quaid said impatiently.

'Right, well, beyond the Mogao Caves in the desert, I can give you a GPS starting point, you should find an area of brick walls. Just old fortifications rotting in the desert. There are dozens of them. Nothing to do with the old casino, just decrepit old buildings. Not much left. Anyway, that's your marker. From the furthest eastern wall, you walk back north for a few hundred yards, then turn until you have a jagged hill in your sights, not a sand dune, and walk for two hundred yards. It's parched there, very hard-packed as opposed to much of the Gobi, which is drifting, unstable.'

Basso went on, imparting a few more directions until Mason's head hurt. Luckily, both Sally and Luciane were typing it all out on their phones. Quaid had a pen and paper and was copying it down old school. Mason turned his attention to the packed casino, the tangle of bodies that seemed to grow thicker the later it got.

He turned and put a hand on Sally's arm. 'Do you have everything?'

She nodded. 'I think so. Assuming our new friend here told the truth.'

'It's all good,' Basso affirmed.

'Excellent.' Mason pulled her to her feet. 'Because we have company. Move. *Move*. We have to get the hell out of here.'

313

Chapter 42

Mason grabbed hold of Phoenix Basso and ran. Or at least, he moved as fast as he could. The casino was packed, heaving with bodies all dressed up for a good night, the chatter and conversation turned up to full volume. With his team, he started threading through them as fast as he could.

What prompted his sudden movement was the unnerving sight of several SED faces entering the casino from the far side, all dressed in black, all searching the crowds for something, taking no interest whatsoever in the surrounding tables and games. Mason recognised them as he was trained to do, saw the purposeful movements of their bodies, the severe looks on their faces, the way their eyes searched for something.

For his team.

He pointed them out surreptitiously. By now, even Sally and Luciane had spotted the SED across the far side. Mason led them around the other side of the vast space for one reason – that was the only way he knew led to an exit. He picked his way between people, easing them out of the way, jostling through. He was forced to pull one man to the side, while staying as low as etiquette would allow and watching his enemy from afar.

At his side, Basso came willingly. He'd seen the men too. Basso was mumbling to himself, clearly rattled. The team spread out, cutting through the crowd, heading for the far wall before following it around to the same exit where the SED had just entered.

For Mason, it was the right move. Leave by the same door your enemy had just used. Let them waste precious time examining the room you'd just vacated. He was moving too fast to take a head count of the enemy, but he'd seen there were at least nine.

Probably thirteen.

He pushed past another couple. A man's wife made a noise of complaint. Mason held a hand up as an apology. They kept moving, tried to blend in as best they could. The casino inside Caesars was lively, upbeat, noisy. People stood and chatted and watched the gambling, oblivious of the scenario playing out amongst them.

Mason, caught in a Catch-22 situation, found himself not wanting to keep turning his head to surveil the enemy, but still needing to keep an eye on them. It was only a matter of time before one of them spotted him. There were too many of them, too many eyes on the prowl for his team to go unnoticed.

And they needed to know when that happened.

Mason pulled Basso along. They reached the far wall, sneaked quickly along its length, treading the carpet and the marble walkways.

There was a man spearheading the other team, a bald, stocky man. Mason saw him clap eyes on Luciane and do a double take. The guy then stopped and held up a hand. Mason kept going, rueing his luck, cursing to himself. If only they could pick up the pace.

They reached the exit, slipped through. By then the men were turning around and making a beeline for them, but the press of bodies got in the way. The SED were having to push their way through and when they did it too roughly they were confronted, which slowed them down even more.

Mason led Basso across a wide, circular area between rooms, the air chilly with AC. He was sweating, looking back. He could see the SED bobbing around back there, seeking a way through the pack of people. He moved faster, slowed by more crowds, then started pushing his way through once more.

Mason passed a cashier's desk with Nobu on the far right, bustling with people. He saw a sign for the Forum Shops and Casino, thought about it but then remembered what time it was. The shops would be closed at this time of night, or at least virtually deserted. Going that way would be a deathtrap. He saw signs for the pool and a buffet, but he ignored them. What he needed was an exit.

They pushed on. Sally came up to his shoulder.

'The main Porte Cochere is that way,' she pointed. 'This way is the Centurion Tower and the Forum Casino.'

Mason made a face and started walking in the right direction. He didn't have to drag Basso along anymore; the guy was walking ahead, practically forging a path. He slid between people, moved them aside, asked politely to be let through, all the while moving as fast as he could. Mason heard comments in his wake, sometimes about rudeness, mostly about losing at the card tables. There was scattered laughter.

Mason looked back. The SED were gaining, not as careful in their push through the crowds. One woman went flying; her companion stood up to the man who'd pushed her until that man stared him down. Another man staggered as the leader went past, raising his voice in the man's wake but attempting nothing. It was packed, and perhaps security envisaged a little jostling, a few shoves and knocks, because they never came running.

Mason saw the way ahead open out. Now it was a vast area, the home of the reception desk, a massive statue and several sets of doors that led outside. Using the suddenly gained space, he darted for the main Porte Cochere, making sure his team was around him. The doors loomed ahead.

He glanced back. The men weren't running, but they were coming fast. They, too, had escaped the crowds now and had a bit of space in front of them. They were closing the gap.

To left and right, people stared, seeing and sensing that something was wrong. Mason needed to escape the situation. He barged through a door and felt the sweltering heat from outside hit him full in the face.

It was surreal. Surely it couldn't be this busy at this time of the night. But the area outside, the wide sweeping road which catered for taxi drop-offs, arrivals requiring valet, and wandering tourists, was packed all the way down to Las Vegas Boulevard. Mason shouldered his way through a crowd, following the pavement.

The team exited the casino through different doors, all charging through at the same time, the flinging doors, the lights shining off the glass, the surging bodies making a spectacle as they dashed outside together. Mason hurried now, with Basso right in front of him.

The SED soldiers exited seconds later. They were close.

They looked excited. Mason saw Roxy and Hassell drop back to deal with them.

But what could they do? Here, in the heart of one of the world's busiest and most glamorous cities? Mason wasn't sure, but he kept going.

Roxy blocked the path with Hassell. Mason didn't know whether the SED would recognise them as individuals, but they slowed momentarily, looking at the road to make their way past. Unfortunately for them, there was a very wide, very noisy G-Wagon idling at the kerb, blocking their way. Mason forged ahead several feet.

A man tried to push his way past Roxy. She tripped him. The guy went sprawling, head first, and struck the pavement with his face. Another man tried the same manoeuvre. Hassell shoved him to the right, into the foliage that lined the path. Mason lost the guy in the greenery, his legs kicking in futile disbelief.

By now, the SED had realised what was going on and had crowded around Roxy and Hassell. The raven-haired American turned towards them.

'Back off,' she said.

The bald, blocky leader walked right up to her. 'You will stand out of the way,' he said with total imperiousness. 'We will speak to that man.'

'You mean *interrogate* him? Kill him, perhaps.'

'If that is what has to happen.'

'And if you fail, will the Shadow Kings execute you for that failure?'

The leader's face didn't crack one bit. 'Stand aside. I will pay you, even give you a bonus.'

'Because here you cannot kill us, right?'

'Do not be too sure of that.' This time the leader's

318

impassive face transformed into a lascivious grin.

It wasn't exactly a stalemate, but it was giving Mason a chance to pull Basso further away. They were nearing Las Vegas Boulevard now, and could see the endless, flowing crowds ahead.

Mason slowed. Ahead, the Strip was painted by a million bright lights; incredible, towering, floodlit façades marching on both sides of the road, golden glasswork and soaring frontages. It filled the senses, pumped the adrenalin. Mason paused, waiting for a moment to jump into the crowds.

Behind, Roxy and Hassell still stood in the way of the SED. This was the moment of truth. How far would their enemies go? That, Mason decided, entirely depended on what orders they'd received.

And they soon showed their true colours.

The SED reacted as their leader barked out an order, drew knives, and, outside a jam-packed Caesars Palace, attacked Roxy and Hassell.

Chapter 43

Roxy flung a hand up, barely able to believe her eyes. She'd expected a rush, a charge of bodies maybe, but she hadn't expected to see knives. She blocked one thrust, staggered back, deflected another. The soldiers came at them en masse, stabbing and thrusting. Roxy felt a knife part her sleeve and then her flesh, felt the blood start to flow. She flung herself aside, unable to stand up to so many weapons at once.

Hassell did the same to her right, throwing himself onto the road in front of an oncoming car. The car braked violently, swerved and hit the kerb to its left, barrelling up it. Hassell stopped rolling, jumped to his feet.

The SED weren't here for them, though. They flowed past, tucking their knives away. Roxy could see shock and disbelief on the faces of several passers-by, as if they couldn't quite believe what they'd just seen. Maybe their eyes were playing tricks on them. Maybe this was a publicity stunt for a stage show. Roxy could see it all going through their minds, and that was why they didn't reach for their phones and call the cops.

It was over almost as quickly as it had begun.

The men swept past. Roxy assessed her bleeding wrist, saw the damage wasn't that bad. She turned and checked on Hassell and then ran after the sprinting soldiers, seeing Mason and Basso up ahead.

Sally and Luciane were first, though. They barged into the running SED men, smashing one man into another until several were falling, tripping to the ground. In front, Mason slipped into the flowing crowds, heading north up the Strip towards the Mirage and the Venetian. Roxy and Hassell caught up to their enemies.

But not all of them. The leader and two men were running hard, also flitting into the crowds and following Mason as fast as they could.

* * *

Mason looked back. He'd seen the knife attack and knew what was coming. The leader – Mason recalled Luciane calling him Miura – was in front, smashing his way through the crowds, now totally unrestrained. Yells went up all around him, and people challenged, only to be struck away by two of Miura's underlings who ran with him.

Mason thought quickly. There really was nowhere to go. He grabbed Basso by the arm and started running, darting in and out of the crowds, looking over at the road but seeing an endless jam of nose-to-bumper traffic. Maybe there was still a chance.

Mason steered Basso towards the road, ran off the kerb and started weaving his way through the cars and vans and trucks. This was quicker. There were no pedestrians to worry about, but a cacophony of horns sounded in his wake, especially when the SED started following them.

Mason slipped between the rows of cars, now angling back towards the kerb and staying as low as possible. The night was brightly lit, narrowing his chances of making a getaway, but that didn't stop him from trying.

'They're right behind us,' Basso suddenly cried out.

Mason whirled. He saw the leader rushing just a few steps behind, saw the violence in his face, his black eyes. He stopped on the spot, ducked, heaved the leader up in the air and deposited him on his spine. On either side, drivers stared, and some screamed. Miura's two cronies came rushing up and drew their knives.

In the middle of Las Vegas Boulevard, surrounded by traffic, with the eternal glow of the Strip's lustrous lights in his eyes, Mason battled the three assassins.

He kicked the man on the ground, making him stay down. He elbowed a second man in the face, sent him stumbling into the side of a car, and then front-kicked the third attacker, stopping him in his tracks. Basso lingered at his side, unsure where to go or what to do. Mason pressed his advantage, grabbing hold of the man who'd struck the car, taking him by the head and smashing him into the side window. The glass cracked. The guy slumped to his knees.

By now, though, Miura was back on his feet.

He drew a knife, slashed at Mason. The blade sliced through Mason's shirt, drawing blood from his chest. Mason skipped back, fell into Basso and tripped. Suddenly, he found himself on the floor, at Miura's feet.

The knife came down. Mason had to roll away, felt the knife slashing at his back. The only recourse was to roll under the nearest car, away from Miura's outstretched hands.

Almost instantly, he heard Basso's high-pitched yell.

Mason swore angrily, kept rolling. He came out the other side, saw boots in front of him, realised Miura's two goons had followed him around the car. He kicked out, smashed a shin, saw two knives gleaming.

Mason scrambled backwards. The men attacked. Mason kept them away by using his feet, scrambling along the asphalt road between cars. But at the same time, he could hear Basso's terrified voice.

'No! No! Please don't hurt me. Don't kill me! I'll tell you anything you want!'

Mason drove his arms down, pivoted and rose from the ground. He saw the knives coming, blocked one and then the other. He didn't fancy his chances, but what else could he do? Basso was in trouble, facing the leader of the SED.

One man swung in low. Mason leapt back, out of range of the slicing blade. He trapped the knife between his body and the nearest car, heard the blade scrape loudly down the metal door. At the same time, he kept his opponent in the way of the other man, giving him no angle to attack.

Mason jabbed upward, struck his enemy in the eyes, made him stagger away. He grabbed the man's knife and thrust it into his right bicep. Just then, the other SED soldier attacked, knife flashing. Mason darted aside and shoved out both hands, grabbing the man by the wrist.

'*Please!*' Basso was screaming. '*Not the knife!*'

In hell, the man was blubbering. Mason's vision was full of angry soldier, but Mason had hold of his knife hand. The man tried to head-butt him. Mason turned his head aside. The guy who'd been stabbed was on his knees, staring at his arm. Mason jerked his opponent first one way and then the other, trying to make him drop the knife.

They smashed into stationary cars, stumbled backwards and forwards. Horns blasted all around them. They fell in front of a car, washed by its bright headlights. Mason used his strength to climb atop his opponent, bore down on the hand that was holding the knife, and snapped the wrist.

There was a cry. The knife clattered to the ground.

Over to his left, Mason could still hear Basso's voice.

'*In the Gobi. Not the Mogao. Further into the desert, there are rows of brick walls…no, no, please don't…*' Basso cried out. Mason heard blood splash. Miura's stentorian, terrible voice, ordering Basso to go on. Mason could hear the pleasure in Miura's voice. There were sirens blasting through the air.

Mason still struggled with his man. The guy was tough. The soldier with the knife in his bicep was back in the picture, too.

Mason took a long, shuddering breath. He couldn't help Basso, but could hear the man blubbering, hear the sound of a knife slashing flesh. Soon, the rest of the SED and his own people would be here, adding to the chaos. Add to that the oncoming sirens and the churning mass of cars and people scattered around, and Mason felt like he was performing in a circus. The bicep guy came at him with one good hand. Mason dodged his attack and struck out at the embedded knife. He hit the hilt. The man screamed and fell to his knees. Mason whirled immediately and dealt with the man with the broken wrist.

He was free. He vaulted over the front of the first car to his left.

His boots came down near Basso's head. He couldn't believe what he was seeing. Miura was on top of the man, astride him. There was blood everywhere, pooling, spreading quickly. Miura's knife was inside Basso, all the way to the hilt. Basso's eyes were wide open, his mouth stretched in a silent, terrified scream. Miura's face was practically touching Basso's, and the smile on Miura's face was unmistakably vicious.

'No!'

Mason darted forward. Miura rose instantly to meet him, holding the knife underhand and crouching in readiness. Mason had half an eye on Basso.

The eyes glazed over as the man breathed his last.

Then Miura was surrounded by his own men, the rest of the team surging through the stationary cars, running down the open rows. For a moment, Mason froze, facing eleven men, and then his own team hit from behind.

It was chaos. Roxy led with her feet, kicking, stepping and then kicking again. She struck men in the small of the back, sent them sprawling. Quaid punched and pushed. Hassell used his momentum and his bodyweight, bowling two men over. The SED smashed into cars or went sprawling or fell to their knees. Some knives clattered away.

It was when flashing blue lights started washing across the façades of nearby establishments that Mason considered the situation. Sirens split the night. There was no way any of them – including the SED – could afford to be caught here tonight.

Mason let out a yell, told everyone to get the hell away from the scene. They all knew the meetup point. Next, if he hadn't seen it in action, he wouldn't have believed it. His team just melted away, slipped between the motionless cars and vanished into the extravagant night. Mason backed away from Miura, giving the man space, felt a car at his back and then slid around it. Miura, breathing heavily, just crouched there and watched him, an animal at rest, his hands coated in blood, his teeth bared.

Mason hurried down the row of cars, then glided across the rows, heading for the far pavement, the side of the road where Casino Royale stood. He made his way past the Imperial Palace and Harrah's, straightening his clothes as he went, smoothing down his hair and wiping the sweat from his face. He checked himself for wounds, for blood, but found nothing serious. His arms and knuckles ached, his right leg was grazed. Many times, he checked back, but saw no sign of Miura and his goons following.

Mason flitted between the crowds, his face washed in swanky lights. He soon recovered from the exertions, his breathing and gait returning to normal. Casino Royale stood ahead, its unmistakable multi-hued sign standing tall above the entrance. There were people crowded around the doors, and Mason joined them, eager to make sure his team was okay. He pushed through into the noisy, cool interior, made his way through the slots and a few tables. He had to ask the way to the main blackjack area but was soon heading towards it, eyes scanning left and right.

His heart leapt. Roxy was staring at him from across the room. Sally and Luciane were pretending to watch a game, but had their eyes on him. Quaid and Hassell were almost immediately at his side.

'I don't know what to say,' Mason said as they gathered. He was stunned.

'Did they kill Basso?' Sally whispered.

Mason nodded. 'I couldn't save him.' The knowledge tore at him inside.

'That bastard Miura looked like he enjoyed it,' Luciane said.

Mason nodded. 'He's a murderous freak.'

'I realise this might be insensitive,' Hassell said. 'But it has to be asked. Did they extract any information out of him before he died?'

Mason nodded. 'Pretty sure they extracted all of it. Miura and his people know exactly where the casino is.'

A brief silence fell over them as they all contemplated what that meant. Luciane spoke up first. 'I understand completely,' she said, 'if you want to end this now. This is my mess, my quest. I started it. I can't ask you to help me finish it.'

Mason and Sally both reached out a hand at the same time. Sally said, 'We're in this together. We want to be. To the end.'

Mason glanced around at the packed room, the absorbed players, the babbling watchers. He couldn't see the wall past a sea of heads and shoulders. At a table, a man shouted in pleasure and a great cheer went up.

Mason turned to the others. 'Assuming Miura makes it to the airport without being arrested, we have to figure he has a head start.'

'We have to get out of here as soon as possible,' Hassell said.

Until now, Quaid had stayed relatively quiet. It was now that he smiled and looked at them all, biting his lower lip.

'And that, my friends, is where I come in. I have an idea.'

'Oh no,' Roxy said. 'Is it as good as your idea to go to Dublin?'

Quaid nodded. 'Better,' he said.

Chapter 44

The flight to the Gobi Desert was a long one, and wouldn't be direct, only they weren't going to the Gobi. Not straightaway.

At Quaid's insistence, they were flying to Italy first.

Mason had been instantly suspicious. He remembered them flying to Italy once before, and the fiery woman they had met. Still, this was the best way, Quaid said. They could fly non-stop to Italy, and then non-stop to China, which would pretty much match or better Miura's speed. Quaid had made a tough phone call before they left McCarran Airport, and then they were off, winging their way through the night.

Mason, in his seat, took several deep breaths. His head felt like the outside of a tornado. It had been bad in Vegas, dreadful, but it had also been illuminating. His soul hurt, hurt for Basso. Mason hated that he hadn't been able to help the man, to save him. He felt bad that he'd dragged Basso into this, but knew the SED would have got to him, anyway.

I should have done better.

You can't save everyone. You should know that by now.

Mason wrestled with it as they flew over the Atlantic.

Roxy sat in the seat beside him, an array of miniature rums on her tray table. There was a packet of pretzels too, but she didn't seem bothered about those. Two of the rums were empty, and Roxy was working on the third.

'That helps,' she said.

'I wish this thing would go quicker,' Mason said.

'A long way to go,' Roxy drew out the word 'long'.

Sally, on the other side, suddenly leaned over. 'I do too,' she said. 'Balancing the books of Quest Investigations is never easy, but we're not getting paid for this.'

Mason blinked. He hadn't even thought of that. It showed how insulated Sally kept them from the highs and woes of running a business, he thought. The flight attendant came around again just then and, in response to Roxy's wistful gaze, deposited another rum on her tray table. Roxy winked at the man as he vanished down the aisle.

'At this rate,' she said, 'I think I'm about thirty minutes away from joining the mile-high club.'

Mason ignored her, still troubled. The feeling of failure wouldn't go away. Vegas had been frantic, sheer madness, but he felt he should have done better. After a moment, he stole one of Roxy's rums, tipped it back and ignored her faux-angry gaze. He unbuckled his seat belt, rose and walked down the aisle to where Quaid and Hassell sat alongside Luciane.

'What's in Italy?' he asked, bending down.

'You know what's in Italy,' Quaid said with a tremble in his voice. 'Anya.'

'Is that wise?' Mason didn't look over at Luciane, but the question in his tone was obvious.

'No,' Quaid said. 'Not at all. But she owns her own plane. It'll put us ahead of the SED. We've used her before.

We know she can get us close to where we need to go. It's the fastest way from America to China, and she can get us in with little fuss.'

'You sure about that?'

'I'm not even sure she won't break me in half. For all sorts of reasons. You know we have a bumpy past, but it's worth the risk.'

Mason was happy with the fastest way from America to China. Luciane looked confused. 'Who's Anya?' she asked.

Nobody answered.

Finally Hassell, who'd spent a week at her home in the Italian lakes, said, 'Lovely lady. Owns her own business. Helped us out a few times. Carries a knife and an attitude. Not happy with Quaid because of their...chequered history.'

Luciane arched her eyebrows. 'Well, actually, that makes two of us.'

Quaid buried his head in his hands.

Mason counted down the hours. Hassell's thoughts soon turned inwards, reflective. Quaid tried not to strike up any kind of conversation. Maybe he was rehearsing his lines for when they met Anya. Sally slept with her laptop open on her knees, and Roxy brooded over her rums. Mason tried not to think about Vegas and Phoenix Basso and the man they still had to beat, Miura.

They landed at Leonardo da Vinci in Rome a few minutes ahead of schedule, deplaned and dashed through customs as fast as they were able. Quaid had asked Anya to meet them here. Now, following the directions on his messages, Quaid guided them through the airport to an area that dealt with private flights and private runways. They showed their passports and were allowed through, directed to a private lounge. As they closed in on their destination, Quaid got more and more nervous.

'I'm not entirely sure this was a good idea,' he said as they walked along the clinically polished hallways.

'It'll be fine,' Roxy told him, a bit inebriated. 'And if it isn't – what the hell? We'll be a man short.'

'Thanks,' Quaid said.

They slowed for a set of double glass doors, pushed through, and found themselves in the private lounge. It was round, with a dimly lit bar to the right and a fresh buffet to the left, and lots of tables in the middle. The temperature was a balmy 21 degrees, the atmosphere in the room airy and laid-back. Mason counted about four people seated in the whole place.

A suited doorman greeted them, checked their passports again. Clearly, Anya had already done something behind the scenes because they strolled through without question or challenge. Mason walked between tables as Roxy headed for the bar.

Before she got there, however, a figure approached, barring her way. The figure was lithe, blue-eyed and wearing denim cut-off jeans with an empty leather sheath dangling from her waistband. She had short blond hair, an inquisitive, suspicious gleam in her eyes and full red lips. A gold Rolex shone on her left wrist, twin diamond bracelets on her ankles. In her left hand was clasped a tumbler full of some amber liquid that Mason knew would be bourbon.

'Anya,' Roxy said with pleasure.

Mason made a beeline for her, holding out his hand. 'Great to see you again.'

Anya shook their hands with a firm grip. Right then, Sally came up, holding her laptop in one hand. 'Do you know what we need?' she asked.

Anya nodded. 'One-way trip to Dunhuang, right? Or as close as I can get.' She pitched her American-accented voice low.

'Can you do it?' Sally asked.

'I have a few strings I can pull.'

Mason didn't need to know any more. Anya was wealthy, connected and liked from sea to shining sea. It was at that moment that Quaid came up, looking sheepish.

'You do right to approach me that way.' Anya glared at him. 'In fact, you should be on your knees.'

'Oh, you'd like that, wouldn't you?'

'I haven't heard from you in months, years before that. In fact, no disrespect to your team intended, but you only ever call me when you need something.'

Quaid spread his arms. 'You're a great connection.' Then he winced.

'*Connection? Connection?* Oh, well, that's amazing. I'm a great *connection*. Well, all I'm saying is it's a damn good job I didn't wait for you.'

Quaid finally met her eyes. 'Yeah, you told me about the pool boy, the car detailer and the window cleaner.'

'Oh, that's just for starters. In the last few months I've—'

Roxy was watching with interest, as was Mason, as Quaid chose that moment to step aside and introduce Luciane.

'And this is Luciane,' he said.

A tension seemed to crackle between the two women as they both realised exactly where they stood in Quaid's life.

'Hi,' Luciane said shortly.

Anya made no move towards the other woman. 'Charmed, I'm sure.'

'Luciane is the main reason we're here,' Quaid went

on, trying to smooth over a moment that was as rocky and jagged as an ocean bed.

'You got no chance.' Roxy laid a comforting hand on his shoulder.

'I'm flying you to China for her?' Anya asked archly.

Quaid winced. 'Well, it's a long story. Why don't we explain it to you on the way?'

Anya stared at him with no expression. 'Actually, I'm looking forward to getting in the air,' she said.

'Why?' Quaid asked tentatively.

'So I can throw you out the goddamn door.'

Anya turned and stalked away. Mason avoided Quaid's eyes and followed, soon joined by Roxy.

'I'm really looking forward to the plane journey,' she said.

Mason risked a glance back, saw Quaid walking with his head down, Luciane following with a stony look on her face. It was a short but tension-laced walk to Anya's Cessna Turbo Stationair, which, Mason remembered, was a six-passenger plane. Lucky. At least that was one less thing to worry about.

They boarded, took their seats. Anya checked through the avionics. At first, nobody mentioned the large box sitting halfway up the aisle between seats; they were too busy getting settled. But then, typically, Roxy pointed it out and asked if they should do anything about it.

Quaid waited until the plane was in the air and had levelled off, then unbuckled his seat belt and set about opening the box. Inside, Mason saw, was a GPR – a Ground Penetrating Radar machine. He'd asked Anya to pick it up on the way.

'We wheel it around the desert,' he said. 'And it tells us when there's a big space underground. We can set the parameters. I used these things several times in the army when we were searching for items of material.'

'A geophysical method,' Sally said, looking the machine over. 'It uses radar pulses to image the subsurface. Detects reflected signals from subsurface structures, like, say, a casino. Walls. Rooms. This is the perfect machine for detecting a void.' She looked over at Quaid. 'Great idea.'

'Thanks,' Anya drawled as she moved into the cabin, having switched the plane to its autopilot setting. 'When the great fool here told me what you were doing, where you were going, this seemed like the best plan to me. Otherwise, you might as well just bring a bucket and spade.'

'I kind of assumed Basso's directions would be spot on,' Sally said with a shrug. 'But the GPR is perfect. Thank you.'

Anya inclined her head before turning the full force of her glare somewhere between Quaid and Luciane.

'Explain,' she breathed.

Quaid told her everything that had happened so far. At first, hearing about Luciane's struggles, Anya's face softened, but then it got harder as Quaid came to the end of his story. 'And how long have you two been an item?' she asked.

'Don't worry,' Quaid assured her. 'We go back to my earlier army days.'

Luciane glanced sideways at Anya. 'Did he run out on you, too?'

Anya snorted. 'Oh, with his tiny tail between his legs.'

'Hey,' Quaid objected.

Luciane laughed. Roxy, clearly listening with her head cocked towards the conversation, let out a chortle.

Mason tapped Quaid on the shoulder. 'I'd leave it alone if I were you. At least they've found some kind of common ground.'

'Yeah, but I'm not sure I like the common ground that they've found.'

Anya settled herself between Luciane and Roxy for a while, and the three chatted and laughed over the drone of the plane. Hours passed. Mason found prepacked sandwiches in a large fridge at the front of the plane and passed them around. One wasn't enough. He opened bottled water and swigged that too, and then started on his second sandwich.

'Where are we landing?' Sally asked at one point.

'Dunhuang Mogao,' Anya told them. 'That's where you want to go, isn't it?'

'Perfect,' Sally said. 'But how the hell did you swing that?'

'It's *always* who you know,' Anya said. 'That's everything. That's life. The best lesson I have ever learned. I cultivated my contacts carefully, and can now land almost anywhere in the world with a cover story. This time, I'm bringing in my best friends as tourists.'

'Luckily, your best friends already have visas,' Mason said.

'I knew that.' Anya briskly returned to the cockpit and took over control of the plane. Soon after, she announced they were descending towards Dunhuang Mogao Airport.

Mason closed his eyes briefly, wondering what the last, irrevocable part of this mission had in store.

Chapter 45

They cleared customs through a private hall inside Dunhuang Mogao Airport. The border patrol officers barely glanced at their passports but hurried them through and, once their backpacks were scanned, had no further interest in them. The visas were still good, the passports all fine. A man wearing a uniform and white gloves investigated the box with the GPR and then waved them onward.

Anya left them in the hall, waving goodbye and ignoring Quaid until the very last moment. As he passed out of sight, she shouted, 'Call me,' and then turned and stalked back to her plane. Mason wasn't sure what favours she'd called on to get them into the country, but he knew they'd be immense. He just hoped he'd be around if Anya ever needed a return favour.

They left the terminal, caught an Uber. As ever, the heat was distracting, the sand in the air a nuisance. They booked into the same hotel as before, took a quick shower and then met in the lobby to discuss their next moves.

It had worked out well for them timewise. They were

losing nothing. It was past eleven p.m. Dunhuang time. The team gathered in plush chairs around a glossy black coffee table and put their teas and coffees on coasters.

'Any thoughts as to the SED?' Mason asked first. 'They surely couldn't have made it much faster than us.'

'Not a chance if they were using civilian transport,' Quaid said. 'Of course,' he shrugged, 'they could have got lucky.'

'But barring that,' Mason said, 'we should have some alone time out on the sands in the morning.'

'What time is sunrise?' Hassell asked.

'Six fifty-nine,' Sally told him.

'Early start,' Roxy said.

'First,' Mason said, 'let's recap what Phoenix Basso told us in Vegas. We have a GPS point, and phone apps with which to use it. We're looking for an area of low brick-built walls. Find the easternmost wall and then walk north a few hundred yards until you have a jagged hill in your sights. Another two hundred yards. That's the point where we break out the GPR.'

'It's a heavy bastard,' Roxy said. 'We're gonna have to take turns carrying it.'

Mason nodded. 'We need people on the GPR. People on the dunes, the high ones, acting as lookouts. We need Sally working her magic, trying to pinpoint the way in. And we need a place to fall back in case Miura and his goons turn up.'

'Weapons?' Roxy asked.

'Great shout. Unfortunately, we have none.'

Roxy grumbled, but then tried to look upbeat. Sally showed them her GPS app and how to use it. Mason figured it was so easy even Quaid could follow it. They split up shortly after and made their way to their rooms. Mason stripped off and fell into bed, asleep as soon as his head hit the pillow.

A five a.m. alarm awakened him the next morning. He groaned, rolled over and stretched, realising he'd slept in the same position all night. He was still exhausted, still aching, and didn't want to move. Then he remembered what this morning represented.

They would search for the ancient casino.

Galvanised, he rose, changed clothes and headed downstairs with his half-empty backpack over one shoulder. The team ate, grabbed an Uber and asked the driver to take them first to a supply store and then to the Mogao Caves, since that was about a twenty-minute hike from their first destination. Mason knew Basso hadn't been too far out when he lied to the collectors about the position of the casino. The Mogao Caves would still be visible.

The Uber dropped them off and drove away. Sally walked around the parking area and stared into the desert, the team at her side. Mason saw hard-packed earth for miles around, punctuated by the inevitable sand dunes, some reaching incredibly high, their tops scoured by winds and producing sandy spindrift which spiralled away in the air. It was cool, with a chilly breeze, the sun not having taken hold of the day yet. The way ahead was marked only by wooden barriers.

Sally put the first foot forward. She held her phone in her hands, a red dot as her destination. A blue triangle indicated their own position. Mason, Hassell and Roxy had already searched the area for enemies and found none. They had new shovels in their backpacks, rope, torches and a small set of binoculars, which Mason now used to scan the horizon. Again, he saw nothing.

'Safe as can be,' he said. 'Let's move.'

They moved out. Hassell was carrying the GPR machine for the first part of the journey; it had fitted inside his backpack but left him unable to zip it up. Mason picked a point on the horizon and started walking towards it, trying not to veer off course. The walk started out easy, but their destination was further than they had thought, and the little blue triangle tended not to move much as they continued.

The morning marched on. A yellow ball rose in the sky, warming the land through. Mason took the GPR and carried it for twenty minutes. Still, they were some way from their journey's end. The going was relatively easy as long as they stayed away from the softer sand. The sun grew hotter and hotter and they were forced to stop often to take out their bottled water.

Finally, though, Mason saw Sally raise a hand. He walked over to her. The red dot on her phone matched perfectly with the blue triangle. He scanned the terrain in every direction. Hassell was already marching up the highest, closest mound, binoculars in hand, to scan the desert for pursuers. Mason saw nothing else, no low brick-built walls, no jagged hills. He put a hand over his eyes and looked up at Hassell, who had now reached the top of the mound.

The team spread out. It was Hassell's shout that drew their attention and, looking up, made them gaze further to the east where, after squinting for an entire minute, Mason made out an irregular-looking shape.

Hassell came rushing down the high mound of sand.

'No SED,' he said. 'We're the only ones out here that I can see. But the walls are off that way.' He pointed east. 'Can you see them?'

'I see something,' Roxy said. 'Could be a wall. Could be a damn elephant. My eyes aren't what they used to be.'

'Hard to see,' Sally agreed. 'Are you sure it's the walls?'

Hassell nodded. 'A whole series of them, just as Basso said. The sand has done a good job of hiding them, but from up there,' he pointed to the top of the mound, 'they're unmistakable.'

Mason moved out with the entire team. They slogged through patches of soft sand, moving slowly, wiping the sweat from their foreheads. By the time they reached the first wall, they were panting.

Mason sat down in the soft sand, swigging water. Sally and Luciane went straight to the first wall and started scooping handfuls of sand from its surface. It didn't take long to reveal the sandy bricks that the wall was built from, a long, straight, uniform structure that could at one time easily have been the wall of a house or similar. Mason let them work for a while, getting the lie of the land, and then moved to the next structure.

Another brick wall, this one irregular and with ragged gaps along its length as if it had been the subject of rockfalls. The third was irregular too and, as Mason moved on, he saw the makings of a small town in the desert, sand-covered straight or jagged shapes stretching in all directions, standing proud of the desert floor but still nothing but rough humps and bulges in the sand, easy to overlook. He broke out the compass, checked for east and then started walking in that direction.

'Let's find the easternmost wall,' he said.

They grouped together, walked through the long-lost town. From here, looking back, they could still see the Mogao Caves, but only barely. They shimmered in the distance, heat haze rising between them. A refreshing wind blew, laced with sand, making them view everything through

340

half-closed eyes. Mason's boots sank into the sand as he walked, but this time it wasn't a long journey.

'Eastern point of the town,' Sally called out.

Mason stopped. There was a wall to his right, the furthest extremity of the brickwork. He stopped and viewed the horizon, looking for a jagged rock or hill.

'I see it,' Roxy said, almost incredulously, as though shocked that Basso hadn't lied to them.

Mason saw it too. The hill looked like three giant fingers had reached down and scooped it out.

'Two hundred yards and break out the GPR,' Hassell said.

Straightaway, they walked the short distance and then started looking around. Nothing stood out, no obvious bulges or depressions in the landscape. Quaid was carrying the machine and now he knelt down in the sand to shrug it off his shoulders and start unpacking.

Sally took a shovel from her backpack. 'Just think,' she said with delight. 'At this very moment, we could be standing over the world's oldest casino.' She was practically grinning.

'Not just that,' Roxy said dryly. 'But also the most dangerous.'

Chapter 46

It was a tremendous team effort.

They unpacked the GPR and took turns wheeling it around the ground. In places, the wheels got stuck, and the machine had to be carried. In others, it worked just perfectly, rolling smartly over the smooth ground. The screen fed back reflected signals from any subsurface structure. The area of their search was pretty vague, Mason admitted to himself, and they did not know what extent to cover, but the GPR was their best bet. They were looking for changes in material properties, voids, cracks.

At first, it was hit and miss, but then Sally and Luciane started conducting the search in the most efficient way, by following a grid pattern. The sun climbed the sky until it reached its zenith and then started down the other side. Twice, Mason had to stop, sit down and pour sand out of his boots. They ate and drank on the go, watching the GPR's screen, searching from side to side. Hassell and, at times, Roxy climbed the nearest mounds and searched the terrain, always reporting the absence of any unwelcome visitors.

Hours after they had arrived, Sally let out a low whoop. The latest radargram showed a vast void under the earth, or so she said. To Mason, it was merely a group of ridges, black lines, bold lines, thin lines, but Sally could roughly interpret the data and Luciane had used one of the machines before.

Together, steadily, they mapped out the void and its edges.

Mason broke out his own shovel and started digging, shovelling the sand away from the edge. The others joined in. Soon, there were six of them hard at work, digging heaps of sand away from the edges and making their own mounds. It was hot, painstaking work, fruitless for the most part, disheartening. They dug two, three, five feet down and found nothing.

But the void was below them.

Mason heard Luciane talking about it but didn't understand half of what she said. Just that it was a wide area, broken in places by walls, and stretched at least ten feet deep, maybe more. Of course, there was no easy way in. The sand had to be resting on a roof of sorts that hadn't collapsed, at least not yet.

Mason took a break, using the downtime to walk to the top of a mound and check the landscape. He could see the Mogao Caves in one direction, high sweeping dunes in another. The jagged hill dominated another direction and there was some scrubland in another. It was vast, dry, empty nothingness for as far as the eye could see. He wiped sweat from his face, sand from his clothing. His hands ached from the shovelling, his calves from all the stretching.

From below, there was a cry. Roxy suddenly disappeared. Mason blinked in surprise, then raced back down the mound, kicking sand in front of him as he went. He ran with a kind of lurching motion, trying to stay upright all the way down, and then hit the firmer ground. Soon, he reached the place where Roxy had disappeared.

Heard her voice.

'It's a tunnel.'

Around him were the others. Sally fell to her knees, listening. Hassell and Quaid were bent over, looking into a black void. Mason saw a ragged hole in the ground through which sand was slowly falling. He knelt down beside Sally.

'You okay?' he shouted to Roxy.

'Yeah, it's not too bad. There's a tunnel down here.'

Sally was already squeezing her lower body through the gap. She shone a torch down and then dropped, landing on her feet. Mason couldn't stop Luciane going next, and then he was poised over the hole.

He looked up.

'Someone has to stand guard,' he said.

Hassell nodded, taking the job.

Mason lowered himself down and then dropped. His booted feet hit a dry, sandy floor. Ahead, Roxy was examining a hole that was held up by a thick doorway lintel. Sand continued to trickle down all around them. The air was musty, but just now it was relatively fresh from the new hole. To left and right, Mason just saw bulging sand. It made him nervous.

'What's through that door?' he asked.

Roxy shrugged. The door had long since rotted away, leaving the stone frame and lintel above. There were no markings, no carvings, nothing to tell them what they were walking into.

'Look at your boots,' Sally said suddenly.

Mason glanced down, sightly worried. At first he saw

nothing, but then a faint gleam caught his eye. He scraped sand away and then reached down and plucked something off the floor.

It was a round coin with serrated edges. Mason wondered how long it had lain in the sand, maybe since the fifteenth century, maybe since Basso and his associates came down here. He turned it over between his fingers.

'Man with a walking stick,' he said, staring at the engraving. 'I have no idea what that means.'

Sally shrugged. 'We'd need an expert on ancient Chinese coins for that,' she said. 'And I'm sure we will find one. Keep it safe for now.'

Roxy pushed forward, ducking inside the doorway and then disappearing, torch in hand. Mason flashed his ahead, illuminating the way, his beam crossed by those of the others.

From inside the doorway, there was a gasp. 'Hey, guys, you won't believe this.'

Mason quickly followed Roxy, but didn't get there before Sally and Luciane. He was fourth in line, followed by Quaid. Together they all entered the dark space, conscious of the weight above their heads, of the sand pressing in from all sides.

But Mason soon forgot about that. Beyond the doorway was a vast room, stretching beyond the scope of their flashlights. He saw thick stone pillars marching away into the distance, a bronze domed roof. Stone tables everywhere with carved legs, their surfaces covered in dust and sand. Piles of coins, both on the tables and on the floor where they'd spilled in the earthquake, heaps of chips on every surface. Mason played his torchlight left and right. He saw golden fittings attached to the pillars, small-framed paintings that glowed in the light. There was a three-foot-tall golden statue of a dragon in what he assumed was the centre of the casino, its teeth bared. More statues were scattered around the room, beside the tables and, so far as they could see, the walls. As Mason walked forward, he saw old parched bones littering the floor, and stepped respectfully around them. The team spread out around the room, passing between pillars and illuminating the far walls. In the torchlight, Mason took a snapshot of the entire room.

There were bags full of coins, their necks wrapped in golden silk. There were stools and chairs and tables that had collapsed, now half buried in sand. And in parts, there was roof wreckage too, shards of strong timber. Above, the interlocking and overlapping crossbeams that had remained intact still looked sturdy. At the far end, the once gracefully turned eaves had fallen in, unable to bear the weight of the sand. Rounded tiles had cracked and shattered on the floor, but some had remained whole and some could still be seen above. The original appearance of the place might have collapsed like the structure, but its inherent beauty could still be seen everywhere, some of it intact, some of it broken.

'From my research,' Sally said, 'I recall the casino had a Hard Hill roof, a main ridge with sloping raised ridges on the gable walls. Two slopes facing front and back. It used encaustic tiles and had a row of what are called Ridge Beasts, mythical creatures from Chinese fairy tales. Look, you can see the remains of some right there.' She pointed to the floor where Mason could make out what might once have been a seahorse and a dragon.

They pushed on inside the vast space. Mason smelled fustiness, the rotting of cloth, the deep stench of the earth. All he could hear was the sound of his own team's scraping footsteps, the sound of coins rattling as Roxy picked up an old bag and shook it. His mouth was dry with excitement. He let his hand scrape past an old pillar, feeling the hardness, the smoothness. He picked a couple of coins up from the ground and let them run through his fingers.

'This is incredible,' Luciane said.

There were many other objects scattered around the place, many still intact on tables, some fallen to the floor, some even crushed. Mason saw broken paintings and prints, jade jars and bowls of exquisite design, an arched bronze plaque, another in the shape of a tiger. There was pottery from different dynasties, from tricolour glazed to purple clay. There was even a twenty-five-stringed instrument hanging precariously on one wall next to a spot where the stone had caved in.

Mason stood near the centre and turned round and round, taking it all in. He could hear something, a deep groan, the groan of weight pressing down from above. It set his nerves on edge.

'We got it,' he said, still smiling despite his misgivings.

'I knew it would look like this,' Luciane gushed. 'I *knew*.'

Quaid picked up another bag full of coins and peered inside. 'There must be forty, fifty bags scattered around here,' he said. 'Not to mentions the individual coins, the chips, the treasures on the walls and the floor. This find should be shared with the world.'

'It will be,' Sally said. Already, she had a camera out and a video recorder and was documenting the place. She walked from table to table, laid out the heaps of coins, gathered up the chips and put them in front of the lens, trained the camera on the walls and the scattered statues. Luciane was with her, doing her own version of the same job.

Mason stood there, gaping from side to side. Dust hung in the air, drifted before his face. He wondered briefly what was going on up top, but knew Hassell would warn them if anything happened. Roxy had explored the furthest so far and was examining the far walls, shining her torch on the hanging pieces, the items on small podiums, the spread out statues. She was facing a closed door with indistinct carvings on the face.

'I wouldn't open that,' Mason said quickly.

'I'm not that daft,' Roxy said. 'I don't want a face full of sand.'

Mason inched his way towards her, taking care not to tread on anything – tiles, bones or streams of coins. A pillar had collapsed nearby, and he took a cautious look up at the roof where it used to stand. The intact tiles were bulging, as if it was only a matter of time before they came streaming down. Mason swallowed heavily. Any kind of disturbance would test the viability of this place.

'Look at these things.' Roxy swept her torch beam across the relics. 'They're priceless, all of them. I don't know where to look next.'

Mason nodded, standing close. It felt good; it felt like they'd done the right thing in seeking the casino out, in documenting it for the world. He turned back towards the entrance to where he had just heard a scraping noise.

Hassell stuck his head through the door. 'Guys,' he said. 'We have company. They're about two miles out, in canvas-backed trucks. At least four men that I can see and that's just the drivers and passengers, all dressed in black, carrying weapons. They're headed straight for us. Has to be the SED.'

'Thirteen then,' Luciane said.

Mason cursed. 'We need more time.'

'You took the words out of my mouth,' Sally said. 'I haven't documented even half of the place yet.'

'You're not gonna get a chance,' Hassell told her.

Sally whirled, seeking Mason. 'Hold them off,' she said. 'This place is *incomparable*. It's beyond imagining, a one-off. We can't let it disappear again into Chinese history—'

Luciane interrupted her. 'Please,' she said. 'The coins, the statues, the wall hangings, the...oh, *everything*. This mind-blowing casino. It's fifteenth-century. It deserves a worldwide audience. This is everything I've been working for.'

Mason saw them turn back to their work, knew they'd be impossible to pull free. He turned back to Hassell in the doorway.

'They're here to kill us,' Hassell told him.

Quaid stepped forward, a precious statue in his hands. 'Then let's see what we can do to modify their thinking,' he said.

Mason knew the SED wouldn't take any prisoners; they would bury them here in the sand. But the fact was they were *here* now, in the exact spot they'd been hunting for. Even if they all left at this moment, the SED would know they'd been here, would search for them unrelentingly.

'No choice,' he said. 'Gear up.'

From the back of the room came Roxy's voice. 'I have a shovel.'

Mason shook his head and motioned Hassell out of the cave. It was time to fight for their prize.

Chapter 47

Mason, Roxy, Quaid and Hassell raced up from the depths below, using a rope that Hassell had anchored to a protruding section of brickwork. They scrambled up as quickly as they could and then dashed to the top of the nearest mound, backpacks in their hands. Mason had already pulled out his binoculars and looked through them even as he came to the top of the sandy slope.

Two trucks, in the near distance, were winding their way through the desert, trying to avoid the deeper sand and bouncing along a narrow track. The trucks were large, red and open bed with canvas stretched across the back, the large tarpaulin hiding whoever was seated there. Mason saw two passengers and two drivers, weapons held between their legs, helmets and sunglasses on. He had no doubt there were other men in the back. The trucks were coming on at a steady pace, probably so someone could read the map and follow a compass. They threw up a haze of mist in their wake.

Mason crouched low in case someone was watching. He

followed the path of the trucks. 'I have an idea,' he said. 'They didn't see you, right?'

Hassell shook his head. 'I doubt it.'

'Good. Well, they're coming here expecting to make an ambush,' Mason said. 'How about we turn the tables?'

'Go aggressive,' Roxy said. 'I like it.'

'Can you tell where they're gonna stop?' Quaid asked.

Mason pointed to a rough patch of ground beyond the brick walls. 'See there? It's an obvious place. You can see the walls from there, but there's space to park a couple of trucks. That's where they'll stop.'

Mason was calling on his experience in the field and on the battlefield. The area was the natural final destination of the trucks if they kept on coming towards the walls, and Mason knew that's exactly what they'd do. Surrounding the area were several low dunes and two tall ones, and then the series of low brick walls. Quaid, also with a military mind, agreed with him.

'Hurry,' Mason said. 'We're gonna have to run if we want to get into position in time.'

They shrugged on their backpacks and ran down the slope, sliding for most of it. Sand flew out in all directions. Mason took the lead, rushing across the firmer sand and back towards the walls. The sun shone high overhead, the slight breeze caressing their faces. They couldn't see the trucks, but could discern the dust tail spiralling above one of the tall dunes.

They split to both sides after discussing strategy, reached the smaller dunes and tucked themselves in behind them. The trucks were so close they could hear the shifting gears, the roar of the engines. Then came the sound of their tyres crunching and rumbling across the earth. Mason ducked low as the trucks came into sight.

To his left and ahead were sand dunes. To his right, open ground towards the low brick walls. He crouched with Roxy; Quaid and Hassell were on the other side of the track.

Mason listened keenly, hunkering down, waiting, until he heard the brakes being applied. The moment he heard that, and the changing engine note, he raced out from under cover and ran towards the trucks. He stayed low, under the eyeline of the driver and passenger, Roxy at his side.

Mason went for the passenger side, Roxy the driver's side.

Mason reached the truck before it had stopped moving, grabbed the door handle and yanked it open. The man sitting above looked down with a shocked expression on his face, just as Roxy threw open the other door. Mason reached up, grabbed the man's wrist and pulled him out of the cab onto the ground below. The man sprawled, too shocked to scream, his gun clattering. He hit the ground face first, sprawling. The truck was still moving, now under its own momentum, as Roxy removed the driver, but coasted inexorably to a stop.

Beside it, as agreed, Quaid and Hassell had copied them with the other truck. Speed was of the essence. They had to incapacitate their opponents before the trucks stopped properly and the men in the back jumped out.

Mason likened it to shock and awe. He didn't pull any punches, stamping on his opponent's spine and then the back of his neck. The guy struggled, but weakly. Mason bent down, scooped up the gun and smashed him over the back of the head with it. They couldn't open fire…yet. He relieved the man of a handgun, magazines and a knife, shoving them all into his backpack and waistband.

Seconds after attacking the truck, he was ready to move.

On the driver's side, Roxy knelt astride her opponent before rendering him unconscious with several blows to the temple. Mason saw her stand up. He ran to the front of the truck, glancing over at Hassell and Quaid.

This was where their entire plan could go to hell. Quaid and Hassell weren't as clinical and highly trained as he and Roxy. He slowed, at the same time ready to act. At the other truck, he saw Quaid beating down with the butt of a rifle, heard the meaty crack of it striking a skull, and then saw Hassell struggling upright with his own enemy. Mason was about to act when Hassell kneed the man in the groin, then struck him under the chin, making him stagger back against the truck. Even that might alert the men in the back, who would be jumping down at any moment. Mason aimed his gun, ready. Hassell slammed his own weapon across his opponent's temple, stunning him, driving him to his knees.

No time to wait.

'Run!' Mason said.

Already, he could hear crunching as the men in the flat bed jumped down to the ground.

Mason whirled and ran for the low brick walls. Roxy was at his side, Quaid and Hassell just a few metres back. As they ran, leaving the trucks behind but still twenty yards away from the walls, crossing a veritable no-man's-land, the first shots rang out. Bullets stitched a path between them, gouging into the sand.

Mason zigzagged, presenting a hard target. Their plan hadn't quite worked, but it had gained them weapons. Another barrage of shots rang out. Now there was shouting, sounds of confusion. Mason and his team were lucky; their enemy was in disarray, possibly even searching for more attackers.

Mason reached the first wall, dived behind it, landed on sand and got a face full. Roxy rolled across his legs in her haste, sand folding all around her. From the other side, Hassell and Quaid appeared, diving headlong just as a volley of bullets ripped the air where they had been.

Mason crouched low, let a few seconds pass, then he was up, positioning his gun on the top of the wall, squinting through the sights and opening fire. The enemy – he counted over a dozen of them – were milling around or running between the two trucks, rushing to help the fallen men or listening to the angry shouts of their boss. Mason lined them up.

Bullets flew among them. One man screamed and twisted, throwing his gun into the air as blood fountained from his throat. This was now kill or be killed, and they weren't in the city anymore. Mason saw another of his rounds hit a man in what could only be a bulletproof vest, sending him staggering backwards and then to the ground.

Roxy, Hassell and Quaid added their own weapons to the mix, scattering the soldiers.

Bullets zinged off the trucks. One hit a large tyre, puncturing it. The SED didn't just take fire; they returned it in kind, leaning out of cover blindly and shooting on automatic. Mason ducked down as a blast of gunfire peppered the wall he was hiding behind, ancient bricks sheared by hot lead.

Sand mushroomed into the air as bullets struck. The brick wall shuddered. Mason stayed low, crawled away and found the next wall. The others did the same. When the SED men ventured out, showing their faces, Mason and the others were in different positions.

The shift in location paid dividends. The soldiers concentrated their gunfire on the wall. Mason popped up and opened fire, striking two of them in the head. One man fell back against the truck, leaving an ugly red smear; the other just collapsed in a heap, dead before he knew it.

By Mason's count, that left ten, including the leader.

He ducked again. Bullets tracked him, striking the wall in front of his head. Roxy collapsed near him, but that was just her throwing herself down, getting a mouthful of sand which she proceeded to spit out. It was heaped all along the wall where it had drifted. On the other side, Quaid and Hassell were knee deep in it.

Mason whirled and started crawling again. This time he found an eastern running wall, dissecting their position, and followed it to come up in a different location again. He didn't surface until he'd stopped crawling, but then rose with his gun in hand and fired until the magazine ran dry.

Quickly, he swopped it for another.

Hassell and Quaid ran and leapt over the wall he'd just crawled to. Bullets chased them, barely missing. Mason shook his head and yelled angrily. It was a stupid decision and had almost taken their lives.

Mason fired again. The SED were still using their trucks as cover. Bullet holes were everywhere. Mason could see several legs beneath the truck and swept his bullets at them, striking at least one man, who started howling.

Focused as they were, they didn't see the two SED men flanking them.

Mason ran back behind another wall, fired three times, and then found another shelter. He didn't stop moving for more than a few minutes, keeping the enemy guessing. He changed mags on the fly, yelling at Roxy for cover, then watching her back as she followed suit. They moved as a team, working for each other and always gaining that shelter together.

Mason moved and fired, moved and fired. That way, he picked off another SED fighter, which now left nine. He could see them communicating through earbuds, reaching into the backs of the trucks for more ammo, sheltering, and then jumping up into one truck. He didn't like the look of that.

Further, he thought. They had to retreat further.

From his left, a shadowy figure appeared. It was far closer than he could have imagined, a shadow blotting out the light. It was above him, flying, and it held a knife.

Mason folded, collapsing under the figure and then spinning in the sand. The SED attacker hit the soft sand hard and then whirled, shooting up several flurries. Mason did the same, kicking out with his feet, catching the guy a glancing blow across the wrist. They were like snakes in the sand, striking, parrying, leaping.

Mason rose, brought his gun around, then ducked as a volley of bullets smashed into the wall that barely covered him. The SED man launched an attack, catching Mason around the waist, striking at him with the knife. Mason got a hand up, parried the weapon and fell back against the wall that was protecting him.

He knew that, from the other side, a similar figure had attacked Hassell.

Mason squirmed and kicked. He threw sand in his opponent's face, rammed the guy's head against the brick wall, saw part of it crumble away and then bullets chip the edges. The SED fighter had to fling himself headlong to avoid shots from his own men.

Mason took advantage of that. He swivelled the gun in his hands, realised it was too big and clunky to use at close range, and then reached for the handgun on his waist. It wasn't there! Mason cast around, saw the weapon lying half-hidden under sand some way off to the right. He dived for it, scooped it up and lined the man's head up.

He fired.

The soldier's head exploded all over the wall.

Mason felt calm flooding his veins. There was no panic here, no raised blood pressure. He had always been an outstanding soldier, and part of the reason was his ability to remain calm in the heat of battle. He thought succinctly, acted without anxiety. He did that now, returning coolly to pick up his rifle as he tucked the handgun away, picking it up and sighting it on Hassell's attacker. When the time was right, Mason pulled the trigger, taking away half the man's head.

Hassell sat up, breathing heavily, covered in blood. He gave Mason a thumbs-up sign.

Roxy and Quaid were at the wall, ducking down, coming up to fire. Bullets peppered the surrounding brick, but they kept their enemy pinned down.

Seven left, Mason knew.

He was in his element, fighting, retreating, fighting again, moving position. He swopped in another mag, saw that he didn't have all that many left, then changed tactics. Now he would wait for targets instead of haphazardly pinning his enemy down. He yelled out for the others to follow suit. Hassell yelled back that he was already using his last mag.

Mason took stock. He hastened once more, using a dissecting wall that ran south-east. He laid low, waiting. For a moment, there was a lull in the battle.

And then they came, the remaining seven mercenaries racing for the first wall that Mason had hidden behind. They were now employing a similar tactic. This was how they would wear Mason's team down.

And Mason knew it would work.

Chapter 48

The SED soldiers made a war of attrition, wearing down their enemy. They raced for the first wall, fired over it, then raced for the next, drawing fire, always hidden, close to death but somehow escaping it. Mason stayed where he was for a while, knowing the enemy was on the move and not wanting to lose sight of them. He kept waiting for the perfect target; it never came. The Shadow Kings' mercenaries ran from wall to wall, crawling through the sand in between, the constant flurries giving their positions away.

One time, Roxy tracked a merc by following his sand flurries, knew exactly where he would pop up, and waited. When the man's head appeared over the parapet, Roxy blew it away, leaving a spurting set of shoulders and then a collapsing body.

Bullets chipped away at the brick walls. Gunfire resounded around the desert, sometimes clamouring back off the high, wavelike dune walls. Mason felt like a heap of sand – the stuff was everywhere, all over him. He checked his weapon, his remaining bullets, remaining magazines, keeping a running count.

Roxy crawled up to him, elbows working double time. 'What's the plan, Joe?'

He shrugged. 'This is the plan.' But he felt responsible for them. He couldn't just let something happen; he had to force it. They were all under his protection – not just Roxy, Quaid and Hassell, but Sally and Luciane back in the casino too.

'We change tack,' he said.

'In what way?'

'Simple,' he said. 'We attack.'

With that said, he signalled Quaid and Hassell, passing on his intentions. Roxy was looking at him as if he were mad, hesitating, but then nodded.

'If you think it'll work.'

He felt gratitude rush through him. Roxy was her own fearsome fighter with a toolbox of experience and tactics. To hear and see her giving him the lead was gratifying, and it shored up his confidence in his ability to lead.

'Move then,' he said.

They crawled in another direction, around the edge of a wall, back towards the trucks. They all stayed low, flicking up very little sand. They took up an attacking position and waited for the mercenaries to make their move.

Which they did.

Seconds later, three fighters rose, firing. Mason waited three seconds, then sprang up, surprising them. His own bullet took out one man, Roxy's another. The third man ducked down before he was hit. Mason coolly leapt over the nearest wall, closing the gap to the SED. His team instantly followed suit.

The Shadow Kings' soldiers rose again. This time, Mason was upon them, crouching behind the same wall. He grabbed a gun, forced it up in the air, heard and felt it discharge. Roxy was at his side, grabbing for another weapon. Mason levered himself upright, forced the gun away and jumped over the wall on top of the SED fighter.

The man fought insanely. Almost immediately, Mason realised he was up against the leader of the SED, the man called Miura. In the flurry of battle, Mason's gun went flying away, landing in the soft sand nearby, so he caught hold of Miura's and wrenched it from side to side. The man tried to head-butt him, but missed. They leapt and tussled and staggered in the sand. Mason put a foot behind the guy's right boot and pushed.

Miura hit the wall, stumbling back. His bald head caught the sun, flashing and sweating and streaked with blood.

'I will end you, scum,' he spat.

'Hey, we want to share.' Mason still had hold of the gun and now wrenched it away from the man. It was too big for close-quarter fighting, so he flung it away, reached for a knife. Miura whipped a black blade out and slashed forward. Mason deflected it with his own.

There in the desert, beside a sweeping sand dune that looked like a wave and under the blistering sun, Mason and Miura struck at each other, back and forth. Mason caught blows intended for his neck and heart, deflected them, tried to make Miura overstretch. But the man was a good knife fighter, striking underhand and skipping aside, already folding into the next move, constantly attacking. Mason went backwards, not because he had to, but to allow Miura time to wear himself out with his incessant attack.

Roxy smashed her enemy across the top of the head, reared back when he caught her in the stomach, fell gasping.

He then bashed her over the head with his weapon, sending her tumbling back into the wall. Roxy struck it head first. Blood flew, leaving a mark on the bricks. Flesh tore. Roxy spun round, lashing out. Her fists struck true, swiping a knife from the man's hand that had been about to bury itself in her neck.

She leapt at him, spitting blood.

Quaid and Hassell rolled across the top of the wall, clutching at their opponents. They landed hard in the sand, but the soft mounds cushioned the fall, and let them slip from the grasp of their enemies. Quaid kicked sand in his enemy's face while Hassell buried his in the sand, pressing down hard on the nape of the man's neck.

Mason retreated a hundred yards, past the last of the brick walls and onto the hard-packed desert. The sun was in his eyes, glaring down. His clothing stuck to him; there was sand in his boots. He slashed left and right, wrists dripping blood as he attempted to keep Miura at bay. The man was stocky, powerful and well-trained.

'Did you find the casino?' Miura asked.

Mason tried to bait him. 'Oh yeah. Footage is gonna be on TV screens any day now.'

It worked. Miura snarled and lunged. Mason sidestepped the attack and sliced with his knife, slashing the man across the face. Two flaps of skin were instantly parted and blood flowed. Mason winced.

'That's gotta smart,' he said.

Miura yelled out a curse and flung himself at Mason, who staggered back further. Now, at his back, he knew the hole that led into the casino was visible.

Miura clapped eyes on it, eyes that widened. He backed off. 'Is that it?'

Mason flung a hand at it. 'Yes, it's the goddamned casino. Why couldn't you back off and stop being murdering bastards and let something of such historical value to the whole world be unearthed? What is wrong with you people?'

'The Shadow Kings take what they want,' Miura said. 'They are far from weak, and will not be bullied.'

Mason saw it now. *Weakness? Bullying?* 'But all that is just political bollocks,' he said. 'Your bosses, they're nothing more than men in positions of power getting greedy. Listen... this is all just a political statement, and you're in the middle of it. Powerful men are always sending men and women off to war to further their own agendas, while they keep their hands clean and take home the money later. It's why my friend quit the army, some of the reason I did. They send boys and girls off to die, to be brought home in body bags, and all for a bit of imagined power that won't matter next year anyhow. They promise them honour, a future, glory, and they give them bloody dirt and exploding missiles. Save the rest of your men now. Call this off.'

Miura almost looked swayed. There was a strange look on his face, something that was almost placid. He opened his mouth, closed it, opened it again.

'There is something in what you say,' he said. 'Something almost pure. I can understand it. But I am part of the agenda. We all are. We are the sword that wields it, that delivers it.'

And Miura struck at him, face changing instantly. Mason backtracked, still catching the blows, hearing the ring of metal on metal. He edged around the hole in the ground and watched as Miura eyed it.

'Don't die for that,' Mason said.

Miura leapt at him, knife raised. The blade came down, slashed Mason's upraised arm and sliced a chunk from it.

Mason flinched, staggered. Blood poured from the wound and dripped to the ground, mingling with the sand.

And Miura disappeared down the hole.

At first, Mason was dumbstruck, wondering where the hell the man had gone. One second he was a flying, terrifying figure, knife silhouetted against the bright, blazing skies, and the next he had disappeared without a sound.

Mason leapt at the rope, grabbed it with one hand and let himself down. His arm burned, blood ran from the wound, soaking his clothes. His eyes adjusted quickly to the sudden dark and he saw Miura crouched below, head in his hands, clearly having taken a knock during his long fall.

Mason landed beside him, grabbed him and threw him back against the wall of the cave. Miura suddenly slid around him with a slinky action, grabbed the rope, and curled it around Mason's neck in one swift movement. Then he leaned back and pulled.

Mason didn't panic. He reached up and grabbed the rope, couldn't find purchase for his fingers beneath it, but created a small gap. He could breathe, barely. But Miura was yanking on the rope with both hands, leaning back. The thick twine tightened around Mason's neck, cutting off his air. He was practically pulled off his feet, nowhere to turn, nowhere to go. He couldn't turn around, couldn't free the rope. He was helpless. The knife fell from his hands as his vision blurred.

Out of the darkness came a screeching blur. It hit Miura in the solar plexus and then the balls, all elbows and knees, practically in flight. It hit harder than a rock, and with bone-crunching accuracy, driving Miura away from the rope. The SED leader let go of the rope and collapsed to the floor, groaning.

Sally stood over him, Luciane at her side.

363

The two women had treasures in their hands, a ceramic bowl and a jade statue, both of which they now used to beat Miura into unconsciousness. As they worked, Mason eased the rope from around his throat.

'Thank...' he gasped. '...you...'

Miura reared up, face twisted, eyes ablaze. His face was a mask of blood; it was dripping off his chin, his nose. He screamed. The knife was suddenly back in his hand, and he lunged straight at Sally.

Mason was all out of choices. He plucked the knife off the floor and, on his knees, threw it end over end at Miura. The blade flashed past Sally's left ear, nicking it and drawing blood, and then slammed point first into Miura's face with a clunk. The impact arrested the man's momentum, stopped him dead in his tracks, and sent him slithering down to the floor.

Sally looked away, felt her ear and turned to Mason.

'Close as fuck.' She didn't usually curse.

Mason let out a deep breath and rubbed his aching throat. 'Help me up.' He grabbed the rope once more, thinking only of Roxy, Quaid and Hassell, and climbed it back out into the blazing day.

Up top, he shaded his eyes and started staggering back towards the ongoing fight. He still couldn't breathe properly, and his lungs were heaving. He saw Roxy flat on the ground, a man atop her, and Quaid and Hassell struggling over to the left.

Mason ran as fast as he could. He didn't stop. He launched himself through the air and struck the man on top of Roxy full in the face with both his knees. He tumbled, rose and, in the blinding heat, shook his head. Sweat droplets flew in all directions, but Mason only had thoughts for his team.

He started running again, smashed into the man fighting Hassell and then flung himself at the one battling Quaid. His actions helped both men gain the advantage.

And then he realised Roxy was at his side. Mason had knocked her opponent out cold with his flying knee attack. He was crouching, hands on knees. He looked up at her.

'You good?'

In front of them, Hassell knifed his man in the chest. A shot rang out – Quaid using a handgun to finish his own opponent. As it was, the final gunshot echoed back off the wavelike sand dune, the sound repeating again and again in their ears. It pinpointed the moment when a profound silence suddenly covered the scene.

Mason looked around, saw the bullet-strewn trucks, the lifeless bodies of the SED men. He fell to his knees in the sand, exhausted.

There was movement in front of him: Sally and Luciane exiting the hole in the ground, backpacks secured, their faces worried as they blinked in the light. Mason waved at them.

'It's safe,' Quaid yelled.

But they hadn't finished yet. Mason knew not all the SED fighters were dead. They set about securing the living, making sure they had no weapons near them but had bottled water they removed from the back of the truck. Mason bit his lower lip when he realised only two of their enemy had survived.

Sally and Luciane came up, bent over under the weight of their backpacks. Both women wore radiant smiles.

'Did you get everything you needed?' Hassell asked.

Sally nodded. 'Incredible footage,' she said, 'of the world's oldest casino. We've removed nothing, stolen nothing. It's all intact.' She said this for the benefit of the listening SED soldiers, though Mason was unsure if they spoke English.

'We have not disturbed the casino's heritage or taken anything from it. We just wanted to share this historic moment with the world,' she finished. They all knew that this meant it was over. The Shadow Kings could not attempt to hoard the casino's treasures for themselves now that the precious archaeological site and its riches had been filmed and put front and centre on the global stage for all to see.

Mason grunted as Roxy fussed over his wound, binding it with a strip of her T-shirt. His own clothes were soaked and would need changing before he embarked on any kind of civilian transport.

Speaking of that, he looked over towards the Mogao Caves. 'One last hike,' he said.

The team gathered around, set their faces to the south, and started on their long journey back.

Chapter 49

Days passed. Mason and the team returned to the West. Mason's wound started healing even as a vacuum of purpose opened up around them. This was the aftermath, the sudden cessation of action. Mason found Sally wanted to stay with Luciane, at least until they had divided the footage of the casino between them and formed a plan of action.

So, days later, he found himself back in Dublin.

It was after six, getting dark. They had seated themselves at the very back of an old pub in central Dublin on O'Connell Street, the city's major thoroughfare. They had pushed two tables together and were ensconced in a little niche, so that nobody bothered them. Half-empty pint glasses and bottles of beer and cut-glass tumblers littered the chipped black table in front of them, along with plates, the remains of hearty meals of steak and chips and burgers and chicken fillets, all loaded with salad that, for some reason, remained on the plates.

Mason was sitting back, watching the band set up on stage. The bar to their left was getting busier and busier. It wrapped around the wall to the entrance, where people were flowing in, more arriving every second. The stage was soon set up, the band pausing over their instruments, waiting for someone to announce them.

Mason took another swig of his beer. His arm still ached, his knuckles were bruised, but otherwise he was fine. His body had been battered time and time again throughout the mission, and was now healing.

Figures started crowding around the stage, filling the spaces between Mason's team and the musicians so they could no longer see them. All they could hear was the sound of a drum kit and then a guitar as they started up, and then the singer's voice crooning a song. Even from the very first beat, the crowd was hooked and started singing along, filling the bar with their voices.

Mason leaned in to Roxy, who was sitting beside him. 'At least we all survived to talk about it.'

She smiled without humour, her raven hair falling across her face. 'There were moments when I thought we wouldn't, especially in the desert.'

'Me too,' Mason agreed. 'But we're here now, and we made a coup.'

Sally leaned over as far as she could, voice faint beneath the music and the crowd. 'The footage we have will form a documentary which will be enhanced by diligent research. It will be great. We can mix modern gambling, say at Vegas and Macau, with the ancient forms, showing how it used to be. The networks will eat it up, especially when we announce the discovery of the world's oldest casino in conjunction with it. Public awareness will be on a high.'

'The Shadow Kings killed to prevent this,' Hassell said mordantly.

'They approached it with pure aggression,' Sally replied. 'They caused all the problems, from the beginning, desperate to sell the relics on the black market for their own gain. All Luciane wanted was a chance to be astonished by history. They came in with all guns blazing.'

'Literally,' Roxy said wryly.

Mason finished his pint. 'Now the most serious question of all,' he intoned – and waited for everyone to look at him. 'Who's going to get up to go to the bloody bar?'

They laughed. Roxy rose at the chance to use her elbows and Quaid went with her. Soon they were back, armed with trays of drinks rather than anything more dangerous. Mason raised his glass and said, 'Cheers.'

'To what comes next,' Roxy said, clinking her rum and Pepsi Max against his pint.

'Any ideas?' Quaid looked at Sally.

The brunette with the blue-tipped hair took her phone out and laid it heavily on the table. She jabbed a finger at it. 'This thing has been going off day and night for a week,' she said. 'There's no shortage of jobs out there.'

'And the good thing is, we can pick and choose,' Mason said. 'I'll drink to that.'

Luciane joined them, raising her own cocktail. Their glasses rose, the bar's lights shining off them and sparkling, the liquid inside reflecting glimmers of amber and gold and green. The glasses lingered for a long time in the air.

And then the team drank, celebrating their success of the moment and far more to come.

THE END

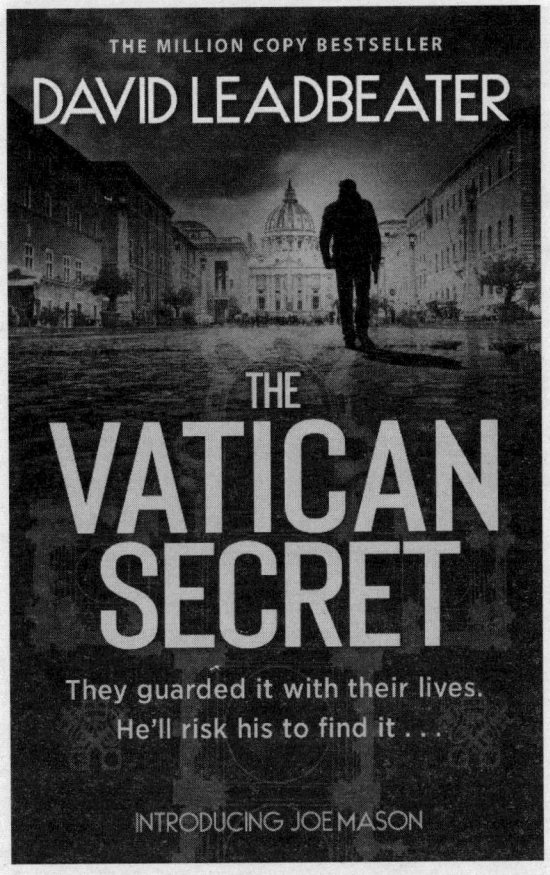

The adventure continues …

Don't miss the second action-packed and
adrenaline-filled instalment.

Available now!

A stolen treasure.
A secret society.
Danger is waiting in the shadows …

Don't miss the third gripping and fast-paced action
adventure in the series.

Available now!

In this game of cat and mouse, the rules are simple:
kill or be killed…

Can he uncover their deadly conspiracy
before they find him first?

THE
BABYLON
PLOT

A JOE MASON THRILLER

DAVID LEADBEATER

THE MILLION COPY BESTSELLER

Don't miss the fourth gripping and fast-paced action
adventure in the series.

Available now!